Bobbie Faye's
(kinda, sorta, not exactly)
Family Jewels

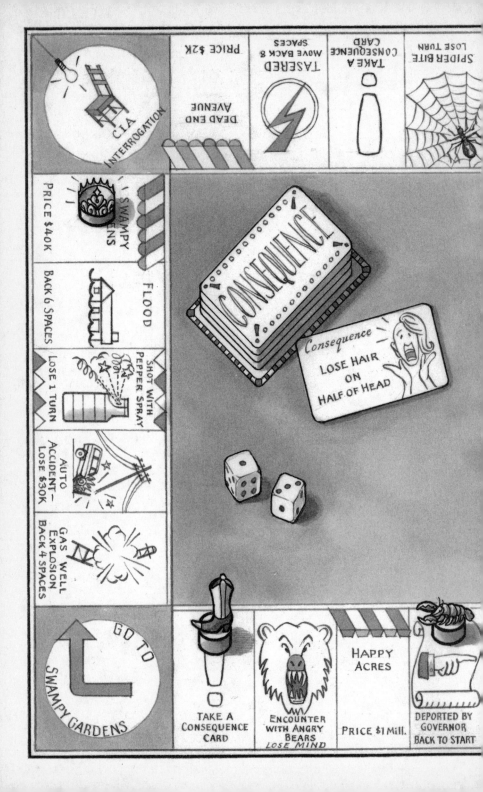

Bobbie Faye's

(kinda, sorta, not exactly)

Family Jewels

TONI McGEE CAUSEY

St. Martin's Griffin

NEW YORK

This is a work of fiction. All of the characters, organizations, and events portrayed in this novel are either products of the author's imagination or are used fictitiously.

www.stmartins.com

Book design by Gretchen Achilles

Illustrated board game by David Cain

LIBRARY OF CONGRESS CATALOGING-IN-PUBLICATION DATA

Causey, Toni McGee.
    Bobbie Faye's (kinda, sorta, not exactly) family jewels / Toni McGee Causey—1st ed.
        p. cm.
    ISBN-13: 978-0-312-35450-3
    ISBN-10: 0-312-35450-9
    1. Cajuns—Fiction. 2. Diamonds—Fiction. 3. Theft—Fiction.
4. Louisiana—Fiction. I. Title.
    PS3603.A8988B59 2008
    813'.6—dc22

                                                    2008009286

First Edition: June 2008

10 9 8 7 6 5 4 3 2 1

For Mom and Dad

Genius has its limitations.
Insanity . . . not so much.

Bobbie Faye's
(kinda, sorta, not exactly)
Family Jewels

Chapter One

Bobbie Faye Sumrall was full up on crazy, thank you very much, and had a side order of cranky to spare. The bank—citing the picky little reason that it didn't want to lend money to people who were routinely shot at—said *no* to a loan for a new (used) car. It wasn't like she'd ever been hit by an actual bullet, for crying out freaking loud. Immediately after that, she couldn't get an insurance company to give her a quote for a start-up business grant application she needed to turn in. (Three insurance giants had gotten restraining orders as soon as they heard who was calling.) (Wusses.) And then the FBI guy she'd been blistering hot and bothered about had dropped off the planet two weeks earlier, and geez, there was only so much rejection a girl could take. She needed to have one night, one measly little night, to sleep well. That wasn't too much to ask, right?

Apparently, the Universe thought it was.

Bobbie Faye and the Universe were like warring spouses locked in an eternal battle, trying to blow each other up rather than admit the other was savvier. (The Universe, by the way? A big fat cheater.)

Still, she tried. She went through her nightly routine: she squeezed into the tiny bathroom of her small, almost-not-ratty trailer, fantasizing about actual hot water while she grabbed a tepid shower. To wind down, she poured herself some juice and nibbled on crackers. (Yeah, her luck was solid. The juice tasted like it had gone bad. And not the good "fermented" kind of gone bad.) Thankfully, her five-year-old niece, Stacey, had been invited to spend the night at a friend's house. No matter how much she loved the little rugrat, she was grateful that tonight there wouldn't be fourteen billion attempts to hogtie the kid into bed for a whole five minutes of sleep before Stacey bounced up again, determined to drive Bobbie Faye out of what little was left of her mind.

When Bobbie Faye did finally stretch out on her lumpy twin mattress, she sank into disturbing, hallucinogenic dreams—all disjointed, a half-step two-step out of rhythm, bits and pieces swirling in a kaleidoscope of confusing colors. At one point, she saw herself as if from afar and damn, she looked odd. She could have sworn her boobs were off kilter, like one was higher than the other, but maybe it was just that striped, butt-ugly shirt she was wearing, the one she'd won back in high school in that dumb "spirit week" contest. She was twenty-freaking-eight years old; why couldn't her subconscious mind be a team player and clothe her in something über cool and sexy? And why did her long and normally loose-flowing brunette hair look so . . . strange? It seemed all wrong. It was stiff, like she'd emptied a can of hair spray and shellacked it into a helmet.

Great. Bad dream *and* bad hair. Just perfect. But at least she wasn't bald, like that little schlumpy guy she was talking to.

Oh. Wait. Make that the schlumpy pot-bellied guy she was shooting.

Why in the hell was she shooting this guy? Five times. Damn, but it was a beautiful pattern. At least her dream got that part right. She leaned over the man as he stared at her off-kilter boobs, saying something about them not being real. The jerk.

He didn't remind her of anyone she knew. Stupid subconscious. Why couldn't it at least let her pretend to take out one of the jerks driving her insane? Mr. No-Extension-For-You IRS Guy would have topped her list. Or maybe Nick Lejeune, the local bookie who kept placing odds on her every move. (Would she wreck today before or after noon? Would she inadvertently blow something up or would it be on purpose? Would she be in jail on her birthday?) He was making a fortune and not even giving her a cut.

But no . . . the dead guy in this dream wasn't the least bit familiar. Bobbie Faye watched herself as she picked up all of the dropped casings, felt for a pulse on the dead guy, and wiped her fingers on her hideous shirt. Then the images churned, and wind rushed at her, tangling her hair, buffeting her arms spread wide open as if she were flying under the streetlights in the small commercial district of her tough, no-nonsense industrial hometown of Lake Charles, Louisiana.

When she woke up, she had a raging headache and her mouth was painfully dry. She peeled her eyes open, and *holy fucking shit*.

There was something definitely . . . bloodlike in her hair. She'd sleepwalked a couple of times as a kid, mostly wandering aimlessly through the house. She had a vague sense of having done it again last night. An almost-memory of having heard something in her sleep—had she gotten up to check? Then banged into something? Her closet door was open, so it was a possibility. She glanced down, dreading what she'd find, but no, she still had on the same t-shirt she'd worn to bed, but there were a couple of bruises on her left arm and a cut on her right that she didn't remember having the night before.

So it *had* been a dream. A way too realistic bad dream. Probably best to ease up on the chocolate suicide cake after dinner.

She sprang up as she felt the weight of cold metal in her right hand, a weight she recognized and instantly wished she didn't. It was her Glock. She froze, her body running cold and clammy. It was supposed to be locked up. It was always locked up, especially with Stacey living there now. Bobbie Faye gingerly sat up and checked the magazine: five bullets were missing.

Clearly, the Universe thought it was payback time.

Chapter Two

Four days later, the memory of the freaky-assed dream hadn't faded, but at least she'd managed to push it out of her mind. Her temporary amnesia would have come in handy while she dealt with the Crazy, Inc., portion of society which believed it absolutely had to be armed and dangerous at 10 A.M.

Bobbie Faye wasn't entirely sure if it was the ninety-five-degree heat searing the June morning, or the fact that Ce Ce's air conditioner had gotten in a snit and shut down for the day, but it felt like the oppressive warmth had the nutjobs out in force; she hadn't been at work fifteen minutes and she was already itching to plunge her head through the nearest wall. Or strip naked and go skinny dipping in Bundick's Lake. With her luck, she'd end up on the five o'clock news like last year when little high-school senior Aubrey Ardoin caught her completely naked, sinking into the lake, using his spanky new digital recorder, the underaged rat bastard. (He'd financed his techno-geek habit through selling "Bobbie Faye debris" on eBay.) Of course, it was the fact that he'd hacked into the LSU Purple and Gold preseason game and aired her naked self on the JumboTron that had gotten her on the national news. Again.

She wouldn't ditch Ce Ce in spite of how much she wanted to

4

escape the oppressive heat and insistent customers. She loved her boss, so she stuck it out, breaking a sweat while doing her dead level best *not* to sell a compact Glock to older-than-dirt Maimee Parsons, a Baptist pillar-of-the-community. It wasn't an easy thing to do. Or not do, rather. As the person in charge of the gun and knife counter at Ce Ce's Cajun Outfitter and Feng Shui Emporium, Bobbie Faye was supposed to sell to anyone who'd passed the state-required security check. Maimee, eighty-five, had just aced that sucker. Not exactly a red-letter day for gun safety.

Bobbie Faye should have known something was wrong when Maimee had shown up in baggy slacks, a mismatched striped shirt, and a baseball cap shoved atop her pert white curls instead of being well coifed and wearing her usual church dress. The old woman frowned down her nose over silver-rimmed bifocals, the glinty look in her eyes incongruent with the sweet round doughy "O" of her face.

The gleam in Miss Maimee's eye was usually because Maimee had long been in charge of the Lord's Supper at the main Baptist church in town and therefore felt she had a lock on exactly who was going to Hell, and she reveled in the knowledge. But today, the gleam seemed slightly maniacal, and Bobbie Faye wondered if Maimee wasn't tilting toward the *husband of fifty years gambled away their retirement and needs a'killin'* manner of thinking. Just her very Baptist presence in Ce Ce's shop—where it was well known that Ce Ce practiced a little voodoo as a sideline business—suggested Maimee had clocked in on the *psychotic break* side of the equation. Maimee wasn't big on second chances unless the Lord Himself granted them and it looked like Edgar Parsons, recent big loser at the gaming tables, was about to come up on the short end of the prayer stick.

Maimee's ability to suss out any remotely minor sin intimidated even the most unrepentant person (her nephew, the governor, included). In spite of that, Bobbie Faye liked her. Maimee had been one of those rare people who had actually helped Bobbie Faye's mom get food on the table, back when most people thought her mom was halfway to certifiable, before they knew she was taking pain killers for the cancer.

As Maimee peered down the barrel of an empty Glock, her spindly legs spread in a stance that would have made Dirty Harry proud, Bobbie Faye scanned the old rambling store, dusty and cram-packed with every imaginable doo-dad and whatchamacallit on the planet. Maybe Maimee could pray over someone instead of buying a gun, but when Bobbie Faye looked around for victims, the store seemed eerily devoid of customers. It was as if the crowd of sinners, knowing Maimee's reputation for her . . . *enthusiasm* . . . in laying-on-of-the-hands prayer mode, had migrated way the hell away from the gun section of the store.

"Miz Maimee, you don't really want a Glock. You want to go home and talk to Mr. Edgar and work out some things."

"Nonsense, girl. This isn't about Edgar. I feel the need for protection." She plunked the Glock down on the glass countertop. "I have the right to buy a gun and you have to sell it to me."

Bobbie Faye rankled at being called *girl*, but she let it slide. It was probably best not to annoy soon-to-be-armed customers. "You don't know how to shoot."

"Well, I heard that you're a crack shot and you give lessons here, so sign me up."

"They're kinda expensive."

"Not a problem. How many lessons will it take for me to be able to pick off an intruder at night?"

"Doesn't Mr. Edgar come in late sometimes?"

"Here's my credit card. Run it on through. And add some ammunition. I'm not sure how much a person needs to defend themselves. A lot, I imagine. Ring that up, too."

This was going to get ugly. Bobbie Faye knew it, knew she was going to be on the blaming end of things if Mr. Edgar should suddenly meet his untimely demise, just as sure as she'd known a couple of months earlier that she had to hijack a truck in order to save her brother who had called with the teeny tiny problem of being kidnapped and held for ransom. She was sorry about destroying nearly half the state while rescuing Roy. Really.

She had a feeling not everyone believed her, though, which made her think briefly of her ex, Detective Cameron Moreau. Sure, he was sexy and he could be charming as hell when he wanted to be (he hadn't been an SEC Championship Quarterback for LSU without gaining a little public relations savvy), but for every ounce of gorgeous, he was also pound-for-pound the bossiest human being on the planet. (Well, okay, slight exaggeration. There were a few people she hadn't met yet and it was statistically possible at least *one* of them was bossier.)

Cam meant well, sure. He had a good heart. She knew that— knew, as they were growing up best friends, that he just wanted what was best for her, even though they butted heads about her choices. There was a moment there at the end of the last chase where she knew he'd been torn between choosing to shoot her and choosing to help her. For about two seconds, she thought they might have had a possibility of being friends again when he decided to help, but true to form, as soon as the crisis was over, he'd reverted back to being ticked off that she hadn't called him for his advice, hadn't let him control her every move.

Yeah, she was really beginning to empathize with Maimee's gun purchase.

She picked up the gun Maimee had set on the counter, palming the weight of the sleek metal. An ill feeling gnawed at the pit of her stomach as she flashed back to her weird dream, seeing herself shooting that schlumpy guy. She could practically taste the acrid gunpowder residue in the air, feel the vibrations of the impact as the man hit the ground.

"Bobbie Faye," Maimee huffed, tap-tap-tapping her credit card on the glass countertop, snapping her back to attention. *It was just a dream. Only a dream.* "Go on now. Ring it up. I've got to get to a prayer meeting."

The word *meeting* hung in the air above Maimee's head just as the front door of the old Acadian-style building yanked open, bell jangling, and in flounced one royal pain-in-the-ass: Francesca Despré—all five-foot-five of her, an inch shorter than Bobbie Faye and slightly flatter chested (something Francesca had never accepted and used push-up bras to mitigate). Francesca's short auburn hair framed a perfectly tanned complexion and her couture clothing shrieked Wannabe Diva! but the actual effect was Newbie Hooker. She teetered on black four-inch stiletto heels and carried a fluffy shockingly pink feathered purse that she clutched in one hand and an alligator-clad makeup sample case in the other. It was the shredded and practically nonexistent black micro-miniskirt which was the *piece de resistance*—a skirt made of such gossamer threads barely strung together, Bobbie Faye suspected there was a dumbfounded spider who woke up that morning wondering where in the hell its web had gone.

Francesca headed straight for the gun counter. No hope that the impending doom of Francesca showing up was unintentional. She sashayed through the store, weaving past the cammo gear and fishing tackle, the tents and Coleman lanterns, rerouting at the last second to avoid the screened-in boxes of live crickets and over-stacked shelves of "Feng Shui" crystals Ce Ce hadn't quite managed to unload.

"Fuck," Bobbie Faye muttered, eyeing the nauseatingly perky Francesca crossing the store.

"Bobbie Faye!" Maimee reproached. "Watch your language!"

"Miz Maimee, you're buying a gun. I'd be willing to bet you just upped Mr. Edgar's life insurance. You don't get to take the high road today."

"Hi, Bobbie Faye," Francesca bubbled when she reached the gun counter. "We have a problem."

Encryption code in: **********
From: Simone
To: JT

Confirmed: BF is inside. F has entered.

(sent via cell)

Encryption code in: ************
From: JT
To: Simone

All plans are go.

(sent via cell)

Bobbie Faye scanned past Francesca and realized that every male customer over the age of two had suddenly found the aisle to the gun counter absolutely essential for their shopping needs. Francesca, for once, seemed not to notice the attention she drew. (Once Francesca went through her *boy-crazy* phase—oh, wait, she was still in that phase—she'd morphed from a partner-in-crime prepubescent tomboy, breaking into the neighborhood "male-only" clubhouses, into a beauty-pageant attention-seeking missile, treating makeup application with the same reverence other people would give to CPR.) Francesca propped her purse and sample case on the counter and immediately proceeded to give Bobbie Faye the earnest expression.

"Oooooohhh no," Bobbie Faye said, having seen that wobbly helpless wide-eyed *please-oh-please-help-me-with-my-homework* pout one time too many. "*We*," Bobbie Faye leaned forward over the counter, gesturing between the two of them to emphasize the point, "do *not* have a problem."

"Bobbie Faye, you have to help. I told them you would." Francesca worked the big doe eyes and pouty lips.

"Nice try. Not happening."

"Wait," Maimee asked Francesca, her shrewd gaze narrowing beneath the brim of her baseball cap, "you're that Lady Marmalade woman, aren't you?"

"Why yes," Francesca preened, turning the makeup sample case to show the Lady Marmalade logo on the front.

Maimee dug into her oversized handbag. "You sell to hookers and pole dancers and big breasted women who frequent gambling parlors, don't you?"

Before Francesca could answer, Bobbie Faye put a hand on Maimee's arm as it heaved out a Bible the size of a mini howitzer. "I don't think we have time for you to pray over her today. It would take hours."

The old woman gave the Bible a little backswing shake. "I was thinking more along the lines of smacking her with it."

Bobbie Faye wanted . . . oh, how she wanted . . . to move out of Maimee's way and let her have at it, but she gently guided the Bible down to the glass counter, and said, "Miz Maimee, have you considered anger management classes?"

"She knows what she's talking about," Francesca said to Maimee. "Bobbie Faye's had to take it three times already. They even give her discounts now."

"Not helping yourself one bit, Frannie. You should be leaving."

"I can't, Bobbie Faye. They're coming!" Francesca nodded toward the door, as if that was self-explanatory. "And if you don't hurry, you're gonna be in trouble."

"And just exactly *why* would I be in trouble?"

"Because I told them you would know where they are. Or how to find them. So now they think you do, or that you can, so you have to or they're gonna kill people."

Chapter Three

Aiden Stewart threw the rest of the soggy chips—what these bloody Americans called fries—into the paper sack and cursed the blasted fast food drive-through. With a place as big as the U.S. he'd have thought there'd have been someone who'd mastered the art of frying a potato.

What he wanted was a whiskey, but Sean MacGreggor, who could be a right sour bastard of a boss, frowned on drinking on the job and had been known to permanently retire a bloke or two when he'd caught 'em at it. Aiden had secretly maintained that it was the Scots side of MacGreggor's Scots-Irish DNA that had ruined him, because no decent Irishman would have blinked over a wee drink on the job.

They had been parked for nearly an hour in a vacant lot located diagonally across from the strangely named store where this Bobbie Faye woman worked. Aiden glanced around the interior of the box truck they'd leased for the job. Sean, their boss, stretched out, looking about as relaxed and friendly as coiled razor wire. The barbed wire scars pocking the left side of his face should have rendered Sean repulsive, but Aiden was damned if it didn't seem to have the opposite effect, especially on the women. Aiden had known Sean since they were kids growing up, scrabbling for existence in Tallaght, west of Dublin. He could no longer remember the first person Sean had killed, but he remembered it had been to help them eat, and they'd followed him ever since.

Mollie, Sean's sprite of a cousin, hunched over the steering wheel and drummed her fingers, irritating the hell (on purpose) out of Robbie, the rat-faced terrier-sized computer geek who'd proven indispensible already. Earlier that morning, Robbie had planted a bugging device on the side of the gun counter Bobbie Faye manned, and now as the women talked, he grinned (fuck, they needed to get him to a dentist and get some teeth in that head).

"Sure, an' d'ye really think the woman'll go along with it?" Aiden asked. He'd read up on several of this Bobbie Faye woman's latest events and getting her to do what she was supposed to do sounded a bit like trying to herd kamikaze bats.

"Aye, she'll no' have a choice," Sean said, and he seemed calm and confident enough, though Aiden knew this was when he was most likely to snap. Aiden wondered—and not for the first time on this job—if having Sean and Bobbie Faye on the same continent wasn't going to be a bit like banging nitroglycerin against a truckload of C-4.

Find *what*?" Bobbie Faye asked Francesca, then hung her head and sighed. She might as well have just opened the door to Hell and said, "Hi, Honey, I'm home!"

Francesca beamed as if Bobbie Faye had somehow tacitly agreed to something. Then she peered around, careful to turn away from Maimee, and whispered, "The *diamonds,* silly. And you don't have much time."

"Bobbie Faye," Maimee snapped, "any day now. I have prayers to attend to and I need that gun."

Somehow, that sentence seemed perfectly normal today.

Bobbie Faye wanted to lie face down on the counter and press her temple into the cool glass, close her eyes, and breathe deeply to keep from beating the crap out of anyone. Later on, maybe a decade from now, when she opened her eyes, they would all be gone and it would be a good day. It wasn't going to happen, though, and from the determined set of Francesca's pout, Bobbie Faye might as well get to the truth; the sooner she did, the sooner she could get rid of this nightmare.

"Frannie, what in the *hell* are you talking about?"

"Mom and Dad had a . . . little . . . disagreement," Francesca continued whispering.

From the way Francesca tensed and hunched her shoulders while her glance darted around, Bobbie Faye knew the disagreement couldn't be little. Nothing with her mom and dad had ever been little—even their beginning had supposedly been epic: a Romeo and Juliet couple caught between warring Cajun (Marie's) and Creole (Emile's) families. They had immediately fallen in love and declared that if they weren't allowed to marry, they would eschew the classic double suicide for something their parents really feared. They would leave LSU and attend the University of Alabama. (Emile's dad staggered around with angina attacks for weeks after that.) Their wedding sealed a shaky truce between the two politically connected families. Marie's rice-farming Cajun clan owned a grain mill and the family could finally afford to do something luxurious, like send Marie off to college to become an artist. Ostensibly in the Mardi Gras bead business, Emile's family earned their money the old-fashioned way: organized crime. Bobbie Faye knew there was some specific bad blood between the families from a couple of generations back, but everyone old enough to know what caused it had incredibly vague patches in their memory when questioned.

"They're getting divorced."

"You're kidding."

"No, I'm *not* kidding," Francesca said, her voice rising with distress "And it's just mean of them, because it's giving me bad dreams and you'd think they'd care at least a little bit, but no, off they go, Daddy with his hoochie fling and Mamma with the diamonds.

That's when Daddy put a hit out on Mamma to make her bring 'em back. Mamma's not gonna and she's gonna get killed and then *you know* that Mamma's family will be after Daddy and these stupid diamonds will *wipe out my family*, Bobbie Faye, and—"

Maimee interrupted, "Could we move this along? People are going to Hell today if I don't get to my prayer meeting soon enough. I need that gun *right now*."

"You don't *need* it right *now*. I'm pretty sure there isn't a new salvation plan where you rush annoying sinners along to their Maker as they beg for forgiveness."

"There could be."

"Yeah, the little known Thou Shalt Carry and Conceal commandment. Do you have some family I could call for you? Friend? Psych ward?" Francesca tapped Bobbie Faye on the arm and she turned to say, "What—" just as two men, pistols in hand, strolled in her direction.

She didn't have anything loaded. Nothing handy. Alarm sang *oh, shit* in a high-pitched squeal in her head. She squinted at a tall, heavyset man whose physique looked put together by an engineer too fond of his T square, with everything about him blocky and wide, even down to basket hands large enough to moonlight as a forklift. There was a bulge under one arm beneath his sports coat where a holster marred the otherwise rectangular lines of his body.

"I think I'm supposed to shoot someone today," he announced, looking directly at Bobbie Faye. "Is it *you*?"

Bobbie Faye blinked. "Did he just ask what I think he just asked?"

"That's Mitch Guillory," Francesca said when Bobbie Faye looked around for an explanation.

"*That's* little Mitchell?" Bobbie Faye asked, not seeing any hint in this refrigerator-square man of the kid so scrawny his mamma called him a toothpick-with-eyes. And then she remembered seeing his mugshot flashed on the news: he'd been wounded in a sting of organized crime in New Orleans.

"You're not supposed to shoot her yet," the other man cautioned Mitch, and Mitch seemed to relax a smidge, but Bobbie Faye kept her eye on his gun.

"But don't I shoot people?" Mitch asked.

"He kinda has a short-term memory problem," Francesca explained. "From being shot."

"I was shot?" Mitch asked, frowning, self-consciously patting himself down.

"Yeah," the other man sighed, having obviously explained this a few times, and Bobbie Faye recognized the sigh—a cringe-inducing recognition as she remembered he was Donny, so boyishly bland that, at thirty, he could almost be mistaken for fifteen. She hadn't seen Donny since he'd gone to L.A. to be an actor, though his career high thus far had been in a hemorrhoid commercial. Donny and Mitch were both Francesca's cousins and always hung around the summers when Francesca's mom sent her to live in Lake Charles with her grandmother.

"You got shot in the head," Donny continued to Mitch. "You keep forgetting stuff." Like, Bobbie Faye remembered from stories at the time, his own alibi or what his defense attorney would tell him, and so he couldn't stand trial. And where Francesca, Mitch, and Donny were, Kit couldn't be—

"Read your instructions," said a woman with a rough, sexy smoker's voice.

—far behind.

Kit, petite, spikey hair, had hidden behind Mitch's bulk. Bobbie Faye recognized her killer good looks as the bratty little cousin who tagged along. She'd always been slightly deranged, the kind of kid who would put cheese in ice cream. To Bobbie Faye she said, "I wrote it all down for him. I think he has a real future as a hit man. He's got great consistency, if we can just clear up this whole *oopsie, wrong target* problem."

"Aren't you . . . a career counselor? For the correctional system?" Bobbie Faye asked while she grabbed the Glock away from

Maimee, just then realizing that the scowling old woman had pulled a box of bullets from the shelf and was trying to figure out how to load them.

"I have a good record in placing people where they have a high aptitude."

"Yeah, why bother with the whole 'and it should be legal' aspect of the job."

"I'd have put you in demolition, for example. You show an exceptional destructive capacity."

"Well, gee, let me update my resumé."

"I'll see what I can find for you," Kit said, missing the sarcasm. "Assuming you live."

"Shhh," Francesca said to Kit, then she spun back to Bobbie Faye. "See? You're perfect for the job."

"Yeah, right after I tattoo STUPID on my forehead."

"Word on the street is that you know how to find the diamonds," Kit explained. "We're helping Francesca keep her parents alive. So that means you have to help."

"You cannot possibly believe Emile would put out a hit on Marie," Bobbie Faye said. Everyone nodded, though Mitch looked to the others for their response before joining in. "No way. Besides, I have things to do. Paperwork for a grant to finish and turn in. I am not chasing after anything just because you show up with some insane story."

Bobbie Faye had to shut and lock the display case to keep Maimee's hands off a SIG.

"But you're our best chance! You saved your brother! Against really bad odds! I watched the whole thing on the news. And I heard Daddy's sending some of his . . . um, workers . . . and Mamma's side said they were, too, and it's going to get *worse* and people are going to die. They're *all* convinced that since you're the Contraband Days Queen, you'd be able to get them."

Bobbie Faye's gaze whiplashed back from where Donny preened for the security camera. Francesca had never been happy about Bobbie Faye being the unofficial queen of the local pirate festival, even though it was strictly a hereditary title. "What in the world has that got to do with anything?"

"You're Cajun. You can find out stuff about Mamma because all her friends are Cajun, so they'll tell you stuff they won't tell me, even though we're cousins."

And there it was, out there. The thing she hadn't allowed herself to think about: this request was about family. Family—specifically from her dad's side. Her dad's sister, Marie, had her life on the line. An aunt who'd been nice to her in spite of the fact that her brother, Bobbie Faye's dad, hadn't ever acknowledged Bobbie Faye, nor she, him. There was a time, when she was very little, she had wished it was different. Now? No way. The only person she'd confided to about her family was Nina, her best friend who owned and ran a questionable quasi S&M modeling agency, but that was because Nina tended to approve of Bobbie Faye's less polite tendencies, particularly if they ran to the homicidal.

Francesca's cousins . . . well . . . technically, two of them were her cousins as well . . . looked at her, hope brimming.

"Maybe you can figure out where Mamma hid them?" Francesca asked. "Because you're really crazy and Mamma's really crazy, so y'all are a lot alike. You probably can think just like her."

"It scares me that you're in sales."

The front window shattered and a bullet whizzed *just* over Bobbie Faye's head and she yelled, "Down!" grabbing the Glock and the bullets on her way to the floor. Allison and Alicia, the twins who worked the front counter, herded the rest of the customers to a back room where there was no flying debris or glass. The cousins spread out, and Mitch shot back, though he clearly was confused as to where to shoot, since he was doing a fantastic job of getting rid of all of the dangerous mannequins lined up in rows in the camo section of the store.

"Mitch!" she yelled, but he couldn't hear her as he picked off a plastic head. Another sniper bullet whizzed past, shattering the tins of gunpowder above Bobbie Faye's head, and black powder showered her and the floor.

Great. Bad hair *and* flammability, all in one move. Yipfucking-whee. She loaded the Glock, and told Francesca to call 911. As she peeked out from behind the counter, she realized Maimee had not, in fact, moved to the ground like everyone else, and while Mitch kept shooting, more sniper bullets slammed into the Coleman lanterns nearby and glass went everywhere.

"Miz Maimee, get down!"

"I'm calling my prayer partners," Maimee announced as she dialed her cell. "We'll just meet here. I think this is God's way of telling me we need matching Glocks."

Bobbie Faye wondered if Mr. Edgar would live long enough to see Maimee in that nice padded cell she was clearly headed for.

"The train's going to block the police," Kit yelled from near the door where she stood at a safe angle, peering out. There was a long-ass train slowly approaching the tracks just a block beyond Ce Ce's store; the cops would have a twenty-minute detour if the damned thing wasn't moving.

"Frannie," Bobbie Faye gripped the woman's arm, hoping to shake her out of her ditzy-fugue state, "*get the cousins out of here. Go to the police.*"

"No way. Daddy's got lots of 'em on the payroll. They'll lock us up before we can help Mamma. We gotta find the diamonds first."

"The FBI—" But Bobbie Faye stopped when Francesca rolled her eyes. Her dad's shady activities had included bribing senators and God knew who else.

"They questioned Mamma, but she didn't have the diamonds on her, so she must've hidden them. We heard she's supposed to be selling them, and if she does that, Daddy will really be mad, so we only have a couple of days, and now we can't find her."

More bullets shattered display cases, embedded in walls, and knocked things off shelves, and Bobbie Faye couldn't tell whether the shooting was from the sniper, Mitch, or Donny joining in for show. When Ce Ce got back from her errand, Bobbie Faye was going to wish one of the bullets had hit its mark. "Who the hell is out there shooting anyway?"

"Maybe somebody who doesn't want us to find the diamonds?" Francesca guessed.

"You're all causing more damage than those stupid diamonds are worth."

"There's about thirty and they're worth a few at least million. Each."

Holy shit, that was a lot, even for diamonds. And Bobbie Faye realized that *why yes, someone probably* would *shoot her for that kind of money.* Actually, there were a few people who'd shoot her for free; add in that kind of money and people were going to line up out the wazoo with guns aimed her direction.

"I'm really sorry to get you involved." Francesca worked her expression from quivering all the way up to full-blown remorse.

The glass fish tank holding the bait minnows shattered from a direct shot and water and minnows whooshed out everywhere. From the other end of the store, she heard a muffled, "Oops."

Then Kit said, "It's okay, Mitch, honey. You shot real good there. Not a single fish shot you back."

Sonofabitch, it was like a bumper crop of crazy in there. They were destroying Ce Ce's, which was bad enough, but now she knew she was going to have to help them. As much as it killed her to admit it, they were family. And there was a part of her, an ingrained sensibility, that just could not let one of them get killed while she stood by and did nothing.

She really fucking hated that stupid sensibility.

FROM THE DESK OF JESSICA TYLER (JT) ELLIS

ASSISTANT TO THE UNDERSECRETARY OF THE UNDERSECRETARY OF
THE SECRETARY OF THE ASSISTANT TO THE DEPARTMENT OF DEFENSE
HOMELAND SECURITY
NEW ORLEANS, LA

Re: progress report stats
(to be filed under field notes, personal, **only**)

Textiles which originated with Marie Despré to be seized for suspicion of acting as a method of smuggling diamonds. Textiles include but are not limited to: purses, belts, shoes, and accessories. Please note that suspect's other hobbies include sculptural art—all known pieces are to be searched, galleries plus private collections. Various offices around the country, including FBI, tasked to help.

Case # 198733BFS / diamond search   field notes: personal

16 items searched
2 movie stars threatening a lawsuit
5 politicians disturbed (with someone other than spouse)
3 paparazzi arrested, cameras confiscated (talk to legal)

1 agent in the field in Lake Charles
1 crazy Cajun woman in the middle of this case
(see fucked, completely—previous case)

Chapter Four

From: Simone
To: JT

Confirmed: shooting inside. Tapped into security via phone. BF alive.
Any luck that end?

(sent via cell)

From: JT
To: Simone

Textile search continues. Three politicians, two not with spouse,
questioned. Several movie stars' homes searched. One agent bitten by
dog.

Encourage BF to work for us. Necessary means.

(sent via cell)

Detective Cameron Moreau leaned back in his chair in his
claustrophobic office in the tiny cinder-block State Police
building. He stretched out his long, lanky six-foot-four frame, his
cowboy boots kicked up onto his desk as he crossed his arms and

contemplated the file in front of him: a murder of a Lake Charles jeweler, known to deal in high-end jewels for very wealthy clients.

The shot pattern and utter lack of forensic evidence made it clear that this wasn't an amateur deal and the PD had almost no leads—information they'd managed to keep completely out of the news for once. Something about the shot pattern had been bothering him, but he'd stared at it now for a couple of days in between the normal chaos of his job, and he couldn't quite place what was making him uneasy.

It hadn't helped that the FBI had swarmed onto the case like mosquitoes, chasing down the leads and questioning his every move and then not sharing information. Fuck them, he was tired of this case already. The FBI wouldn't tell him why in the hell this jeweler meant so much to them, and normally, he'd have just stowed the case away, cooperating only when the Bureau got around to calling . . . only this time, there was that shot pattern making him uneasy.

He'd been feeling seriously wary all morning, in fact. Some people could predict when it was going to rain by when their bones ached. Cam could predict impending doom. Maybe it was just because he'd dated Bobbie Faye too long. Or maybe it was all of the years prior to that when they'd been best friends. He'd weathered more than enough of her disasters and the experience had made him alert to any signs of catastrophe bouncing off the horizon and heading his direction. He was trailing after a shooter with no evidence, the freaking FBI was so far up his ass they ought to have medical degrees, and the headache clawing the inside of his skull was getting worse.

Activity picked up in the station. Cops' voices reached a steady thrum of excitement. Jason, one of the dispatchers, hurried down the hall, stuck his head in Cam's door, and said, "You know there's gunshots over at Ce Ce's?"

Adrenaline shot up his spine. Jesus H. *Christ.*

He bit back the *is Bobbie Faye okay?* question. She wasn't his concern anymore. They'd broken up, it had been a year, and she had made it crystal fucking clear she had no interest in him. Didn't need him, didn't want his help. Got pissed off at him anytime he tried to tell her how to handle something when all he'd been trying to do was help. Which was fine, actually. Better than fine. He was dating Winna now. A very sweet, very pretty schoolteacher. A nice person who didn't tear up half of the state. A woman who actually called him and asked his advice on anything from cars to career. She was quiet. Normal. Thank God.

When Cam didn't respond, Jason kept going down the hall and Cam exhaled. He was permanently out of the Bobbie Faye business—someone else could take care of her disasters.

His phone rang and he grabbed it up. One of his street sources had promised a clue to the shooter in the jeweler case. But instead of his source, Cam heard gunshots and glass crashing. And then Bobbie Faye, as calmly as if she were ordering pizza, said, "Um, Cam? Do you think you could go pick up Stacey from camp and bring her to your mom's for me? I've got a mess to deal with here—I don't think I'm going to make it over there on time."

"What the hell is going on?"

"Oh, just a little disagreement. Don't have time to explain. Look, you said I should have asked you to help last time, and I am and it's important because it's Stacey, and—Hey!" she shouted at someone in the store as the sound of ordnance and background screaming cranked up in volume on his phone.

"Bobbie Faye!" he shouted.

"This is not my fault," she snapped before he could finish his thought. "Look, you can bust my ass for it later, okay?"

"I'm coming there."

"No, damnit. Just go get Stacey."

She hung up the phone, but not before he heard rapid-fire shots close by, and he was pretty sure Bobbie Faye was shooting back. And just like that, he was sucked in.

Why in the hell couldn't she just PMS like the rest of 'em?

From: Simone
To: JT

Fuck. **Sniper.** *NOT OURS. Looks to be after BF.*

(sent via cell)

From: JT
To: Simone

On it. Ordering back-up. Send coordinates.

(sent via cell)

Stop the damned shooting!" Bobbie Faye shouted over the hail-storm of bullets. She'd wanted to explain to Cam what was happening, but he'd never believe she hadn't brought this on herself. And frankly, she didn't want half of her family in jail while she tried to solve the problem and, knowing Cam, that's exactly what would happen if she'd told him. He had a very nasty habit of being a cop first. She needed time to find the diamonds. She didn't know where the hell Marie had put the damned things, but she did know Marie was a creature of comfort, and there were a few family members who would house her. Then there was Marie's business to search, her friends to talk to, and if Bobbie Faye had to turn the whole freaking state upside down and shake it, she would find those fucking diamonds and beat the living crap out of her relatives with them.

Sirens blared at a distance and she eased over to a side window near the end cap of camping gear: the train was dead still on the tracks, blocking the police. Another bullet zinged in through the front.

She'd have to go out the side porch where she could circle around to her car. She grabbed her purse and shoved in the loaded

Glock, pocketing the keys to the gun cases in case Maimee decided that God was all about forgiveness and she'd have a heavenly get-out-of-hell free card just for the asking if she accidentally liberated one of the other pistols in the case.

"C'mon," Bobbie Faye said to the cousins, and led them to the side exit as Francesca re-explained to Mitch that no, he didn't have to shoot anyone. Yet.

From: Simone
To: JT

They're coming out. SIDE DOOR. Necessary means engaged.

(sent via cell)

C am shouted instructions as he ran through the station house. Even if he hadn't been the Detective Sergeant on duty, his CO would have called him in. He was kidding himself if he thought he'd be able to avoid Bobbie Faye's swath of destruction. If she wasn't already dead, he just might kill her himself.

On his way out to his car, Cam pulled out Trevor Cormier's card from his wallet—the FBI agent tangled up in Bobbie Faye's last unholy mess. The bastard who'd had incredibly possessive body language toward Bobbie Faye when Cam had finally tracked them down. Not that it mattered to Cam if Trevor was attracted to Bobbie Faye. The man, Cam had learned, had been Special Ops before he was FBI, and the majority of his records were classified. Sure, he'd proven himself more than capable when Bobbie Faye's brother had been kidnapped, but still . . . Special Ops in Afghanistan and Syria and God knows where else meant, in all likelihood, that Trevor had multiple kills under his belt. Multiple strategic kills . . . *offensive* kills . . . had to change a man. Harden him. Rumor had it that Trevor had no qualms about using anyone he needed to get what he wanted when he was undercover. It was part of the job. And his record indicated that he was exceptionally good at his job.

Trevor had asked Cam to contact him if Bobbie Faye ran into any trouble while Trevor was back at Quantico dealing with the fall-out from Roy's kidnapping. Cam wasn't sure why he hesitated calling Trevor, but he did. He put the card back in his wallet and hopped in his car.

Bobbie Faye stepped outside into the bright summer sun and felt the sweat immediately start to trickle down the back of her neck beneath her heavy hair. She hadn't gone four feet when she slammed straight into a guy who, by all appearances, was rounding the corner, coming from the coffee shop adjacent to Ce Ce's. Her first thought was to determine whether he'd been the id-iot shooting into the store, but he didn't appear to be armed and, oddly, she could still hear ordnance pinging into the store behind her. Parking Lot Guy seemed to be heading toward his gleaming black Harley waiting a few yards away. Her second impression was that it was almost like . . . he'd detoured . . . in order to run into her.

Geez, paranoid much?

In his scuffed biker boots, he stood a little taller than six foot, a baseball cap pulled low over longish brown hair in a ponytail; a mustache and goatee registered but mostly, she'd first focused at her eye level where incredibly tanned, muscled arms were covered with tats and scars. She registered the hottie factor, the flat abs and nice ass, in the moment it took her to try to sidestep and spin away from where they'd rammed into each other. Something intangible, some scent, jumpstarted her Hormones, which backpedaled with a *whoa* and in an overriding show of power, halted her entire body with a flood of heat, and that was kinda weird because the last time that happened was when Trevor . . . *holy shit.*

Trevor was here. *Undercover.*

She stumbled as she caught the expression in his eyes that warned her to not show she knew who he was, and his hands were instantly on her waist, keeping her from crashing into the concrete parking lot. Those hands felt *goooooooooooood. Thank you, Jesus, for loving me a little.* Trevor slid his right hand just a little beneath the hem of her shirt, and Bobbie Faye was about to amend that *little* to *a lot* when she felt him stick something like a Band-Aid just above the top of her jeans. For a second there, she flashed on all of those hot talks, practically phone sex, they'd had when he'd been in Quantico after Roy's kidnapping. She had to fight against the reflex of jumping up, landing on him, and circling her legs around his waist. That might have given things away a tiny bit. She was such the pro.

"Holy freaking geez, asshole, keep your damned hands to yourself," she griped for Francesca's benefit as she and the cousins caught up. Bobbie Faye stepped away from Trevor, pushing against a bicep (and she wanted an Oscar for resisting licking it, thank you very much).

"Hey, bitch. You fell on me. *Watch your step.*"

He pushed past her, climbed on his bike and kick-started the roaring engine . . . and seemed to be stalling, checking gauges. It dawned on her that his *watch your step* had been said with a *heads up* tone. She spun, checking out her surroundings to see if Trevor had been alluding to any specific impending danger. The train whistle sliced through the normal morning traffic noises as she walked toward her Honda Civic—a sad, rusted, and dented little box of a car that had recently wheezed past the two-hundred-and-forty-thousand-mile mark on the odometer. Bobbie Faye glanced back over her shoulder as Trevor pulled out a flask and ostensibly consulted some sort of map, though from this angle, she could have sworn he was actually looking at her instead. Other than the menacing-looking biker image he projected, everything seemed quiet on the tree-lined side street.

Well, other than that white van, bearing down on her.

Which then proceeded to stop as the side door slid open and hands grabbed her, yanking her inside while someone shoved a sack over her head.

Chapter Five

From: Simone
To: JT

Oh, shit. BF yanked off street. Another player. No audio. Visual on van. Sending license plate . . . now.

(sent via cell)

From: JT
To: Simone

Where's Trevor?

(sent via cell)

From: Simone
To: JT

Following.

(sent via cell)

From: JT
To: Simone

Does he know you're there?

(sent via cell)

From: Simone
To: JT

Unknown.

(sent via cell)

Holy fuck, someone had actually kidnapped her. Could chocolate give you hallucinations? Was she having flashbacks from her heavy M&M benders in the fifth grade? Because seriously, what the hell?

One of the hijackers in the van twisted her arms behind her, holding her in place as the van door slid and clicked shut, and then the van accelerated . . . slowly.

"Your *famiglia*, Bobbie Faye, they are to get you killed, *si*?" a gruff, Italian-accented male asked.

"Look, if Roy owes you money, I don't—"

"This ain't about your brother," a creepy, raspy voice said on her left, surprising her. After Roy's kidnapping and the subsequent press about her rescuing him, quite a few people had surfaced trying to coerce her to pay his debts. (Or there were husbands and boyfriends of women he was seeing who kindly wanted to rearrange his face.) She had grown so accustomed to surprise visits, Fear had taken to napping somewhere in the back room of her brain.

Raspy poked her with a gun barrel. Fear was now definitely awake, and kicking its idiot partners, Run and Scream, who'd been seriously falling down on the job.

The van turned right. *Huh?* She knew from memory that the street they'd just turned on was not the path to take if they were trying to rush away from the city with her. They seemed to be . . . going around the block.

"*Non*, no about *il vostra fratello*—ah, your, brother, *non*. This is about the *diamante*," the Italian voice supplied.

"The diamonds?" she asked, struggling with the jerk holding her arms as the van made another right-hand turn. "You have got to be kidding me." She hadn't been helping Francesca fifteen whole minutes and dealing with the repercussions of assisting her family was already about to get her killed.

"We know your idiot cousin," Raspy explained, "asked you to help find those diamonds. And we're telling you, you *don't* wanna find them."

"Gee, if you know me that well, you know I just love a big strong guy to boss me around." She tried to kick out, and someone sat on her legs while the guy behind her wrenched her arm. Fuck, that was gonna bruise.

"*Magnifico*," the Italian said, clearly losing something in the translation. "Tell her you are . . . finished . . . sì? That you no want to help her!"

He was clearly overjoyed. Idiot. "I've told her that ever since seventh grade. In our family, we do Stubborn like other people do Olympics."

"We do it better," Raspy said. "We're here for the buyers. The diamonds belong to us, and everything is set. You interfere? You're dead. Come down with the flu. Convince her you're out."

"Gee, I'm feeling positively queasy as we speak."

"Good girl," Raspy said, and she wanted to deck him for the *girl* crap. What the hell was it with people? She wasn't twelve.

"So, and not that this is *anything* like a brainstorming session, but why kidnap me to tell me to not find the diamonds when you already had a sniper trying to take me out?"

There was a distinct hesitation before the Italian said, "Ah, sì, the . . . sniper, he is good, *non*?"

"No," she said, realizing what had been bothering her at a gut level about the shots aimed into Ce Ce's. Well, other than the whole "being shot at" thing. "He kinda sucked. He could have just killed me."

They made another right-hand turn, which, by her calculations meant . . . clearly her brain was leaking out her ears, because *holy crap*. They'd made the block?

"The buyer," the Italian said, "he want to no kill you, first chance."

"A warning," Raspy supplied. "You get one warning. They said they're not cold-blooded."

"Well, gee, they're practically nominees for the Nobel Peace Prize."

"*They* may not be cold-blooded," Raspy laughed, "but I am. You don't listen? We start killing your family."

The van stopped abruptly and they shoved her out, leaving the sack on her head. She struggled for a moment to pull it off, and as she looked up, she realized she was in essentially the same spot she'd been in before being grabbed. The brilliant cousins pulled up in a gleaming yellow Hummer, which stunned her senses with its brightness. Not exactly a stealthy, anonymous choice for oh, say, finding millions in diamonds or following hijackers.

She was probably lucky Francesca hadn't decorated it with sparklers.

When Bobbie Faye glanced over at Trevor's original position, he was gone, and she tried not to make it obvious that she was disappointed or that she swept her gaze around, looking for him as she turned to go to her car . . . stepping out of the way of the black SUV . . . then realizing, too late, that it had swerved at her. She saw the door opening, the maw of darkness inside the vehicle obscuring faces as she turned to run, because holy shit, twice in one day?

And then something light and soft covered her head and someone yanked her backward, hard, and she banged into the frame as someone hauled her into the backseat. Before she knew what had happened, her arms were zip-tied behind her back.

She was sensing a theme.

From: Simone
To: JT

Got her.

(sent via cell)

Bobbie Faye," a woman's silky voice caressed, almost as soft as the folds of material covering Bobbie Faye's face, "we know your cousin planned to ask for your help finding the diamonds."

"Jesus. Did Francesca take out a freaking ad in the paper or something?" She felt the car drive slowly and then turn right.

"Close. She let it be known that she thought you were the answer to her problems."

Great. Just fucking great. "Let me guess—you don't want me to find the diamonds, either."

There was a hairsbreadth of a pause, and the woman chuckled. "Ah, so that's what the last group wanted. Interesting that they let you live."

"Yeah, that was my favorite part."

"Well, now you are going to find the diamonds and bring them to us. And *only* us, or your life as you know it is over."

"Who the hell *are* you people?" Another right turn. What the fuck? Were they going around the same block? Who knew the side exit of the store led to the Bermuda Triangle of Hijack-land?

"We," Silky said rather matter-of-factly, "are the people who can take away every single thing you ever had, ever loved, or ever wanted."

"Can I keep the lava lamp? Because I'm *really* fond of the lava lamp." She felt a gun press into her check. "Fine. Geez. You can

33

have the lava lamp." They didn't want her dead. Good. They could bite it.

Someone clocked her on the side of the head. As they yanked her back, she swore she could feel a lump rising at the point of impact, front and side. Something sticky trickled down her chin and she was pretty sure that slam had cut her forehead. Maybe she should learn not to taunt the armed and crazy wackos.

"Here's how we're going to handle this," Silky said. "You're going to find the diamonds and give them to us. At that point, if you've been a very good girl and haven't pissed me off, we'll give you a finder's fee. An extremely large finder's fee, which should help you with the previous cretins who threatened your family."

"Riiiiiiiigggggggghhhht. And I'll bet I get a set of steak knives thrown in for free, too." So much for shutting up. She really needed to practice that, she thought, as someone clocked her again, same spot. "Cut it out!"

"You don't have a lot of choice," the woman laughed. "You really don't want to see me displeased. We'll be watching, Bobbie Faye."

Someone cut the zip-ties that held her hands, and the SUV stopped abruptly, just as the van had. The door opened and she was tossed out onto the street. Bobbie Faye yanked off what turned out to be a pillowcase (high thread count, very nice) and stared after the vehicle as it sped away down the same block the van had taken. She looked around and Trevor was now across the street, on his bike, apparently having followed the SUV around the block. There was something incredibly—furious—about his tension, in spite of the poker face he held.

She brushed her hands beneath her shirt and felt the small Band-Aid–sized patch Trevor had stuck on her. On the off-chance that it was a voice transmitter, she turned away from Francesca and the cousins as they gaped from the Hummer, and said, "Welcome to Bobbie Faye World where we don't charge extra for all the crazies you can stand."

He cracked a smile, confirming he could hear her. The relief that washed over her as she turned back toward her own crappy car was palpable. He was *here*. Helping her. She didn't know how or why. She'd missed him, missed their banter. The memory of his voice, talking to her until she was languid with comfort and sleep, flooded back to her. Which is why she wasn't paying all that much attention to the big boxy moving-type truck until it slowed and she thought *no way, not again . . . not even in* my *life*, just as the back door scrolled up and open. She tried leaping out of their grasp, but it happened so fast, she tripped, dropping her purse, and fell straight into their grasp.

She had always had lovely timing.

When Bobbie Faye disappeared into the back of that truck, fury vibrated through Trevor as steadily as the hum of the Harley's engine. This whole goddamned thing should never have happened. The Agency could have alerted him sooner. If her name hadn't popped up on the radar of his own personal contacts when it did, he wouldn't have known to get here. He was too late to change the forward momentum when he'd first arrived, which gave him only option #2—infiltrate. Let her be used as bait, try to keep the agency's mismanagement from getting her killed.

He shoved the rage aside. Anger was a luxury that had no place in an op, even though this set of players in the moving van had not been on the Agency's goddamned radar. The first kidnapper: yes. They were the target—stop the buyers. The second had been rumored, and now he had his own suspicions, but this third hadn't even appeared as a blip. At least not in the intel he'd been given, and his clearance was pretty fucking high. Which meant either the Agency had been caught off guard or someone wasn't playing well with others when it came to information. Trevor didn't know what was worse—that Bobbie Faye was in a terrible position, or that she didn't even know yet just how bad it was.

He knew myriad ways of killing people, and at the rate of the threats to Bobbie Faye's life, he might need every single one. That was fine, if it kept her safe. Or better yet, throw all of the assholes in a room and let her have at them. That would teach them.

He amped up the volume in his earpiece and heard Bobbie Faye . . . and it sounded like a steady . . . growl. She knew he had miked her. She was letting him know she couldn't talk.

"We're just checkin' ye for wires, woman," an odd Irish lilt spilled into his earpiece.

Sonofabitch. He closed his distance to the truck. Exhaled. Thought through his options, stomping down the emotions. Two of his men were positioned across the vacant parking lot, "repairing" an old beat-up car, their "iPods" direct links to a mic of his own that he could key to alert them for fast response. He turned the bike, deciding to run counterclockwise to the van and face it; he wanted to get a look at the driver.

They'd *gagged* her. Had she missed some freaking forecast somewhere? One hundred percent chance of kidnapping today, with a fair-to-likely chance of morning bruises and bound hands?

That was it. When this was over, assuming she lived (she was going to indulge in that pretty fantasy world for a moment), she was going to take karate again and get that black belt she'd been wanting. (Of course, there was the niggly little problem of the karate teacher not letting her back into his dojo after she accidentally shattered his nose last year, and the judo teacher broke out in hives when she'd tried to sign up at his studio. Maybe there was a jujitsu teacher somewhere who hadn't heard of her. But by God, she was going to take something.)

She noticed the hand of the asshole holding her arm—he was missing two fingers. The guy who appeared to be the boss knelt in front of her, patting her down. He had a SIG in a shoulder harness, another smaller gun in an ankle strap, a third at his waist, and a Ka-

Bar knife strapped to his belt. All he needed was a bazooka strapped on his back. (Slacker.) He wore a relaxed expression of power, the kind people get when they know they can take a life as easily as let it be. She'd seen that kind of menace before in her ex-boyfriend Alex, who had turned out to be more than just bad-boy rebellious; he'd been a criminal, a gunrunner. Geez, she needed some sort of pill for her nagging case of "Dating the Worst Possible Guy, Stupid," and while she was at it, maybe they had shots for "Wrong Place, Wrong Time, You Idiot." Hell, she'd probably need a double dose.

"Aye, she's clear," the Irish boss said, and she glared at him so she wouldn't sigh in relief that he had missed the little microphone patch. He watched her with an intensity that scraped her raw nerves. "Ye're quite the popular woman today. Now, ye're goin' to follow my instructions, or ye're goin' to die. Do ye understand this? Nod if ye do." She nodded, noting they made another right turn. Maybe there was a per-mile charge in the Kidnappers' Union?

"I think it's about time for the train to finish up, boss," a small, hunch-shouldered guy called from the front passenger seat. "The cops are on the other side."

The boss continued, unconcerned. "We have seen the two other groups; we had intended on makin' your acquaintance first, but there is always the advantage of lettin' the amateurs have their go. I'd imagine they were quite emphatic about ye findin' the diamonds and deliverin' only to them."

She nodded.

"Aye, yes, that is to be expected. I'm certain they made quite the elaborate threats against you, or your family, should you not comply."

She nodded again as the truck made another right turn. The sound of a motorcycle rumbled louder; Trevor had somehow circled around to approach the truck. For a brief moment, she thought he was going to play chicken with the driver, but he turned into a driveway as if that had been his intended destination.

"Fine, this is fine," the boss continued. "However, ye should know that they are local . . . freelancers. They carry no real weight and either group could easily be bought off, should ye want to eliminate their threat." Okay, this wasn't sounding so bad. "I, however, canna' be bought in any way. I'll be having those diamonds, *álainn*, or many people will die." He leaned closer. "An' I'll make sure the world knows they die as a result of your choices. Do ye understand this? Ye may nod." His voice rumbled low and soft, the Irish lilt tugging at the corners of the words, gving them just the right amount of spring to imply that he had a bit of humor sprinkled on top of his psychotic murderous intent. Oh, goody, a *happy* murderer. *Much* better than a cranky one.

She nodded, and felt them turn again.

"Good. Ye'll find the diamonds and ye'll wait for me. Ye should be aware I know exactly what they are, what they're worth, and how many there are. Ye will not be able to fool me so do not try. Ye'll not be smart enough."

She seethed and didn't nod. *Not smart enough. You bastard, I'll show you not smart*—and then he pulled his knife and used it to start slicing the front of her shirt.

"I can get to ye any time I want, *álainn*. Do ye understand?"

Chapter Six

Trevor kept one eye on his high-tech monitor, which would have appeared to anyone else to be nothing more than a fancy cell phone. Fortunately, it was capable of more than even the agency understood. The number spiking in the corner of the handheld's screen: Bobbie Faye's heart rate. Fuck, he wanted her out of there. She didn't whimper, didn't give him a cue that he'd better move in, get her out now. No, this asshole didn't want her dead. Yet. Just scared.

Her heartbeat steadied, but hadn't dropped back to normal.

The phone vibrated. Trevor checked the caller ID and slapped off the phone, in spite of the fact that it was going to piss off his so-called "boss." He already knew what the man wanted. Rather, *who* the man wanted.

And she was in the truck, her heart rate high, unable to talk.

From: Simone
To: JT

Third player. Want me to pull her out?

(sent via cell)

From: JT
To: Simone

No. She's expendable. Track the player.

(sent via cell)

C am listened over his radio to the frustrated cops grousing about being forced to wait for the train to pass in order to reach Ce Ce's. Two squad cars had peeled off to drive around the unusually long train; no one could tell him what was going on over there. Calls to Ce Ce's snagged against a busy signal. Maybe the phone had been destroyed, or maybe someone was calling out, but it was killing him not to know if Bobbie Faye was okay. He looked in his rearview mirror to where Stacey sat buckled in, her face sticky with the ice cream he'd bought for her. His mom was going to kill him later when she had to deal with Stacey on a sugar high.

"Uncle Cam, is people shootin' at Aunt Bobbie Faye again?"

Jesus Christ, where'd the kid learn to put stuff together. Five-year-olds weren't supposed to be this sharp.

"Ah, she's fine, honey. She's just busy and you were only supposed to have a half-a-day at camp today, so she thought you'd like to go over to Me Maw's to swim." Stacey referred to his mom with the same affectionate nickname as did her "regular" grandchildren. His mom still hadn't accepted the fact that he wasn't dating Bobbie Faye and Stacey wasn't going to be another one of her official brood.

Cam strained to hear any details from his radio. He didn't want to turn it up on the off chance bad news was broadcast—at least at this setting, he could slam the volume down before the kid heard anything damaging.

"When I get big, I'm gonna shoot people 'fore they can shoot me," Stacey announced, and Cam's headache cranked up another notch.

"No, honey, you're not gonna shoot anyone. Nobody's gonna shoot at you and you're going to grow up and be normal."

Dear God, he hoped.

The Irish bastard slit most of her shirt down the front, letting the knife scratch against her skin just enough to create a welt, the sting of skin broken as if by a razor's edge, each inch of the cut drawn out with a teasing smile. He was waiting for her to nod, to agree that she wasn't smart enough to outwit him. He'd probably start slicing some other clothing item if she didn't agree.

She glared at him. Common Sense had sounded all of the alarms, begging her to play along as "the frightened prisoner" but the Glaring? That had a mind of its own. Because who in the *fuck* did this guy think he was?

Um, probably a psycho killer, Common Sense offered. Still, the Glaring wouldn't back down.

The bastard *laughed.* "Very good. I see we have *tuiscint dá chéile,* a mutual understanding, ye see." He spoke into her ear, his warm breath pulsing against her neck, "I like ye, *álainn,* and would like to keep ye without harmin' ye."

Keep? Oh, holy *hell.* She ran rapid fire through Alarm, Fear, Repulsion, and Loathing when Fascination stepped up and said, *Oh, so this is what psychotic bad guys look like.*

Mid-shudder, the truck stopped and they tossed her out. She tumbled onto the asphalt, looking up in time to watch the tires spin as they raced away. She yanked the gag from her mouth, spitting out the taste of sweat-soaked cotton. Bobbie Faye spun where she stood on the off chance there were any more criminals who wanted to take her for a test-drive today. The road was clear, except for Trevor on his bike, heading for her, and the cousins in the Hummer, parked, managing to block the "escape route" of the truck . . . *after* it had already driven safely away. Well, give them two points for finally thinking of that little trick, three kidnappers later. God help her if she was ever on fire. They'd probably figure out to call the fire department when there was nothing left but ashes.

She looked down at her sliced and gaping-open shirt; it had been one of her favorites, and of course, she'd chosen that day to wear her almost-see-through bra. Her hands shook as she ripped the rest of the shirt down the front so she could tie the halves together. The heat of the day baked her skin as she stood in the morning sun, her pulse throbbing so hard she could feel it in her fingertips, too aware of every single drop of sweat running down her skin. She knew she was going into shock, especially since she didn't really register how close the motorcycle was until Trevor closed his hand over hers. It was everything she could do to keep from leaping forward and throwing her arms around him. His gaze fell to the sliced shirt and the welt still visible. He squeezed her hand, his thumb circling over hers, calming, though the anger shining in his eyes was clear.

"Play along," he warned as he yanked her to him, throwing her off balance so that she landed against his side and had to grab his arm to keep from falling to the pavement. "Look pissed off for our viewers. Go straight to your Aunt Marie's house, and whatever you do, when you see me there, you need to be afraid."

If he kept looking like he'd be happy to go on a murder spree, she didn't think looking afraid was going to be a real stretch. He shoved her away and pointed at her car, as if he was giving her instructions. She stalked toward the Civic, scooping up her purse from where she'd dropped it before.

"Bobbie Faye, yooohoooooooo, Bobbie Faye," Francesca called, heading on a direct intercept course between Bobbie Faye and her car. "We decided you'd be safer if I rode with you! So I can protect you if those bad guys come back!"

She looked up to heaven. *Seriously, God, didja just get bored with the pestilence, plague, and a horde of crickets?*

•   •   •

FROM THE DESK OF JESSICA TYLER (JT) ELLIS

ASSISTANT TO THE UNDERSECRETARY OF THE UNDERSECRETARY OF
THE SECRETARY OF THE ASSISTANT TO THE DEPARTMENT OF DEFENSE
HOMELAND SECURITY
NEW ORLEANS, LA

Re: progress report stats
(to be filed under field notes, personal, **only**)

Textiles which originated with Marie Despré to be seized for suspicion of acting as a method of smuggling diamonds. Textiles include
but are not limited to: purses, belts, shoes, and accessories. Please
note that suspect's other hobbies include sculptural art—all known
pieces are to be searched, galleries plus private collections. Various offices around the country, including FBI, tasked to help.

Case # 198733BFS / diamond search   field notes: personal

27 ~~16~~ items searched
9 ~~2~~ movie stars threatening a lawsuit
7 ~~5~~ politicians disturbed (with someone other than spouse)
3 paparazzi arrested, cameras confiscated (talk to legal)
2 medical claims (cuts & bruises) (see above)
1 agent treated for human bite (dog owner) (see above)
6 defense attorneys filing harrassment suits

1 agent in the field in Lake Charles kidnapped? can we be so lucky?
1 crazy Cajun woman ~~in the middle~~ of this case
(see fucked, completely—previous case)

C am drove away from his mom's house where Stacey had managed to shove two chocolate chip cookies into her mouth before she'd been there one whole minute. She was such a determined little kid, he just prayed that whatever she decided to do when she grew up was legal. He hated to think about the damage someone with Bobbie Faye's genes could do if she actually *planned* it.

The radio crackled with officers finally on the scene at Ce Ce's. The gunmen, whoever they were, had begun shooting after Francesca had entered the store. Given Francesca's dad's mob ties, this could not bode well for Bobbie Faye, though Bobbie Faye seemed to have gone willingly. The officer called in a "last reported sighting" location and the direction the witnesses believed Bobbie Faye had driven away. Cam spun his car, stomping the gas. There was a chance—a small chance—he could intercept them and find out what the hell was going on.

I f Bobbie Faye's car had started on the first, or even the third try, Fluffy-head would have been stuck riding with the other cousins and Bobbie Faye could have had the few minutes' ride to Marie's to think through the day's events. Instead, Francesca had made it to the car in time to join her and was now practically trying to levitate above the torn-and-duct-taped ICEE-stained seat in order to avoid touching anything.

"Bobbie Faye, you really need to get a new car. With leather seats. You should get leather for days like today when you're cut and bleeding—leather wipes off easier."

"Right, because the seats are the thing I should be worried about when I'm bleeding."

"Just don't let anyone Luminol them. Leather really isn't ever the same after that, I don't care what the detectives tell you."

"You never really had a chance at a normal upbringing, either, did you?"

"We're normal," Francesca answered, hurt, her voice petulant.

"Frannie, anyone whose dad routinely heads out to the garage with an Uzi in one hand and a pistol in the other is not leading a normal life."

"There were raccoons that tore up our trash. Daddy was just scaring them off. We're *normal*."

"Uh-huh. Three of the references you listed for your first job after college were in prison for organized crime."

"Oooh, that was the job at Cosmetics Heaven! They loved me over there. I did the best makeovers, *ever*. I got so good, they gave me all of the hard cases."

Bobbie Faye accelerated, weaving through the back streets, neatly avoiding the multitude of cop cars zooming toward Ce Ce's. It was a sad commentary on her life that Bobbie Faye knew which side streets to take to accomplish this feat. She knew from the decibel level of the sirens that Benoit, Cam's best friend, was leaving Rosie's Diner four blocks away and heading her direction, and that he'd probably be biting into a shrimp po'boy with juice dripping down his chin, and forgetting to look to his left, where she passed by just a block away. She resisted waving to his profile as he did just that.

"You need a complete overhaul," Francesca said, pushing a finger against Bobbie Faye's cheek. "You have to do something about those pores. You could park a truck in there."

Bobbie Faye had the sudden impulse that an animal in a trap would have: chew anything off just to escape.

While Francesca catalogued every facial product she thought Bobbie Faye needed (and there were many), Bobbie Faye headed north on Highway 171, past the train car switching station, beyond an industrial park of businesses, and then through the heavily treed neighborhoods that lined the highway. Her little car coughed thick clouds of black smoke every single mile. There was no gas station for miles to check her engine until she got well past the bridge. With each new blast of smoke from her exhaust, the Hummer backed off so as not to Hoover up the nasty fumes. Bobbie

Faye and Francesca, however, weren't as lucky. As the oily vapor seeped into the interior, Bobbie Faye rolled down a window and Francesca had a coughing fit.

"Where are we going, anyway?"

"To your mom's"

"When she disappeared, we tried there first. Pick somewhere else."

"It's not exactly like I'm equipped with onboard 'diamond MapQuest' in my ass, Frannie. Maybe she left a clue at her house to give us some sort of starting point." Bobbie Faye couldn't exactly say they had to go there first because the FBI hottie she'd been lusting after had told her to.

Sooty fog shot through the dash. "I think we should ride with the cousins," Francesca wheezed. She flapped her hands to fan the smoke away. "The Hummer is new and clean and smells pretty and it doesn't have that awful ticking sound."

"Nice try, but my car doesn't tick."

"Does so."

Bobbie Faye approached a bridge that spanned a swollen bayou.

"I'm sure I hear ticking," Francesca pouted.

Her cell phone rang, and Bobbie Faye dug it out of her purse, noting Cam's caller ID. "I'm kinda busy right now," she answered.

"Where the hell are you? The men said Ce Ce's looked like a war zone."

"Bobbie Faye!" Francesca tugged on her arm. "I really do hear ticking."

"I have a little errand," Bobbie Faye told Cam. "You did the thing?"

"Who's that with you? And what's ticking?" he asked.

"Nobody and nothing. Did you—"

"Yes. She's safe with my mom. What's—"

"Just because I'm pretty doesn't mean I don't hear things," Francesca groused. "And there's ticking."

"Nothing's ticking, Francesca, so give it a rest!"

"There's ticking?" Cam asked, and Bobbie Faye hated that forceful, controlled freaking-out sound he had at times like this. "What's ticking?"

"Nothing, Cam. Everything's fine."

"There *is* ticking!" Francesca shouted, vindicated. "Look!" She gestured wildly to the floorboard of the back seat. Then her face elongated as her eyebrows went up and her chin dropped. "Uh-oh. Is that a bomb?"

Oh holy hell.

From: Simone
To: JT

Audio in BF's car. Something about a bomb.

(sent via cell)

From: JT
To: Simone

You are fucking kidding me.

(sent via cell)

"A bomb?" Cam asked, the horror in his voice evident.

"Um, yeah, well, busy now. Gotta go."

He shouted as she hung up, but there was no time to explain. Not that she could explain anything, actually, because when had her life ever made sense? Especially now? She was mid-bridge with a car that was spewing so much smoke, she expected a Hazmat team to parachute in any minute now, not to mention the teeny-tiny problem of there being something very bomblike in her backseat. Was there a timer on that thing? Then again, why would she trust a person trying to blow her up to show her how long she had left to live? She pulled over, and she and Francesca hopped out.

Damn, *Sonofabitch*. Oncoming traffic. She waved them off, stopping them from entering the bridge. Francesca grabbed her arm and tried to drag her back toward the Hummer.

"I don't wanna walk all the way to the end. Let's just ride with the cousins."

"I can't let other people blow up, Frannie," Bobbie Faye said, digging her phone back out and dialing 911. It was a good thing she had some warning. . . .

Wait. How often do bombs actually *tick* anymore? In this age of C-4 plastique explosives, bombs didn't still *tick*, right? How convenient that it ticked long enough for her to get safely out. She thought about the first abductors and their warning to stop trying to find the diamonds and realized: it was a con. They were trying to scare her off. And she *fell* for it. Geez, she felt like she should give back some of her IQ points.

She spun and headed for her car. Maybe she could coax it a little farther, at least to a gas station.

"Bobbie Faye! You're crazier 'n your mamma, and that's a bunch of crazy!"

At which point, the car, apparently eager to help punctuate the point . . . detonated.

Chapter Seven

The concussion slammed Bobbie Faye against Francesca and they crashed to the road. Car parts and shrapnel flew in every direction as a fireball rolled out and upward. After what might have been an eternity, but was maybe only a half a second, the car debris rained down as the side of the bridge near her car started caving toward the water. *Huh. Bombs can still tick. Valuable little piece of information there.*

"Ooooooooh," Francesca singsang, sounding like she did back in fifth grade when she ratted Bobbie Faye out for selling those Popsicles made of holy water. "The mayor's gonna have a heart attack."

"Again," Bobbie Faye agreed.

"Maybe you can send him an apology?"

"Yeah, because I'm sure there's a Hallmark card for that somewhere: sorry about the bridge, please don't die." A piece of the bridge fell into the bayou below. "I wonder if they sell postage stamps in prison?"

Bobbie Faye's ears rang, and the arched structure shook as she and Francesca got unsteadily to their feet. The hole near her burning car prevented the Hummer from moving forward. Her phone chirped as she tried to decide which direction to go: back across the unsteady bridge toward her cousins, or onward to the opposite bank. Caller ID: Nina. Her best friend was in Italy doing a fashion spread for her new magazine (having branched off from her quasi S&M modeling agency to a quasi S&M magazine).

"Hey," Nina said by way of hello, "you're not going to believe where I am."

"I betcha I got ya beat."

"I'm a guest in an Italian villa, where they're serving me tagliolini with crab meat and aubergine sauce."

"I'm standing on a bridge where my car just exploded and part of the bridge is falling into the water. But hey! The good news is, I think we've avoided the sniper!"

"Okay, I'm not playing this game with you anymore. You always win."

Nina leaned forward on the silk divan in the gorgeous sixteenth-century salon while the photographer's assistant adjusted the lighting. "Are you okay?" She waved off the waiters who were hovering with trays of food, eyeing the models; they'd gotten amazingly good service at the villa.

"Oh yeah. Cuts, bruises, bad hair, people trying to kill me. Normal day."

"Tell me what's wrong," Nina said, popping open her laptop. "I can catch a corporate flight out tomorrow."

"No, you stay. This is going to be fine. I just have to find some stuff. It'll all be over before you could get home anyway."

"I want to help. What can I do?"

"Pray. A lot."

"Do you remember the time you put a voice-activated tape recorder in Father Patrick's confessional and ended up breaking up at least eleven marriages that we know about?"

"Can I help it if Father Patrick was a lot busier than we thought?"

"Well, I think God's still mad at you for that one. You might need more than prayer."

Trevor saw a bullet whiz past Bobbie Faye. The *hell?* It had been close enough to slice the top of her shirt at the shoulder, and she hit the deck of the bridge, lying on her stomach, palms down, ready to crawl whichever direction she could determine was safe. As he scanned the banks of the bayou down and to his left, he radioed his men to get the fucking Hummer out of his way. He couldn't see where the sniper hid in the rampant overgrowth of reedy grasses and thick green brush.

We're done," John said, checking his sights on his rifle scope. The crazy bitch had dropped below the bridge railing. And this was after she got out of the shitty car in time. He hadn't had the supplies to do a fancy remote detonator. He hated this fucking job; he coulda been done earlier if they'd just let him pick her off in the first place. One quick shot to the head on her way into work this morning and *bam,* he woulda gotten his payoff. Instead, he was belly down on this Godforsaken bank of a bayou, up to his ass in bugs and mosquitoes and probably snakes. At least there was so much muddy crap growing out here, he coulda had a party and no one woulda seen 'im.

"Ah, but you missed," Otto, his Italian partner said, low and annoyed. "Like the other sniper. You try again, no?"

The fucking other sniper, whoever the hell he was, couldn't hit a drunk in a bar. Fired too wild. Stupid amateurs. John checked his sights again. "Too many people. I told you we shoulda taken her out from the beginning."

"This is not what the buyer wanted," Otto said, and it gave John a helluva lot of satisfaction that the man had been forced to crawl in the mud in his expensive clothes. Why in the hell would some asshole wear leather pants in the South in summer? "He only want," Otto continued, "to say *go away.*"

"Yeah, well I don't think she's big on listening."

John tried to tell 'em that. But now he was going to make her wish she had.

From: JT
To: Simone

The bridge? Her car blew the bridge? And there's a sniper again? How many people hate this woman?

(sent via cell)

From: Simone
To: JT

Apparently, a lot.

(sent via cell)

Relief flooded Bobbie Faye when she heard the motorcycle. She pushed up, her face just inches off the hot asphalt that burned her hands, small pebbles biting into her palms, and she looked down the length of the bridge where two men held guns on the cousins. Damn, she'd wanted to do that all morning. Trevor wove past the Hummer and then the hole and the debris, stopping between her and the direction the sniper bullet had come from—a bullet that was way too close for comfort. She was still shaking from it.

"Get up," he barked at her. He was in character, Bobbie Faye realized, for Francesca's benefit. She hoped. Because that look on his face? Scarier than the fact that the sniper was apparently still determined to finish her off. And strangely, a lot better shot than he had been at the store. Unless there were two snipers? Noooo . . . not even . . . fuck. Who was she kidding? She wouldn't be a bit surprised if there was some sort of sniper contest going on.

"Get on the bike," he ordered. When she didn't stand up immediately, (Brain: *move now*. Legs: *fuck you*.), Trevor pulled out his SIG, pointed her direction as his expression hardened into murderous. "Get on the bike. *Now*."

"Where are you taking her?" Francesca demanded, standing, her hands on her hips, her toe tapping in her stiletto as if he wasn't frightening enough to make Satan feel insecure in his job description.

It surprised Bobbie Faye that Trevor paused to answer.

"I've got a message for you from your dad," he told her at gunpoint as Francesca's eyes narrowed into a glare. "Stay out of it. She," he angled his head back toward Bobbie Faye, "is working for him now."

Of course she was. Because having four psycho cousins, three crazy hijacking groups of morons, a sniper, *and* a sneaky FBI guy wasn't quite enough insanity for one day.

C am waited at the foot of the bridge, watching as the fire department prepared to douse the remains of Bobbie Faye's car. Most of the car had blown up and forward, landing on a section of intact pavement; there was a gaping hole in the bridge behind where the car currently burned. Parts of the car littered the bridge and dead fish floated in the slow-moving bayou, while cops and bystanders alike shouted in vain against the blaring sirens. He stood there in sunglasses, his sleeves rolled up to his elbows, sweat trickling into his collar, ignoring the oven-level heat. The advantage of being tall allowed him to see above most of the other officers milling around, and he scanned the road beyond the smoking bridge, looking for a sign she was okay.

Patrolmen canvassed witnesses, occasionally glancing his direction with a small shake of the head to indicate no specific sighting. The car was probably too charred for the crime scene team to know yet if there were remains inside. Bitter-tasting smoke billowed up and hung in the otherwise crystal blue sky, casting an ugly haze over the surrounding run-down waterfront property. Not even the lush green of the cypress and birch could offset the smoggy cloud hovering over the fishing area.

Cam tried to see past the smoke to gaze back south at the city. He wanted to feel its rhythm, the hum of Lake Charles's industry situated smack in the middle of farmland on one side and swamp and fishing on the other. Sometimes, he could detach himself from the harsh reality of crime, feel the heat of the small city, listen to its heart, its good intentions that offset the bad stuff happening, and that sustained him.

Then there were days like this that killed him. He didn't know if she was dead in that car, or maybe at the bottom of the bayou, or if she'd escaped. (How? And had gone where?) This was why he couldn't have married her, he reminded himself. This was why that engagement ring was at the bottom of the lake behind his house, Bobbie Faye never the wiser. Because, ultimately, he would have gotten the phone call. He knew so many cops' wives and husbands dreaded that call, and yet, he had always known that if he'd married Bobbie Faye, even though he was the cop, he'd have been the one on the receiving end. Too many times he'd tried to get her to be safe. Too many times he'd tried to make her see if she just asked for help, she wouldn't have to face this sort of danger. Too many times he'd told her she could keep this sort of chaos from happening, she could have an easier life, a real life. She never listened. Goddamnit, she never listened.

Right now he had to do something—anything—because thinking was just no damned good.

Ce Ce scanned over the disaster zone that had been her store, her long braids swinging as she turned and turned her ample body, trying to take it all in. The pieces of four display cases filled the aisles around the gun counter where Bobbie Faye had holed up, the merchandise shot all to hell. There was no blood, so Ce Ce breathed a sigh of relief. How could this have happened? Ce Ce felt wholly at fault, wholly unworthy. People knew her for her good voodoo. She ran an entire side business on her reputation for getting results. She'd cast several protection spells for Bobbie Faye recently and they should have been in effect. Those incantations should have prevented any craziness from getting in the store and bothering Bobbie Faye. Every angle should have been covered.

Wait. *Multiple* spells. Could they have cancelled one another out? Oh, Lord. She looked around the old mazelike store. Half of the wooden floors sagged from age, and dust coated some items that maybe hadn't been such good purchases at the time (she didn't know how she was going to unload those Pet Rock Vacation Spas that were cluttering aisle twelve). Somewhere in that store was an inlet for the bad, and it had gotten her girl.

The twins joined her—Alicia with streaked hair now so that Ce Ce could tell them apart. They all watched the cops range through the aisles as they interviewed witnesses, took photos and fingerprints, and bagged evidence.

"Bobbie Faye was just minding her own business," Alicia whispered in awe.

"Trying to talk Maimee out of buying that gun," Allison agreed. At nineteen, the twins had seen a lot of Bobbie Faye disasters, but nothing quite this up close and personal.

Ce Ce looked over at Maimee, who was giving her statement to the cops and who was now extremely disgruntled at being detained. Several other customers gathered at the worn, chipped red Formica tables over in the little breakfast nook Ce Ce had installed near one of the counters where she sold biscuits and gravy and chicken tenders to the fishermen heading out for a day on the lake. Those who weren't answering the cops' questions had their attention riveted to the little TV mounted above the food counter, where footage from the local TV news showed a crater in the Highway 171 bridge. Ce Ce grabbed Alicia's arm to steady herself as the camera zoomed to the remains of a Honda Civic with telltale

Bondo and duct tape holding on the rear quarter panel—or what was left of it.

"That's Bobbie Faye's car," Alicia whispered, and Ce Ce swallowed hard.

Ce Ce's best friend, Monique, bustled out from the back office area and gaped. Monique, a mom of four hellions, was squat and heavy, red hair and freckles, and looked like the safest, sweetest, nicest person on the planet. Her sunny disposition was probably a result of having a flask handy twenty-four/seven—something Ce Ce didn't entirely fault her for.

"How did you get into a crime scene?" Ce Ce asked her. As the owner, they'd let Ce Ce in, but no one else was supposed to get past the perimeter until the cops were done with the evidence collection.

"Oh, honey, I used to babysit Earl over there," Monique waved at one of the cops. "Hey," Monique said as she took in the extent of the damage, "I thought we cast a bunch of wahootsie thingies to keep Bobbie Faye safe in here."

Monique had insisted that she wanted to learn how to cast the spells, but her extreme lack of attention to detail (especially as she'd drink whatever was in the flask throughout the lesson) was going to get them killed if Ce Ce wasn't careful.

"Honey, whatever we did wasn't strong enough."

Excitement brimmed in Monique's big blue eyes. "Are we about to go all kick-butt in the voodoo-rama department?"

Ce Ce scanned the room and then turned toward the storage area where she kept her supplies. "You bet your sweet freckled ass we are."

Cam stood near the crime scene tech as she checked over the car. It reeked of burnt rubber and the sour tang of seared metal. The tech, Maggie, was older than God, and she always wore a nice suit with a red flower in the lapel. A short woman who barely came up to Cam's sternum and was as wide as she was tall,

Maggie nonetheless moved with an elegant grace that made Cam think of ballet lessons and etiquette classes instead of the grisly reality that was Maggie's day job. None of this whole scene was improved by the dead fish smell wafting upward from the bayou below them.

"I'm not seeing remains," she said to Cam in a volume low enough, Cam suspected, that the news couldn't catch it on their boom mikes, which were extended as far out from the police barrier as possible. It was always an insane feeding frenzy with a Bobbie Faye case—the news ratings usually spiked on days when she created a wide path of destruction, and per usual, every TV station, radio station, newspaper (even high school), and Internet news site was represented. Cam tried to stand between Maggie and the cameras as she worked, but the cameras had set up on both ends of the bridge just beyond police barricades, so there was no avoiding them. "I'll get you something more conclusive once we go over the debris," she told him, "but I think your girl must've gotten out before the bomb blew." She leaned into the car through the missing doorway. "Looks like we got a good fire crew this time—they did the best they could not to destroy the evidence. I might get lucky."

Cam allowed himself a small sigh of relief even while he flinched a little at the *your girl* part. When in the hell was this freaking town going to let him forget they'd once been together?

"What about the bomb?"

"Looks real basic from the little bit I'm seeing, nothing fancy, but that's nothing more than an educated guess at this point, since we'll have to put divers in the bayou to try to find out if there's any more evidence below us. I'll have something more for you by tomorrow."

He didn't have to tell Maggie that this was a priority case. Bobbie Faye related events automatically got the mayor's and the governor's attention and their urgency to make it go away, fast. Maggie went back to supervising the collection of evidence and Cam surveyed the crowd. Somewhere, there was someone who'd seen what happened. The damned frustrating part about investigating anything that the Contraband Days Queen did: most of the town felt a sense of loyalty, as if she were really some sort of crowned royalty of their own, and they wouldn't rat her out if they thought it would help her get away. Of course, as soon as it was clear she'd gotten away, he'd have fifty people claiming to have been running from the car with her when it blew up, just to get themselves on TV.

He kept scanning the crowd, looking for an expression of . . . confidence. Of someone who already knew that Bobbie Faye hadn't been in that car. But most of the people were scowling with curiosity or worry. Then he landed on a familiar face.

His headache instantly got ten times worse.

From: Cam
To: Bobbie Faye

Where the hell are you? This is my SEVENTH message! Call me.

(sent via cell)

Bobbie Faye pressed her face into Trevor's back as she rode behind him on the Harley, the wind whipping her hair against her, stinging her face until she had to close her eyes. Which meant she couldn't see the curves ahead as Trevor sped through them, leaning into the road, going so fast that the terrain was a blur and she was in serious risk of becoming asphalt décor.

She made a mental list of asses that needed to be kicked, and it was getting freakishly long. Who in the hell did these people think they were? How was it okay for them to just ram into her life and threaten her and her family? She knew Francesca's dad was a scary guy, well connected to organized crime if the rumors were anything to go by. (Nothing had ever been proven.) Someone like that probably would order a hit on his ex-wife, to do whatever it took to get something back that he wanted. Him, she understood. But these other people . . . trying to kill her? Who were these people trying to manipulate her for their own ends . . . were they insane? Did they think she'd recoil in fear and do what she was told, like she operated on common sense or something. . . .

. . . *Oh. Wait.* Okay, maybe she didn't. Maybe she should, but at this point, she was fucking pissed off. And sore. Blood ran down her left arm from scrapes and scratches she'd gotten when she was thrown from the explosion. She could only imagine what the cut on her forehead looked like from that second abduction; she was probably going to be turning purple from bruises at any point.

The adrenaline must be subsiding, because her arms felt loose and weak and she had the shakes. She pressed closer to Trevor, and he let go of one of the handlebars and covered her hand with his. Then he turned left off 171 onto Sam Houston Jones Parkway and then a right into a gorgeous neighborhood—something about "Park Manor" on the sign, but she missed some of the name.

Marie had moved into this exclusive enclave after she'd left Emile. Mature trees filled the lawns, including stunning live oaks with lush, green canopies and massive limbs that dipped down almost to the ground, colorful crepe myrtles with a riot of pale pink flowers, and stately pecan trees. Each mansion sported at least two stories, many of them, three. Trevor drove to the back of the neighborhood, one of the last streets fully developed. There were obviously developers with plenty of optimism in Lake Charles: a new huge section of the neighborhood was under construction on the street behind Marie's place.

Bobbie Faye would have picked the Victorian as having been her aunt's, in spite of having not seen it before. It was quintessential Marie: pinkish siding with deep fuchsia flowers that overflowed from every inch of the yard and porch. As soon as they came within sight of the house, Trevor stiffened and quit holding her hand. They parked at a side entry, and Trevor moved so quickly she didn't realize what he was doing until he'd done it: he'd zip-tied her hands.

"What do you people do, buy these in bulk?" She felt the claustrophobic freak-out factor click on. "Get these off."

He pointed to where he'd notched the plastic tie; the notch was nearly all of the way across the middle of the tie, which meant one good twist of her wrist and she should be free.

"Don't even *think* about this being a regular habit," she muttered.

He grabbed her wrists to lead her inside. He bent down to whisper in her ear, a hint of a smile in his voice. "I wouldn't bet on that." They stepped inside the house and her really crappy day just went all to hell.

Chapter Eight

Reggie "Buzz Saw" O'Connor and her cameraman walked toward the police perimeter where Cam stood on the bridge, and his mood worsened with her every step. She was a beautiful woman, though Cam refused to acknowledge that maybe he felt that way because she was a Bobbie Faye type: long, lean, and a little curvy. Unfortunately, the beauty hadn't made it past her skin. Reggie was extremely manipulative and the kind of reporter who would not only plant a banana peel in someone's path, but who would be there for the fall and probably have paid a hooker to pile on while she took the photos. She called herself an "investigative" reporter, and if there was no news, then by God, she created it, even if it meant blowing a case detectives had worked more than a year to put together.

"Cam," she said, when she confronted him. "You look like shit, as usual. Still missing Bobbie Faye, I see." She looked over to the burnt car. "Literally."

"How's the ex doing? Still annoying you by breathing?"

"Hey, at least I know how to get his attention. You got anything for the record?" she asked, shoving a microphone in his face as her colleague aimed his camera at Cam.

He looked at her like she'd lost her mind. Come to think of it, considering how bitter her divorce and well-publicized custody battle had become, she probably *had* lost her mind.

"So," Reggie said, talking into the mic, "what would you say if I had inside information that says that Bobbie Faye might be working for organized crime, setting up some big heist. I hear she's in deep trouble."

"You know I never give a statement, Reg. Whatever game you're playing, you're wasting my time."

Reggie laughed. "I'm not playing, Cameron, but that's okay, you'll catch up soon enough." She turned to walk away and the cameraman followed until she stopped and peered over her shoulder. "You know, it has got to be really debilitating for a girl like Bobbie Faye to be dead broke all of the time. She's got a niece to raise and no real decent place to live . . . what if she were to suddenly come across a way to be wealthy, even if it's a little fuzzy, morally? I know—" she stopped him before he could respond "—no comment. But personally, I think she'd be tempted. In fact, I don't think you know her as well as you think you do. You really don't know what a woman pushed to the edge is capable of doing. I, however, don't have any illusions about your Bobbie Faye."

Cam just stared at her, poker-faced, until she turned around and left.

Sonofabitch. What was that all about? He knew Bobbie Faye had shaved a rule a time or ten when she thought they were dumb or in the way and weren't really necessary, but Reggie was hinting at something bigger, something that brought out the feral, competitive reporter in her.

So what in the hell was Bobbie Faye up to?

The first thought Bobbie Faye had when entering the all-pink living room was that she was going to have to bleach her eyes. Every single item in the room was some shade of pink, peach, rose, or blush. Even the plastic casing on the large flat-screen TV had been somehow painted pink, which was an affront to TVs everywhere. She'd barely had time to blink and adjust her eyes from the bright noon sun when three men stepped into the room from the kitchen.

Emile. Great. She'd apparently missed the fact that today was Rat Bastard *day.*

Bobbie Faye swallowed the distaste that automatically flooded her as her uncle stood flanked by two bodyguards. Clearly, her uncle had a no-neck, "must be the size of a small planet" hiring policy when it came to his goons. Sandwiched between them, Emile seemed almost tiny, though he was nearly as tall as Trevor. His dark, exotic looks were still handsome; only the crinkles around his eyes indicated he was closer to sixty than a first glance would have indicated.

Bobbie Faye could imagine him as he'd been in college when Marie met him: bright, funny, beautiful, and rich. Every girl's dream. But somewhere along the way, he'd grown into a man who ran a multimillion-dollar Mardi Gras bead business, which, by allegations the federal government had never been able to prove, had also given him access to a wide organized crime network—a network he joined back then and now led.

"What," he said, grinning, white teeth bright against his darker complexion, his arms spread wide. "No hug for your uncle?"

She tamped down the anger and fear she felt as she held up her zip-tied hands in front of him as a way of blocking his hug; she wasn't fooled. She hadn't ever been fooled, not even as a kid, when Emile would bring along sacks of candy and ostentatious presents the few times he ventured into Cajun land when picking up Francesca from her grandmother's in order to drag her back to New Orleans for the school year. He was the kind of guy who bought a watchdog, then shot it for barking and waking him up. Or so the rumor had gone.

"I don't think uncles send pit vipers to pick up their nieces, but I could be confused by this whole *family* concept."

Emile chuckled, glancing at Trevor, who'd taken up a stance on the opposite side of the room from the bodyguards. Trevor folded his arms across his chest. His biceps bulged, the tattoos on his shoulders above them flexed just a bit, almost imperceptibly. He looked chiseled out of stone and she got distracted for a second there, wondering where he got those tattoos—and if she could forget those, what else did she not know about him? Then his forearm flexed, and she felt the tension radiate off him, in spite of his practiced, calm demeanor. That was the first time Bobbie Faye registered that somewhere along the way, he'd put on a shoulder-holster—and his right hand, tucked into the crook of his elbow, was probably resting on the butt of his gun. He wasn't exactly inspiring her to relax.

"Oh, *chérie*," Emile said, nodding toward Trevor, whose expression was that of a stone cold killer, "he's an insurance policy, nothing more."

"Somehow, I'm pretty sure he doesn't work for State Farm."

"I want my diamonds back, Bobbie Faye." Emile's voice had gone soft and deadly. She had to blink away images of poisonous snakes slithering across the floor, but her skin crawled with apprehension, just the same. "So you can stop playing your little game and tell me where they are."

Game? *Game?* She could see the headline now: *Woman's head explodes, takes out city.*

"You have lost your mind, along with the rest of the idiots from today. I have . . . had . . . a car with duct-taped seats—that are now completely burnt to a crisp, by the way—and a *huge* expanse of a trailer that's barely big enough to fit two lightbulbs . . . so just what about all of my opulent lifestyle has led you to this stellar conclusion that I know where the fuck your stupid diamonds are?"

She may have been shouting. The great big men with the great big guns put their great big meaty palms on the butts of said guns. Maybe shouting at a murderous organized crime king wasn't such a hot idea. Especially when tied up.

"One of these days, Bobbie Faye, your mouth is going to write a check your ass can't cash," Emile said.

"My ass has cashed *plenty* of checks." Wait. *Damn.*

The gunmen laughed. Even Trevor had to look away to maintain his stony stare.

Emile strolled to the coffee table and snapped open a day planner, thumbed through to whatever he was looking for and tapped it.

"What's that?"

"Marie's itinerary. She writes down everything. One of the wonderful things I can count on about my dear ex-wife is that she doodles on everything. Even a burled walnut desk which cost me ten grand," he seethed, getting carried away, then paused, regaining his composure. "Take a look."

Bobbie Faye eased around the rose-colored leather chairs and bent over the day planner. It was one of the larger weekly calendar versions, with notes scribbled in and around and over the appointment time slots in no orderly fashion. There were annotations for hair, nails, dress fittings, lunches with friends, and business appointments for the textile business she'd started—an outgrowth from her weird art sculptures that had made her famous. She now created purses and shoes out of oddball "found" objects and beads of all types. Her work sold well in galleries and the textile business had rocketed when a couple of skanky-but-popular young starlets had been photographed wearing her belts on the cover of *People* and *InStyle*.

Bobbie Faye nudged the book at an angle so she could make better sense of the blocks of time X'd out for shopping, crazy unclear notations of supplies, as well as a couple of recipes. She got dizzy just thinking about how much time it took to write all of that on one day, much less do it. Then the initials caught her eye. *b.f.* She had to turn the book sideways (Marie had filled every margin) and read a hodgepodge ramble of words that wrapped from the outer edge to the top of the page:

d's safe check copies check b.f. knows where

The tingling sensation started at the back of her skull and raced down to her fingertips, numbing her hands. *b.f. knows where* seemed to grow larger and larger as she stared, and she closed her eyes, rubbed them, then looked again.

Yep, still there. What the fuck? What in the hell had Marie been thinking?

"Does Marie have a boyfriend? What?"

"Quit playing dumb."

"I have no idea what this is." Then something occurred to her. "Is this why Francesca thinks I can help find the damned things?"

"I'm sure my daughter has rifled through the entire place, so I imagine so. The more important point is, *I'm* sure you know where they are, and I want them back."

"Right. You bet. I'll get right on that."

She waited for him to threaten her, waited for the obligatory *I'm going to kill your family,* that everyone had resorted to so far. But instead, Emile just smiled. Which made her shudder.

"If Aunt Marie had completely lost her mind—and in this family, that's not a terrible stretch—and she had planned on telling me where they were, she didn't get around to it before she disappeared. So, dear Uncle, if you want me to find the damned things, you're going to have to let me search this place for clues."

Emile seared her with a hateful glare.

"Or, we could just stare at each other while someone else finds them first. Totally up to you." She looked pointedly at the pink decor. "I'm not promising not to throw up if you keep me in this house, though."

The goons nodded in agreement with her assessment of the pink. Emile thought it over and then said, "Fine. You have one hour to search. You don't come up with anything, I start tearing apart everything you own and everyone you love until I find the diamonds or you bring them to me."

"Yeah? You'll have to take a number on that one; it seems to be the popular flavor of the day."

"I'll post my men at the doors, so don't even think about trying to escape."

"Wouldn't dream of it. I'll take Tweedledee over there," she said, smiling and pointing to the biggest of the two guards.

The man actually flinched. And then looked ashamed when Emile cut him a scathing glare. "You'll get that one," Emile said, nodding to Trevor.

"The assassin guy? *No fucking way.* How am I supposed to figure out clues if I'm worried he's going to cut my throat?"

"I'd suggest you move quickly, then. I have calls to make," Emile answered, stepping toward the front porch. "One hour, Bobbie Faye. And not a minute more."

From: Simone
To: JT

Confirmed that Trevor has her.

(sent via cell)

From: JT
To: Simone

Agency won't confirm if he's off the reservation with permission. Do not trust.

(sent via cell)

From: Simone
To: JT

Think it's a coincidence he helped her with the tiara which was a map to a fortune . . . and now he's back when the diamonds are worth a fortune?

(sent via cell)

From: JT
To: Simone

I don't believe in coincidences.

(sent via cell)

Benoit worked the bridge accident with Cam, sweat dripping from both of them in the mounting heat. Somehow, Cam managed to look cool and collected (probably all of that experience wearing LSU football gear as a star quarterback—high pressure and high heat in the first games of the season made him immune to the temperatures now). Benoit, on the other hand, felt like he'd been swimming. It was too hot even to talk, though they'd been friends so long, they didn't have to do much more than a subtle shake of the head. Cam, a good eight inches taller than Benoit, was still scanning the crowds gathered at the foot of the bridge. If anyone had actually seen Bobbie Faye walk away from the accident, they had one helluva poker face.

Another gorgeous, long-legged, and curvy LSU fan approached Cam for an autograph (he always obliged) and Benoit waited until the woman walked away before quipping, "You need to carry some of them glamour shots, *cher*."

"Go to hell."

They worked the crowd, trying to cull witnesses from media-seekers, and Benoit was amazed all over again at the grace Cam could display in crisis. The man handled the football fans with aplomb, though he was completely focused on the task: finding Bobbie Faye. Lots of people had asked Benoit over the years why Cam hadn't gotten a job outside of Lake Charles at some fancy corporation—there were many who'd have been willing to put a famous ex-football star on the payroll, especially as a company spokesman. But those people never really understood the man and how much his hometown meant to him. The town was family.

There was another reason Cam had stayed, though he'd never said as much to Benoit: Bobbie Faye would have never left her home, and Cam wasn't going to leave Bobbie Faye.

Well, until the dumb sonofabitch caused their breakup.

Benoit's cell phone rang then, and it was Diane in dispatch.

"I've got a call to forward to you," she said, "from someone who says they have something important about the jeweler murder you and Cam been workin'."

Benoit had her put the caller through, and he heard a man's voice speaking with the thick Cajun accent, thicker than his own, indigenous to these Acadiana parishes.

"Son," the man said, "I done worried me about this now, an' as much as I figure on to likin' her, I got to call it in."

"Call what in?" Benoit asked, once he had the man's name and address.

"Well, now, you got to come see. Me, I don't want to cause her no grief, an' if it was just a'blowin' up somethin', *cher*, I wouldn'ta minded, her being the Contraband Days Queen an' all, but this here, well, there's killin' when someone needs it, and then there's just killin'."

Benoit couldn't get anything else out of the man except when and where to meet. The PD didn't normally get calls like this in a Bobbie Faye case; people were usually lining up to be her alibi. He closed his cell phone and watched Cam scowling at the back of another autograph seeker as she walked away.

"What was that?" Cam asked.

"Nothing, *cher*, 'til it's something, and I'll let ya know."

The television on the wall blared the news coverage of the bridge accident and the sound echoed off the rehab hospital's walls. Every square inch of the nasty aqua-green TV room sprouted some cranky, bitchy, angry, not-quite-dried-out addict of something or other, all glued to the chaos on the screen as if it was some blockbuster film, with her freaking sister the action star. Lori Ann was thankful right about then that she only favored Bobbie Faye around the eyes and possibly the chin; she curled her petite frame in the corner of the horribly uncomfortable sofa, made tortuous, she was sure, because every day without drinking was going to be hell and they wanted the inmates—okay, okay, *patients*—to start experiencing hell as soon as possible so they'd learn to cope.

The viewpoint of the footage on the TV screen widened to show multiple news helicopters hovering alongside the helo apparently shooting the footage. On the ground below, there were at least a dozen cop cars, two fire trucks, paramedic units, a crowd of a couple of thousand onlookers, traffic snarled for miles, and reporters like fleas on a dog. One of her fellow patients was passing around a big bag of popcorn, for crying out loud. Lori Ann glanced over at her counselor, an older, conservative social worker who looked like he'd had all of the fun beaten out of him a thousand years ago.

"Another Bobbie Faye day," he said, acknowledging her glance. "Looks like she's blowing things up again."

"Yeah," Lori Ann said, "and somehow *I'm* the fuck-up of the family."

Chapter Nine

Michele pulled her glasses off as she leaned her slender frame against the ornate bedroom door inside the governor's mansion, her ear pressed to its raised panels. She knocked a few times, then listened again. She'd been at this for an hour.

"Sir? You have appointments." She tried to control the rising panic in her voice. "And the benefit tomorrow night! It's going to be televised! Everyone will take it as a personal affront if you don't show! I can't just tell them you've canceled!"

She listened to the muffled reply and rolled her eyes at Kitty, the governor's assistant secretary and Michele's right hand, who approached from the intersecting hallway. Kitty leaned in to the door, listening as well.

"Is he . . . crying?" Kitty asked.

"He says he's not leaving this room until 'that woman' is found and hog-tied."

"He's hiding from—"

"Shhhhh," Michele stopped her. "Ever since she acciden- tally blew up his limo, he gets real twitchy when he hears her name."

"Geez, if the Democrats only knew."

•   •   •

revor closed the door to the neon pink master bedroom—he suppressed a shudder—as Bobbie Faye paced. Frustration billowed from her as her long legs made short work of the wide space by the bed. He'd cut the wrist-binding as soon as he sent the two guards to their posts, and she pumped her arms with each step as if she'd like to strike something. Hell, who was he kidding? She'd like to strike *someone*, probably *him*.

"If your head spins off your shoulders," he teased, "I'm going to be *completely* grossed out."

She stared at the opposite wall, but he could tell she fought against a smile.

Her phone rang, jarring her and she jumped, knocking over the crystal lamp, which shattered on the wood floor. She snatched her phone open after checking the caller ID with, "Hello, Frannie. No. *No.* Bite me," and hung up. She glared at the opposite wall, not quite facing him. "I have a ride home. And an appointment to get a facial and highlights, should I live."

She paused, a ragged breath shuddering through her. "Why would Emile hire you?"

"Suffice it to say he thinks he's got the most cutthroat, successful mercenary available for the job in me."

"Emile's not easily fooled." She eyed him, and he could see she was trying to calculate just how much of his cover was real, and how much was for show.

"There's enough verifiable truth there for him to be a believer." He watched her. He knew how easily it would be to lie. He could pretend his cover had been completely fabricated, that he'd simply played a role. But he wouldn't—she'd had enough of lies in her lifetime.

"Oh, well that's just *great*. First I date a guy who turns out to be a gunrunner, then I date a guy who's a cop who would prefer to arrest my sister and destroy my family, and now I like a guy who could probably give lessons in one-hundred-and-one-ways to dispose of pesky corpses. I swear, the next guy I am remotely interested in, I am getting a resumé with full references."

"I think you have seriously underestimated me if you think there's going to be a *next* guy."

She frowned at him, her energy crackling the air in the room, and he waited, his arms crossed. She was a little dangerous when she was on edge. He liked dangerous, so that worked. In fact, it worked a lot, as did her curves in the killer t-shirt now tied beneath her breasts, the thought of which reminded him of the welt the asshole Irish guy had apparently created. Trevor had to smooth out a scowl. No need to remind her of that event; she was already wired and deadly as it was.

"So I don't suppose," she asked, staring now at the opposite wall, which, he was sure, was an indication of how annoyed she was, that she didn't want to look him in the eye, "that it was a complete accident that *you*—the guy I'd been talking to on the phone, the guy I had all of those hot conversations with, who didn't hint at all about going undercover—just happened to be assigned to this case about the same time I had my ass dragged into this mess?"

His first thought was that *hot* didn't even begin to describe those conversations, but she'd have tried to deck him if he pointed that out right now.

"No," he said, watching her tense, "it was not a coincidence."

Bobbie Faye hated the way Trevor stood there, watching her, emotionless, his arms crossed, leaning his hip against the dresser as if they were having a casual conversation about the weather. He was so damned unreadable, it drove her crazy, although she was beginning to think if someone Googled the word "crazy," there'd be a star over her trailer, so maybe she'd already arrived there. She also hated, just for the record, the fact that there was a low hum to her body whenever he was nearby, that simply being aware that he stood not five feet away made her body ache.

Somehow, the dresser drawer broke. Possibly slamming it was a bad idea. She didn't even remember opening it. Then he did the thing she hadn't realized she'd been wanting: he stepped into her space and pulled her into his arms.

"I don't think the dresser ever did anything to you."

"Bastard." The word didn't have as much force muffled the way it was into his chest. Geez, he felt good.

"I had to move fast, once your name popped up. I couldn't contact you, Sundance. Your cell and work phones were tapped, and you were being watched."

"Because of that crazy note in Marie's day planner."

"Right. The Agency has been surveilling Emile for over a year now—we'd suspected he was behind the original theft of the diamonds, but they never resurfaced until Marie took them from him."

"Why in the hell would all of you people be so fired up over diamonds? I mean, sure, a few million is a lot, but really—"

"They're not exactly your typical diamonds," he interrupted, "and they're worth closer to a half a billion."

She stood completely still, stupefied by the number. "I think you just broke my brain."

Reggie mulled over her plan as she sat in her car while her cameraman, DJ, grabbed a few minutes of B-roll of the crowd and the burned-out car. She had already found two people to confirm that Bobbie Faye was alive after the explosion, though there were too many variations of how she'd left the scene, and with whom, to know which story was correct. It was amazing what people were willing to do to be a "star" on TV—they'd tell her stuff they'd never mention to the police. Reggie was glad Bobbie Faye was alive—the nutcase was worth more alive to her than dead right now.

She gazed at a small photo she had of her four-year-old son, Nathan, pinned to the back of her visor: he was laughing as he reeled in his very first fish, a bream half the size of a Twinkie. She'd have sworn it was a ten pounder from the sheer joy in his eyes. His dad stood off in the background on his cell phone, completely oblivious to his son's elation.

It felt like acid eating away at her heart to know that her asshole ex only fought for custody of Nathan because he knew she wanted him. He'd traded in his aggressive, active wife and her regular investigative beats—which conflicted with his intense desire to hide his clients' illegal activities—for wife number three, a far more passive model whose great ambition was to make sure her highlights were kept up consistently. Harold used custody of Nathan as a way to hold Reggie in check. She couldn't reveal his little detours beyond the law (particularly when he was skimming off his partner's accounts) for fear he'd sail off to some island with her son, forever. He had the money and the bastard gene to do it, which is why she simply *had* to even the playing field.

A playing field that was going to change with this story. Reggie could smell victory. Usually, Reggie, like the rest of the media, was on the sidelines, a little behind the Bobbie Faye action curve, and not quite fast enough to get exclusives, which were the currency of rising in the business. Anyone who could get an exclusive on Bobbie Faye, who could catch her on camera in the midst of one of her exploits, would be on national TV. No one had gotten Bobbie Faye making a statement, midcarnage. And if the reporter who got Bobbie Faye on camera also happened to catch her in the middle of a crime? Well, national news desk, look out, because Reggie had a plan to get both of those things.

She watched DJ saunter back to her car, which meant he'd probably gotten a few shots of some skimpily clad hot twenty-somethings that he knew would make it on the air. He winked at her and shot her his wicked smile. She wished she'd taken him up on his offer to off her ex when it would have helped. Instead, she'd waited too long, thinking she'd spring the evidence of his affair on him and that would break his pre-nup, but she should have known a sneaky bastard like her husband would have a judge on the payroll and she'd end up with nothing.

DJ climbed inside the car and gave her a big sloppy kiss. They headed back to the station so he could upload his tape while she did a little recon to finish their plan.

Aiden watched Sean roll dice through his knuckles, a sure sign he was agitated. Robbie's face flushed with concentration over his computer as he typed in commands, listened on a headset, and then frantically typed in more.

"Still no' getting' anythin'?" he asked.

"No' a damned thing," Robbie answered. "No' even residual sound, like it fell off."

"Probably in the explosion," Mollie offered, and Robbie threw her a grateful glance.

Sean had spent a great deal of money tracking the diamonds when they'd disappeared on him a couple of years ago when Emile stole them out from under him. At least, Sean believed it to be Emile, but had never known for sure. Until now. Sean wasn't going to be very happy. Sean didn't take failure very well, which usually meant the employee in question got a bullet. In fact, he was humming the "Dear Liza" song, and Aiden couldn't help but think of the way he'd altered the lyrics, ending with:

> There's a hole in his bucket, dear Liza, dear Liza,
> There's a hole, well just fuckit, put a tag on his toe.

"There!" Robbie said, pointing at the screen. "The GPS is up again. She moves, we got 'er." Sean quit humming and smiled.

Bobbie Faye stood still in the circle of Trevor's arms. The half-billion-dollar figure of the vast worth of the diamonds ricocheted through her ragged mind, demolishing the few cells left standing. She sighed.

"So you're not really here to rescue me, are you?"

He leaned back and held her gaze. "You want me to believe that just because I showed up, you'd have abdicated helping your family?"

"I mighta," she fibbed.

"Yeah, Sundance, and then after that, you'd be strapping on a pink tutu and ballet slippers and dancing to Mozart."

"Jerk," she said, but he'd made her smile. "Let me guess: the FBI thinks it's possible I'm involved because of that note, and so does everyone else. So the Feds think I'm supposed to be working with you while I'm pretending to be scared of you *while* I'm working for the people who want me to find the diamonds *and* the people who don't want me to find the diamonds, all of whom seem to fall into the 'shoot first, oh look, something shiny,' school of logic."

"You forgot the facial and highlights with Francesca."

"If she waves fingernail polish at me, I'd better get a pass for shooting her."

He smiled, and started brushing the debris from her hair, taking a moment to examine the cut on her forehead. She probably looked like some sort of horror movie victim, since he paled a little bit. He dragged her to the adjoining bathroom and she flinched at her reflection: she looked like a battered rag doll on crack—a metric buttload worse than one of those "before" shots on those makeover beauty shows. If there was a World of Fug Ugly, she was its president. Her hair had tangled from the motorcycle ride, and there was dried blood on her forehead and cheek, scrapes on her arm, ground-in asphalt and dirt stained her shirt from where she'd landed on the bridge.

He dug around in the cabinets, brought out a washcloth, then wet it and went to work on her.

"If y'all have been watching Emile for a year—how are *you*

here? You were busy working for Vincent." The wonderfully now-dead asshole who'd kidnapped her brother.

He wiped her face clean. "My cover as a mercenary was never blown—no one outside the Agency besides you and Cam know who I am."

"So you just happened to be available for this mess?" When he focused on her arms, she made the connection. "You told them to watch me!"

"No," he said, finishing the other arm. "I told them to let me know if you were in any danger. I thought someone might try to go after you, thinking you still had the tiara." Her mom's tiara—the rusted piece of crown that her great-great-great-great-grandfather, who happened to be Lafitte, had made for his daughter and that had been handed down through the generations. The one that turned out to be pretty damned valuable after all.

"And so the Agency called you in to help?"

There was a pause, and when he didn't answer, she tapped his shoulder.

"When I heard they were going to use you as bait, I didn't exactly give them a choice."

She watched him, remembering their one movie date, a western they didn't get to see the end of because he got marching orders to get back to Quantico that night. Then there had been all of those hot phone calls, but she'd never really let herself hope that maybe there was more between them than just chemistry. Okay, maybe she'd hoped, a little, that there would be something more. If she'd had a clue he cared—with the connection she felt to him—she'd have begged, borrowed, or stolen a ride to Virginia.

Pizza.

That image popped into her head. She stared into his sincere expression as he ran the cloth down her scraped arms, and she thought how going out for pizza would have been a terrific second date. There was a cozy little mom-and-pop place she knew, funky and fun. Casual enough to relax and get to know each other, not too "hang out at your place, automatic sex" casual, though. She could have dressed up in something sexy. He would look great in whatever he showed up in. He'd have opened a door for her and insisted on doing so even when she rolled her eyes at him. It would have been really amazing. There probably would have been an stunningly hot goodnight kiss.

"I hope the FBI has some sort of Universal Platinum Card," she said, her voice choked on the emotion, overwhelmed, and she stepped away from him, "because you're paying for whatever blows up."

"You find the diamonds, we'll pick up the charges," he answered, matching her light tone while studying her, frowning at her abrupt withdrawal. "Although it would be nice if we left the state intact."

She went back to the bedroom, heading for the dresser drawers, intent on rummaging. "It's not like I plan these things."

"God help us if you did."

John climbed back into the van, which he'd parked down the street from the seller's house. Otto was on the phone to the buyer, babbling in Italian, which John hated, since he didn't understand a word. When Otto arched an eyebrow, John said, "She's still inside."

Otto said something else, listened, and then hung up. "Buyer say he make no more promises to seller. Bobbie Faye woman needs to not come out."

John pulled out his sniper rifle, handed it to Otto. "Here. If she's smart, she'll stay out from in front of the window." He opened the van door.

Otto frowned at the rifle. "But I am not so good as you. You should do this."

"Ain't gonna help one fuckin' bit if she don't step in front of a window. I got me an idea. You just make sure she don't come out of the house."

With that, John ran off toward the new development. He definitely had a great idea.

Chapter Ten

The master bedroom turned out to be devoid of a single freaking clue. No big neon sign with an arrow saying, "Diamonds this way, stupid." Emile's deadline loomed as Bobbie Faye and Trevor climbed to the third floor, an airy workshop with sunlight streaming in from a bank of windows overlooking the new section of the development.

Bobbie Faye had never seen so much junk piled in one spot. Not even Ce Ce's haphazard arrangement matched this heap of crap. Overturned boxes of supplies looked as if they'd been rummaged through and the contents spilled now all over the little floor space not taken up by massive work tables. More boxes were crammed underneath. From the look of the jars and bowls on the table, Marie made her textiles out of anything odd, from the natural (leaves encased in polymer) to the surreal (hoses? seriously?), to shiny beads and faux gems. Bobbie Faye reached for an indescent red purse and drew back when it pricked her.

"Ow!" She looked closer. It was made of hundreds of little stiletto heels, all of them apparently razor sharp. "Who the fuck would want to carry this around? You'd have to have your own paramedic on tap."

Trevor pointed at a framed photo of an eight-page layout in

InStyle magazine where the hottest young TV actress sported a purse just like it in blue.

"I wonder how many bandages they had to airbrush out of that?"

There were dozens more framed photos of celebrities, politicians, and even a couple of world leaders, all sporting Marie's textiles, or standing before a piece of her sculptural art. Bobbie Faye had known her as Weird-Aunt Marie who was always stopping to pick up some oddball item from the ground whenever they were over at the family home. Marie, who hadn't met a flea market she didn't love, in spite of being married to one of the wealthiest men in the state. She'd never thought of her aunt as famous, as someone who had a life, an art.

"I'll bet a lot of that went away when Emile's money dried up," she mused out loud and Trevor followed her gaze down the length of the photo wall. "It takes real money to run this kind of business—there's no profit for years, and to get invited to the right parties, you have to have the right connections. She must've gotten desperate."

Beneath those photos, a nightmare of a desk where a snowdrift of random paperwork threatened to avalanche: calendars, invoices, business cards, receipts, postcards, flyers, advertisements for her upcoming shows, newspaper clippings reviewing shows, ticket stubs from old movies, phone numbers and incoherent scribbling, random abbreviations.

"How in the hell would y'all know if the diamonds weren't here? It'd take forever to go through this."

"They're not your normal diamonds—they're tagged with a radioactive isotope. We scanned the house and we can tell that they were here, but they're not here now." He glanced around the room. "Are you sure this is where you want to start?"

She nodded, weaving through the junk to the desk. "Marie could be a thousand places right now, especially with the help of her . . . my . . . family. I'm assuming y'all are already tracking everything like bank accounts and travel?" She looked up from the paper-work and he nodded. "And I know Marie. Well, I used to know Marie. She's clever. Whenever they'd play cards or board games when I was little, everyone wanted Marie on their team because she'd win. She was smart enough to get the diamonds from her hus-band, and that couldn't have been easy. But she's also kinda sloppy."

"I hadn't noticed. So you're looking for?"

"I don't know. Some idea of where she's been, where she's go-ing. I know we could go out and interrogate all of her friends—"

"The Agency has every friend and relative's credit card tagged. We're watching every place on her calendar."

Bobbie Faye leafed through posters for upcoming shows; in some of the photos of the work Marie was going to showcase, she'd taken her textiles (her purses, shoes) and turned them into sculptures. *Way to repurpose, there, Aunt Marie.* If something doesn't sell, stick it in a pile and call it art. Bobbie Faye was soooo going to use that strategy for her next garage sale.

"And we could rip apart everything she ever made or sold—" She put her hand up to stop him. "I know. You're already on it. But if I were Marie? No way in hell would I put those diamonds some-where I couldn't personally check, to make sure they're safe. Emile has tentacles into too many banks. She wouldn't trust a safety deposit box. And she sure as hell wouldn't trust our family."

She sifted through the dome of papers, shoving some stuff in her purse 'til it was overflowing. She separated out some of the items and made a "look through more thoroughly" pile. It was hard to focus since Trevor stood very close, helping, but bumping into her as she threaded her way around the stacks of samples at their feet. Marie had left the air conditioner off when she decided to disappear, and the third floor plus the whole "heat rising" thing, plus the June temperatures, had turned the workshop into an oven. The heat made her feel light-headed and soft, like she was melting into the floor. Or maybe that was Trevor's presence, his sudden reappearance doing that to her, confusing her.

He'd barely been in her life when he'd disappeared. She'd resigned herself that he wasn't coming back. Except here he was, brushing against her, concentrating on stacks of papers, reaching around her and how in the hell could two adrenaline junkies like them even think about dating? Okay, she'd thought about dating. A lot. "Dating" being that euphemism for "lots of hot monkey sex" because geez, look at the man.

"You okay?" he asked, and she realized her focus had gone fuzzy, staring at him. She looked down to what she held in her hand: rice husks. Pre-drying, just harvested rice husks. She had had an important thought about them, but whatever she'd been thinking flitted back out again, dissolving in the suffocating heat with the rest of her.

Bobbie Faye crossed to the window, desperate for some ventilation. She fought to yank it open and instantly regretted the jangle and vibration of noise from the construction site across the street and the dust the moving machines kicked up that coated her mouth as she inhaled. Trevor stepped up behind her a second later and tugged the window back down, his arms on either side of her and she bit the inside of her lip to keep from leaning back into him.

And then there was the tiniest of a "plink" sound, almost inaudible, barely registering as separate from the construction noise. It was as if someone had tossed a rock at the window. A tiny sound, really, something she shouldn't have heard, except that the window directly in front of her forehead spider-webbed. Wasn't that odd? Someone had thrown a rock three stories up, and then, oh, look, there was another one and she marveled for a moment at how a piece of glass had managed not to break altogether. There was a part of her brain that wanted to congratulate the contractor, or maybe the window manufacturer, for building a window of such sure and strong design that it could withstand a rock. Instead, she was hitting the floor, underneath Trevor as he yelled something she couldn't hear because maybe the blood was rushing to her head or maybe she was screaming. (It was a toss-up.)

"Bulletproof glass," he said, as she tuned in mid-sentence. Trevor scanned the room, seeming to forget for a moment that he was on top of her, supporting his weight in a permanent semi-push-up with the length of him covering the length of her. While Fear and Screaming tried to make up for having been such lazy-assed slackers earlier, yelling *bulletproof glass cracking, means* bullets, *dummy, firing at you, pay attention here,* the rest of her brain rocked out on the *mmmmmmmmmmmm, biceps* view and was now focusing rather intently on the abs. And the shoulders. And wonderfully muscled legs pressed into her.

Maybe it was shock. Or denial. Or both. On steroids. But apparently, the slutty part of her brain did not want to pay attention to the yammering about bullet this and dying that and she stroked his bicep and wow, did she have his attention.

"*Jesus,* Sundance."

She grinned. "Almost being killed again is sort of making me reevaluate priorities." The smart part of her brain said *I give up* and her body wriggled a little beneath his.

He stared at her for what seemed like forever. She wasn't entirely sure he breathed, so intent was that look.

"What?" she asked finally.

"I'm trying to figure out how to get someone to shoot at you every day."

"Somehow, I'm beginning to think that's not going to be a problem."

Which reminded him of the shooter, damnit. He rolled off her and knelt, trying to peer above the sill to see where the sniper was located. Two more pings hit the window above his head.

Benoit rocked back on his heels at the sight of the video; it was absolutely the last thing he'd expected. The little haberdashery tucked into the last corner of the refurbished-and-now-flourishing downtown shopping center had all of the latest high-tech security equipment, which seemed completely incongruent with the dapper, old-fashioned, little Cajun Mr. Beaureagard, who owned the place. Mr. Beau had been in business forty years, and in spite of the radical changes in clothing styles, as well as the hard-hitting economic times the city had suffered—especially after Hurricane Rita—he had managed a successful shop. His good business acumen and foresight had led him to rent nice prom tuxes to kids of the affluent executives of the surrounding chemical plants. The downside to the high school business was that every once in a while, there was graffiti or break-ins, one of which had recently made the papers. The boy had gotten off because the old video was too fuzzy to convict him. After that incident, Mr. Beau had installed extra security cameras.

"Rewind it and let me see it again," Benoit said, and the old man adjusted his bifocals on his acorn nose, squinting at the console, confused over the array of buttons. Finally the selection was made, the recordable DVD jumped back to the beginning of the pertinent section, and Benoit leaned in closer to get a careful look.

"For true," the old man said, his Cajun accent rolling thick up and over and down again with a singsong inflection. "I don't like to call against her, she's a good girl, *cher*. And Sal? He's a little on the shady side, so I figure, *mais no*, he's been doing something against her. So if she has a good reason, no way I like to get her in trouble, no."

Benoit watched the footage in silence. He'd have to get a drink or two into Cam before he let his friend see it. Benoit hit the button to slow the speed of the images.

Sal—Salavadore Frenetti—the jeweler who'd been murdered four days ago, had a shop diagonally opposite of Mr. Beau's place. The jewelry store catered to upscale clients in much the same way as Mr. Beau did their teenagers. The police—and then the FBI—had canvassed every single shop owner and only two had a camera pointed anywhere in the direction of the jewelry store or alley next to it. Oddly, one camera had not been "functioning" the night of the murder and the other surveillance tape had "accidentally" been erased. Benoit and Cam had suspected a mob hit, given the perfect symmetry of the shot pattern, and thought maybe someone in the syndicate had leaned heavily—but quietly—on the shop owners to conveniently manage a collective amnesia. Now Benoit wondered if the amnesia was more a result of protecting the Contraband Days Queen. As a Cajun, Benoit knew his people tended to close ranks and shield their own.

Benoit certainly hadn't expected to see that Queen on this footage—especially as she pulled a Glock on Sal and loaded him with five rounds.

The camera hadn't caught her image directly; instead, the camera had been aimed down the sidewalk (the common escape route for graffiti artists) and at the end of that sidewalk, the antique storefront jutted out, its entire front bay window full of antique armoires. The largest armoire had a mirrored front, and it was set at an angle in the store that caught a reflection of the alley, in much the same way security mirrors could see "around" corners in stores.

A woman, who was about the same build as Bobbie Faye met up with Sal in the alley. He seemed surprised to see her. They argued and for a brief moment, she stepped forward and the streetlight illuminated her face fully. She looked so much like Bobbie Faye, Benoit felt dread thrum through to his soul. The woman pulled the Glock, Sal looked at first as if he was going to laugh, and then he peered over into the shadows. Benoit thought he saw movement there, someone else . . . maybe two people? When Sal faced the woman again, his demeanor had changed from dismissal to blatant fear. He appeared to be begging, and then the woman planted the five shots straight into his chest. Sal fell, slow-motion, to his knees, then half-rolled, half-fell to his back. He seemed to be talking for a minute; she leaned over him and listened, then seemed even more agitated. The woman hunted around on the ground in the gravel alley. Bobbie

Faye—the suspect, he amended his thoughts—picked up all of the casings, checked the man for a pulse, and wiped her hands on her shirt. She stood there for a second, looked back at someone in the shadows, and casually walked off.

Benoit froze the screen at the one moment she looked back over her shoulder, and even in the harsh shadows cast by the streetlight, there was Bobbie Faye's angular face, the same shaped eyes and nose . . . everything. *Sacre merde.* He wasn't a hundred percent sure that it was Bobbie Faye, but the fact that he could even think in percentages shocked him and set him rocking on his heels again, trying to reel in the thoughts. There was the odd angle of the mirror to contend with and the fact that the faces couldn't be seen clearly on the tape. A couple of times, there was a weird double-image, probably caused by the shape of the mirror or a reflection in the antique store's bay window. The footage was relatively dark in spite of the streetlight, and he wasn't sure if there was a man in those shadows or not. Still.

He stared at that frozen image, at that slight hint of a smile. He knew Bobbie Faye. He'd grown up with her. He knew her character, inside and out, and he knew she'd never kill a man. He'd have bet his life on it. And yet, that was her face staring out of that frozen image. Her smile. Benoit couldn't believe it. Didn't want to believe it. There was *no way* he could believe what he was seeing, and if the video had been presented to him by anyone other than Mr. Beau, a man so honorable he'd driven all the way back to Baton Rouge once to return an overpayment that the IRS had given him—a whopping five dollars—Benoit would have immediately assumed the footage had been altered. But there stood Mr. Beau, clearly heartbroken for having to turn in someone he liked, anguished over this in a way that all Benoit's years as a detective told him was sincere. Benoit had to believe that the footage was legit.

Just how in the hell was he supposed to tell Cam that the

woman that he loved—and up until ten minutes ago, the woman Benoit had been certain Cam should have married—might be a murderer?

The clean-up in Ce Ce's store had begun, now that the police released the crime scene and left. While the store was slowly put back in order and the contractor measured for new windows, (she'd been through this enough times to have a great contractor on a hefty retainer), Ce Ce worked in her office. She poured over spell books, incantations, and old translations she'd gathered in her private voodoo library. And she fretted. Somehow, her protection spells hadn't worked. The sniper should have been compelled not to shoot; the cousins should never have been able to talk Bobbie Faye into leaving with them. Ce Ce had failed, and she was going to rectify that.

Ce Ce's insurance agent, Neil, an incredibly tall, reedy man whose bland complexion blended perfectly with his light gray suit, gray tie, and gray shoes, hovered in her doorway. The only thing of color on Neil was the stain on his shirt; he'd apparently had pizza for lunch. He scratched his head, worry deepening his permanent frown.

"They're going to want to write a clause excluding 'events' by Bobbie Faye," he sighed, ruffling through his thin gray hair.

"They're not going to get it, hon," she said, flipping to another page in the spell book she was investigating. "Don't make me call my attorney again."

The poor agent mopped his forehead with his tie. The last time Ce Ce had turned in a claim, his agency had tried to cancel her. The company had intended on excluding any expenses pertaining to Bobbie Faye's existence, and they reamed poor Neil out when he'd signed a renewal policy with Ce Ce without that exclusion. But when the company balked at paying, Ce Ce's attorney had made a simple and brief phone call, which had convinced them to keep the policy intact. (Ce Ce had given the attorney a love spell which he'd used on his drop-dead gorgeous wife. He wanted refills for life. Ce Ce wasn't about to explain to him that the potion really only worked once, and would wear off if the two people weren't really meant for each other; as long as the attorney was convinced he needed it, Ce Ce was happy to supply it.)

"I'm going to get fired, Ce Ce!"

He was starting to look ruddy in the heat, and for Neil, actual color in his face was probably a sign that he was nearly apoplectic. Poor thing was, Ce Ce realized, a victim of the Bobbie Faye event, too, and she patted his hand as she passed by him on her way to her storage room. "You wait right here, hon. I've got just the thing for you."

In her storeroom, she rooted around among the hundreds of vials she had stocked. With all of the shelves crammed floor-to-ceiling, the room was barely navigable. Ce Ce had to squeeze her pudgy, made-for-lovin' body through the narrow openings. Dust covered many of the ingredients as well as the vials, and none of the latter were labeled. She'd discovered a long time ago that unlabeled potions were safe from theft, because no one wanted to accidentally use a shrink-a-penis potion or a make-him-think-he's-a-lizard potion instead of a get-rich potion or a love potion.

"Whatcha doin'?" Monique slurred, startling the crap out of Ce Ce as she nearly knocked over an entire shelf.

Ce Ce eyed her friend, who grinned that goofy on-her-way-through-flask-number-one-for-the-day smile. "Just finding something to help Neil." She held up a vial that barely glowed amber in the light.

"That looks kinda like water. Only dirty. Ooohhhh, are we gonna make Neil a dirty old man?"

"No." Since her friend had a problem with keeping secrets, she wasn't about to tell Monique that she was giving an insurance man the power of "yes." It was a weak potion—Neil probably couldn't handle anything too strong. "It's just a protection spell, honey." Better to avoid the direct truth here. Ce Ce wouldn't want Neil to abuse the power she was temporarily giving him to survive his boss's wrath.

"Maybe you need to freshen those up a bit," Monique said, all wide-eyed, innocently observing the overcrowded, dusty shelves.

Ce Ce frowned, assessing her stock. Maybe the vials were a little old . . . a little . . . expired. Maybe that's why the protection spells hadn't worked as well for Bobbie Faye. She traded the barely amber vial for one twice as dark.

"See!" Monique exclaimed as she followed Ce Ce out of the storage room, "I can be a big help! You gotta teach me stuff, like what these are." Monique held up delicately dried curlicues of iguana entrails, which were hard to come by, because the lizards had to die naturally. Ce Ce removed them from Monique's hand carefully.

"Maybe later. I think you need to start on something simpler that won't kill our customers if your ingredient measurements are off by a milliliter." Ce Ce turned and handed the vial to Neil, catching him in the act of leafing through her spell book. He jumped back, having the decency to look guilty. "Here, hon. This is all you can handle right now."

"It's a protection spell!" Monique blabbed. "A really strong one. Double strength."

"There's that discretion I know and love," Ce Ce said dryly. To Neil, she said, "Just drink it after your evening meal. Be sure not to eat anything yellow, though. It tends to give you indigestion if you do."

Neil thanked her, took the vial, and loped out of the room looking a little more afraid than when he came in, which was a shame, Ce Ce thought. She'd meant to help.

Which reminded her: find a spell for Bobbie Faye. Ce Ce needed something that was all-purpose, portable, and definitely powerful. She turned back to her open spell book and started to flip back to the incantation she'd been contemplating, when the one displayed on the pages Neil had opened to caught her eye.

The spell was *wonderful*. Except for the part where Bobbie Faye would probably kill her for doing it, but other than that? It was *perfect*.

Chapter Eleven

As Bobbie Faye rolled to a sitting position near where Trevor knelt beside the window, a vibration rumbled through the building. Items on the desk quaked with the increasing shaking of the floor and the walls, several photos crashed on the hardwood planks, and a weird sculptural art piece fell next. Boxes danced off the top of other boxes, spilling plastic pellets and beads and buttons and God knows what else.

Trevor and Bobbie Faye slid across the floor to the window on the corner of the house and peeked above that sill to see a bulldozer heading their way from the construction site. Without a driver.

"How?" she asked.

"Bulldozers can keep going, once the gear's engaged."

Construction workers on the far end of the development site saw it cross the street; they ran, but had acres to cover before they'd reach Marie's house.

But this wasn't just any bulldozer. No little Tinkertoy version for her life, yippeefuckingskip. This was a big Cat daddy of all bulldozers with a giant blade that came to a "V" in the front, the kind they used to shear huge trees when clearing land. It climbed over the curb, knocking off a fire hydrant, which spewed water against the window. And without a driver, it plowed straight ahead, cleaving through the back deck and *into* Marie's house.

The blade ate through the back porch and then kept going, splitting the flooring, wedging open the pier-type foundation. The entire house canted forward, its underpinnings crumbling as the machine continued to push. Tables slid, slamming against one another as supplies and papers from the interior wall tumbled directly toward Bobbie Faye and Trevor. They scrambled, climbing up the now-sloping floor to get to the staircase. Beads rolled underfoot out of overturned boxes.

They stumbled and clawed their way across the floor, which dropped hard to a slope as another support beam bit the dust below them. The waxed hardwood gave no grip, except where boards popped up, unable to bend with the twisting frame of the house. Part of the exterior wall right where they'd been kneeling wrenched, Sheetrock and studs snapped, glass cracking, then falling in great chunks. Subflooring ripped away, exposing the two floors below through holes that gaped larger and larger with each passing second. The giant machine on the ground kept going, slowed down only by the weight and volume of its victim. Pipes clanged as they broke and sheared through walls, water spurting through the now-missing sections of the floor as the room kept tilting. Something hissed, and Bobbie Faye and Trevor smelled the additive the nice helpful utility company puts in the natural gas so you'll know when there's a gas leak and, oh, yeah, you're about to go *boom*.

They looked down through the holes in the floor, all the way down into the kitchen. A white light flashed, as the gas caught fire, blue white and then orange flames shot out of the feed to the formerly gorgeous stainless-steel range, torching the massive cherry and granite island in front of it. Somewhere above the din, Bobbie Faye thought she heard the shrill beep of a smoke alarm. Good thing that sucker was in working order.

And then she was falling. The dozer had inched through the dining area, taking another supporting wall with it as well as the joists Bobbie Faye had been standing on as they scrambled for a stairway that simply wasn't there anymore. Down she went, registering Trevor's furious movements to grab for her, and she landed on top of an armoire . . . which rocked and tilted and started to fall through the second floor. She leapt, grabbing onto a pipe protruding from the ceiling. Trevor swung down through the same floor opening, yelling something she couldn't hear above the roar of the machine and the house crashing around them, but he pointed, and she saw what he wanted: head for the front window, because the last thing they'd want to do is head for the back and have the house fall on them.

Which it was proceeding to do. The house creaked and snapped and vibrated, groaning as it shuddered against the onslaught. The dozer's massive treads dug into the ground, losing purchase as the earth became sloppy mud from the spurting pipes, until some piece of debris or other fell underneath the tread, giving it traction. The machine lurched forward a couple of inches and the walls jerked apart from the roof and fell a bit more. She and Trevor clamored over floors that were now sagging all across the back wall of the house, the supports falling apart beneath them, and she remembered now why she hated the fucking obstacle course in P.E. She'd declared rather obstinately to her fifth-hour teacher that she was never going to use this stupid physical education stuff. There was no freaking *rock climbing* in freaking *Louisiana*, she'd insisted, and she was never, ever in her freaking life going to need to know how to do a hand-over-hand climb up a stupid freaking rope. (Said hand-over-hand technique coming in rather handy as she scaled the electrical cord to the lamp wedged near the front window to keep from falling into the burning kitchen below.)

Behind her, Trevor fell, and just in time, snagged a grip on molding from the ceiling, cutting his hand on the protruding nails as he climbed toward the window. As more of the house gave away, she swung out, on the dangling cord, *Hi Tarzan, Me Jane*–style, planting both feet in the gigantic front window as the entire glass popped out, squeezed as it was by the torque of the twisting outer walls. Bobbie Faye latched onto the sill and as the house caved in behind her, Trevor leapt toward her. They both tumbled through the window, sliding two stories down the now-sloping exterior as the house collapsed away from them.

Safe. They were safe.

She glimpsed Emile and his two bodyguards running away from the house, frantic. The guards shoved their boss into his car, doing their job, protecting him. But not before he caught sight of her and Trevor.

A sniper bullet whizzed past just as Bobbie Faye leaned forward to check out a cut across Trevor's shoulder.

From: JT
To: Simone

Jesus Christ, I am so fired. The whole fucking house collapsed?

(sent via cell)

It had taken John five minutes to find where Otto had moved the van in the wooded lot across from Marie's—he'd apparently moved it so that he could watch the front of the house to make sure the bitch didn't come crawling out. John expected to find a very pleased Otto and a confirmation that his fee would be wired to his account. The dozer had been the perfect tool for the perfect accident: no Bobbie Faye, no house, no clues, no worries. The buyer would be thrilled. What he found, instead, was Otto on the roof of the van, dead. Sniper rifle in hand. Cell phone ringing. John guessed the dumb fuck had climbed up there to have a better line-of-sight above the cars parked in the front drive of Marie's house. A motorcycle raced by and he looked up in time to see that bastard mercenary Emile had hired riding off with Bobbie Faye.

The caller ID on the phone showed: unknown. John answered,

because the only person Otto had been talking to on that phone had been the buyer. By the time John explained the situation, the buyer had wired extra money into John's account so he could hire the help he'd wanted in the first place.

Sean and Aiden climbed back into their box truck.

"Happy huntin'?" Mollie asked, and Aiden nodded. They'd seen the man climbing onto the top of the van, aiming a sniper rifle at Marie's.

"Who d'ye think he was?" she asked. "Feds?"

"No' likely. Too amateur," Sean answered.

"Ye still got 'er?" Aiden asked Robbie, who nodded, focused completely on his computer system and the GPS signal he was tracking.

Cam stood in the front yard of Marie's collapsed house. The fire department had turned off the main gas supply and had trucks in front and in back, putting out the flames.

"We can't get to the upper floors," Jordan, the local precinct captain told him. The man was a friend, who also happened to have married Cam's middle sister. "The building's barely standing," Jordan continued. "We gotta get the fire out on the ground floor and then get an assessment of structural stability before we can try to get in there to sift through the debris," he shouted above the sirens and the roar of water rushing through hoses onto the house. "I heard you got a couple'a witnesses say they saw her climb outta there."

Cam nodded. It wasn't anything he could keep secret, particularly with the media interviewing everyone and their dog who lived in the neighborhood—an upscale place where the home-owner's association preached the neighborhood watch program. Jordan grinned, relieved. He'd always liked Bobbie Faye—hell, all of the firemen in the city had been especially appreciative of her since she'd lobbied hard and very publicly to get them a raise *and* new equipment after the last disaster. Cam envied feeling that pure, simple, happy relief. Bobbie Faye was alive, and she hadn't even fucking called him. She'd been shot at, had a fucking bomb explode her car—not to mention a *bridge*—and she hadn't even called him to let him know she was breathing. He pressed the heel of his hand to his right eye, in the vicinity of the bitch of a headache he was nursing.

"Your sister wants to know if you and Winna are still coming over Saturday for the bar-b-que," Jordan said, and Cam threw an *are-you-freaking-kidding-me?* expression in Jordan's direction. They were standing in the middle of another Bobbie Faye disaster— how in the hell could he be thinking about something like a date?

"Hey, don't kill the messenger. You know Gracie—she's inherited the Moreau control-freak gene," his brother-in-law said, but he smiled. He and Gracie had been married three years and seemed pretty happy about it. Gracie, in turn, was determined to see the last of her brothers shackled, as if it was something of a personal affront that her oldest brother had somehow evaded her matchmaking skills. She taught school with Winna, who, Cam had to admit, was very pretty, sweet, stable, and refreshingly interesting. They'd been dating for about two months—often enough, as far as his sister was concerned, to be an official couple.

Cam's phone rang and he recognized the crime scene tech's number. He knew she'd already dispatched a team to Marie's and it was entirely too soon for her to have any sort of findings on the bomb or even the evidence they'd bagged from the car. Jordan went back to his job as Cam took the call.

"Your girl is keeping me too damned busy," she said, getting straight to the point. "I feel like I can give you a pre-lim that there were no remains in the car—it's looking pretty good that whoever was in there got out before detonation."

This was good, but he already had the wit's descriptions of Bobbie Faye leaving Marie's, and he'd told Maggie that earlier. "What's up, Maggie?"

"I have something here I need to run to confirm, so this is guesswork, but given the case's profile, I thought you needed a heads-up. You know I got hair and blood from the bridge." Cam tensed, but he'd seen the spots she'd scraped—there wasn't enough blood to indicate a serious injury. "It's the hair," she said when he hadn't responded. "Before we got called out today, I'd been running a hair sample from our diamond jeweler case."

"I thought the Feds took all of the forensic evidence?"

"Not all," she said, and he could practically hear her smile. "A couple of pieces of evidence had been misplaced and we've been working *real* hard on finding them. Anyway, while I was waiting on them to ask me for this stuff again, I had a DNA run—the lab owed me a favor—there were no known matches. It seemed like a dead end."

"Why do I get the feeling there is a 'but' here."

"Yes. I don't have a DNA on file for Bobbie Faye."

"Why would you need one?"

"I was supervising the cataloguing of the samples from the bridge, and something about the hair sample we found next to her handprint struck me as familiar." Cam knew that they *did* have Bobbie Faye's fingerprints on file. Hell, the PD practically made them must-reads for all new cadets. "And then I realized why it was so familiar—I'd just seen it—from the jeweler case. I've checked it under the microscope and I'll get a DNA to see if the two match, but I won't know if they are positively Bobbie Faye's hair unless we get a DNA on her."

No fucking way. Bobbie Faye would never be involved in an actual murder.

A large section of Marie's roof gave way and crashed in under the blast of water from the fire hoses.

Fuck, he did not have time for this. He did not want to have to go through the freaking ordeal of chasing her down again and arresting her.

He had to get a DNA sample.

Bobbie Faye and Trevor walked through her trailer, checking closets and beneath beds and in the bathroom—making certain no one, especially not a persistent assassin, was hiding. Then relief hit her—the endorphin rush after the adrenaline subsided. She plopped down at her tiny kitchen table, tearing open the paper bag of food they'd bought on their way to her trailer. Within seconds, she'd shoved a bite of the chili cheese dog her into her mouth and nearly collapsed with joy.

When she noted Trevor's amusement at her expression, she said, "Apparently, blowing up things gives me the munchies."

"Dear God, we'd better stock up."

She'd have made a face at him, but that would have slowed down the eating. Besides, there were magical powers of healing a great chili cheese dog could have over all things insane. Especially the dogs made by the Ardoin brothers, because they were a Cajun version of the American classic, using smoked sausage and Cajun spices and three kinds of cheeses and she wasn't sure what was in the chili, but if she could mainline it, she would. She tried to remember when she'd told him of her unholy obsession with the Ardoin's hotdog stand, how she'd actually save her change so she and Stacey could have chili dog Saturdays. She heard him chuckling and when she looked up, she saw a crooked white smile against tan skin, and holy geez, that was even better than the chili. He bent down and kissed the corner of her mouth, stealing a little chili she was sure was smeared there and her brain sort of exploded as two of her favorite things in the world collided. Suddenly chili cheese dogs were associated with lust and all things sex and her unholy obsession just got a lot unholier.

Her phone rang: Nina, returning her call. Bobbie Faye would have assumed Nina was sleepy from the lazy sound in her voice and the time difference, but knowing Nina the way she did, the woman probably had just finished with some Italian count. Or two.

"What can I get you?" Nina asked.

"Your condo, if that's okay? I need a place to hole up and think."

"Sure thing."

"Hang on, not so fast. I should probably warn you that the house I was just at is no longer an actual house."

"Is it a puppy?"

"Ha."

"You have a spare key and the code. Have at it. I've been meaning to remodel that kitchen anyway."

They said their good-byes and in less than ten minutes, she'd cleaned up the food wrappers, thrown some clothes and toiletries in a satchel, and met Trevor in the living room. He was standing by the side of the window, scanning the front.

"We'll have to go out the back," he said, and she eased up close to him and peered past where his hand barely parted the curtains: two different TV stations had set up cameras. The manager had kept them from entering the premises since it was privately owned; odds were they were setting up at every exit. Front and center, though, was Reggie O'Connor. Bobbie Faye gritted her teeth. People had warned her that Reggie was the kind of person who'd look in your face while she put a knife in your gut, but Bobbie Faye hadn't believed the warnings. It was tough being a strong woman, as Bobbie Faye knew directly, because there was the constant expectation to be demure, deferential, a good little Southern belle. That crap could just bite it, and she understood the kind of flak Reggie had gotten trying to muscle her way into a bigger market by scooping her male colleagues. Bobbie Faye would have thought that would have created a bond between them, maybe something supportive they could have shared. Then Reggie targeted Bobbie Faye. It was probably the show entitled BOBBIE FAYE: SHOULD SHE BE SPAYED? which was most memorable, though the BOBBIE FAYE: FORCE OF EVIL OR JUST PLAIN STUPID? was a close runner-up.

She wasn't overly fond of Reggie.

Bobbie Faye looked at Trevor and knew what he was thinking: sugarcane field. The trailer park backed up to a huge field with green sugarcane about a man's height, and the rows were just far enough apart for a motorcycle to fit in between the stalks. It was going to be a pain to push it through the tight space—they would get smacked with every stalk they passed. They'd parked three trailers down when they'd arrived because Trevor didn't want to be obvious, and they were leaving the same way they'd entered: out the back door. They were barely down the back steps into the privacy-fenced yard (a tiny twelve-by-twelve-foot "patio") when the wooden gate to her fence started to open.

From: Simone
To: JT

Alert—cell phone activity. Incoming to BF. Signal originated in Italy.

(sent via cell)

From: JT
To: Simone

Shit. Buyer's from Italy. Do you think BF is planning to sell?

(sent via cell)

From: Simon
To: JT

We have to assume yes.

(sent via cell)

Chapter Twelve

Cam slipped through the back gate of Bobbie Faye's patio area, his gun drawn. He listened: no noise coming from her home. He eased toward the back door and nothing seemed disturbed. Still, given the day's events, there was no assuming that all was okay.

He'd seen the TV cameras set up in the front of the trailer park, so he'd hidden his truck a half-mile down the road and taken to the sugarcane field to avoid the media. The back door was locked. He glanced overhead—no news helos. Yet. They were all probably too busy covering the bridge or Marie's. He put his gun away long enough to jimmy the lock; he kept a nice lock pick set hidden in what looked like a regular pocket knife. It wasn't something he advertised. Hell, it wasn't something he ever used, except the rare occasions when someone's life had been at stake. He'd had to go into an old apartment Bobbie Faye had before they'd started dating, before he'd become a cop, and stop an asshole who'd trapped her there. He hadn't had a pick that time, and all Cam had been able to hear was her yelling and a lot of things crashing and breaking. He destroyed the door that time. It had only been when he'd finally broken through the door that he realized she'd kicked the bastard's ass and the crying had come from the idiot as he whimpered for her to just let him leave.

This time, he didn't want to show forced entry.

Cam stood just inside Bobbie Faye's back door, in the living room/dining room combination and the place smelled like . . . chili cheese dogs. She'd been here recently, for the aroma to be that strong. He looked in the kitchen trash and sure enough, Ardoin's take-out bags were crumpled there. Sonofabitch, he'd missed her. He pulled out his cell phone to call her and there was a missed text message from her—had to have been delayed when he'd hit the crappy wireless reception area on his way to her trailer.

From: Bobbie Faye
To: Cam

I'm 5× 5.

(sent via cell)

F ive by five. Slang for *wonderful.* Which was her way of saying *I'm breathing, but let's not get too hopeful about it.*

Cam scanned the room, his cop's eyes picking up every detail that was different from her last trailer. He hadn't actually been inside this slightly less-beat-up model, ("newer" would have been too generous). He could see she salvaged a few of her things— some family photos, that dumb clock Stacey loved, some toys, and a few oddball knickknacks which had meaning to Bobbie Faye but probably to no one else. Except him. He knew that French drip coffee pot was the one they'd found at a flea market one lazy summer afternoon; she'd loved the red enamel color and kept it at her place to make him coffee on Saturday mornings when he stayed over. Next to it was a rock about the size of his palm, only it wasn't a standard rock, but a piece of silica he'd found once and thrown against her window when they were kids. He hadn't expected to break the damned glass, and she'd landed in huge trouble, but she'd saved it, all silvery and black. There were other things, but he forced himself to look away from the old to see what was different: a new TV and VCR; well, used-for-new. Probably bought them down at Dusty's Thrift Shoppe.

The place smelled like her perfume—light, airy, something called Angel, he thought, which if the marketers had had a clue, should have been called Temptation. Or Damnation. He eased back toward her bedroom and he closed his mind to the scent as he moved in and out of the rooms. Clearly she wasn't there, and he should have already finished his mission and left. He sure didn't need memory lane. He just needed that DNA sample. One that would show that it wasn't her hair at the murder site. One that would show that the killer had also been on that bridge, though how it had happened to be next to Bobbie Faye's bloody handprint was going to take some explanation.

He stopped in her bedroom, noticing the open closet door, the empty hangers on her bed, the look of her dresser drawers having been shut and not quite closed, as if she'd left in a hurry, and a cold trickle of worry pricked at the base of his spine. It looked like she'd taken some clothes, and her makeup bag was gone from the tiny bathroom. And so was her favorite hairbrush. He rummaged around in the cabinet, knowing her habits as well as he knew his own, and in a basket on a top shelf, there were a dozen or so ponytail bands. Two had caught hairs in them. These should suffice for Maggie to match to determine if one or both hairs from the two different scenes were Bobbie Faye's.

He hadn't thought, 'til that moment, what he would do if they were a match. Could he be handing the DA the very information he'd need to make a good case against Bobbie Faye? Circumstantial as all hell, but then many cases came down to circumstantial evidence.

Cam faced the mirror, arms braced on either side of the sink. The hairs he had weren't admissible—he had no warrant, no permission, and they definitely weren't something discarded in public he could have simply picked up. Nor could he argue she'd left hair behind on a brush in his house—he'd given everything of hers back. Maggie wasn't supposed to still have the hair from the murder site, and her conjecture that the hair on the bridge was a match to Bobbie Faye's was just that—a conjecture. Still . . . would knowing ahead of time that the DNA was a match help the DA focus on Bobbie Faye?

He was breaking ten kinds of laws, not to mention ethics, just being there. She wasn't his girlfriend, hadn't wanted his help, and they hadn't been able to have much more than a barely civil conversation in a year. Even if she *had* been his girlfriend, he'd have been duty-bound to comply with any search warrants, and if she'd been staying at his place, he'd have handed over anything he'd owned, like his hairbrush, if it had been on the warrant's list. So what was he doing here?

His cell phone rang, and he saw it was Benoit. He hesitated; Benoit would ask him the kind of questions he wasn't sure he wanted to answer just yet (like had he lost his mind?).

"Yeah," he answered.

"Can you meet me at your house?"

"I've got some leads to follow up."

"Yeah, *cher*. You're gonna want to meet me. Twenty minutes."

Benoit hung up, and Cam's worry ratcheted into overdrive. It wasn't like his best friend to be anything but laid-back.

Cam pinched the bridge of his nose, clenching his eyes shut, and tried to shove away the awareness of the headache throbbing. When he opened his eyes, he blinked, adjusting back to the light, and that's when something shiny glinted from the small space where the bathroom vanity didn't quite meet the wall in the cheap-ass trailer. He leaned closer, assuming it was a piece of jewelry, and he had his pocketknife out on reflex, planning to fish it out for her (ignoring his constant inner argument over not being the guy who was supposed to be doing that sort of stuff for her anymore), and that's when he realized it was larger than jewelry, and it was brass.

Brass *casings*. In the bathroom? *Weird* was his first thought, and then, as he bent over to inspect it more closely without having to touch the brass, he knew something about this was beyond weird. And wrong. There were at least four casings back there. Bobbie Faye didn't typically pick up her brass after shooting at Ce Ce's firing range—she knew the twins were dead broke and needed to recycle the brass to make extra money. If it had been just a single casing, he'd have assumed it was something Stacey had somehow found and wedged behind the sink with the typical wily behavior of a five-year-old, but he found it odd that she'd have a single casing to play with, much less four. Bobbie Faye would have never let Stacey play with anything that might make the five-year-old think bullets were toys. His ex might be crazy, but she was exceptionally careful about that kid.

Cam used his pocketknife to pry the top casing out and laid it on the vanity countertop. He then retrieved a second, and then a third, and the dread that swamped him forced him to admit what he was thinking about: there were five missing casings from the jeweler murder scene. Five. And as he pulled the fourth casing out from the spot behind the vanity, he saw a fifth which had fallen in a little ways further. It took using a pair of scissors with the pocketknife to maneuver the shell out without touching it, but there it was, lying next to the other four.

Cam didn't really believe in coincidences. Five missing casings. A jeweler murder. Rumor that Francesca had been saying something about diamonds when she was at Ce Ce's. (Well, if Maimee was to be believed, and frankly, he'd never seen a woman go so clean off her rocker so fast as Maimee had gone after Edgar had lost their retirement and life savings.) Then there was Maggie's phone call about the hair on the bridge matching the hair at the murder scene. And on the other side of all of those coincidences was the woman he'd intended on marrying.

• • •

It was surreal that she and Trevor were pushing a motorcycle through the rows of the sugarcane field behind her trailer park—Bobbie Faye was pretty sure she'd hopscotched over reality two explosions ago—but what she really couldn't reconcile was the fact that Cam had broken into her home. From their hiding place, they'd watched him come through that gate and go up to her door and then pick the damned lock. Even if he was just checking to see if she was okay, and if he thought that maybe she wasn't, that maybe she'd needed help, he would normally have knocked and shouted for her to come to the damned door. In fact, he'd have started by banging on the front door and then he'd have barreled around to the back, on the off chance that she'd dragged her bleeding body to the back door by mistake, and then he *still* would have knocked. Normally.

Except, he hadn't. He'd broken into her trailer, big as you please. He was the man who'd been so hell-bent on adhering to doing what was "right" that he'd arrested her sister for a DUI instead of calling Bobbie Faye and letting her get Lori Ann into rehab, quietly. When she'd gotten upset over that, he'd made it clear he was a good cop who didn't bend the rules. He made it crystal fucking clear she was the one kind of girlfriend a good cop would never want. So why was it o-freaking-kay for him to bend the rules when *he* wanted something? What in the *hell* he'd wanted, she had no clue.

She glanced over at Trevor. He'd been watching her, aware she was stewing.

"Do you want to go back and kick his butt?" Trevor asked with a mischievous glint.

"No," she said. The last thing she needed was a shouting match with Cam right now, and she particularly didn't want to have to answer questions about Francesca or diamonds or explosions or anything until she'd had time to think. She looked down the row she and Trevor navigated, taking in the sight of the thin sugarcane leaves at least a couple of feet taller than Trevor, shooting up and then drooping open, umbrella-like, forming a canopy of green overhead, as far as the eye could see. It looked like she was going to have a while to think—Trevor had wanted to push the bike 'til they were far enough away from the trailer so as to not risk drawing anyone's attention when the Harley's loud engine revved.

"If you ever come back to Louisiana again, I promise I'll show you something prettier than exploding houses and stifling hot farms." Maybe she'd even have gotten the grant to start up her South Louisiana tour business, and could afford to treat him to something nice, like a fancy dinner out. She absently stuck her hand in her purse, feeling for the papers she had to fill out before the stupid deadline.

"I'll have plenty of time."

"Oh? You think they'll let you hang around, assuming I don't get you killed first?" She tried her dead level best not to sound too hopeful (about the staying, not about the killing). Probably sounded hopeful. Shit.

"They'd better, since I transferred here." He pushed the bike onto a trail that she hadn't known existed—it bisected the field.

"You . . . huh?" Had her brain melted out her ears? "When did you do this?"

"Transfer?"

She nodded.

"Last month."

Last month. That would have been a couple of weeks after the disaster with Roy . . . oh *hell*. She paused as he moved forward. "You got demoted. Oh, Jesus, Trevor, I'm sorry."

He stopped pushing the bike and frowned at her. "Your brain is a very scary place sometimes."

"Like that's news."

"I did *not* get demoted," he said, in that amused, smug male sort of way. "C'mon," he said, holding out a hand to her. "We need to get out of here."

"You *requested* the move? You're not like, terminally ill and figured suicide by Bobbie Faye disaster would be a quick way to go, right?"

He responded with a very slow, sultry, wicked, holy-geez, where-was-a-bed-when-you-needed-one sweep of a gaze that started at her toes and when he met her eyes, he held the gaze and she was pretty sure she was going to need CPR.

"Let's just say I intend on having that second date."

Cam went back to Bobbie Faye's kitchen, grabbed a plastic zippered baggie, and returned to the bathroom; he scooped the casings carefully into the bag, then sealed it. He avoided his reflection in the bathroom mirror. If he tagged 'em and bagged 'em and turned them into evidence, he'd still get the shit kicked out of him by his captain for not getting a proper search warrant. Moving the casings like this was tantamount to throwing the case into the toilet, if it turned out that these were, indeed, the casings missing from the jeweler's murder. He didn't have a warrant. Any good defense attorney could have the casings declared inadmissible. Oh, sure, he could say he had a permanent invitation to her home, that he'd been taking care of Stacey and she needed something. It was weak, the DA would know it was weak, and so would a judge. The casings could end up inadmissible and, if that happened, and they were the one clue needed to prove someone was a killer, he'd have thrown away the evidence for what? An ex who drove him nuts?

The most likely motive for them being in her trailer was that whoever had put them there wanted Bobbie Faye implicated. For all he knew, these shells had Bobbie Faye's prints on them. She'd taught shooting lessons to plenty of people at the range, she never picked up her own brass. Bobbie Faye was a pain-in-the-ass, but she was a smart pain-in-the-ass—she wasn't dumb enough to kill someone and hide the shells in her own home . . . not with three bayous between her trailer and the murder site she could have tossed them into. For the casings to be there, in the trailer, hidden, but not quite hidden well *enough*, reeked of someone framing her. Could he count on a good attorney getting her off?

With her luck?

He could save his ass right here, put the casings back, let the investigative process run its course. Because moving these casings? Illegal. He'd be canned. Charged with tampering with evidence, impeding an investigation, and probably a dozen other charges. His career would be over. Maybe Bobbie Faye would never be a suspect in the jeweler murder, maybe that wasn't her hair at the murder site, and maybe she was going to turn into Mary Poppins and start singing and flying—they all had about the same chances of coming true.

Cam walked back to the kitchen and dug around in the medicine cabinet and found the headache meds she kept—mostly for him, since she didn't have headaches. He filled a glass with ice water, took the meds, and left the glass and the meds on the counter where she'd see them when she came home. He wasn't sure why he'd done that—maybe he wanted to annoy the hell out of her when she realized he'd been inside without permission. It was easier to focus on her being angry, on how they'd probably fight about it; almost anything was easier than thinking about that plastic bag in his pocket.

He slipped out the back door and that's when he noticed it: her storage shed door. It had definitely been closed when he arrived. Now it was standing open. He pulled his gun out, pointed down, and toed the door open a little more. No one was inside, but he saw two sets of prints in the dust on the floor—a man and a woman's. Overlapping, like they'd been in there at the same time, moving around. Witnesses had placed her on the back of a Harley leaving Marie's with a rider that fit Trevor's general description. The Feds were all over this case—could Trevor be involved? Or was it a possibility that the people who'd pulled her into her vehicles earlier—according to the twins who were at Ce Ce's when it all went down this morning—had decided to take her again?

Fuck.

He tracked the prints to the sugarcane field. He hadn't gone far before he crossed a furrow where the dirt had a single tire track—from a motorcycle—and a man's footprints on one side and a woman's on the other. From the way the balls of her feet had dug into the soil, it looked like she'd been pushing something—probably the bike. As had the man. Maybe they hadn't wanted to draw attention by revving the engine. The fact that she was on the opposite side of a heavy bike, helping to push suggested she was not being forced.

Cam squatted, gauging how long it had been since the tracks had been made, and he'd guess not longer than a few minutes. She was on the run, and whether she liked it or not, she was going to have to tell him why.

Reggie couldn't help but notice the bright yellow Hummer when it pulled into the trailer park; most of the residents appeared to have gotten their cars through Ed's Swifty Thrifty Lot, where no clunker would prove too dilapidated to sell. The Hummer was not only sorely out of place, but it pulled directly up to the front of Bobbie Faye's trailer and a woman popped out and went to bang on Bobbie Faye's door.

Reggie looked through DJ's zoom lens, and there was Donny, the stupid sap. If she had to hear one more time about him bragging about all of the acting roles he almost had before he left L.A., and all of the things he was going to be able to do once he landed a new agent, she was going to slam a microphone against his head.

She mentally shook herself and repeated her mantra: whatever it takes.

Donny pulled his smile for the camera as he casually ambled over, like they'd never met before, hadn't been talking, and to anyone watching, it would seem believable. Maybe he could make a decent actor after all.

Chapter Thirteen

Cam was late getting home—he'd followed the motorcycle tire print until it reached a trail, and without his truck, he couldn't catch up. His truck wouldn't fit the narrow trail, even if he could have found the trail's opening and backtracked. Benoit had been waiting for him with a six-pack of ice cold beer and had handed one to Cam when he met Cam at the door.

"Thanks," Cam said, taking the beer and swigging it before he reached his living room. "It's been a shitty day."

"It's about to get worse, *cher.*"

Cam hadn't thought it was possible, but as the footage from the surveillance DVD rolled on his high-def big flat screen TV, he felt as if he'd been plowed by the biggest, meanest sonofabitch SEC lineman to walk the gridiron. He'd been standing, and then he was sitting in a chair Benoit must've pulled up for him.

While his friend and partner moved to the sofa, Cam sat directly in front of the screen, rewinding the images, rewatching it at slower and slower speeds. He paused it several times when the picture was a little blurry, or there seemed to be shadows of other people, and the rational detective part of his brain tried to think it through, to make sense of how in the hell he was seeing the woman he'd known since they were kids . . . shooting a man in cold blood. Because there was no doubt, it wasn't anywhere near self-defense.

He and Benoit watched as she picked up the five casings and, without moving, he could feel the weight of the brass in his pocket. Cam didn't say a word about them to his partner. Benoit was his best friend and would take a bullet for Cam, but Cam wasn't going to let Benoit derail his own career just because Cam had gotten sucked into another Bobbie Faye disaster. And *goddamnit,* this was a disaster she might not get out of. He squinted at the image again when he paused it—she was standing underneath the streetlight, and she looked distorted in the harsh light and strange angle. The whole perspective was off.

Cam thought about that.

"This can't be her," he told Benoit, who said nothing for a long time. And there she was, her hand holding a Glock, planting five slugs into the jeweler in a pattern he'd known all along was familiar—and now he knew why. "Can't be," he said again.

Holy Christ, he had the slugs in his pocket. What had he done? *Fuck,* what had *she* done? Could someone have forced her?

"It could be someone else," Benoit said, though Cam felt his friend's uncertainty in the too-calm delivery of the thought. "Maybe someone dressed up like her. They had to have known about the other video cameras—maybe the assumption was that we'd get those tapes, too."

"True," Cam said, remembering the footage from one store was erased and the other videotape broken. "Bad angle. Bad lighting. It could be someone else."

Could be? He'd said *could* be. Not *is.* Not *it* is *someone else.*

"I'm not going by the PD this evening," Benoit said. Which Cam knew meant he wouldn't be logging this evidence in tonight. As soon as it was logged in, they'd have to arrest Bobbie Faye.

"I can't ask you to do that," Cam said. "She's not my . . . she's not anything to me." Except someone who pissed him off on a regular basis.

"She's still my friend, Cam," Benoit said. "An' she's yours. Even if you're never going to marry her."

"Marry her? God no. My life would be like this every fucking week. No thank you."

"Well, *cher,* I want a day to see what else I can find out, first. I'll have to log it in tomorrow. But maybe I can shake the trees and drop something that'll help."

Cam nodded, and used his computer to burn a copy of the DVD. He would find Bobbie Faye. Ask her some questions before Benoit logged this in.

Trevor padded barefoot through Nina's expansive, ultra-chic loft; freshly showered, hair still damp, clad only in jeans, (something Bobbie Faye's Hormones were busy writing thank-you notes about). He appeared to be quadruple-checking the security system. Bobbie Faye stood at the big antique mahogany dining room table, glad to have showered away the debris from the day, though she didn't really want to think about what had actually happened. She wondered if there was some sort of job she could get as a Specialist in Denial and Compartmentalization because she was a freaking pro. Come to think of it, there were entire governmental departments she could probably apply to. Of course, then she'd have to answer for entire departments running screaming in the streets, so maybe it was best just to quietly freak out by herself.

She caught Trevor's reflection in the huge loft windows—the dark outside had turned them into mirrors, and when she didn't think he noticed her watching, she caught how his gaze swept the length of her and stayed on her ass. She was soooo second-guessing the short silk pjs she'd grabbed for comfort. They were a little slutty. Maybe too slutty. (Was there such a thing as half-slutty? Kinda up there with sort-of innocent and a little pregnant.)

She refocused and scrutinized the junk she'd shoved in her purse from Marie's place. Trevor made another lap past the walls filled with gorgeous paintings and the African masks (original, not

Pier 1 copies, Bobbie Faye had learned when she'd inadvertently dropped one once). There were chic polished metal lamps and deep, plush rugs that were more comfortable to lie on than the bed Bobbie Faye had at home. There were two bedrooms, and the spare was fully stocked with clothing of all sorts—for Nina's models, Nina had told her once. Bobbie Faye didn't ask about any of the S&M props Nina had stored there for use in the magazine, or why Nina had gotten started in this business in the first place. Well, she hadn't asked any direct questions; Nina was a very private person, ironically, and Bobbie Faye knew that Nina told her more than she told anyone else in the world, but as they'd grown older, there were more and more gaps. Bobbie Faye wondered about that, and if Nina had seemed unhappy, Bobbie Faye would have pressed her friend for more information. Nina, though, seemed perfectly well-adjusted. Probably was the only well-adjusted sane person Bobbie Faye knew.

"That's at least your fourth time around the place," she commented when he passed her again.

"Tenth," Trevor said absently from across the room. She looked up, since he seemed amused. He tapped the huge window that overlooked Lake Charles—its dark, still surface reflecting the moon; the bright lights from the casino boat undulated, hypnotic in the light breeze coming off the water. "Do all of your friends and family automatically install bulletproof glass?"

"Yeah. They ask for the Bobbie Faye 'cranky nutcase' discount."

"Good to know."

Trevor kept moving, and he reminded her of a panther she'd seen as a kid when her mom visited an old friend deep in the swamps; he was lethal, sinewy, graceful, strong. He was also sending text messages via his fancy cell phone—encoded, he'd explained—to his field office, getting updates, updating them. She wasn't using hers anymore since he said it was being traced.

"Won't they trace us from your phone?" It was something she should have thought of earlier, but she was so tired, so utterly wired and exhausted at the same time, she wasn't thinking clearly.

"They think so."

"You're not being a good agent and giving them an accurate signal, are you?" He shrugged. "So just out of curiosity, if we were where the signal said we were, where would we be?"

"Cut Off."

She laughed. The southernmost tip of habitable Louisiana land that wasn't a barrier reef island, down at the toe of the boot. She appreciated his irony.

His phone rang as he joined her at the table and his expression clicked into impassive as he answered. "Yeah."

"I want her here," Emile shouted. "She destroyed Marie's house. Clearly, you can't control her. I want her where I can watch her."

"You want her alive so she can find the diamonds?" Trevor asked, and Bobbie Faye stilled. Emile sputtered something incomprehensible and Trevor waited 'til he was done. "She didn't blow up the house—someone else went after her. So if you want to terminate the contract, that's fine with me. She's a royal fucking pain to control—" she stuck her tongue out at him and he grinned "—and I don't know who the hell else I'm up against. I'd just as soon cut this one loose. But she'll be dead five minutes after I move her, I promise you that."

"Do you think she has them?"

"I think she's closing in on finding them."

Emile fumed, but finally said, "I want reports. She so much as twitches an eyelash, I want a report."

Trevor hung up and said, "Try not to twitch an eyelash."

"I'll see what I can do."

From: Simone
To: JT

What do you mean, we don't have any trace of where Nina lives? How could we have a gap in our records like that?

(sent via cell)

From: JT
To: Simone

I don't know, but it's a serious concern. First, the best friend happens to be in Italy . . . where the buyer's located. Now, we can't find BF because she's staying at the home of said friend, who doesn't exist in any of our records.

(sent via cell)

From: Simone
To: JT

They went to high school together. She existed.

(sent via cell)

From: JT
To: Simone

We have a record of a Nina McVey—starting at age 7. Her grandma's name is Rhoda McVey, and her life seems to begin right there, same year. Working on a home location for Nina. High priority.

(sent via cell)

Aiden handed Sean the binoculars; they lay belly down on a rooftop across from the loft where Bobbie Faye was holed up with some guy no one knew—just that he seemed to be helping the woman and, from the number of times he "casually" brushed her arm, rubbed a shoulder, or watched her when she was studying the junk laid out on the table, he was pretty fucking interested.

"Ye takin' the first shift," Sean instructed, handing Aiden the binoculars back. "An' wake Mollie up in a couple o' hours t' replace ye."

Aiden nodded as Sean picked himself up and headed down the back fire escape to where the box truck was parked and where Robbie was probably still monitoring the GPS tracking bug. When Aiden focused the sights again on the woman, he felt a twinge of sorrow. She looked to be about dead on her feet, worry etched across her pretty face. He knew that Sean intended on taking her along with the diamonds—if she disappeared the same time as the stones, the world would think she'd taken off with them, and none the wiser that Sean had lifted 'em for himself from her before escorting her back to Ireland. Sean would enjoy breaking her—the more stubborn they were, the more fun Sean had.

He let the twinge of guilt go. The team had made a lot of money together with Sean's leadership. They were wanted everywhere, and this was the heist they needed to buy their freedom. Enough money to buy off officials or buy a private island. Sean had gotten them this far, from their days on the streets, juggling for coins. Aiden wasn't about to second guess the man now.

How many do we have out there?" Trevor asked his man, Dave, as he spoke into his phone, looking out of the expansive kitchen window. He had the lights off and could see the buildings across the street. Nina's loft had fantastic views in both front, back, and on the south side—only the north side was taken up by the wall of the adjoining building on this block, and that building she'd converted into a gym and garage.

"Two groups, that we can see," Dave answered. Trevor had Dave positioned on Nina's roof, and two other agents running surveillance—one in the building across the street, second story; one on the ground. "Looks like group number three from this morning is over on the roof opposite you, as you expected." Trevor had numbered the groups in the order of their abductions of Bobbie Faye earlier just to keep it simple over the airwaves. "Number two clocked in down on the street, still in their SUV. You were right about them."

Fuck. Homeland Security. He knew he was being lied to by his boss. He was also pretty sure he knew why.

"And group number one? The buyer?"

"No idea. I'll keep you posted if anyone else shows."

They hung up and Trevor stood still in the dark, focused across the street. He didn't have his night-vision goggles with him, or he'd have gotten a better look at the prick. As it was, he could see an outline where the man had huddled against the low wall surrounding the roof, his own binoculars trained on the dining room window. If Trevor craned his view down and to the left, he could see the SUV parked on the street; someone's cell phone lit up briefly as a call came in.

Bobbie Faye's eyes blurred from going over the piles of paper she had on the table. There were mailers that someone had produced for a couple of events showing off Marie's brand-new line of accessories, a newspaper article about the charity auction of one of her art pieces, an invitation to an awards benefit, a couple of lunches, a flurry of notes about pedicures and manicures and hair stylists and fittings—clearly Marie was planning on a big event or a trip somewhere and needed to be in top form. Next to all of that was the one clue Bobbie Faye understood that she was pretty sure no one else had thought to pursue: the rice hulls.

Her attention suddenly riveted up to the doorway to the kitchen; she didn't know how long he'd been watching her, but Trevor leaned against that archway with a simple elegance that made her think of every spy movie she'd ever seen, his biceps bulging in arms crossed over his chest, and when she was finally able to tear her eyes away from that gorgeous sight and move upward, he had a huge smile. Smile? Huh?

"Did you know," he asked, "that you were in here singing the 'Oscar Mayer Weiner' song?"

Oh, shit, that was out loud? Quick. What do crazy people usually do when caught?

"Shut *up*," she said, and when he raised a brow, realized she'd said it instead of thought it. "Um, not you. The shut-up part. Inside my head. Very noisy in there right now."

"Out here, too."

"Was not."

"The neighbors called. Wondered what cat we were killing and were we going to be through anytime soon."

"Fine. Keep it up and I'm going to serenade you with my version of the *Sesame Street* song."

"Dear God, no. I don't get hazard pay."

"Didn't you have phone calls or something productive you were supposed to be doing instead of leaning against the doorways looking sexy?" He grinned. Jesus Christ, but her brain was tired, skidding straight through Self-Preservation without even bothering to brake until she reached Abject Humiliation. At this rate, she should just get nekkid and dance. (And the Hormones said *Amen.*) "Stop it," she said to his smile. "Phone calls?"

"Yeah, a couple. The originating agent's having an orgasm because all of the players appeared."

"Oh, well, yipfuckingwhee. Tell him—"

"Her."

"Her—next time, *she* can be the one looking into those weird amber eyes."

Trevor stopped all movement. "You saw the Irish guy?"

"Yeah."

"I saw you fall out of the truck and you rolled away from me. I couldn't see you well until you stood again. You were pulling something off—"

"The gag. They didn't cover my head like the other two."

The pause and his cast-iron expression made her glad she was sitting. She pulled her knees to her chest, curling into a tight ball. Trevor stepped in front of the chair and squatted, eyes level with hers. "He has a medium build, shorter than me, scary looks but has a charming smile in spite of the barbed-wire scar?"

She shuddered. "Yep, that's him. Well, he didn't smile much until the end, and he kept calling me Ally or something, but yeah."

"*Álainn*. Which means *beautiful*."

"Great, because that makes being kidnapped all warm and fuzzy."

"And he *let* you see him," he continued, ignoring her. "You didn't just work off a blindfold or something?"

"Hi," she waved at him, "already scared stupid, here, thank you." Panic was threatening a coup and Bravery was booking the next flight out to Tahiti.

He caught her expression and his own softened. "That's Sean MacGreggor. As you've no doubt guessed from his accent, he's Irish. Scots-Irish to be exact." Trevor stood, and she felt, more than saw, him reigning in control of his demeanor. "He's a butcher, essentially. Started out in simple theft when he was a kid, graduated to B & E, mostly to get enough money to get off the streets. Took a liking to it. He's been suspected as the mastermind behind several heists and money-laundering deals in Europe and the UK, and he never leaves behind a witness."

"Um, never?"

"Never."

"Can we go back in time and pretend like I'm a dainty flower kinda girl who faints at bad news?"

"You're my partner, Sundance, and you need to know this stuff."

"Let's take a vote: all for *denial*, raise your hand." She raised both.

"If he didn't mind that you saw him, then he's got some sort of strategy where you seeing him doesn't matter to him."

"Great. I didn't feel like there was enough challenge yet, thank you."

"Sean knows our procedures enough to know the Agency would be following you as soon as word got out that you might be able to find the diamonds, and he doesn't care if you see him or report that he's here," he continued, tapping her on the forehead to make her pay attention. "And *that* means he's got an escape plan."

"You don't sound surprised he's here."

"Rumor had it that he was trying to lift the diamonds when Emile snagged them out from under him. Two of MacGreggor's original gang were dead when it was done and MacGreggor disappeared. He's been vapor ever since, and there'd been no word from Homeland Security, who was supposed to be tracking him, that he'd entered the U.S."

"But you had a feeling," she guessed from his expression.

"Let's just say it was a hunch that he'd show up. The diamonds are worth a half a billion. That's his ballpark. And MacGreggor's big on revenge, so he'll want to pay back Emile. Don't let the charm fool you—MacGreggor's deadly. He didn't come to play."

"Gee, Trevor, maybe I can find some kittens for you to terrorize next."

"If it helps any," his voice rumbled low as he braced himself on the arms of her chair and leaned in, "I didn't come to play, either."

Was she drooling? She was probably drooling. She'd heard drooling was unattractive, but damned if she could shut her mouth. The tan and the biceps and the long hair falling forward over incorrigible blue eyes and that wicked, wicked smile were all right there, and she was pretty sure smoke just spurted out her ears from all of the brain gears grinding to a halt.

"You're exhausted," he pronounced. *Yeah, that's what every girl wants to hear.* "We need to get you to bed."

"Bed?" Was that her voice that squeaked? *Bed* was *much* better than *exhausted.*

"For sleep."

The likelihood of sleep happening was about as great a possibility as Bobbie Faye getting the Pulitzer for astrophysics, but he seemed intent on steering her to the spare bedroom and all of her Hormones were so eager, they threatened a massive stroke if she opened her mouth and ruined the moment. Like with the yawning.

Geez, she was yawning. There were the *abs* for crying out loud, and she *yawned*. "It's not you," she said, and then yawned again.

"I know."

"We really have to work on that low self-esteem you have there, Trevor."

"Oh, we will. Later. But right now, you're going to sleep."

He placed his SIG on the nightstand within easy reach, and he pushed a little snub-nosed .38 she hadn't seen before underneath his pillow. He climbed in and patted the covers, and she knew sleeping next to him wasn't going to work. He tucked her into his chest, his right hand near the snub-nose, the SIG near his left, and after settling in and yawning again, she said, "God, you smell good." And then, "Damnit, did I just say that out loud?" He chuckled and held her and she was dimly aware that he talked to her, stories about growing up with three sisters and maybe there was something else in there and then something about baseball and something else about pretty cars and she drifted off. As her body felt liquid and languid and safe, she remembered she'd forgotten to tell him what the rice husks meant, but it was too hard to force words back up to the surface and so she thought: tomorrow.

FROM THE DESK OF JESSICA TYLER (JT) ELLIS

ASSISTANT TO THE UNDERSECRETARY OF THE UNDERSECRETARY OF
THE SECRETARY OF THE ASSISTANT TO THE DEPARTMENT OF DEFENSE
HOMELAND SECURITY
NEW ORLEANS, LA

Re: progress report stats
(to be filed under field notes, personal, **only**)

Textiles which originated with Marie Despré to be seized for suspicion of acting as a method of smuggling diamonds. Textiles include
but are not limited to: purses, belts, shoes, and accessories. Please
note that suspect's other hobbies include sculptural art—all known
pieces are to be searched, galleries plus private collections. Various offices around the country, including FBI, tasked to help.

Case # 198733BFS / diamond search   field notes: personal

35
~~27~~ ~~36~~ items searched   ★ Sean MacGregor!
~~11~~ ~~9~~ 2 movie stars threatening a lawsuit   sent Trevor backup
~~13~~ ~~7~~ 5 politicians disturbed (with someone other than spouse)
   3 paparazzi arrested, cameras confiscated (talk to legal)
~~6~~ 2 medical claims (cuts & bruises) (see above)
   1 agent treated for human bite (dog owner) (see above)
~~8~~ 6 defense attorneys filing harrassment suits
   3 women arrested, attempts to bribe to keep their items
   5 people called Oprah   ⎫ HAVE PR HANDLE
   17 people called Fox News   ⎭
   -have someone call InStyle, deflect interest in Marie's items

                                                            ★ reminder—it is wrong to kill a civilian!

   1 agent in the field in Lake Charles ~~kidnapped? can we be so lucky?~~
   1 crazy Cajun woman ~~in the middle~~ of this case
   (see fucked, completely—previous case)
   3 "warnings"—Sean & who else?

Chapter Fourteen

Bobbie Faye sensed someone stirring and she woke with a start, then realized she was still in Trevor's arms the way they'd lain together the night before. She relaxed back into his embrace as he grinned against her temple. The glowing red numbers on the bedside clock indicated it was nearing six-thirty in the morning. They'd gotten about four hours of sleep—a Godsend. She stretched against the length of him, too aware he still had on jeans and she still had on pjs. Damnit.

Trevor quietly stroked her hair, moved it away from her face, and she wished on everything holy that this day could officially not start so she wouldn't have to get out of bed. He ran his hand over her shoulder and down the curve of her hip and the heat of his touch electrified the rest of her body and it struck her with such a force that *she wanted this man*. So very much. Not just that she was lonely, or cranked up on lust, or that he was revenge, but *choice*. The way he held her, talked to her like an equal, looked at her, teased her. It was stupid and insane. She didn't know enough about him. Not really, not beyond the few stories she could barely remember he'd lulled her to sleep with.

She must be certifiable, because right then, she didn't really care.

He shifted as if he sensed what she was thinking. Of course, her running a hand across his chest may have given him a clue.

"We don't have time," he murmured.

"It's not even seven a.m." *Plenty* of freaking time.

"When I start on your body, I'd like us to have a few hours. And a lot less . . ." he hesitated, as she slid her hand up and over his chest, ". . . audience."

"Audience?" Um, what? He looked annoyed with himself for his word choice. Perhaps her hands sliding down to his abs had done a much better job of distracting him than she'd realized and he was just confused.

"I'm pretty sure we've got the Irish outside on a roof, and Homeland Security are across the street in their SUV. This isn't counting the buyer's people, if they tracked you, or my own men outside, and to be perfectly honest," he kissed the line of her jaw, "I'd like our first time to be private."

Her foggy brain just wasn't keeping up. "Hey, I know you're all Super Agent Guy and protective—but all of those people are in a place we civilians call the *out*side and we are on the *in*side, and there's bulletproof glass and a security system that would keep out God, so we're okay. Unless you think Nina's got cameras up in here or something, but I'd kill her and she'd have had sense enough to warn me. So see?" She unbuttoned the top of his jeans. "Com*pletely* private."

"No," he said, but he paused to kiss her stupid as he pressed her into the bed. Every part of her body caught fire. If she could just get a little closer and a whole lot more nekkid . . .

He stopped himself, rolling away, lying on his side to face her. "Jesus, Sundance, the world goes away too easily when you're around. But we have to stop. You don't want to do this in front of cameras."

Cameras? For real? She studied his expression and crap, he was serious. She sat bolt upright. "How in the hell did they get cameras in here? Past Nina's security? And why are we still here? And—"

"Whoa. Slow down. Not *in* here, per se." He sighed. Damnit, Trevor was not a "sigher." "They'll probably have thermal optics."

"Hang on . . . thermal-whats?"

"Optics. They allow the viewer to see heat signatures through walls. Anything that generates heat will show up, glowing red, while everything else remains black."

"That sounds like something they made up for the movies."

"It's very real, and some of the units are pretty sophisticated."

"How sophisticated? What all . . ."

"People, animals . . ." he hesitated, then a sexy grin spread across his face, ". . . appliances." She followed his glance over to the big armoire Nina had in the corner—the one they'd discovered housed all sorts of sex toys for Nina's S&M magazine modeling shoots—and then she made the connection he implied, from Nina's toys to her own, remembering just what was in her top dresser drawer back at her trailer. An item which generated a helluva lot of heat. Amusement lit his sinful blue eyes.

"So," she stammered out, grabbing for a sheet to cover herself more. "You're telling me that you used thermalwhatsits on me . . . at my trailer . . . and . . . and . . . you know all about . . ." She gestured back at the armoire, indicating the toys, not actually able to say the word "vibrator." Oh, sonofa*bitch*. She jumped out of bed like she'd been hit with a 220 volt of electrical current, and she didn't know what to do or where to run. Instead, all she could manage was to gape at him, open-mouthed. It didn't help that she was standing there in front of him, dressed in skimpy pjs, with Trevor grinning at her with a dead sexy grin as if this was all funny and just—Goddamnit! She threw the nearest thing she could lay a hand to—a candle—straight at his head. He ducked, the bastard. Laughing.

"It wasn't *always* in your dresser drawer." He growled. She narrowed her gaze, and he moved his SIG to the other side of where he sat, out of her reach. "Though I didn't realize what you had gotten out of the drawer the first time—and only time—I saw what you were doing. You made my life a living hell. I had to force myself to turn off the thermals whenever you went near that dresser. Talk about killing a man."

Had her head spun entirely off her shoulders? Had she completely levitated, while her head rolled across the floor? Because it felt like it had. So *this* was how he always knew all of the right little things to do to seem so intuitive about her, like buy the goddamned chili dogs. Or exactly where Nina lived, without her having to tell him. Or a dozen other little things he'd done that made it so comfortable to be with him. Her inner fourth grader wanted to kick him.

"You *spied* on me. Gathered . . . data? And probably made reports."

"Not about that," he said, nodding toward the armoire, indicating the vibrator they had managed not to name thus far. "Never about that. But pretty much everything else, yes."

She couldn't believe how nonchalant he was. Who in the fuck was this guy? Where did he get off?

Oh, baaaad word choice, and she blushed all of the way to her ears.

"Sundance," he said, sitting forward, closing into her space where she stood beside the bed, "you were the focus of the attention of a master money launderer—he had your name as the owner of that tiara a long time before he put your brother's kidnapping into play. You were a big variable, and it's my job to know the variables. My job was to investigate you while I was working for him; we had to know where you stood, ethically, what kind of person you were, especially if you could be bought."

"Like I'd betray my own brother."

"You'd be surprised how many people would. Look," he said, standing, "I know you're uncomfortable with this. I know how much your privacy means to you."

"Well, I guess you would, now, wouldn't you?"

"I was going to tell you."

"When? When you had me in bed, knew all of my secrets while not telling me any of yours? You've used information to make me comfortable. To manipulate me. How am I supposed to know if all of this—" she gestured between the two of them "—isn't just so you can keep track of me and the diamonds. Keep me close, get your hands on them." And then a realization dawned on her. "Or that guy, MacGreggor? You knew he was here, looking for the diamonds! So you conveniently show up, all sexy and hot and romancy and Jesus! I fell for it."

"You're pissed off."

"Well, isn't that a firm grasp on the obvious. You should look into being a spy or something."

"This," he said, gesturing between them as she'd done, "is not about this case. Or *any* case. I want you." She blinked, shocked at his bluntness. "I want you for *you*. Not for any other reason. And I think you know that."

"How in the world do I know that? *I don't even* know *you*."

"Like hell, you don't." He stepped closer, inches away. Had she done it again? Believed in smoke and mirrors, believed in something that was just, simply, not true. Of *course* he was arguing his position—he still needed her for the case. If there was a reality TV show for the World's Worst Judge of Men, she'd win, hands down. "We," he said, leaning into her, "are nowhere near done. I care about you more than you know."

"Very pretty words, Trevor. Well rehearsed. They almost sound real."

His cell phone rang from the nightstand, shrill, and she jumped from the noise. He glanced at the screen, then back to her. She could tell he wanted to say something, but he pulled on his t-shirt instead, grabbed the phone and, just when she thought he was going to leave without saying anything else, he spun, yanked her to him, and kissed her.

Hard.

She tried pulling away, but he held her tighter, and holy Mother of God if the man didn't know exactly how to make her completely insane with lust. Even though she hated him. (That's when Hormones piped up with the argument that they were perfectly okay with being a slut while hating him, and Common Sense threatened to turn in its resignation.)

She pushed him away. "I am so not falling for you." Shit. For *that*. She meant to say falling for *that*.

He raked her with a gaze, up and down, and watched her blush again. "Wanna bet?"

He left the room, and she sunk down on the bed, her head spinning. Fact, fiction, everything blurred. It was Alex, the gunrunner's web of lies all over again. Wasn't it? She sat there for a few minutes in a fog of fury when she heard someone pounding on the front door. He must've gone outside and forgotten the code to get back in, and she realized she actually wanted him to come back so they could finish that argument. Because now that she'd had time to adjust to the fact that their entire relationship was based on lies—or omissions, rather—she was ready to tear his ass to pieces. The sonofabitch had *spied* on her.

She jumped up, dropped the sheet, grabbed a robe, and hurried to the front door, only to see it opening. She slid abruptly into the sofa, trying to scramble backward as she realized the hair of the man coming in her front door was much darker than Trevor's, and shit, she needed Maimee's Glock from her purse, and it was over on the table. . . .

And then she realized she was looking at Cam, who was about as livid as she'd seen him in a long, long time. Which probably meant he was going to be awarded a *Guinness Book of World Records* entry for "most pissed off in one person."

Just perfect. Apparently, some time in the middle of the night, she'd taken the express elevator to the second level of Hell, Know-It-All Asshole Division.

• • •

Cam wasn't sure how long he'd stood there just inside Nina's front door when a hand smacked him in the chest and he realized Bobbie Faye was standing so close he could smell the shampoo in her hair, that stupid fruity stuff he'd liked so much. He could tell she hadn't blown her hair dry after her shower because it was curly, framing her face as she looked up at him expectantly. *Jesus*, this was a bad idea. He should have sent Benoit. Or hell, even Jason from dispatch would have been better at questioning her without being distracted, especially with this freaking headache, which would have made normal conversation strained, and just added a layer of refried pain on top of their conflict.

"Cam?" There was panic in her voice. "Is something wrong with Stacey?"

"No." He shook himself out of his stupor. "No, she's okay. I checked on her before I left for work. Mom said she was a little wired last night—after you called, Stacey wrangled too many cookies and didn't want to fall asleep, but she's having fun."

She pulled her hand away, and he could feel the heated imprint through his cotton shirt as if she'd branded him. Then he felt something at the back of his neck, almost like a wisp of smoke, and he had his gun out as he spun to face the kitchen archway; Trevor stood leaning against the door frame, arms crossed, gaze narrowed at Cam. The bastard hadn't even flinched when a gun was drawn on him, and Cam and the agent stared at each other over the barrel of Cam's gun.

"Nice to see you, too, Detective," Trevor said.

Cam lowered his gun. "What the hell are you doing here?"

"Staying in a safe place, I thought," Bobbie Faye answered. "I had this wacky concept, call me crazy, that if the door was *locked*, people would stay on the *other side* and knock."

"For someone trying to stay safe," Cam sidestepped the issue, "you're being stunningly sloppy. I could have been *anyone* barging in here."

"If you had been anyone else," Trevor said, "you'd have been dead before you stepped in the door."

Bobbie Faye glared at Trevor. "The phone call. You knew he was on his way up here, and you didn't tell me."

"We were a little busy," Trevor said, and Cam snapped his attention to the agent, and back to Bobbie Faye. He wasn't sure of the meaning, since the agent remained poker-faced, but Bobbie Faye's expression was steeped in anger. "Breakfast in ten."

"At least he has sense enough to keep you out of the kitchen," Cam muttered, and Bobbie Faye smacked him on the arm.

"That toaster had it in for me, it is not my fault it caught your kitchen on fire, so quit bringing it up. And back to the point, what the hell are you doing? Specializing in breaking and entering now? Have you lost your mind?"

"I need to speak to Bobbie Faye," he told Trevor, but Cam's gaze stayed on her face. Cam understood, then, from the way she returned his gaze, that she hadn't just been referring to him barging into Nina's with her "locks" comment—she must have seen him breaking into her trailer. He turned back to the agent. "Privately."

"Well *that* would be new," Bobbie Faye countered.

Trevor nodded to Cam and left the room as quietly as he'd entered.

Benoit squatted at the entrance to the alley where Sal had been shot; the remnants of the police tape fluttered from the streetlight a few feet away. He wasn't sure what he hoped to find that might help Bobbie Faye. The PD and crime scene techs and FBI had all been over the alley with meticulous precision. He had low expectations of finding a single clue, much less something that would help his friend, but he'd resolved—somewhere in the tug of war between duty and instinct—that he ultimately had to side with the fact that he'd known Bobbie Faye since high school, and she couldn't be a murderer.

The scene looked so entirely different in the early morning light than it had on the surveillance footage. He slowly scanned the turn-of-the-century buildings which had been refurbished just a few years back; rustic, faded red brick warehouses that sported the patina of more than a hundred years of weather made the place warm and welcoming, while simultaneously, the up-dated tinted windows, freshly painted trim, and extravagant moldings gave the place the feeling of luxury.

As he looked over the area, he paid particular attention to where the two surveillance cameras that should have captured the activities in the alley were located.

Interesting.

He walked over to where the murderer had stood, and looked back at the cameras, double-checking his theory: the murder had taken place in the direct line of sight of both cameras. Ten feet deeper into the alley, and only one camera would have caught the activity. Another five feet, and the murder would have been out of the range of vision of both cameras.

If the woman brought a gun and shot the man in cold blood— which she'd clearly done—did it make any sense that she wouldn't have at least cased the place prior to the event? It didn't look like a crime of passion, or a spontaneous decision, and it was clearly not self-defense. So, then, if she'd walked the alley even once to scope out the security, surely she would have noticed that she could have lured the jeweler a little deeper into the alley with-out risk of being caught on camera. The streetlight—located at the entrance of the passage—hadn't illuminated the back part of the area, if Benoit's memory served him well. In fact, he mused as he walked farther to the back of the road, the murderer had nodded to someone who'd remained in the shadows right here . . . so was it intentional that she chose to stop where she did to shoot Sal?

Why bother to fake Bobbie Faye's identity if the murderer hadn't known, for certain, that she'd be recorded? She could have just worn a cap or hat, or some sort of disguise to cover her head and face, and she would have remained anonymous, especially if she'd chosen the shadows. And if this line of thinking was correct . . . then how angry was she now that the two surveillance tapes had disappeared without exposing the Bobbie Faye identity to the police? If someone had set that up as a frame, what would they do next?

And not a single bit of this reasoning helped Bobbie Faye.

Benoit looked at the case from the point of view of a cop, as well as that of the DA, who was also his friend. Bobbie Faye had a reputation for helping people out of jams, even if that meant bending and breaking the law a time or ten. She'd skated off the last disaster without being charged (and there were a multitude of charges which could have been levied, starting with destruction of public property to reckless endangerment . . . crap, the list was too long to think about); he suspected the only thing that had saved her ass then was Cam and, possibly, the Fed, Trevor, pulling strings. (Of course Cam, the idiot, hadn't told her he'd called two senators on her behalf.) Even without a clear cut motive, a good DA—and his friend was damned good—could argue that she *habitually* allowed the means to justify the ends, that she had grown accustomed to the law not holding her accountable, and so she'd come to the point where she believed that she could get away with killing Sal.

For what reason? Benoit didn't know, but with the sheer number of crises involving Bobbie Faye yesterday, he was willing to bet his badge that something major was up. It wouldn't be all that hard for a DA, and probably most any jury, to leap to the conclusion that anything that would drive Bobbie Faye as hard as she was driven the day before was probably extremely compelling, and if she'd mangle a house and blow up a bridge, was murder all that hard to believe?

John watched through the sights of his scope as Bobbie Faye talked to the asshole cop, Cam. They both looked over at someone else in the room, but that person remained out of John's sight. Now they focused completely on each other again. Arguing, it looked like. They were usually arguing, though, so it was no surprise.

He didn't have a shot. Neither did the men he'd hired.

It had taken a couple of hours from the time he'd made the call to the time his assistants had arrived. Once he had the operating budget wired into his account from the buyer, John worked fast, hiring the best he knew in the merc business. There was a brief moment when he thought about going after the diamonds himself, but he'd decided he'd rather not turn into the target. Besides, the rewards were going to be significant: enough freaking money to live on for a couple of years and getting even with Bobbie Faye.

The two hours he'd waited for the mercs to arrive had been passed scouting out where Bobbie Faye had gone after she left Marie's. Lake Charles was a small town, and there weren't that many hotels to check. Discreetly spreading around cash got him past the morals of a host of hotel clerks, and since every one of them had been a dead end, he moved on to Bobbie Faye's friends. Nina was the closest friend, and her place wasn't on any four-one-one, but John knew a couple of the models Nina used for her agency. Now, if Bobbie Faye would just move into his sights, everything would be perfect.

Nina had no intention of going to sleep—she'd get her job done there in Taormina, wrap things up with the photo shoot in the villa, both of which would probably take a couple more hours. There was a corporate jet fueled up on the runway at Catania; thank God it was a military base—she'd get first preference flight out. Flight time back to Louisiana was about twelve hours, if they pushed it, and she had a feeling she needed to be home. She dialed Bobbie Faye's phone number, only to smile when she heard her friend's extremely grumpy hello.

"So," Bobbie Faye said, "do you keep any weapons in this place? Because I am feeling an extreme need for weapons this morning."

Nina was pretty sure she heard Cam in the background. "Obviously you haven't looked in the exercise suite."

"Exercise? Why would you keep . . . oh. Don't answer that. Don't you have Italian men to handcuff or something?"

"Already done. And I'm heading home, so I'll be on a plane for a while—I'll call you when I hit New York. Try not to blow up the state before I get there—I want to move some of my art to a safe place."

"One of these days, you're going to call me and I'm going to tell you that absolutely *nothing* is going on, everything is quiet, and people aren't yelling at me."

"Sure, B. And when you do, I'll know that they are treating you very nicely in the padded cell."

Cam peppered her with so many questions about yesterday, Bobbie Faye wanted to kick him, but she'd learned her lesson: no kicking big things without her boots on. Right then, she was barefoot, which was the only goddamned thing that saved Cam's shins. She plopped down on the sofa and stalled answering—as much to annoy him as to take a moment to remember that Punching Big Cops was a Bad Thing. Even if he was an ex-boyfriend. Not only was he being a cop, he was being a *jerk* cop, using his interrogation tone and cutting off her attempts to ask him what he'd been up to in her trailer. He grew agitated with each ensuing detail, so she gave him only the minimum highlights of the day's activities and the search for the diamonds. He didn't need to know about Marie's day planner note.

"So you're helping Francesca? Are you nuts? What am I talking about?" He threw his hands up, and paced in a circle. "You practically have the label *Crazy, Inc.* trademarked."

"And I'm getting it tattooed on my ass, too."

"You don't even *like* the woman. She always competed for everything you had, all through school."

Bobbie Faye didn't want to get into the whole "Francesca's family could get killed, and by the way, they're my extended family, too," since she'd never explained that connection to Cam before. "Francesca competed with everyone, Cam. I mean, holy geez, with a dad like Emile, she learned competition from birth. Besides, she never really went after anything I cared all that much about."

"Yeah. Got it. Thanks."

"You know what I mean. You hated her. You don't count."

"And the warm and fuzzy just keeps on coming."

"Well, gee, Cam, the next time you barge in to announce to me what an idiot I am, I'll be sure to dial the decade back to the fifties and—what the hell—I'll have some tea and crumpets and a nice side dish of Don't-Mind-Me, I'm-A-Doormat disorder waiting for you while I tie my apron on. Now, if that's all you want, I have diamonds to find."

"Where were you Saturday night?"

"Why?"

"Just answer the question, Bobbie Faye," he barked. He paced away from her, fighting his temper. He rubbed the bridge of his nose, as he usually did with a headache. "Can't you ever just answer a damned question?" He looked like crap, from the bloodshot eyes to the rumpled slept-in look of his clothes.

With his arm bent and his muscles flexed, she realized again how sexy Cam was. Taller and lankier than Trevor, at six-four, he intimidated a lot of people, particularly with that cop glare he'd perfected, and he was an unusually natural leader, both on the football field and off. He had always been sexy to her, even when he was a gangly fourteen-year-old to her scrawny twelve. But she also always saw the guy she'd grown up with. The guy who'd let her drive (and, oops, wreck) his first car, the one who would have never admitted, in a million years, that he liked the movie *E.T.* She especially noticed his biceps as he stood there, and how his sweaty shirt plastered against ripped abs. *Oh, God.* She was a bicep and abs junkie. She was going to have to quit, cold turkey, because look where it got her: one guy who'd conned her into complete humiliation, another one who was determined to continually berate her for everything she'd ever done wrong. She probably didn't even breathe right. So that was it. AA. Abs Anonymous, here she comes. She wondered if there was a patch for that.

"I was home alone," she finally answered when he'd leaned in, about to ask again.

"All night?"

"Well, yeah." He'd been demanding in his tone before, but now Cam verged on belligerent.

"Alone?"

"Cam!"

"Well? I have to know. Were you alone?"

"What in holy hell crawled up your ass and died?"

Chapter Fifteen

It's police business, Bobbie Faye." Cam's voice hammered the air and echoed off the loft walls. "*Yes* or *no*, were you alone?"

He watched her carefully as she leaned forward, confusion spreading across her eyes, and her robe fell open and dear fucking Lord, there was her cleavage spilling over next-to-nothing pjs and he had to look away.

"Yes. Alone. What's going on?"

"Is there anybody who can confirm you stayed home? Was Stacey there?"

"No, she spent the night at Janie's down the street. Did something happen Saturday night?"

He breathed in and out a minute, his gaze fixed across the room on a plant by the window, pushing away the image that open robe had seared in his mind. It reminded him, too much, of weekends they'd laze around, barely bothering to dress. "Yeah," he finally said, "something happened." He couldn't exactly tell her that she was now a suspect in the murder of the jeweler, and he wasn't about to tell her about the casings he'd found or, dear God, the surveillance footage Benoit hadn't turned in yet. He'd already made one lapse in judgment, had already bent rules he'd sworn never to bend, much less break. Giving her details of an ongoing investigation where she was the suspect? Wrong. Plain and simple.

"And you're sure you don't have anyone who can confirm you were there all night?"

"No. No one. It's not like I go home to the male equivalent of Winna, so what do you expect?"

She said it so low, so quietly, but certainly not calmly, and he couldn't look away. Why in the hell hadn't he thought about the fact that everyone that gossiped to him about her would also make it a point to fill her in on every single fucking thing he did? He knew if the Winna thing kept going, he'd eventually mention it to Bobbie Faye. Not that she cared, he knew, because if she cared, they wouldn't have broken up. But he'd planned . . . hell, he didn't know what he'd planned. He knew he hadn't thought he'd be sitting across from her, while she sat in a robe and skimpy pjs, with a (if rumor was true) rogue agent in the other room, doing God knows what, having this discussion on the heels of her being a suspect in a major murder case.

"I don't expect anything from you, Bobbie Faye." His tone was so cold, he might as well have ice-picked her.

"Obviously." Freezing temps right back at him.

He should shut up. He should get up and leave, since he'd gotten the answers he needed. He should stand up right fucking now and walk out that door.

"You know," he said, his voice hard and cutting, "that's what happens after you leave a person. They move on."

An utter look of shock played across her green eyes. She leaned forward as if a little gut-punched, and he didn't know what she wanted from him. To never date anyone else while she blithely went on with her life? To always be that guy she rejected, pining away? The one she kept as a backup plan? To hell with that.

"You . . . you're trying to say that *I'm* the one who left?"

"Of course you left."

She stared at him like she was seeing him for the very first time, and something tingled on the back of his neck, something that told him the picture had just shifted a bit to the right, but hadn't clicked quite into place, and she started shaking her head in disbelief. Then she chuckled, but without any mirth or joy. No, it was more along the line of total incredulity.

"That," she said, hopping up and yanking the front door open, "is just like you. How someone can be as good a detective as you are and still be blind as a fucking bat is flat beyond me. Now you got your answers to your questions. You can leave."

Benoit approached the antique shop, reaching for the door handle when he heard Reggie O'Connor say, "So, Benoit, you're looking good."

He turned to face her, wowed by her bright red low-cut shirt, just the right amount of cleavage for her job as an on-air reporter, and her long hair curled in messy waves that looked natural. She beamed a perfect, blinding white toothy smile and if he hadn't known her reputation for being a cutthroat reporter, he'd have immediately asked her out. Or given in one of the number of times she'd propositioned him. But he wasn't completely insane. Dating Reggie would be a bit like dating a piranha; it wasn't a matter of *if* you'd be eaten . . . just *when*.

"Aw, *chère,* you say that to everyone. Might as well cut to the chase."

"Benoit, sugar, one of these days, you're gonna realize I will be the best thing that happens to you. But right now—" she flicked a hand and Benoit caught a subtle signal and realized her cameraman was standing off to the side, rolling "—I want to know what's the story about how Bobbie Faye has been caught on tape shooting our jeweler vic?"

It was a damned good thing he'd played poker for most of his life; he feigned surprise and leaned in to her a little. "I don't know what you're talking about, *chère,* but this sounds real interesting. Where'd you hear this?"

"Apparently, Mr. Beauregard told his wife, who told her sister, who called her ladies group at her church, and it pretty much spread from there. Mr. Beau said you have the only copy. Care to comment?"

"Now, *chère,* you know I don't comment."

"Not even for your friend, who looks like she gunned a man down in cold blood?"

"You have a good day, now, Reggie. I like your shirt."

He stepped inside the antique shop, ignoring Reggie's swearing under her breath; he knew Reggie's boss would love to air something—anything at all—on this story. It had ratings written all over it. If Reggie could get someone to comment, she'd run with the story live and there wasn't going to be a helluva lot he could do about it. Once it became officially public, he'd have to log the DVD footage (and the original hard drive) into evidence and he could just imagine the DA's delight at finally getting to press charges against Bobbie Faye.

Cam strode past Bobbie Faye and took the corridor to the garage area where Nina stored her cars. He replayed the argument, especially Bobbie Faye's parting shot, and ran slap into Francesca, who nearly fell off her stilettos onto her flaming pink ass. He caught her and averted his eyes from the micro-mini that should have required him to have an ob-gyn license, and he sure as hell didn't want to encourage Francesca. In high school—when everyone else knew he was nuts about Bobbie Faye and they were best friends and he hadn't figured out how to change their status without ruining the friendship—Francesca's version of "flirting" had been to show up in his bedroom every weekend of one summer. Naked. In his bed. He finally figured out she was conning his youngest brother into leaving Cam's window unlocked, but locking it didn't seem to give her the message—she just switched to waiting for him after the summer football practices.

"Ooooooh, Cam," she cooed, her voice dropping an octave to a sultry whisper. "You're single now . . . I'm single now . . . you wanna catch up later? Maybe have some drinks? I mean, after I help poor Bobbie Faye with her makeover and some other stuff?"

"Oh *hell* no," Bobbie Faye said from behind Cam, and he heard her slam Nina's door shut. He distinctly heard the lock click.

"No thanks, Frannie."

"It'd be fun." She pressed a well-manicured nail lightly into his chest and started to stroke downward. "We haven't caught up in a long time."

He caught her hand and pressed it away from him. He tried to pull back his anger and frustration with Bobbie Faye to keep it from spilling over. "No, Frannie."

Her eyes shone a little bit, and he felt like he'd just kicked a puppy. "Well, if you change your mind." She smiled.

As she walked toward Nina's door, he turned back to her and asked, "By the way, how did you know where to find Bobbie Faye?" He was certain his ex hadn't called Francesca, even though Bobbie Faye was trying to help her—Bobbie Faye's patience with *Annoying, Unlimited* was about as thin as an amoeba. Nina's physical address—her newest physical address in an everchanging list of homes—wasn't listed. Cam had the security code only because Nina wanted one cop on the force to know it when she was out of town.

"I followed *you,* silly," Francesca said, and she gave him the little cheerleader wave as she pranced toward the door.

From: Simone
To: JT

There was another call from Italy? We can't get a trace?

(sent via cell)

From: JT
To: Simone

Italy's only a guess, since the signal is bouncing off satellites like crazy. Someone has something pretty high-tech to block our tracking software. It's as good as ours.

(sent via cell)

Ce Ce stirred the concoction in the glass bowl very carefully, watching the clear liquid thicken into a jelly consistency. She glanced around her workroom and noted (for probably the hundredth time) that all of the talismans were hanging in their proper places: rosemary on the north wall, thyme on the east, sage on the south, and mint on the west. She'd become a little obsessive about the placement of the talismans ever since Monique had traded one out for a rubber chicken as a joke, and the three love spells Ce Ce had concocted after that had had disastrous results. (Although the banker who started the chicken farm seemed quite happy.)

The worn butcher block countertop where Ce Ce worked had been sprinkled with her own mixture of primrose, powdered olive, and crushed beeswax. She'd mixed the first set of ingredients the night before (thank goodness the berries were in season) and had set the bowl out beneath the full moon to absorb its powers. To this mixture, she added powdered lodestone, hematite, sea glass, and then aloe. She tried to ignore the incessant knocking on the door and Monique, on the other side, imploring Ce Ce to let her in.

"I won't mess up this one, I promise," Monique pleaded, as she hiccupped. The hiccups told Ce Ce her pudgy redheaded friend had hit her hidden flasks again.

"No way, honey. You just wait out there. I'm almost done."

"What do you want me to do about the prayer group?"

"The what?" Ce Ce's head whipped up from the bowl to the

door; she couldn't stop what she was doing to let Monique in—the timing of the addition of the last two ingredients was critical.

"Miz Maimee's back and now she has her prayer group with her. She says God has called her to the Glock counter until you sell her one. And her prayer partners are laying hands on anyone who moves on that side of the store."

Ce Ce eyed the mixture in her bowl, judging it time for the lavender as she called out to Monique, "Just let 'em be, honey." The last thing she needed was Maimee and her group even more upset, bringing strong, negative energy into the store. On the other hand, a little positive energy flow would be welcome. "Tell her I'll be with her in a little bit."

"Okay, but she says they're doing some sort of cleansing prayer."

"It's all good, honey," she told Monique as she added the hyssop, and then looked at the jar and couldn't remember if she'd added it in already. There appeared to be more missing from the jar than she'd intended to take. Surely not. Surely she hadn't added too much.

Heading toward the kitchen, ignoring Francesca's knocks on Nina's front door, Bobbie Faye was still steamed from her conversation with Cam *and* still humiliated from her previous argument with Trevor.

She fully intended on confronting him—and then the wonderful aroma permeating the kitchen overwhelmed her. There was the mouthwatering scent of bacon and mushrooms and chives and eggs and where on earth had he found this stuff? She was pretty sure Nina's version of a "stocked kitchen" was a full drawer of take-out menus. As soon as she stepped through the doorway, Trevor set down a glass of orange juice on the granite bar in front of her; he stayed focused on his tasks, moving away from her in that tight t-shirt, maneuvering pans and easing around the room as fluid and beautiful as water flowing over stones. How was it that a man so lethal could simultaneously look so comforting?

The delicious saturation of flavors drenched the air, and the fact that *he'd* created them stunned her senses, and she drank the orange juice without thinking. As the cold tang hit her palate, something awful scratched at her memory. Something dark and wrong and deeply horrific and she shuddered and couldn't quite place what it was, but she set the orange juice down as Trevor glanced up from the stove top. He stopped moving and focused completely on her.

"Did he upset you?"

"Who?" she asked, glancing back at the orange juice with an eerie feeling climbing her spine, reminding her of that weird, psychotic dream, and she shook it off and shifted her attention back to Trevor. "Cam?"

"You're pale." He plated the omelet and set it in front of the bar stool next to where she stood.

"Cam always manages to upset me." She didn't know why the orange juice bothered her, because it tasted fine. "That's his Standard Operating Procedure." She looked down at the plate and her stomach growled.

"Eat." He slid the utensils in front of her. When she didn't pick up the fork, he added, "Eating this in no way indicates that you're not still angry with me."

She sat down at the bar. "Nice try at the reverse psychology. You're seriously deluded if you think I'm that easy." She stared at the omelet; damn, there were two kinds of cheeses. Maybe even three.

"Sundance, in all of the history of women, you would be the last one that someone would label 'easy.' "

"Good," she said, then, "Wait." He smiled. "I'm *not* going to be manipulated."

"Okay." He reached for the plate and Instinct took over and she grabbed it, protecting it, and he waited, his hand still on the rim.

"I never said I didn't want it."

"*Do* you want it?"

She eyed him, wary, unsure if they were still talking about the omelet. He snagged her fork with his other hand, cut the omelet, and fed her a bite. She should have been annoyed at his blatant manipulation, and she should have kept her lips closed, but Hunger vetoed and took over her mouth and she had to close her eyes once the food passed her lips because *oh. dear. Lord.* She had no idea anyone could do something so sublime to an omelet. She wasn't even sure what he'd done, but it had melted in her mouth and she'd nearly had an orgasm. When she opened her eyes, he was clearly enjoying her response.

"You jerk," she said, but it was hard to sound really angry when she'd taken the fork and was stuffing her mouth with the next bite. When he arched an eyebrow, quizzically, she angled the utensil toward the omelet. "You're not playing fair."

"I have no intention of playing fair."

She wanted to take that growling statement and the wave of sexual energy emanating from him as purely flirting, but Trevor was the kind of guy who'd managed to out-strategize people while undercover—even people prone to tremendous paranoia, like the mob types he'd indicated he'd had to associate with in the past. Why in the hell would she be any less of an obstacle if he thought she had something he needed, and any less deserving of exploitation?

His goal was to find the diamonds and to trap this MacGreggor guy, not have a real relationship with her, and it was time for her to learn a little self-preservation for a change. She'd seriously screwed up her life trusting two different guys in the past—she just flat didn't need the third strike. She wasn't entirely sure she could handle it, and she pushed that thought away, because she'd have to investigate the *why* of that notion, and there was no way she was going to do that. Not with him standing there looking like Sex Incarnate and *feeding* her, for crying out loud. Good freaking grief, he was *smart*.

"Well, good thing you don't have to play anymore," she said, and he frowned, his blue eyes in his deeply tanned face snapping to *confused*. "I know where to start looking for the diamonds." She pushed off the bar stool before he could respond, went to the dining room, and picked up what she needed from the dining table. When she spun to return, she slammed straight into him.

"Jesus, we need to hang a bell on you." His eyes narrowed as she held up her fist and opened it, palm up, to show him what she'd retrieved. *Let's just see how well he'd researched her.*

There in her palm were the empty rice husks she'd found at Marie's. He stared at them a moment, then some recognition dawned, and she felt the sting of humiliation all over again: her privacy really and truly had been completely invaded, since he clearly knew she had family—butt-crack crazy family—because that's where the hulls had come from. And how could he be attracted to *her*? Any man who knew the level of insanity she belonged to wouldn't come near her with a ten foot pole.

She'd never discussed who she was related to, except with Nina, and even then, it was just in a cursory exchange: Nina's parents had died when she was young and she'd moved Lake Charles to live with her grandmother. Bobbie Faye's dad hadn't acknowledged her and her mom had turned into a loon, which everyone gossiped about until her mom got cancer, and then for the longest time, she thought her mom's name had changed to "Poor Necia, bless her heart" because that's how every sentence started when people talked about the latest crazy thing her mom had done. Bobbie Faye had never told Cam; they'd met when she was twelve after her family moved into his school district—and he'd just accepted the fact that she didn't have a dad.

"We're going to your dad's house?"

"Yeah, so if you'll excuse me, I've got to go figure out what to wear to Demented Central."

Chapter Sixteen

Benoit met the owner of the antique store. She turned out to be near seventy-five, her leathery skin creased with so many lines, she looked like someone had used her face for multiple games of tic-tac-toe. Her smoker's cough echoed in the big main room as she dragged her oxygen bottle around with her, though the fact that she was wobbling around with a flammable liquid didn't prevent her from lighting up another cigarette while she told him about her bunions.

When she finally meandered back to his question she said, "Aw sweet-heart," in the way old southern women always "sweet-hearted" everyone, "the only young women I seen for sure are my customers, so of course they'd be coming in kinda often. Got all sizes and shapes of girls coming in here, and some of them come once a year, some once a week."

She was lying. The old woman inhaled another drag on her cigarette, shifted her feet, and kept scanning off to the back of the store as if she had a customer, somewhere, she could go attend. The place was empty.

"It would be *beaucoup* help for her, Mrs. Oubillard, if you could tell me whether or not you saw anyone that looked like Bobbie Faye here that night."

"Help her, huh?" she asked, and then another drag. "Well. If you're sure?"

He nodded.

"Well, she was here. A little weird, though, and I couldn't figure out half of what she was talking about, but then my hearing aid acts up sometimes."

"She was here? Talking to you?" Couldn't be possible.

"Oh, not directly to me. She was over there," she pointed to the alley where Sal had been shot. "I couldn't see who she was talking to, though."

"You're sure it was her? And not someone who looked like her? That is a long way away, *chère*."

"Sweetheart, I'm sure. You see that shelf in the back?" She pointed to a display case in the far back of the big store. "I can read all of those magazine covers from here."

Benoit squinted. He could barely make out the colors, much less the headlines. He eyed her suspiciously.

"Got me some cataract surgery last year," she explained. "Multifocal lenses. I needed to be able to see the customers across the store, keep up with merchandise that tries to walk out. I know who I saw in the alley. I was up in my room," she pointed above the store. "An' she waved at me. I had the window open, on account of the smoke." She adjusted the oxygen tube going to her nose and then took another drag. "'Course, I went to bed then. Didn't know old Sal was gonna bite it. I'd a stayed up for that."

Benoit followed her up to her room, decorated in leftover antiques that she'd probably never be able to sell. He took out a small digital camera he always carried now and snapped photos from her window overlooking the alley and noted that she could only see a portion of it. Still, her certainty was absolute, and she'd convince any jury.

They would completely believe Bobbie Faye was in that alley.

"Do you remember the time you saw her?"

"I think maybe a little bit after the *Tonight Show* goes off. I'm not sure, I mighta dozed a little with the light on. I saw her after that, though. Clear as a bell."

Benoit asked her a few more random questions, but she hadn't seen anyone else—hadn't even seen Sal or Sal's lights on. Didn't think anything was suspicious because Bobbie Faye is always doing crazy things, so of course she was in an alley at midnight.

He left as she went to attend to a new batch of customers who'd come clanging in the doorway. The dry cleaners had opened up for the day across the courtyard, and he headed that direction. Then something orange beneath the shrubbery in the center courtyard area caught his eye. Curiosity compelled him forward, and when he bent to see what it was, he felt a sense of alarm. It was a shirt. More importantly, it had the same stripes as the shirt seen on the murderer in the surveillance footage.

Benoit stood and scanned the area to see if anyone was watching his actions. He knew that if the shirt had been in this location after the murder, the police or FBI or crime scene techs would have found it. This grouping of shrubs was less than thirty feet from the alley entrance. So how did it get here? Now?

He didn't see anyone watching him. There weren't many people shopping yet that morning. After a few minutes, he pulled out his camera again and photographed the location of the shirt from every angle. Once documented, he used a pen to lift a corner of the shirt and found blood spatters consistent with what he'd seen on the murder video. Equally worrisome, though, was the fact that the tag had the initials "BF" scrawled with a permanent type of marker.

Benoit hadn't needed to see the initials to guess where the shirt had come from: it was a shirt given out to the winners in a high-school spirit-week competition. He remembered how all of the kids had joked about how ugly the shirts were that year—they were more of a punishment than a reward—though it hadn't deterred them all from entering the contest. The challenge had been to come up with a big, visual event to generate excitement for the football team, and Bobbie Faye had staged a bonfire near the local water tower. She'd convinced a couple of idiot boys (he and Cam) to climb the tower and string Christmas lights, spelling out their school name. No one anticipated someone tossing an ember from the bonfire into nearby shrubs. Fire spread to the trees at the base of the tower, which melted the welds of the old structure and, before anyone knew what was happening, the tower swayed and then toppled. There was a minor flood (but at least it put the fire out). She was the only sophomore whose stunt made the national news, so she'd won the most spirited contest, although the nuns promptly banned her from all future spirit-planning activities. She probably would have been expelled, but when one reporter shoved his microphone in her face and asked her what she was thinking, she said, "Go, Tigers!" and all was forgiven. (Football. Second only to oxygen in Louisiana.)

He snapped on a pair of latex gloves, pulled out an evidence bag, and gently placed the shirt inside.

So because those rice husks are fresh," Trevor asked when she rejoined him in Nina's dining area, "you think Marie's been to your dad's recently." He waved a gadget over her as she nodded, and a damned alarm went off, scaring the bejesus out of her.

"Holy crap, this shirt isn't *that* ugly." He'd already made her change out of the red shirt she'd started off with as her first choice with the picky little detail of her being a better target in red. Now she had on a tiny green t-shirt she'd brought, and she looked down to see what he was frowning at.

"This isn't for the shirt," he said, indicating the contraption, "though it's still heart-attack worthy. There's a GPS on you somewhere."

"Where'd you get that?" she asked as he waved the wand slowly down to her tennis shoes, then over her purse—where it went all bells and whistles, pining its little gadget heart out.

"When I had one of my men bring in the food, I asked for this."

"So you suspected I had a GPS on me . . . all night?"

"I knew they'd found us somehow. They were outside Nina's within a few minutes of us arriving."

"And we didn't leave because?"

"You were tired and needed to rest."

He dumped her purse out on the table and she immediately started grabbing the more embarrassing items (tampons, a nightlight—she really fucking hated the dark—and Binky, a little stuffed lion she'd had since she was a kid and she was going to pretend that belonged to Stacey, though why in the hell she bothered, she wasn't sure, because the man had seen her with a *vibrator* for crying out loud. He'd known when she was going to the bathroom . . . could she please just fall through the floor now? Oh, wait. Already did that. She looked up at God and thought, *this is for all those times I put the jar of bugs in Sister Elizabeth's desk in fifth grade, isn't it?*

Trevor had continued talking, ignoring her blush, saying, "They weren't getting inside or close to the building without me knowing. Besides . . . this will come in handy." He lifted out a tiny little square and held it up for her inspection.

From: Simone
To: JT

They're on the move. And we have company.

(sent via cell)

Cam listened as Benoit described the shirt he'd found and the antique store owner's eyewitness account. They used secure lines to talk, but it would have been better for Cam if Benoit had told him to leave the office while he delivered this news. He hung up the phone, slamming it so hard the cradle cracked. Great. Now he had to requisition a new phone. Explaining that one was going to be fun. He tried shoving the plastic casing back together and when it looked like it might work, he dug in his desk for some tape, jerking the middle drawer open, which jarred the precarious folders piled high in front of him, and the entire jeweler murder file scattered onto the floor.

He stood, planting a fist through the drywall. His knuckles hurt like a sonofabitch, but still didn't match the screaming headache which hadn't subsided in spite of the pills he'd taken at Bobbie Faye's that morning. So much for being the guy known for his control under pressure. He'd quarterbacked games where the entire season rode on one last throw, one final Hail Mary into the end zone to win the coveted SEC championship, and he'd done it, in spite of a fractured wrist and ninety-thousand fans going absolutely ape shit in Death Valley, LSU's Tiger stadium. He'd scrambled out of an oncoming blitz with his own offensive linemen fighting for inches and he was always, always cool. In control.

"At least you had the common sense not to pick a cinder block wall," his captain said from the hallway. "Little problem this morning?"

"No, sir. Nothing. Just. Frustration, sir."

"Frustration, huh?" the captain asked, his stomach hanging over his belt more than it used to, and his ruddy complexion going redder with his annoyance at Cam's destruction. "Well, son, I don't think that belongs here, do you?"

"No, sir, it doesn't."

"Then make sure it doesn't show up again. And call maintenance and have them fix this. Charges are to be deducted from your paycheck."

The captain left and Cam raked his hands through his short-cropped hair and rubbed the back of his neck. He didn't know what in the hell was happening to him. He couldn't even fathom what he'd done already. He'd never withheld evidence. He'd never even

considered the possibility of withholding evidence, not for any reason. He'd never cheated on an exam, even when people wanted to
give him the answers. He was a winning quarterback and there were
a lot of people in Louisiana who thought that was akin to being a
king and deserving of special dispensation. A lot of people wanted
to give him things, allow him to take the easy way out instead of adhering to the rules and he'd never even been tempted. And yet, in
his pocket, still, was a Ziploc bag of casings that he thought may
very well be from a murder case. Casings which were removed from
their location without benefit of a warrant.

How in the hell had he lost his common sense? How in the
world had he gotten to this point? This wasn't like him.

He squatted and began picking up the scattered pages of the
jeweler murder file, collecting the photos of the murder scene into
one stack. The top photo was an overview of the scene with the
body still in position. Several numbered plastic markers stood
next to items found at the scene and within close enough proximity to the body that the items had to be reviewed as potential evidence. One was an old string of pearls. It might have once been a
necklace, but if so, at least half of it was missing, as was the clasp.
There had been no way to know if it had been an item dropped at
the time of the murder or weeks prior. Every time he'd seen the
photo, he'd thought "necklace" because that's how the item had
been logged.

Except now, with his thoughts so focused on Bobbie Faye, he
suddenly recognized it; it wasn't a necklace. It was a bracelet. His
heart went cold at the thought.

He remembered when Bobbie Faye was a freshman at LSU and
he'd been a junior. He'd wanted their relationship to be something
more than just friends, and hadn't found the way to deepen it without jeopardizing the friendship. He'd given her a pearl bracelet for
her birthday; pearls were the June birthstone. They'd never really
exchanged fancy birthday presents before, and he'd hoped she
would understand what it meant.

He picked up the photo and took a closer look, and another day slammed back at him, that day they'd argued. It was a few months after her birthday and he'd reached for her arm, trying to keep her from storming away from him, and his hand slid down to her wrist and accidentally snagged the bracelet, ripping it off. She'd gasped, and then picked it up. They had been fighting over the asshole she'd been dating and was giving yet another "second chance" to. Alex. A guy he now knew was a gunrunner and back then, the guy he knew was the bastard who'd turned her inside out with lies and betrayals. He'd wanted her to break up with Alex. What he'd really wanted was to date her, but he'd stopped short of saying that, and she'd stood there, holding the broken bracelet, her face grim.

"Why in the hell can't you resist doing something as brainless as dating this guy?" he'd asked. Stupid, he knew now. Stupid, stupid, stupid.

"You just can't resist bossing me around," she'd answered.

If he could go back and shake himself, he'd have said, "I can't resist *you*." Corny? Hell yeah. Truth? Absolutely. Instead, he'd said, "If you didn't act like an idiot, I wouldn't need to."

Cam stared at the photo and dropped into his chair, the wind sucker-punched out of his lungs. First, her hair was found at the murder site. Then he'd found the casings hidden in her trailer. Not that the casings were proof positive of wrongdoing, because they could have been from some other shooting event, since she was the world's worst at picking up her brass. Next, there was surveillance footage, which was damning all by itself, and then the shirt and eyewitness account Benoit had just told him about.

Now, her bracelet.

He didn't want to think it was possible that she could have actually pulled that trigger. He hadn't thought it was possible, really. Until now. But what if she was in trouble so deep that she'd thought murder was her only way out? Would she have done it for herself? No. But to save someone? Or if pushed to do so by some outside force? Cam remembered only too well how crazed she got when her brother had been kidnapped—he was pretty sure she'd have done *anything* to save Roy.

How could he think this? He didn't know. Whether she was being framed, or whether she'd been coerced, he just didn't know. He only knew that this was something he might not be able to save her from.

John had lost Bobbie Faye in Iowa, the tiny town to the east of Lake Charles, where Highway 165 intersected with I-10. The Harley had stopped to gas up, and when he'd followed the bike at a distance, he thought it was still Bobbie Faye and Emile's lackey, but when they were a few miles up 165 near Kinder, he got a little closer and realized he'd been had. There was some other couple on the bike—Emile's guy and Bobbie Faye must've switched rides.

This was not going as planned. The night before, it should have been easy, but it turned into a fucking nightmare. Neither he nor his men had been able to get a shot at her, and there were several Fed types positioned all around the perimeter of the building—he couldn't get close enough to set off an explosion without getting himself caught.

He radioed the men he'd hired and they all turned back toward Lake Charles. He knew Bobbie Faye had been heading east when they first left the city, but he didn't know her ultimate destination. He did, however, think he knew someone who might know. It was a simple matter of timing.

Chapter Seventeen

The advantage to having Mollie along, Aiden grinned, was that she could put on a wig and slip into just about any place and not a soul would pay her any mind. It was not that she wasn't good-looking, because to Aiden, she was beautiful. She just had a chameleon quality to her—something Sean appreciated.

"Ye see her, then?" Sean asked when Mollie got back from the rest room in the gas station and climbed in the Subaru they'd switched to driving.

"Sure, an' she's getting in a red GTO." Mollie pointed to the muscle car and Aiden saw Sean smile. It was the second vehicle change that morning—and Mollie had spied both by simply hanging around when Bobbie Faye had hurried through a store or, in this case, a gas station. "She's definitely carryin' a different purse." She looked a little impish. "I asked 'er for a light."

"Ye're supposed to stay in the background," Sean griped.

Mollie pulled off her blond wig. "She tumbled into me, what would ye 'ave me do? I had to say something."

"Ye've an accent, ye idiot." Sean looked like he was on the verge of clocking Mollie upside the head—something he'd routinely done with other women, but never with his cousin. He'd practically raised Mollie.

She smiled, and drawled in a great honey-filled southern accent, "I hate to bother you, but do you have a light?" She was spot on for American. Maybe not one from south Louisiana, but at a truck stop, there were always tourists and travelers. Aiden beamed, quite proud of her, though Sean remained grumpy.

"Sure, an' see to it next time ye just do what I say, and nothing extra."

"Oh, sure, Sean, an' then I wouldn'ta had the chance to drop the new little tracker thing into 'er purse."

"Fuck, woman, say so next time," Sean spat, and Robbie already had the laptop humming.

I can't believe that guy at the gas station let you borrow this car," Bobbie Faye said to Trevor, her hand running across the immaculate black leather seat of the fully restored classic 1966 GTO.

"I gave him enough money to buy it three times over, but yeah, if this thing gets scratched, the car gods are going to burn me at the stake."

"Why do I feel like there's a cosmic short-order cook who just shouted *order up, one Federal agent, extra crispy?*"

He chuckled and she went back to staring out the window. She had to ignore how he made her feel. *Manipulation*, she reminded herself. That's what he used. Just because he made her think she could have more—have *him*—didn't mean she ever could and the sooner she accepted that the better. Besides, even *she* could learn to use common sense when it came to a guy. Damn it to hell.

Bobbie Faye could see the silos of the grain-drying mill long before they turned off the interstate just west of Crowley. If she closed her eyes, she could see the images still, the same as when she was a kid. Seven huge cylindrical buildings, some ten, twelve storeys tall, one or two about half that height, grouped at a 45-degree angle to the dual driveways (one for eighteen-wheelers, one for cars). When she opened her eyes again, she noticed the subtle differences twenty years had wrought: the once shiny metal buildings were faded, more worn-looking, as if they were slowly becoming an organic part of the landscape. There was an office building, low and squat, at the base of the silos, with rough limestone parking.

On this summer day, a fine silt dust—created when the rice hulls were dumped into the silos from the conveyors at the top of the buildings—settled over everything in sight. Even the trees and the house set much farther back and on the opposite side of the driveways looked muted and bland.

Trevor stopped in front of the house, and she stared at the one place she'd sworn she'd never set foot in for the rest of her life: a plain brown-brick ranch-style home, its low-slung roof shadowed by the oaks surrounding it. There was—well, there had been—a swing set in the backyard. A slide that was already rusted all those years ago. As the memories flooded back, she mostly remembered knees. She'd been young, small, and kept occupied digging for odd treasures in the furniture cushions (a pocket watch, the tires off a toy truck of one of her cousins, a nail file, and more spare change than she'd typically see in a month). She remembered the smell of coffee strong enough to get up and walk, the thrum of overhead fans beating a rhythm against the summer heat, and the always-full candy dish on the kitchen counter that she could reach on her tiptoes.

Mostly, she remembered the arguing of her mom and the man she'd sort-of known was supposed to be her dad, though he'd never claimed her and seemed to resent the hell out of her presence when they did attend Sunday dinners. Her mom had said at the time that they had to try to maintain family—that family was everything, even though she and Bobbie Faye's dad hadn't worked out. Her mother never explained the yelling, only that she wasn't supposed to worry about it, but it was kinda hard to ignore when she heard her own father say he'd never wanted a brat. She'd flat refused to go back with her mom after that lovely day.

When she climbed out of her memories, she realized Trevor

stood on her side of the car, holding her door open, his hand out to her. She wasn't entirely sure how long he'd been standing there.

"We're not visiting a guillotine," he reminded her.

"At least that would be more fun." They heard a rifle ratchet a round into a chamber, that distinct slide of metal against metal, and then there were two more. She and Trevor looked at the house, where rifle barrels poked out of the two front windows as well as the slightly opened front door. "Yeah, there's no place like home."

The front door cracked open another inch.

"Hi, Aunt V'rai. It's Bobbie Faye. I need to talk to you."

The door swung out to reveal a woman in her sixties. Bobbie Faye gaped, startled. She hadn't seen V'rai since she was eight, and now it was like looking at an aged version of herself. Even Trevor seemed awed by the shocking mirror image. V'rai's once brunette hair was shot through with gray, and she had laugh lines creasing her eyes—eyes which didn't focus on anyone or anything. V'rai could make out light and dark, Bobbie Faye knew, but was mostly blind . . . something that made her holding that rifle just a tad scary. She was about an inch shorter than Bobbie Faye and slightly stoop-shouldered, and she tilted the bolt-action rifle toward the ground.

"I figured you'd be showing up," V'rai said, her Cajun accent light—but then, she'd lived all the way over in Baton Rouge, "but that damned circus isn't coming in with you."

"What circus?" Bobbie Faye asked, and then heard a loud vehicle turn off the highway into the drive and when she turned around, she saw the Hummer. "Oh. Fuck."

"I'll second that," V'rai said as the Hummer stopped and all four cousins bailed out and jogged (Francesca in purple stiletto heels) toward the front door. "Hold on, Missy," V'rai said, aiming her gun toward Francesca, who clutched her hideously pink purse to her chest. Feathers clung to her cleavage. The purse was molting.

"Good grief, Frannie. Somewhere, there's a really embarrassed naked flamingo," Bobbie Faye said. "How'd you find me?"

"Oh! That was easy. Aunt V'rai told Aunt Aimee that she

thought you were coming by today and Aunt Aimee told her hair-dresser that she couldn't come in today because she had to be here, and her hairdresser told her sister, who told her mom, who lives next door to Kit's mom, who called Kit, who told me."

Bobbie Faye looked at Trevor. "GPS has nothing on the Southern Gossip System."

"How'd your Aunt V'rai know?" Trevor asked her and she had to smile. So his research hadn't told him everything. The poor man just did not know what he was getting into.

"You'll see."

"Hi, Aunt V'rai," Francesca called over Bobbie Faye's shoulder. "I came to help, too."

"Hell no," V'rai said. "You and your cousins just need to climb on back into that contraption and go on back down that driveway. You've caused enough trouble for your mamma as it is."

"But I'm trying to help!" Francesca whined.

Trevor moved between them, back in fine form as an asshole mercenary as he grabbed Bobbie Faye's elbow and steered her toward the door.

"Go in, now," he said, and to Francesca, he threatened, "You, go home. Your dad's warned you: he'll put a hit out on *you* if you interfere and I'll be happy to give him a discounted rate if you get in my way."

"I'm supposed to shoot someone," Mitch said helpfully. "I think it's her," and he pointed to Bobbie Faye.

"Not Bobbie Faye," Donny said. "Not yet, anyway."

"Donny, your mamma's going to be real upset with you."

"She's gonna be proud of me, Aunt V'rai. Just you watch. I've got agents already interested in taking me on."

"Get your butt in here," V'rai said to Bobbie Faye, and as she stepped over the threshold, she motioned to Trevor. "And bring him."

"But Aunt V'rai!" Francesca griped. "Mamma's your baby sister! You *can't* let him in there. He's one of Daddy's thugs!"

"Hmph," V'rai said. "I can do whatever I want. You go home."

From: Simone
To: JT

Damn it. We lost them. Any sign of the cousin, Francesca?

(sent via cell)

From: JT
To: Simone

Sending coordinates now.

(sent via cell)

L ori Ann stood at the pay phone in the rec room of the rehab hospital, tucking and untucking her short blond hair behind her ear. She'd gotten Roy's voice mail three times in a row, and wanted to reach out and smack him. She knew he was sleeping at some bimbo's house. When he finally answered with a muffled 'lo,' she didn't know whether to be relieved or pissed off that he was barely awake. *She'd* had to wake up at freaking 7 A.M. because the state wanted to wring out every single second of torture that they could in a day of sobriety.

"Have you talked to Bobbie Faye?" she asked him, once she was certain he was alert enough to comprehend language.

"Why on earth would I do that this early?" he asked. "I don't have a death wish."

"I meant since yesterday."

"Again—no death wish. She's still ticked off at me for last month."

"She's still ticked off at you for trying to date the mayor's wife when the woman came in for out-patient surgery on the day you were recuperating in the hospital, you moron. Bobbie Faye already had enough grief from the city and state as it was."

"Since when do you care? You and Bobbie Faye haven't talked since you got arrested."

"Just because we're not talking doesn't mean I don't care. Besides, she didn't call here last night or this morning. She always calls."

"I'm confused," he said, and she could tell he was waking up a little more. "Y'all don't talk, but she calls?"

"She calls and I say 'hello' and then 'good-bye' and then I hang up on her. It's a thing. We have a *thing*. And we do it *every day*. Except for yesterday, when she didn't call."

"Well what am I supposed to do about it?"

Lori Ann knew Roy would be about as enthusiastic about finding Bobbie Faye as a mouse would be to snuggle up to a python. "I want you to start asking around and see if she's okay."

"No way. I might find her. I kinda owe some people some money and I think they got it from her, and I don't have it to pay her back, yet."

"Roy," Lori Ann sighed, staring at the graffiti on the wall above the pay phone, "let me put it like this: I have learned everything I know about annoying the living hell out of someone from our big sister, and I'm *sober* with nothing else to do but concentrate on *you*."

He swore, hesitated a moment, and finally said, "I'll look for her. But it's your fault if she kills me."

"I can live with that."

The ancient parquet floor in the foyer creaked as they made their way into a living room which had remained firmly ensconced in the early seventies. Bobbie Faye remembered the green Naugahyde sofa and the gold starburst clock above it, though about half of the gold had flaked off since she last saw it. What she didn't remember was the kitschy artwork adorning every wall, nook, and surface. She had seen some of Marie's artwork in the now-demolished workshop, of course, and there were a few pieces of Marie's work hung in corporate offices and galleries around town. Some of the pieces V'rai had were retro-modern, and Bobbie Faye found herself liking it.

"You remember your Aunt Aimee," V'rai asked, pointing to her older sister, who was sitting with her rifle aimed out the dining room window. Aimee waved to Bobbie Faye and then went back to staring out at the cousins in the front yard.

"We'll talk later, sweetie," Aimee chirped. "I've got brownies in the kitchen if you want 'em."

Just like when Bobbie Faye was five. Aimee had never married and had always lived at the homestead-turned-grain-mill. V'rai had moved back when her husband died years ago.

"You'll have to go say hello to Lizzie in the bedroom, and Antoine's out guarding the back deck," V'rai said as she felt her way through the living room/dining room. They passed the metal-and-Formica-topped dining room table which held a two-foot tall mound of rifle shells, handguns, bullets, clips, and their own clip re-loader.

Trevor looked from the table to Bobbie Faye. "It scares me to think you might be the calm one."

"Bite me."

He grinned and she ignored him. She was not going to be charmed back into his good graces.

V'rai turned her unseeing gaze in Trevor's general direction. "Go ahead, son. I know you're itching to."

He narrowed his eyes, and glanced at Bobbie Faye for clarification. He'd been doing his best glowering, scary, menacing presence routine.

"She means it's okay for you to check out the place."

"How does—" He stopped, then turned to V'rai. "I work for Emile."

"He's one of Emile's hitmen," Bobbie Faye added cheerfully, and he rolled his eyes.

"Hmph. My ass he is." She nodded toward Trevor. "Go on."

"Yes ma'am." He was a real polite menacing presence.

V'rai gave him a dismissive wave and Trevor eyed her a bit like one would a very strange alien who just might possibly lunch on his brains, though he took the opportunity to move around the living area, looking out every window.

"Your daddy wants to have a word with you," V'rai said, and Bobbie Faye stiffened. "He's on his way here now."

"I don't have a dad, V'rai."

The old woman snorted. "Child, you don't get a say in that one. And I believe this visitor is here for you."

There was a knock at the door, which startled Bobbie Faye. Trevor had his gun out just as Ce Ce burst in, sweat gleaming off her dark skin. She waddled to Bobbie Faye, carting a huge satchel-purse that looked to be nearly as heavy as she was. Trevor glanced between V'rai and the door and then to Bobbie Faye, looking confused, but before she could explain how V'rai had known Ce Ce was there, Francesca had stomped toward the open door in an attempt to follow Ce Ce inside. She stopped when Aimee raised her rifle.

"Back up, *chère,*" Aimee said. "I don't think that crap you're wearing could look any worse, but I'd hate to find out."

"That is so not fair!" Francesca complained. "Y'all always liked Bobbie Faye better. I'm just as much your niece as she is, and it's *my* mom we're trying to help. I should get to come in."

"If you want to help, then go home," V'rai said, and she shut the door in Francesca's face.

From: JT
To: Simone

Rumor of surveillance footage—BF killed the jeweler. Locals have it—not logged in yet.

(sent via cell)

From: Simone
To: JT

Do we bring her in?

(sent via cell)

From: JT
To: Simone

After she finds the stones, yes.

(sent via cell)

Bobbie Faye turned back to Ce Ce, who was still sucking air and sweating, her braids tangled as if she'd been running hard.

"'Scuse me, baby girl." Ce Ce put her big palm on Bobbie Faye's arm to balance herself while she caught her breath. "But I gotta do this spell quick-like before the timing's all wrong. This one's going to work." Then she looked around as if she'd just noticed the tension in the room and saw Trevor. Bobbie Faye knew it was Ce Ce's first time to meet the man, and while Bobbie Faye had described him as accurately as possible, Ce Ce's grip tightened on Bobbie Faye's arm as if she just might slide to the floor in a puddle of goo. "Oh, *my*." She leaned in and whispered a little too loudly in Bobbie Faye's ear. "Honey, 'sex on a stick' doesn't even *begin* to cover it."

Trevor turned from the window, decidedly amused and possibly even a little smug.

"Geez, Ceece. Thanks. I was running a couple of quarts low on humiliation today."

"Young man," V'rai said, "come on in this kitchen and help me make some coffee. And while you're at it, you and I are going to have a talk."

Bobbie Faye blanched as Trevor said, "Talk? That isn't a Southern euphemism for 'I'm going to take you out back and shoot you' is it?"

"Not today," V'rai said. "Are you coming?" She held out an arm for him to guide, which Bobbie Faye knew was a complete ruse, because V'rai had bat sonar and had been negotiating that room for more than thirty years. She probably just wanted an excuse to feel Trevor's biceps for herself; he slipped her hand into the crook of his arm and the old woman smiled back at Bobbie Faye. She wasn't entirely sure what her favorite part was—her aunt getting a cheap thrill or Trevor having to meet her crazy family and his big bad agency self looking just a little bit . . . awkward.

Okay, the second one was definitely her favorite.

"So . . . how is it?" Ce Ce asked, nodding Trevor's direction as she unpacked containers of a clear gel from her big satchel.

"What? No. *No.* Not happening. I've come to my senses."

"Are those the 'I'm Stupid' senses? Because girlfriend, you are in serious need of a U-turn if you're headed that way."

"I second that," Aimee said from where she held the rifle out the dining room window. "Besides, V'rai said he was hotter than—"

"Aimee!" V'rai interrupted all the way from the kitchen. "You are not supposed to gossip."

"Damned bat ears," Aimee grumbled, but she clammed up and went back to watching the activity on the front lawn.

"How did V'rai already tell you that when we just got here— oh." She saw Aimee's look of asperity. "Right." V'rai's "sight" was a royal pain-in-the-ass to the family. She'd known things about everyone, could see things no one ought to be able to see, and could predict things, though she generally refused to tell anyone, unless it suited some purpose she had, which had been damned inconvenient at times when Bobbie Faye was a little girl. Her own mom had been very intimidated by V'rai's talent. Emile had pretty much avoided interacting with his sister-in-law. (Bobbie Faye suspected he didn't want to know what V'rai saw for him, on the off chance she saw he was going to die a terribly painful death . . . because that was one case where V'rai probably would have been happy to disclose the vision.)

"Then it's unanimous," Ce Ce said, smearing some of the gel on Bobbie Faye's left shoulder. "If V'rai says he's hot, then you just need to—"

"Wait—how do you know V'rai? I've been working for you since I was sixteen and you've never mentioned knowing my aunt and she's never been in the store."

"Well, I know a lot of people we don't talk about." She dabbed some of the gel on Bobbie Faye's left cheek just as Trevor laughed in the kitchen. Not just chuckling, but a deep, gorgeous laugh, and Bobbie Faye wondered what he and V'rai were talking about to make him laugh like that. "I do special delivery for all of these Landrys. V'rai don't drive anymore—"

"She drove? I thought she'd been blind since birth."

"Oh, she had a system worked out with Lizzie." Lizzie was the oldest sister among several siblings. "V'rai's got that foot thing."

"The prosthetic?" All Bobbie Faye knew was that Lizzie had been in some sort of car wreck when she was little and had lost a foot.

"Yeah. She can't feel the pedals, but she can see, and V'rai can work the gas pedal *and* the brakes, and they had a system worked out—"

"So much for hoping the crazy wasn't genetic."

"—until that time V'rai ran smack into the courthouse," Aimee said. "That's when the sheriff made her quit driving."

"Yeah, that was quick thinking."

Ce Ce smeared more gel on Bobbie Faye's left arm and Bobbie Faye asked Aimee, "Has Marie been here lately?"

"Can't say." Aimee glanced at the kitchen and then hunkered down over the rifle.

"Who's hiding her?"

"I could really do for some coffee," Aimee said. "Here." She set the rifle down. "I'll be back in a minute."

Bobbie Faye resisted the urge to shout *chicken*. As Aimee ambled toward the kitchen, Bobbie Faye looked down at her arm, expecting to see clear gel smeared everywhere in preparation for whatever weird spell Ce Ce was about to do and when she saw what Ce Ce had done, she damn near had a heart attack.

Chapter Eighteen

"C eece! What the hell are you doing?" Bobbie Faye stared at her left arm—it was royal blue. Down to her fingertips.

"A spell, honey. A really strong protection spell. I think I figured out what wasn't working with the other ones."

"I somehow wasn't scary enough?"

"Oh, no, you were plenty scary."

"Now *there's* an endorsement everyone wants to hear from their employer. I would really like to get through this disaster without looking like a recruitment poster for Blueberry: Fruit of the Month Club."

"It's not bad. It's just a *little* blue," Ce Ce said, not really looking Bobbie Faye directly in the eye when she said it, and she started packing up the empty containers, putting a lid on the one with left-over gel. "Maybe it was the prayer that turned it a little darker."

"Prayer?"

"Maimee and her bunch. They were in the store. Lots of praying might have made this a lot bluer than I remembered."

"Might? If this was prayed over by Maimee, I'm probably lucky I didn't just burst into flames. So what's the chant thing we need to do?"

The incantation. Ah. Ce Ce still didn't meet her gaze. "There's no chant thing for this one—the spell's already in the gel."

"I'm done? I can go wash this off, now?"

"No," Ce Ce said, moving toward the front door.

"I really do not want to walk around looking like a Smurf exploded on me."

"Honey, it worked for Mel in *Braveheart*."

"Ceece—that side *lost*. The main character was drawn and quartered by the end of that movie."

"He probably tried to wash it off. Just don't do that. Especially in the next couple of hours, because I'm not entirely sure about the exploding quality."

"Exploding?" Bobbie Faye felt her insides go squiggly.

"You won't explode dear. I don't think. But the protection spell has to have something to work on or it can go a little haywire. Which is why I have to get the rest of this back to a safe place," she said, tapping her big purse where she'd stored the other containers. "Oh, and I think I may have accidentally solved that insurance quote problem you had. You be sure to live so I can tell you, okay? Bye now!"

Ce Ce toddled out V'rai's front door as Bobbie Faye looked in the living room mirror and stifled a yelp.

John and the men he'd hired got into position at the mill; he watched through his binoculars as the crazy-assed voodoo priestess came barreling out the front door of the house, practically plowing over the idiots hovering between the door and their Hummer. He'd known that following Ce Ce was the way to pick up the trail—eventually, in just about any disaster, Bobbie Faye's boss showed up to try to help the insane ditz. It was poetic justice that the same woman who'd hexed him years ago (and it took two fucking years for all of the warts to go away) should be the source of his finding Bobbie Faye and putting an end to her.

He had three men spread out, and if she came out with the diamonds, they were his. Regardless, she was dead, out of his hair for good, and he'd still get the payoff. Sweet.

Trevor listened to V'rai as he followed her out of the kitchen and the only tag Bobbie Faye could put to that expression was . . . deeply bothered. Though it turned into complete disbelief when he looked up and saw her. He stopped dead in his tracks.

"Shut up," she said before he could form a sentence.

"How?" he asked, incredulous, joining her in the living room. "I only left you alone for five minutes. The mind reels at the damage you could do with a half an hour."

"Okay, seriously? I hate you. Shut up."

He stood way the hell too close, leaning into her space. "I believe we have established that you do *not* hate me."

"And I believe we have established," she said in her best maniacally perky Martha Stewart voice, "that you're a manipulative bastard." She smiled brightly just to put a period on that statement. "What gives?" She nodded toward Aunt V'rai because he had already reverted back to looking uncomfortable—which earned V'rai bonus points, as far as Bobbie Faye was concerned.

"Your aunt apparently has 'the sight'—something you might have mentioned." He muttered, low to her, "Your family? Is nuttier than you are, and I would have said that was impossible."

"Boy," V'rai said, "I'm blind, not deaf."

Trevor nodded toward V'rai. "She said your dad has a different kind of sight—that he can find anything that's missing."

"Oh, yeah, anything that he *wants* to find. Which is why I'm here."

"Not just because Marie's been here?"

She wanted to be there about as much as she wanted a lobotomy. Come to think of it, a lobotomy would have been *much* more fun. Having to put herself in the position of asking her dad for anything? Made her want to shoot something. Several times. And then maybe kick it. "No," she finally answered. "Not just because of that. The rice husks tell me she's been here and it's still a big guess about why. We could spend days looking for her, and we don't have days."

"So, you're going to ask him to help track the diamonds."

She realized Trevor had given up trying to hide anything from V'rai, which meant V'rai had really impressed him with her freaky-assed "sight" skills with whatever it was she'd been able to see about him. Bobbie Faye wished she could ask V'rai what she had seen, what about Trevor made her trust him—because V'rai seemed to be so comfortable with him—but her aunt was exceptionally closed-mouthed about that sort of thing. Of all of the people in all of the freaking South, where everyone would tell you anything if you stood in their proximity, up to and including anything that could completely humiliate a member of their own family, Bobbie Faye had to have the *one* aunt who actually *knew* stuff and wouldn't talk about it.

She turned back to Trevor's question. "Old Man Landry—"

"Bobbie Faye," V'rai chastised, "he's your dad. Call him something proper."

"Cranky Old Bastard," she said pointedly, and V'rai shook her head, annoyed. "He doesn't need to *track* them. He just sees stuff. Wherever it is. Even if it's a couple of thousand miles away, he can pinpoint it." Trevor raised an eyebrow, disbelief evident. "Yeah, I didn't believe it either, but people call him from all over the country sometimes and he tells them where their stuff is. Unless, of course, it's a tiara that could be the map to a lot of pirate treasure." Her mom's Contraband Days Queen tiara. A map old Lafitte had made for his daughter to his treasure. Lost now somewhere in the Mississippi River mud. Then she registered that Trevor had tensed, looking over her shoulder at the kitchen entrance.

"That treasure wouldn't be nuttin but trouble," a man's voice barked, a Cajun accent thicker than V'rai's, and Bobbie Faye turned to face Old Man Landry—Etienne—where he glowered at them. "An' you don't need no more of dat."

"Gee, millions to live on. Dear God, the suffering I'd go through."

"An' everybody on the planet tryin' to take dat from you."

"I don't exactly recall you giving a shit before, so you can stuff it now."

"You don't know nuttin'. You a crazy damn *coo-yôn* for lettin' yo' 'elf get mixed up in all of this—you don't got a single damned bit of common sense, girl, do you?"

Bobbie Faye bristled and Trevor dropped an arm around her shoulder.

"At least I have guts," she told Old Man Landry as he strolled into the living room, setting his cowboy hat down on top of the armory on the dining room table. His tanned leathery face, loose baggy skin, and white hair broadcast his age, though his voice was still strong. But it was his cataract-white eyes that tended to grab people's attention.

"Guts will get you killed," he snapped, and V'rai stepped between them and put a placating hand on her brother's arm.

"She needs help, Etienne."

"Marie's in trouble," the old man said, and then he looked at Bobbie Faye. "She's the baby of the family and we're all that's standin' between her and a bullet from Emile. I'm not holdin' a grudge against you, girl, I'm telling you for true."

"Holding a grudge?" Trevor asked.

"She shot him a while back," V'rai answered, as airily as if she were saying, "and then we all had ice cream."

Trevor arched a brow at Bobbie Faye.

"It was a minor disagreement," she said. "I should have aimed better."

"Remind me not to piss you off."

"Too late," she said, and then back to Old Man Landry, "So you're really not going to help."

"*Mais non*, I'm helpin'—you just too damned stubborn to listen. Go home. I got dis covered."

"And while I'm at it, maybe I should just bake cookies for the people who are trying to kill me—maybe I can Betty Crocker them into a diabetic coma and they'll conveniently forget all about me."

Trevor chuckled and when she glanced up at him, she knew the bastard had one more thing in his research on her than she'd like. "Oh, bite me. It's not my fault those PTA people got sick on the cookies I sent that time."

"Although I think fourteen people getting their stomach pumped in one night was a new record for the hospital here."

"So totally hating you right now."

"You'll get over it."

She hadn't quite pinged on the fact that he had his arm around her and she wanted to smack the crap out of him, but she was too aware of her dad and V'rai watching them, smug little smiles on their faces. "What?"

Landry jerked a thumb toward Trevor and asked V'rai, "He's the one?"

"Yep. He's the one."

"The one what?" Bobbie Faye asked, and neither of them answered. Instead, they appraised Trevor. Well, it was possible they were appraising him—they'd turned toward him, heads cocked, chins lifted, but since V'rai was blind and Etienne had cataracts the size of a small car, they could just as easily have tuned into some sort of Cosmic Nutcase Radio.

"You," Old Man Landry said, pointing a finger at Trevor, "better take care of her. She's a handful, but anythin' happens to her, I'll be huntin' your *coo-yôn* ass down, you got dat?"

"Where in the hell do you get off acting like you care about—" Bobbie Faye's voice rose and cracked and her heart thudded against her chest because all of those years, all of those goddamned years, there wasn't so much as a freaking birthday card, and he was going to stand there and act like he cared? She felt her nails dig into the palms of her hands and it pissed her off that the old man could get to her.

Trevor stopped her with a squeeze, which confused her, and the confusion turned to downright amazement when she caught his furious, disgusted expression aimed at her dad. "She can handle herself," he warned, and there was no doubt it was a threat. "And if she needs me, I've got her back."

Bobbie Faye tried not to let her breath sound ragged as she exhaled, but she might have tucked herself a little closer to Trevor, might have hooked a thumb in the back belt loop of his jeans, all purely accidental, of course.

V'rai cracked a wide smile and chuckled. "He'll do," she said to her brother.

"You'd better be right," the old man answered.

"Right about what?" Bobbie Faye asked and they all were suddenly preoccupied with the ceiling or the floor. Even Trevor.

Great. Just what Bobbie Faye needed—V'rai to start being cryptic. She hated *cryptic*. Cryptic sawed on her last fucking nerve, jangling its keys and blowing smoke in her eyes. Bobbie Faye started to retort, but V'rai stopped her as she felt her way over to an end table overflowing with photo albums and scrapbooks.

"*Mais non*, hush, *bebe*, you'll see later. As for now, I want you to have *teet chôse*."

"A little something," Bobbie Faye translated for Trevor when he didn't recognize the Cajun.

Old Man Landry snapped out something in Cajun Bobbie Faye couldn't quite follow, and V'rai tsked him, and said, "Hush, Etienne. Just some family photos."

"I don't want family photos," Bobbie Faye said as V'rai rummaged through a stack. How she knew which photos she plucked from the group, Bobbie Faye couldn't tell—there didn't seem to be any bend or tear or mark on the photo surface that she noticed right away—then again, Bobbie Faye pointedly didn't do more than glance at them as V'rai thrust them in her hands.

"Nonsense, *bebe*, you will. One day, you'll want to get to know this part of the family, an' you'll be glad you have these. You're a big part of what's missing here—" V'rai touched her own heart "—An' one day, you'll see."

Bobbie Faye took the photos and shoved them in her back jeans pocket. "So you're not going to help me find Marie?" Sadness crept over V'rai as she glanced at her brother's set, stubborn face.

"You've got your path, *bebe,*" V'rai said, "and we've got ours. I can't set you on a path. You got to go your way, or die for sure."

"You don't need us," Old Man Landry said, and he sauntered out of the room.

"Just watch your back, *bebe.*" V'rai turned to follow her brother, and then reluctantly, as if a second thought, she said, "You're teeterin' on the edge of the precipice there, and you watch your back."

Iain't sayin' I did, an' I ain't saying I didn't," the scrawny old woman told Benoit. She rocked on the front porch of manager's unit in Bobbie Faye's trailer park, a basket of peas in her lap, her fingers ripping through the hulls as she shelled them. She plunked the empty hull over her shoulder into a larger bucket. "She mighta been here, she mighta been gone. Had the TV on, couldn't hear a thing."

Yeah, right. Benoit would be willing to bet next week's paycheck the woman heard every damned thing that went on in that trailer park. He glanced down at his notes. So far, Walter Coullion who lived in the trailer just in front of Bobbie Faye swore he was in a cutthroat game of dominoes with his drinking buddies, for which they did not place monetary bets as that would be strictly against the law. They did not see anything, except maybe a couple of women who may or may not have taken off their clothes. Benoit still had a contact high from Walter's breath, so there probably was no use in bringing him in for questioning and hoping he sobered up enough to remember anything.

Bethany Meyers lived in the trailer across from Walter, and

Bethany had probably been one of the not-dressed women at the domino "tournament," and she was having a hard time remembering how to button her shirt when Benoit had questioned her.

His one hope was that little Aubrey Ardoin, not related to the Ardoins of the chili cheese dog stands, had defied the restraining order Bobbie Faye had gotten on the kid to keep him from taking photos of her and selling them (for a fortune) on the Internet. Aubrey was driving around in a used Porsche when his parents could only afford the double-wide trailer sitting toward the front of the trailer park, and he certainly hadn't earned the money from after-school part-time work. Benoit was fairly sure that if Aubrey was to meet up with real work, he'd faint dead away. The problem was that as greedy as the kid was, he was that much more scared of Bobbie Faye since she'd pinned him to a wall—upside down—with well-placed knives the last time she found a cable running into her trailer, which had a tiny little camera on the end . . . which was placed in her shower. If he had a photo of Bobbie Faye, he probably would die before admitting it.

"She's in trouble, Mrs. Abilene," he said to the trailer park manager. "Big trouble. Knowing where she was could really help her."

The old woman popped another pea hull open and raked the peas out, a little bit of the juice staining the tips of her fingers ever greener with each victim. She dipped her bony hand into the basket, scooping up the peas, letting them run through her fingers and studying them the way fortune-tellers study runes. Benoit stifled an irrational urge to bow to the peas. She cocked a wary eye Benoit's direction.

"Well, if knowing she was here would be a' help, then I reckon you oughta be talkin' to dem people."

"People? What people?" Mrs. Abilene's lips thinned in a tight line, but Benoit pressed on. "Honestly, I'm a friend of hers. I really am trying to help."

Mrs. Abilene weighed the peas once more. "Well, since I done seen you pass by here, lookin' out for her with that boyfriend of hers, I figure you alright. But if she tells me different, you're in a world of trouble."

"Yes ma'am," seemed like the wisest answer. And he wasn't about to correct her impression that Cam was still Bobbie Faye's boyfriend.

"I don't know who dey were, dem folks. Dey come quiet like, middle of the night. Went into her trailer like they owned the place. It wasn't like dey was sneakin' in or nothin'—dey turned on the trailer lights. I started to call y'all since it was so late and some people, dey just give our girl a hard time, but then she came out with 'em, and I done reckon she was intendin' to go with 'em."

"How many?"

"Two—a man and a woman."

"You get a good enough look at them?"

"Nah, once I saw she was with 'em, I came on in to watch the rest of my show. Didn't see 'em close enough to tell you more'n dat."

"About what time was that?"

"Oh, 'bout 11:30. I know because my show was right about halfway over."

The coroner had originally placed the murder between 12:00 and 1:00 and now that Benoit had gone frame-by-frame through the DVD the night before with Cam, they knew the time-stamp for the murder was 12:23. Benoit questioned Mrs. Abilene a few more minutes, but if she knew anything else, she wasn't volunteering it. He thanked her and walked away from her office—which was the front room of the first trailer in the lot. He thought about setting up a roadblock and questioning every neighbor as they came home that evening, but he needed to find Bobbie Faye and question her directly. For whatever reason, she'd told Cam she was alone—all night. Now the manager said Bobbie Faye not only hadn't been alone, she'd left her trailer with two people and Mrs. Oubillard had definitely placed her at the scene. The one immutable fact about Bobbie Faye—which had gotten her ass jammed into a world of hard places over the years—was that she didn't lie. So how could she be home alone, but not?

So far, all he'd managed to do was prove that she was there and could have done it, that there were no witnesses who'd place her at home during the murder, not to mention he also had the video of a woman who could easily have been Bobbie Faye pulling the trigger.

Some friend he'd turned out to be.

Chapter Nineteen

You remember what I told you, boy," V'rai said to Trevor as
he followed Bobbie Faye to her aunt's front door while her
aunt felt her way back toward the kitchen. When they
were alone, Bobbie Faye turned to him, expecting an explanation,
but his expression had shuttered to neutral.

"What did she tell you?"

"You know," he dissembled, "I think the blue works for you."

"You've got a serious death wish, there, Trevor. And you're
avoiding the question."

"Yes, I am." He tucked a random stray hair behind her ear and
ran his finger across the line of blue running diagonally across her
face. "You need to ask me later."

"Well, sure, but only because I am the master of patience."
Hell she had the freaking patience of Job and she could wait. She
could so *totally* wait and not be the *least* bit curious, and not wonder what lurid secrets her aunt had "foreseen" and then told him
about her. Okay, it didn't matter. She didn't need to know. Didn't
need to ask. She was completely immune to curiosity. "Was it
good or bad?"

"Neither, Obi Wan. And you can ask me later."

"Fine. *Be* all Zen. Have you ever noticed all those monks are
bald?"

BOBBIE FAYE'S (kinda, sorta, not exactly) FAMILY JEWELS

"Nice try, Sundance."

"Don't say I didn't warn you." She stepped back from him and peeked out the sidelight window. "I want to talk to a couple of Marie's friends—these women are Cajun and very private. Francesca might have been onto something that they would talk to me, but they're never going to talk in front of this many people. It feels like I'm being followed by a tsunami of morons."

"I'll handle that—I'll have my men slow them down and we'll lose them. Where to?"

She thought over all of the names she'd seen yesterday on that day planner page of Marie's—some which she'd crossreferenced when she had all of the papers she'd taken from Marie's spread out on Nina's dining room table.

"D's safe," she said, and it took Trevor a second to realize what she was referring to.

"The note on the day planner," he said, and she nodded.

"Maybe she meant the diamonds were safe. And she said 'check' next to that—maybe she'd just checked on them, knew they were okay. Two of her friends were listed on the last day's entry—she could have reached either one of them from here within a few minutes, and I know she was here recently from the condition of the hulls. It makes sense to check their homes first, see if there's a safe."

"You have a clue which one?"

"Well, she's good friends with them both—they always came to the Sunday dinners we had here when I was a kid. But Miz Pooks's house is closer—maybe we should try there, first."

"Pooks?"

"Family nickname. Miz Patricia Burroughs."

"Sounds good," he nodded, and he began texting someone instructions.

"So you're just letting me lead this thing? The entire FBI at your disposal, and I'm the best you can come up with?"

"Pretty much, yes."

"Man, we're in deep shit."

He stepped in front of her so he would be first out of the door, and as he rested his hand on the doorknob, he paused. "As far as your cousins are concerned, until we get rid of them, I'm still forcing you to work for Emile."

"Right. Badass. Check."

"Which means I'll have to get rough with you in front of everyone."

"Don't worry," she said absently, "I've had worse." She glanced at him when he didn't answer, and he seemed pissed. Badass squared was kinda scary.

"When this is over," he said, "we're getting on a mat."

"Sparring?" He nodded. "Do you have really good health insurance? Because in the Big Book of Stupid Things to Do, sparring with me is entry number two."

"Sundance, the day you hurt me is the day I deserve it."

"Geez, you're cocky, you know that?"

"You'll get used to it."

"I wouldn't count on that."

He looped his free arm around her and pulled her tight to kiss her temple, then whispered, "Oh, I definitely would. What's entry number one?"

She started to retort *dating me*, but something outside the window caught her eye and she realized it was movement . . . out on the front lawn.

"Sonofabitch. It's the press."

The oppressive heat hit them first as Trevor opened the door. The everpresent dust from the silos mixed with the heavy, humid air, and it was like slogging through mud as they pushed outside toward the bright red car. Fuck, the press was going to be able to follow that car. Bobbie Faye barely had time to register her cousins and the men on the motorcycles who'd helped Trevor on the bridge yesterday as they all moved toward them expectantly, when something buzzed by overhead and clanked into a nearby old metal tub filled with droopy roses. Two more pops and the two driver's side tires of the GTO deflated. Trevor pushed Bobbie Faye behind a bay window protrusion—which, unfortunately, blocked them from returning to the front door. Everyone in the front yard—the cousins, the two "motorcycle" agents who'd been with Trevor, and the press—all dropped to the ground and scrambled for cover.

C am reviewed the jeweler murder file. There had to be something in there, some lead he could follow, that would point to the actual murderer and why that person would want to frame Bobbie Faye. He knew that Salvadore ran an upscale place, which was ironic in that Lake Charles wasn't exactly what anyone would consider an upscale town. Hardworking, blue collar, industrial. The store, however, was a part of a larger chain of stores in the southeast—and Salvadore's expansion was picture perfect: never a hint of scandal, never failed an IRS audit, never had any customers that didn't appear to be the blandest, most law-abiding citizens of the state.

He had to be crooked as sin.

Cam flipped through the thick file to the printed database of all of Sal's customers and contacts from the last ten years. The list had been compiled from Sal's sales records, mailing list, personal itemized phone bills, and files. Hundreds of names. Needle in a fucking haystack.

Was it a coincidence a jeweler was murdered and then four days later, several people showed up to pressure Bobbie Faye into finding missing diamonds? Yeah, right. And he held the deed on Tiger Stadium and would sell it for a buck. Was there someone she'd pissed off (well, that would cover at least half of the city, that wasn't helpful) . . . someone she'd done some real damage to, who might want serious revenge? Serious . . . damage . . . made him think of Marie's destroyed house and the rumor that Bobbie Faye had been seen riding away from it. On instinct, he flipped through to the D's and saw "Despre, Marie" as one of Sal's clients. Great. The jeweler was dead and Bobbie Faye was after diamonds and then she destroyed one of the jeweler's biggest client's home. Throw in the hair at the scene, the video, the shirt, the bracelet and *Jesus Christ* she'd be in prison for the rest of her life. And that was without the casings in evidence (which were still shoved in his pocket). His gut turned to acid and he cradled his head. She never, ever made things easy. Why in the hell couldn't the woman just make things easy?

"Cam," Jason shouted from the door, and he looked up, surprised Jason was in the room. He hadn't heard him enter. "I said there was shooting at Old Man Landry's mill."

"Someone's finally taking shots at the old crank—why am I not surprised?"

"Bobbie Faye's been sighted there."

"Sonofabitch." He jumped up from the desk, nearly knocking the file back over. "Get—"

"Already got it—chopper's ready to go."

Cam barreled out of the room, slamming into Winna in her pretty pink sundress. He caught her before she hit the floor.

"Winna? I'm sorry, I'm in a hurry. Everything okay?"

"Oh! Um, no, no worries. We were just going to have lunch."

Shit. He felt like an ass. He hadn't even remembered setting the lunch date. "I'll call you later," he said, and she smiled and waved at him just before he ran outside.

"Anyone hurt?" he asked Jason, who jogged alongside him, and Cam was thankful yet again that the governor felt so anti-Bobbie Faye, he'd personally pushed through a brand new sleek Bell 207 for the State Police Troop D.

"Dunno. One of the neighboring farms called it in—said there's press camped out in front of Landry's Mill and that they heard shots and everyone flattened to the ground."

•   •   •

Trevor had his SIG out; he pulled Bobbie Faye behind him, stepping between her and the sniper while she fumbled in her purse for Maimee's almost-forgotten Glock. As she pushed her cell phone out of the way, it rang and she noticed the caller ID.

"Wow. An insurance company," she muttered, and ignored the continued ringing as another hailstorm of bullets thudded into the roofline above them.

"How many does that make?" Trevor asked as he assessed the sniper's position.

Fuck.

She knew he was using distraction to keep her from panicking, but *damn*. She glared at him. This was another annoying fucking example of him knowing something because her phones had been tapped. She certainly hadn't told him about the grant application. Or the insurance rejections. He was still scanning for the sniper, but he managed to also be aware she was glaring at him. He looked amused.

"Fine" she conceded. "It's a tough sell. But there've only been twenty-five rejections."

"Because 'only' fits into that sentence so well. I'm surprised they call at all."

"I don't mind when they shriek when they find out who I am; I just hate it when they start crying and babbling about a suicide hotline number." More shots knocked off rust from a nearby mailbox.

"How many companies do you have left?"

"Two. Somebody in this state is bound to be crazier than me."

"I think we may need to work on that pitch a little."

Wild shots pinged off trees in the yard and clanged against a dusty aluminum flag pole near the front door, where the faded American flag hung limp in the windless morning. Bobbie Faye eyed the cousins: Donny looked torn between hiding every shred of his ass behind rusted lawn furniture and wanting to look heroic for the press cameras out beyond the driveway—he stepped out and immediately dove for cover again when a shot pinged against the birdhouse near his head. Mitch had hidden himself really well behind a big three-hundred-gallon metal tank V'rai had installed many hurricanes ago.

"Mitch," Bobbie Faye yelled, "could you get away from the propane?"

"You want me to shoot somebody?"

"No," she said, as matter-of-fact as she could, "I thought it would be better to not blow up any cousins today."

"Okay."

Kit scurried over to him and then led Mitch back to her hidey spot behind a big oak tree. Only Francesca remained in her original location, sitting up, frantically checking her nails and then looking over at where Bobbie Faye was half-hidden behind Trevor.

"Bobbie Faye, you look different somehow." Francesca frowned, puzzled. She flinched as a bullet hit the roof above Bobbie Faye's head. "See," she said, pulling out a compact mirror to check her makeup, "you have to come with us. If you just stayed with us, nobody would be shooting at you. We'd protect you and then you could find the diamonds."

What did she mean, nobody would be shooting at her? Everyone was always shooting at her.

Did Francesca know the shooter?

A bullet pierced the compact mirror, a shot that had come over Francesca's shoulder and this time from a different silo, and Francesca flopped on the ground. "Shit!"

Simultaneous in Bobbie Faye's mind was *Francesca cursed!* and *another sniper?* Trevor backed her up and she realized he was trying to reach the carport on the side of the house so they could slip away from the sniper's line of sight.

"Is that just more of Uncle Etienne's family?" Francesca asked Bobbie Faye as another bullet hit a bush she was scrambling toward.

"Franny, we have really got to define how family is supposed to function for you."

From: Simone
To: JT

They're pinned down. Sniper . . . maybe two. Trying to move in
closer without blowing cover.

(sent via cell)

From: JT
To: Simone

I hate my job.

(sent via cell)

Trevor and Bobbie Faye eased to the only escape route: the carport. They moved quickly in unison until the moment Bobbie
Faye felt the barrel of a gun at the base of her skull.

"Move and I'll kill her," a man said, and a hand reached around
Bobbie Faye, taking Maimee's Glock.

Trevor glanced over his shoulder, past Bobbie Faye to the man
she couldn't yet see. With his right hand hidden from the gunman,
Trevor hooked two fingers in the waistband of her jeans, as if he
was about to yank her out of the way. But he couldn't spin and fire
faster than the guy could pull his own trigger, and as soon as she
moved, the gunman would have a dead drop on Trevor. She was too
aware, with her left hand on his waist, that he wasn't wearing body
armor. Bobbie Faye saw him eye one of his cohort FBI guys, who
was peering from behind a tree, but frankly, there was no way the
guy would get a shot until Bobbie Faye was completely out of the
way, and that extra second would cost Trevor his life. She felt his
fingers tense. It was an insane strategy for a stupid bunch of diamonds, no matter how valuable they were.

She caught his hand, stopping him. "They're not worth this."

He muttered something that sounded too much like "you are"
and "freaking aggravating woman" as his grip tightened and holy

fuck, Adrenaline joined Hormones and staged a coup on her brain and she whirled around, facing the gunman.

"What do you want?"

The big, dark "O" of the gun barrel shoved closer to her nose; sweat beaded up on the man's clammy hand.

"Did you know you were . . . blue?" the gunman asked. He was a young guy, maybe twenty, still with pimples and dimples and a cowlick of red hair that made him look a bit like a gangly rooster.

"Have you ever heard about how some women get all puffy and splotchy and hormonal just before that time of the month, and they're so cranky, they completely lose it over the *least* little thing, and they go all homicidal and could bite off your head in between spoonfuls of chocolate and not even notice?"

"Um, yeah."

"Well, being *blue* is much *much* worse. Get the fucking gun *out of my face.*"

He actually started to lower the gun, then seemed to realize what he was doing and held it chest high. "You can't fool me. Just because I'm an intern, doesn't mean you don't have to listen." He tapped the gun. "This says so."

"Jayden?" Kit called from behind a tree. "Is that you honey? How's the new gig working out?"

"Oh, you have got to be kidding me," Bobbie Faye said. Then to Kit, "He's one of yours?"

"She placed me last week," Jayden answered, rather proudly. "And our firm just got hired yesterday. This is my first assignment."

"He has high potential," Kit said. "Lots of petty B & E's, but now he's ready to step up."

"That's what my boss said! That's why he sent me over here to get the stuff from you."

"He sent you over here," Trevor said, "because you're expendable. And if I shot you, he wouldn't give a damn."

"But you're going to put down your gun because I could shoot her. And I'm kinda nervous, so you probably better hurry." Sweat dropped from his chin, past his skinny chest and hit the ground. With his finger on the trigger, he'd probably shoot her anyway, but she'd have zero chance if he flinched.

"If y'all move, the other guys are supposed to shoot her dead. But I kinda don't want to, because my mom's a real big fan. She'll get mad at me if I shoot the Contraband Days Queen. But she'll get madder at me if I'm fired, so please don't make me shoot you."

Trevor slowly lowered his gun, and Bobbie Faye knew he had another SIG in a side holster the oblivious kid had completely missed, but as he crouched and before he could reach the second gun, Jayden squeezed off a shot at his arm. It grazed Trevor's shoulder and he flinched back as Bobbie Faye yelped, and Jayden's eyes widened. "Oops. Really. I didn't mean to shoot you yet." And he pressed his gun deep into her side.

"Well, that's reassuring," Trevor said, as he appeared to be checking the flesh wound, but was, instead, easing to a position where he could overtake the kid.

"I need the stuff," Jayden said to Bobbie Faye as she tried to turn to help Trevor. Jayden pressed the gun deeper into her side and said, "Really. They had one of those listening dishes and they know your aunt gave you something. I have to get it." He began patting her down.

Reggie thought she might be having an orgasm. "Please, God, tell me you're getting this?"

DJ grinned behind the eyepiece of his camera. "I'm getting it."

Reggie watched through a small set of binoculars. The tip-off of where Bobbie Faye had gone that morning was right, and everything Reggie wanted was falling into place. She and DJ weren't the only reporters on the scene, but they had been the first there and had the best position to capture the events unfolding at the front of the house. She'd get the top story slot for the evening news. Bobbie Faye

Sumrall, in action, with a gun on her. Jesus, this was great. Then she squinted, paying closer attention as the gunman patted the woman down.

"Is she . . . blue?"

"Um, yeah," DJ said. "She's blue."

"This just keeps getting better and better."

A iden lay belly-down in the loft window of the barn across the country road from Landry's Mill and aimed his rifle and scope at the woman. When he finally registered what he was really seeing, he backed off the eyepiece a second, rubbed his eyes, and then looked again.

"What's wrong?" Sean said in his ear, peering out the barn's upper window alongside him.

"She's . . . I swear, I havena' been drinking, Sean. She's blue. See for ye-self."

He handed his boss the rifle and Sean squinted through it. "She's wearing the *woad*," he said, referring to the blue dye across Bobbie Faye's face and arms.

"Sure, an' do ye think she knows who ye are?" Aiden asked. "Maybe she's declarin' war against ye."

"No' that it'll do 'er any good," Sean said. "Can ye get a bead on that bloke pattin' 'er down?"

Aiden checked the scope and shook his head. "No' without hittin' 'er. Or takin' out that fella Emile hired."

"I don' much care for that one, anyways."

"Sure. So, plan B?"

"Aye."

"Ye don' think the woman will give ye too much trouble?"

Sean smiled that sick smile Aiden had learned to dread; the kind of smile of a man about to hurt someone for the pure fun of it. "I'm countin' on it, boyo."

Chapter Twenty

Roy sat glued to the little TV in the back of the black stretch limo, tuned into Reggie O'Connor's news: she whispered into the mic as the camera focused first on her, then on the scene playing out in front of Bobbie Faye's dad's house (didn't she shoot him the last time she saw him?). Roy's jeans were half on and a very naked and impatient governor's wife stretched out next to him. Unfortunately, watching a gunman pat his sister down had completely killed off his libido—something he frankly hadn't thought possible, but there was always a first.

Of course, the heaping mouthful of guilt he felt for having lied to Lori Ann that he would look for their sister might have also diminished his lust; he hadn't known he could feel that level of guilt and he would really like to not have made that little discovery. His life had rocked along just fine . . . well, with the minor detail of sometimes being chased by husbands and boyfriends intent on murder because they didn't take too well to him sleeping with their women. Or the people he owed money to. (Those could be really scary.) He wasn't quite sure where the guilt was coming from because it wasn't like Bobbie Faye was out there with a gun pointed at her this time because of him. Except that she'd had to deal with a lot of those husbands and boyfriends and money collectors and maybe, just maybe, she had other stuff to do. Like avoid being shot at by someone.

And painting herself blue.

"Oh, thank God," the very nubile-for-her-age woman said as she sat up and stared at the screen. "It's a Bobbie Faye day. You know what this means?" she asked, turning to Roy, her ample cleavage distracting him to the point where he wasn't entirely sure what she'd asked. "This means," she said when he failed to be able to use language, "that Delano, my idiot 'tough on crime' husband, is going to hunker down and cry and hide until the stupid benefit. We have *all day*." She grinned, sliding her hand down his chest to his boxers, using her other hand to slap off the TV.

For the first time in his life, he said, "Baby, no," and then, "I have to make sure my sister's okay."

Whoa. That was like, all grown up or something. Bobbie Faye would be so proud. Assuming she hadn't gone all Xena, Warrior Goddess crazy already.

When Jayden, the kid gunman, had begun patting Bobbie Faye down, Trevor radiated energy, itching to have a go at the guy. She was pretty sure Trevor paused only because the gun was pressed so deeply into her side, one twitch and Jayden could put a hole through her. While she was a big fan of downsizing, that did not extend to internal organs, and she'd like to keep them inside her body, if that was okay with everyone. Jayden pulled the photos from her back pocket and grinned. He checked her tennis shoes and she was pretty sure the only thing that stopped him from checking her bra was Trevor's murderous expression when he'd made her lift her shirt. Besides, that bra hid almost nothing, a fact that wasn't lost on either man, or, for that matter, probably the entire TV audience now tuning in thanks to the press just beyond the front lawn. Bobbie Faye was pretty sure she saw Reggie out there high five her cameraman.

"Could you sign this?" Jayden asked her as he pulled a Contraband Days beer coaster out of his pocket. "My mom would really go bonkers if you signed it 'Love, Bobbie Faye.'"

"Oh, sure, and why don't I draw a little stick figure with a gun in my side and a heart over it while I'm at it?"

"Would you?"

She grabbed the coaster and the pen he offered as Trevor said, "You have got to be kidding me." She signed it for the kid and he grinned, then looked sad.

"They told me they were going to kill you anyway," Jayden said, backing off away from her as she shoved her feet back into her tennis shoes. "I'm not supposed to tell you, but I think my mom would be real upset with me if I didn't. Though if you die, I think the coaster would be worth more."

"Gee. Thanks. I think."

Jayden backed off, waving the gun at her and Trevor, the barrel still shaking enough to force them to wait 'til he was a safe distance from them before Trevor picked up his own SIG. It was then that she registered that the kid really had taken her photos. Did she have a normal brain that went *whew* or *close call* or *let's go get drunk?* No. No, she did not. Instead, her brain (which clearly needed a good spring cleaning) said *those are my photos*, and in spite of the fact that Common Sense was down on its knees, begging her to listen, as soon as Jayden stepped around the corner, Bobbie Faye grabbed Trevor's SIG, said, "Cover me," and went after her heritage.

If Cam could push the helicopter faster, he would have, but the pilot had a firm grip on the controls and wasn't about to release them to someone who was damned near frothing at the mouth. Picky bastard. Jason (who was back in dispatch) radioed over Cam's headset. "We've got confirmation from reports on scene that there is at least one gunman. He seems to be holding a gun on Bobbie Faye. Patrol cars in route, ETA six minutes."

Fuck. The ETA sucked, but the mill was out in the countryside and the sheriffs were spread thin in that part of the parish.

The acid in his gut went into overdrive. This was not going to be the day he found her dead, goddamnit, because he was going to wring her freaking neck, and anybody getting in the way of that was going to die first.

Bobbie Faye barely rounded the corner of the house when she heard Trevor behind her, muttering something that greatly featured the words "blue" and "crazy" and seemed to include a plan for her and rope, and not in a good way. She chose to focus on Jayden as he fled for a snazzy, new green pickup truck parked just in front of the complex of grain dryers.

"The other agents?" she asked.

"Pinned down still, too far from the house to make it around the corner like we did."

At least in her current location, the sniper couldn't nail her. Well, *if* he stayed in his original position in the silo closest to the road—from there, he'd had a good, clear shot at the yard in front of the house, but the dryer facility blocked his shot toward the back of the house and the closer she could get to the dryers, the safer she was. She could hear shots landing in the front yard, and return fire, with Mitch asking questions and Kit cheering.

Jayden turned and shot wildly at her, and while the first two rounds missed by several yards, the third ricocheted off the dirt near her feet. She dodged behind a big water well pipe as the next bullet bounced off it, just missing her arm when she banged into the valve. She couldn't even count the bruises starting to show up from the day before (though one slight advantage to being painted blue? Not as many bruises showed. Yipfuckingwhee.).

Trevor angled to her right, firing at Jayden as he fled toward the truck; the kid had a good fifty yards on Bobbie Faye, and if he made it to the truck, he'd get away. She ran and aimed at the back tire, her arm wobbling as she squeezed off a shot and she'd forgotten that the gas tank to this particular model was situated just to the front of the rear wheel. Okay, maybe she didn't *quite* forget that and maybe she was just a little bit fucking tired of people telling her what she could and could not do and taking her stuff, like her photos and maybe, just maybe, she aimed that shot, which went through the tire and into the tank. The truck promptly exploded.

It made a very satisfying fireball.

Jayden stopped, his jaw hanging in surprise, then he took off to gain cover behind a tractor.

Trevor joined Bobbie Faye and he eyed the flaming truck. "It's hard to imagine why every insurance adjuster in the state has had your photo made into a dartboard."

"I'm just loveable like that, I guess."

He gave her an unreadable appraisal as they made their way through parked equipment—harvesters, tractors, a front-end loader—trying to sneak up on the kid, but Jayden ran toward the silos. He slowed down long enough to hand off the photos to a small scrappy man dressed all in black. Which is the precise moment a shot churned up loose gravel at his feet, and it was all the invitation Jayden needed to squeal and run away, his arms flailing above his head like errant kite tails. Scrappy guy, on the other hand, spun and ran between the two nearest silos.

Trevor noted the emptiness of the office building. No workers on a weekday probably meant Bobbie Faye's Aunt V'rai had "known" something far enough in advance to keep her employees home. It bothered him on a level he didn't want to think about, especially after she'd warned him Bobbie Faye would die today. He was used to thinking any day was a day *he* could die. You didn't crawl on your belly across desert scrub behind enemy lines or slip into an encampment in the dead of night for a snatch 'n grab or disarm a warehouse full of terrorists without being aware of the risks. He was used to knowing his men were well trained, when he was the elite Delta Force.

She would die today, the aunt had said, unless she followed her instincts, and even then, the odds weren't high she'd live, but it was better odds than if he forced her to stay behind.

And Bobbie Faye, clearly, wanted to follow the asshole who stole the photos.

It was the last fucking thing on earth he wanted right now. He was trained, he'd spent years hunting men, years defending, killing; there was no way she was sufficiently prepared to play cat-and-mouse with a gunman, much less with snipers in the mix. As much as he wanted to treat her like an equal—and she deserved that, she'd earned it—the fact was, he hadn't had time to train her. She could get hurt. How in the hell was he supposed to let her walk into these silos? Then the echo of her aunt's warning thrummed through his chest. Was he a complete fucking fool to even allow for the possibility the aunt may have some ability to predict an outcome? If the crazy old aunt had not just told him things about his missions no one knew, he'd have ignored her. But now? *Fuck.*

They moved forward as he scanned the area. His men were pinned down. Logistically, by himself, he couldn't corner this guy with the photos. Obviously, they were important and the man was likely getting away, even as Trevor hesitated. *Fuck.* His men were still pinned down in front of the house, there was no help coming fast enough, and if the diamonds were sold to the black market, the money they'd raise for any terrorist would be a goddamned nightmare.

"You're thinking 'clusterfuck' and 'epic proportions' right now, aren't you?" Bobbie Faye asked, and he cut her a glance. "If your muscles were any tenser, they'd be corded steel. Not that I *mind* the whole corded steel look, because hey, kind of a fan there, but I

BOBBIE FAYE'S (kinda, sorta, not exactly) FAMILY JEWELS

can handle this. Unless you're going to go all His Standard FBI Agentness on me and try to stop me."

"I swear to God, if you get hurt, I'm going to kick your ass."

"Hey, it's entirely possible I have a plan."

He couldn't resist. "You? Have a plan?"

"I thought I'd go with 'get the photos' and 'don't get dead.'"

"It's focused. I like it," he said, "especially the last part." He kissed her, quick, on the forehead. "Try not to start the Apocalypse. I hate having to fill out reports."

Lori Ann tapped her foot in the rehab rec room. All of the other inmates hunched forward, trying to see the footage on the bad excuse for a TV as Reggie O'Connor's live Bobbie Faye report aired.

"Why is she blue?" the woman with the unicorn tattoo on her cheek asked, because *unicorns* on one's face was *normal*. "Is it some sort of commentary on her emotional state? I think she needs a hug."

"I'll bet she's joined that group," a tall black man with basset hound eyes said.

"What? The Blue Man Group?" Unicorn asked.

"She can't join that group, she's a woman," a prim, neat little man said. (She'd learned he was an accountant.)(Rumor had it that he was really IRS.)(He had a very nasty crying habit she wished he'd break.)

"Maybe she's going to be part-time," Basset Hound said, "because she's like, only half-blue."

Lori Ann snapped, hopping up to face the group, who, as a unit, cringed. "People are *shooting* at my *sister* and all you can think of is to wonder why she's blue!"

"Well, people are always shooting at your sister," Basset Hound said. "She's never been blue before."

Lori Ann glared over at the counselor, who shrugged. "He has a point."

Bobbie Faye watched Trevor veer off to circle around behind the silos as she stepped into the shadows of the giants, grateful for the shade in the smothering morning heat. The buildings loomed, sentries for a forbidden world.

She hated these buildings. They glinted in the sun and glared at her. She shoved her imagination and memories down and focused, instead, on navigating beneath steel staircases that led to catwalks, passing enormous metal framework pedestals for various generators and heaters for the grain dryer itself.

She paused before every man-sized nook, listening for the sound of breathing, smelling the heavy humid air; she knew what the harvested grain-air should smell like—the distinct scent of rice mixed with a little bit of diesel fuel and oil from the eighteen-wheeler truck that rolled through there from the various farms. Hot asphalt, soil, and the bitter scent of drying stalks of grass layered in with the other odors. In addition, men, God bless 'em, *smelled*. And since there were no other workers on the premises, and she had apparently imprinted Trevor's specific smell on her brain, any other male scent was going to be the photo-toting jerk.

A slight crunch brushed against the silence and she recognized the sound: filmy dried rice hulls crushed underfoot. She stole behind a metal scaffold that held a generator bigger than her trailer, (and thankfully, it wasn't running, or the roar would have been deafening). She squatted there, angled to her right, and peered beneath the crisscrossed support posts through a crawl space where she'd hidden as a kid. Black rubber-soled combat boots came into view on the other side of the structure and she knew Trevor had on battle-scarred cowboy boots for his biker/mercenary façade.

Bobbie Faye palmed a pebble and tossed it away from her position to entice the photo thief to move; he inched out toward the sound. She watched his progress and then crept forward softly, careful to keep her sneakers from crunching anything and giving her away. Just as she came up behind him, though keeping herself still hidden, two things happened at once: Trevor popped out sandwiching the thief between them, and behind Trevor, a man with a sniper rifle appeared on a catwalk encircling one of the silos. *Sonofabitch.* The sniper moved into a position with a bead on Trevor. She felt herself go icy cold. Two thoughts ran back-to-back: Trevor could die and *hell no,* he's *not.*

She moved. The thief held a Walther P, but it did not matter, and she would have to think about that later, if there was a later. Trevor's expression as she put herself in jeopardy raced from surprise to anger to confusion all in the nanosecond it took her to raise her own gun and aim—not at the thief between them, but above and to the right of where Trevor stood. The sniper saw her, and his delay, his slight, split-second blink of noticing someone else outside of the crosshairs, was all it took for her to put a shot in his left shoulder, jerking him out of position so that the shot he squeezed off went wild and pinged off the silo.

And then a second shot rang out and the sniper's chest blossomed red; Trevor spun to Bobbie Faye, who hadn't shot the man again, and the thief between them looked just as shocked as they were. Trevor shot the thief, center mass, but the man dove, tumbling, and then he sprang up, running between the silos, clearly wearing some sort of body armor.

Aiden nodded to Sean: the sniper who'd been shooting at Bobbie Faye was down. He'd missed the original kid who'd taken what looked like photos from the woman. They'd had to regroup fast and hadn't had a shot at the second man who now held the photos, but one of the snipers had been eliminated. Sean couldn't have cared less for the woman's welfare except the lass was his best ticket to the diamonds, but not if she was dead.

"Sure," Sean said, "an' there's more to do."

"Ye thinkin' we end this?"

"Aye."

Aiden and Sean were better shots than Mollie and Robbie and had left the latter to man the car and wait for their signal.

John seethed. Sending the kid, Jayden, had been a mistake—one he'd realized as soon as the kid got chatty with that freaking hurricane of a woman, and so he'd sent Alonzo in to retrieve the photos from the kid. John had been positioned where he could aim a parabolic at the house and he'd heard the majority of the conversation—enough to know the asshole Emile had hired was a Fed, working undercover. Now *that* was interesting, but it ultimately didn't matter. John had hired the best hitter in the business, and he'd have nailed the bitch and the whole thing would have ended. Or should have ended, except Bobbie Faye had shot the sniper first.

But hadn't killed him. Someone *else* had, and she'd looked stunned. If John had been in range, he'd have put a bullet in the middle of that stunned expression and man, that would have been the best fucking score and really, he'd have almost paid to have had that pleasure, but he'd set up too far away. He signaled his last man to go in; the last thing he needed was for Bobbie Faye or Trevor to live now. Especially now that he was close to having the clues as to where the diamonds were. Because at this point, he was realizing he could have his cake and kill her, too. All in all, an absolutely excellent day.

Bobbie Faye and Trevor shared a gaze and his was way-the-hell more furious than she'd expected.

"He could have shot *you*," Trevor said, and she realized he was seething. "Goddamnit, you focus on the 'don't get dead' part."

"He was aiming at you, you idiot." Where the hell did he get off, getting mad at her?

"Not the sniper—this guy here," he pointed between them. "For the love of God, don't do that again."

And then a man was on him, having come up behind Trevor from an angle neither of them could see, and she ran toward them, to help.

"No!" Trevor shouted. "Get the photos." But she kept going, her gut not letting her go after something else if he was . . . *oh*. Okay. Maybe he wasn't. In trouble, that is. Trevor spun and with a few simple moves that bespoke of way more experience at this whole killing-with-the-bare-hands-thing than she'd thought about, he dispatched the would-be assailant. Holy shit. Trevor wasn't even breathing hard from the exertion, though there was a moment she caught a primal look, something dark and lethal, and then he shuttered his expression back to neutral.

"The photos," he said, and she turned and followed the thief.

Chapter Twenty-one

From: Simone
To: JT

I've lost her. But we hear gunshots. Investigating.

(sent via cell)

From: JT
To: Simone

I wonder what our medical coverage is for therapy? Because I am seriously going to need it. A lot of it.

(sent via cell)

The freaking thief had gone up the staircase to the catwalk three storeys up on the biggest silo. Three fucking craptastic storeys up. She *hated* heights. She was seven all over again, when she'd climbed up a silo and slipped. She would have died if she hadn't landed in a bed of grain in a small dump truck—would have definitely died if it hadn't been for the fast action of that trucker who'd seen her tumbling off the catwalk in his rearview mirror. She fell through the grain with such momentum that it had seemed alive, sucking her into its belly where it was dark. She'd been screaming on the way down and her mouth filled with rice hulls and the dust gagged her. The trucker had pulled her free.

Bobbie Faye didn't think it would really help to say to the thief, "Pardon me, sir, would you mind terribly letting me chase you over flat ground? Thank you, most helpful, much obliged."

Instead, she sprinted up the stairs, her thighs screaming, having shoved Trevor's SIG into the back of her jeans (ouch, fuck). The thief ran around the catwalk to a ladder, and up he went, which meant up she went, hand-over-hand. Surely he wasn't going into the silo's topmost door, surely he wasn't that stupid, surely he knew how danger—

Apparently not, because the gunman scrambled from the ladder to the highest catwalk and circled to the hatch where the conveyors dumped grain inside. The hatch was used for emergency purposes and to vent the silo of highly ignitable grain dust. Bobbie Faye arrived at the dark opening the gunman had entered and waited just outside, adjusting her breathing, careful not to look down the . . . holy fuck, she was at least seven storeys up. Her Heart started writing its Farewell Speech and it was in such a hurry, it wasn't even bothering to spell correctly. Bravery was standing by with spare pens, so it wasn't a helluva lot of help, either.

A distant *whap-whap-whap* of helicopter rotors beat the air, and she glanced around to see tiny dots on the horizon—no way to tell if they were news or police helos. Someone down below shouted something, and a slight breeze barely made the direct sun tolerable, but mostly, there was just the black maw of that hatch opening, and total silence inside the silo. Then metal creaked from somewhere inside, and when she peeked through the opening, light filtered in from a point opposite her and she didn't know if the asshole had run around the interior via a catwalk and found another way out. This particular ladder that she stood on ended right there; she'd have to follow inside if she wanted to keep up with the thief.

Which meant stepping into the dark, onto a narrow catwalk, into a silo full of semi-dry grain. Why hadn't she called in sick yesterday? Better yet, why hadn't she had that lobotomy she'd been contemplating? Anything . . . *anything* would be better than this. Bobbie Faye pulled the SIG out and ducked into the hatch opening, her lungs fighting the dust she'd disturbed as she felt the solid metal grating of the catwalk beneath her shoe. She sighed with relief. Safe. There was even a handrail. She wasn't going to pitch forward into the abyss of grain.

A gun jammed into the back of her head. What the fuck? Did they teach gun-jamming in bad-guy school?

V'rai's words echoed in her head: *you're standing on a precipice, Bobbie Faye. Watch your back.* Holy fucking *geez*. Would it have killed her to have been a little clearer?

"Got her," the gunman said, and he relayed their location to someone, apparently talking into a cell phone she couldn't see as he stood behind her. She heard the phone click off. "John's on his way—he wants to do the kill himself."

"Please tell me he's traveling from Helsinki or something."

"Man, he wasn't kidding. You never stop. You just can't keep from being *you*."

"I'm seriously contemplating multiple personalities right now. I think passive is real doable," she offered. "How about I go practice—I know! I could sit home, making animals out of dryer lint."

She tried to step away from him and he shoved the gun harder. He apparently had taken the advance lesson in bad-guy school: how not to be confused by random victim babbling.

"Lower the gun," Trevor said from somewhere behind the man, "slowly."

Bobbie Faye would have done the happy dance, if it were not for the fact that she was seven storeys up on a catwalk in the dark with sure death all around. Sure death tended to put a crimp in happy dancing.

The gunman started to lower the gun, and in the next heart-beat, ducked and spun. Trevor leapt over the man's outstretched leg, pinning his arm against the catwalk and knocking his gun down into the grain . . . just as the gunman wrenched Bobbie Faye's ankle. She slammed against the deck of the catwalk, the momentum rolling her underneath the waist-high safety railing toward the gaping cavern of the silo, out in the big open black-ness. Trevor shouted something she couldn't hear as she pin-wheeled her arms, clawing for purchase of the metal grating, the dusty surface slipping from her fingers.

Time crawled. She saw the stark shock in Trevor's expression—that and something more. Something deeper and pure and raw and she shot an arm out, knowing she had to stay with that emotion, knowing she had to somehow allow herself to believe in it, because the connection she felt with him at that moment was something she'd never known before. Then the world sped up again as her left hand, sticky with blue gel, latched onto one of the metal support braces for the catwalk at the same time Trevor reached beneath the railing and fisted a handful of her t-shirt.

"Watch out," she shouted as the gunman tried to elbow Trevor in the back of the head. Trevor kicked with a powerful jolt to the man's knee and the gunman crumpled to the catwalk. Bobbie Faye reached above her, groping for the outer edge of the catwalk and claiming, instead, the front of the gunman's shirt where he lay on the grating. She clutched that as Trevor helped haul her up and as he did, the gunman tried to scramble away. . . .

Only she wasn't completely back up on the catwalk, so she wasn't about to let go of the gunman's shirt; she held onto the photos in his front pocket as the idiot pulled another gun from his ankle holster. He tried to jerk up and away from her while Trevor held her with one hand and tried to bat away the gun with the other, yelling at Bobbie Faye for her to let go, that it wasn't worth it, wasn't worth losing her, but her fingers had a will of their own: those photos could not go with that man. Trevor used his weight to pull her from the gun in the man's hand as it lifted up and up and up and his shirt pocket finally ripped as Trevor yanked her away. The gunman grabbed at the photos with his free hand. She resisted . . . and before she knew what was happening, the photos were in her hand and the man plunged over the rail and down toward the loose, quicksand-like oblivion of the dry grain.

As he fell, the soft light from the hatch openings captured him in that first second, and he had his gun up, aimed at them, whether he meant to fire out of anger or if it was just reflex, she couldn't tell. Bobbie Faye knew in that instant—that one-hundredth of a second which drew out into eternity—that they were so very dead. The bullet emerged amid a flash, and even though the shot went wild, that tiny burst of flame from the barrel of the gun ignited the dust around it, and the ball of explosion rolled outward, every direction, growing and eating everything in its path. Trevor yanked her up and outside the silo, (which is when she had the thought that he was real pretty but maybe not so sharp because they could not fly and, *hello, seven storeys up*, jumping was as bad as the fire). He pulled her anyway, leaping out into the fresh air, and then they fell, flailing from the seventy-foot height of the hatch as the silo exploded above and around them, the thrust of the explosion propelling them farther outward and away and then there was the baby silo below them, looming, slamming toward them faster than Bobbie Faye could fathom.

Trevor took the brunt of the landing, cradling her on top of him, and they started sliding along the angled curve of the dome roof as the giant silo next to them detonated fireballs into the sky. Sparks and burning debris rained down on the metal roof beneath them as they plunged down its slope, both of them fighting to find a handhold. Bobbie Faye toppled over and in that same second, Trevor grabbed her hand and with his other, snagged the lip of the roof, holding all of his weight and all of hers by his fingertips. She should be dead. Instead, she dangled forty feet above the hard asphalt, Trevor the only lifeline she had. The big silo rocked with another blast and she could see his muscles cording under the strain and she met his gaze and she'd never seen anyone look so furious and determined in her entire life.

She shoved the photo remnants—wadded in her right hand still—into her back pocket. Burning debris bounced and singed her arm as he nodded toward a catwalk below her, off to the right, and she nodded back, sickened, but knowing they had no choice. Trevor swung her from side-to-side, helping her gain momentum, and then he released her, and she flew, fell, prayed, promising God a whole lotta things He wasn't even going to buy, not even on sale, not even at a heavy three-for-one specially discounted Deity Savings Rate, but she promised them anyway. And then that catwalk railing loomed up and up and she reached out for it, felt the now-warm metal in her palm, and she stopped falling so abruptly, it nearly pulled her arm out of its socket. She clambered onto the catwalk deck and as she looked up at Trevor, a large piece of burning debris sliced through the smaller silo's roof. He launched off toward her and a living, breathing, fireball chased after him.

He wasn't going to make it. He didn't have a chance to angle enough in the catwalk's direction before he'd leapt, and he was going to fall four storeys.

Bobbie Faye jerked off her purse from across her chest, her stupid, cheap, *holy shit, please hold up,* purse and looped it out toward him and he grabbed it. She fell backward onto the grating, his momentum pulling her forward and she planted her feet on a crossbar to brace against his falling weight and he dangled there, below her. *Thank you for not smoking crack that day, dear anonymous purse-seam person, and doing a double-stitch like you were supposed to.*

She didn't think she'd ever been happier to see a man's fingers before—bloody, scraped, but gripping the catwalk grating, and he maneuvered until he could swing himself up onto the structure next to her. Another pocket of grain roiled in a new blast, and it was as if the world had decided to catch fire; the other silos stood by, silent bombs begging to blow. Their catwalk canted to the left;

the last explosion had ripped apart some of the framework below. One of the poles that should have held it in place was loose from the metal walkway, but still cemented into its base below, like a very long fireman's pole.

"We've gotta take this, slide down," he shouted above the roar of the fire.

Sliding. *Down.* Why was she always plummeting to her death? She should have gone into accounting. Accountants very rarely plummeted to their deaths. That was a real perk they ought to be putting in those accounting description courses in college.

Trevor didn't give her a chance to answer (probably a wise decision). He went first, and she gripped the metal pole and stepped out over forever and slid. When he caught her at the bottom, she didn't even have time to relish being alive as the silo on the other side of the first one to burn erupted into flames.

Ce Ce and Monique sat outside an opulent office in one of the few high rise buildings in Lake Charles (four floors) where they waited for Neil, the insurance agent who had assured Ce Ce that the company would be cutting her a check that day. Between them on the little coffee table sat the leftover blue gel in the container. Ce Ce hunched forward, nervous, wringing her hands with every spike and wiggle and rotation the gel made inside its plastic prison. Tied psychically to Bobbie Faye for as long as she was covered with a part of it, it looked like a demented hurricane, flipping and spinning and thrashing and contorting in on itself.

"That's a little scary," Monique whispered, her eyes darting to the secretary a few feet away, who watched the blue goo with stark terror. "Does it always do that?"

"Not that I've ever seen, Hon, but then, I haven't ever used the gel with Bobbie Faye. It's supposed to be okay as long as I keep it separated from her—if it's too close, it tries to get to the person it's tied to and that makes it volatile; it can explode."

Monique knitted her brows together as the container hopped across the table and the secretary fled the room. "I think it's trying to escape."

"It's taking all of the bad karma aimed at Bobbie Faye and absorbing it away from her."

The container flipped over on its side and started sliding across the table.

"Man, that girl has the stinky jinx all over her."

"Which worries me. The gel has a fairly short life span if it's put through too much, and at the rate she's needing protection, I don't know if it's going to last. I'm going to have to find a backup spell."

"Ce Ce?" a voice said next to them, and they looked up at the beautifully suited man standing there, smiling. She had to blink twice to recognize him as the demoralized, bland, nearly invisible agent who'd been in her store yesterday.

"Neil?" Ce Ce asked, then suddenly remembered: she'd given him the power of yes in a potion the day before. She'd given the power of *yes* to an insurance salesman. Oh, heavens, what evil had she created?

Cam saw the silo explode as they flew in and pain flared through his chest and down his left arm. Bobbie Faye was at that mill. Could she be near the explosions? Dear God. *No.*

All of the news helicopters backed off from the site as each concussive blast rocked them; any closer, they'd risk becoming part of the story. The PD helo landed in the long field across the street from the Landry front yard and he was out of his seat before the third silo blew. It was a madhouse on the ground. There was Reggie and her cameraman way too damned close. Everything was on fire. Cam turned and turned, scanning as much of the property as he could, looking over everyone's head for Bobbie Faye. Fire trucks blared in and he saw his brother-in-law's grim expression as he dismounted. Police cars followed, though one was already on scene. He jogged over to that car, noting they had several people corralled and were questioning them.

"We don't know where she is," the officer said once Cam explained who he was and who he was looking for. "We were working a DUI, but we heard the first explosion and we were first on scene. Some of these fine folks—" he indicated a group of disgruntled-looking people, some of whom were Bobbie Faye's cousins "—were attempting to leave, so we've invited them to stay for questioning. All I've gotten so far is that Bobbie Faye was last seen heading for the silos, chasing after something. No one here seems to know what that was."

Cam faced the shreds left of the silos. The largest seemed to have the most damage, though three others were burning as well. Was today the *day*? She was going to be twenty-nine tomorrow. He wondered if she knew he hadn't forgotten. He always had something for her, even when they hadn't been speaking. She'd always had something for him. He tried not to remember all of the times she'd joked that she wasn't going to live to be thirty. She couldn't even get that right—she wasn't going to live to be twenty-nine.

There was nothing to hit, nothing to shoot, nothing to do but stand there and watch the whole useless world on fire.

From: JT
To: Simone

She blew up what? No. How the hell am I going to explain that one on the expense report?

(sent via cell)

Bobbie Faye and Trevor dodged past flaming pieces of silo and equipment and as they sprinted around the last building, they saw the house. She couldn't process what she was seeing and when her brain finally made sense of the images in front of her—the blaze that had been her family's home—she didn't think. She ran toward the back of the house, toward her aunts and uncle, until Trevor overtook her, picking her up, holding her back in spite of how hard she fought. He pulled her deep into the fields on the back side of the property, beneath another stand of trees, far from the sight of the house and the black smoke, and she kicked and hit and tried to twist out of his arms, and then she registered what he'd been saying: *they're gone.*

"Gone?" All of her energy swamped away from her. Her despair flooded in its wake.

"Not dead. *Out.* I saw them leaving when I followed you away from the house.

She swallowed a knot in her throat, a deep ache in her chest. "This is my fault. I've destroyed everything. I *destroy* everything I touch."

"*No.*" Trevor ripped the hem from his shirt and wrapped a makeshift bandage around her hand to stem the bleeding. "You didn't start this, you didn't ask to be here, and you sure as hell didn't make them steal the photos from you or put a gun to your head in there. It sounded to me like your aunt had an idea of what was about to happen, though she wouldn't tell me what it was, and if *she* didn't stop it, how can you blame yourself?"

One of the FBI guys scared the bejesus out of her when he suddenly appeared next to them, though Trevor didn't seem surprised.

"This is Yazzy," Trevor said of the man whose nose and chin belonged on a man a foot taller. "He just arrived as backup." Then to the man, "You called Bihari?"

"Yeah," the man said, trying not to stare at Bobbie Faye. "She's pissed. She thinks we're making things worse, says we're to find the diamonds her way. She wants you to bring Bobbie Faye in for questioning."

"Tell her I said 'no.' You can report you warned me, and cover your ass, but there are too many players and not enough time to

stop and have a committee meeting. We have a lead and we're going after it."

Bobbie Faye knew he meant the photos, though she wasn't
sure they were a real clue, but she kept quiet. She'd rather chase
around after a bogus clue than sit in the loving (ha) embrace of
the FBI.

"It's not just Bihari that's the issue now," Yazzy said. "She indicated HS was involved."

"I know." When he caught her puzzled expression, Trevor explained, "Homeland Security."

"Crap. You mentioned them earlier and I got distracted. Why
in the hell is Homeland Security following me around?"

"They probably think you're working with MacGreggor,"
Trevor said, and Yazzy blanched.

"You told her?"

"She saw him. We don't have time to debrief—where are the
keys?"

"You're in way too deep, man," Yazzy said as Bobbie Faye
looked around to see what the keys Trevor requested might be for.
Then she saw the motorcycle parked a half a football field away.

"How—"

"Backup plan," Trevor said, cutting off her question. So that's
what he'd been texting on their way to the mill that morning.
"And I'm fine," he said, addressing Yazzy's comment. But there
was something about the way they glared at each other that didn't
really scream "fine" and she looked back and forth.

"He's not supposed to get involved emotionally with a Confi-
dential Informant," Yazzy said, not taking his eyes off Trevor.
"Jeopardizes the whole fucking case, not to mention it's illegal."

"Unless it's been cleared that there was a relationship before
she become a CI," Trevor said, his voice strained with fury.
"Which I did."

"When?" she asked.

"The evening after your brother was kidnapped."

Her head spun. That was after their first melt-her-clothes-off kiss, but long before their conversations. Before she'd even thought he might really want to date her. So the question was, how does a man know to notify his superior that there's a relationship, when there isn't one yet? He could only do that if he planned to start one. But . . . why? After all, the only thing they'd done, interaction-wise, was blow up parts of the state and nearly get themselves killed. Which meant that the next question was, did he plan to start one because it was something he wanted to do, or was it because having a relationship with her was merely an extension of his undercover work and his surveillance? How far ahead *had* he known about these diamonds and that note in Marie's day planner?

"The helicopters are landing," he continued, "and we've got to get out of here. The last thing she needs is to be plastered on TV right now or arrested. Keys."

Trevor held out a hand and, for a minute there, Bobbie Faye thought the other agent was going to refuse. He finally handed Trevor a set of keys before he spun and ran off toward the house and sirens.

She crossed her arms, hiding her shaking hands. It was all too much to comprehend, especially with a fire raging. She focused, instead, on Trevor, on his sure movements toward the bike, on the certainty in how he put his hands on the small of her back.

"Do you always have a backup plan?" *How much is seducing me a part of that?* she wanted to ask. It was right there, tip of her tongue, jumping on the edge of the diving board, too freaking scared to go ahead and attempt that half-gainer into the water. Bravery scuttled back off the board and hid under a towel and Self Mockery was having a stellar moment, making clucking noises.

"Not when it comes to you."

Trevor pulled her to him, and she rocked against the hard planes of his body, which was just so wrong to think about with everything going on around them, but felt so freaking *good*.

They were a pair. Both cut and bruised, bloody and standing

alone in the world, all sound falling away; she trumped him with the blue dye, but he had burns and scrapes that tied her in the crazy-looking department. He didn't seem aware of any of it. Instead, he kissed her, lacing one hand through her hair, and the kiss was gentle, startling her, and she leaned back to see that same expression of fear and hunger and loss and something else, something more, like he'd had when she went over that catwalk rail. And then they heard the click of another freaking gun.

The voice, that cold-blooded Irish sonofabitch voice said, "Which jus' goes t' prove, ye can only depend on women t' fuck ye up. I think we'll take her from here."

FROM THE DESK OF JESSICA TYLER (JT) ELLIS

ASSISTANT TO THE UNDERSECRETARY OF THE UNDERSECRETARY OF

THE SECRETARY OF THE ASSISTANT TO THE DEPARTMENT OF DEFENSE

HOMELAND SECURITY

NEW ORLEANS, LA

Re: progress report stats
(to be filed under field notes, personal, **only**)

Textiles which originated with Marie Despré to be seized for suspicion of acting as a method of smuggling diamonds. Textiles include but are not limited to: purses, belts, shoes, and accessories. Please note that suspect's other hobbies include sculptural art—all known pieces are to be searched, galleries plus private collections. Various offices around the country, including FBI, tasked to help.

Case # 198733BFS / diamond search   field notes: ~~personal~~

35 ~~41~~
~~27~~ 16 items searched
11 ~~9~~ 2 movie stars threatening a lawsuit
~~187~~ 23! ~~5~~ politicians disturbed (with someone other than spouse)
~~3~~ 6 2 ~~3~~ paparazzi arrested, cameras confiscated (talk to legal)
     2 medical claims (cuts & bruises) (see above)
   1 agent treated for human bite (dog owner) (see above)
8 16 defense attorneys filing harrassment suits
7 8 women arrested, attempts to bribe to keep their items
   5 people called Oprah   HAVE PR HANDLE
19 14 people called Fox News   ~~get them extra~~ help
   —have someone call InStyle, deflect interest in Marie's items

SILOS!! FIRE!! Is there nothing this woman can't destroy?

9 sightings of Marie—all false

←1 agent in the field in Lake Charles kidnapped? can we be so lucky?
  1 crazy Cajun woman ~~in the middle~~ of this case
  (see fucked, completely—previous case)
  3 "warnings"—Sean & who else?

*Sean MacGregor!
sent Trevor backup

Where is Trevor? must bring in Bobbie Faye.

★reminder—it is wrong to kill a civilian! mostly

Chapter Twenty-two

Aiden glanced at his boss to his right as they all—he, Sean, Mollie, and Robbie—held guns on the couple. More accurately, they held their guns on Bobbie Faye, whose back was to them. *Special ops* Sean had said when they saw the guy bail out of the silo and keep Bobbie Faye from falling to her death. *Needs to die* had been all he'd said after that, which sucked for the spec ops guy, because when Sean wanted 'em dead, they ended up dead.

The man looked over Bobbie Faye's shoulder at them, poker-faced, though Aiden knew he had to be pissed off for letting them sneak up on him; had he not stopped to kiss her, they might not have found 'em in time.

"You don' want the girl shot," Sean said, smiling, "so let 'er walk over here and I'll return 'er when I'm don' wit' 'er." The man couldn't draw his gun on them without putting her in immediate harm's way, so Aiden and Robbie swept out from Sean; spec ops was as good as dead as soon as she stepped away. "Or," Sean continued when neither of them moved to comply, "I can hurt 'er an' make 'er work through the pain. Your call." Sean let his gaze drift over her backside and he grinned as she turned slightly and looked over her left shoulder, her right hand still around the man's waist.

"I thought you wanted me to find the diamonds and bring them to you. Why the change?"

"Let's jus' say I'm no' happy with everyone slowin' ye down, lass."

"I think," the ops guy said, "that you're asking for a lot more trouble than you realize. She's a handful."

"There you go again," Bobbie Faye said, and Aiden saw anger flash, and something else as she recoiled away from the man, "always insulting me to the bad guys the split second things . . ." she whirled, throwing a knife, ". . . get nasty."

Fuck, the woman was talented with knives, and the ops guy always had one . . . they'd forgotten that in their satisfaction of having them cornered and outnumbered. Aiden heard Robbie's muffled groans and realized the woman had impaled his right shoulder against a tree. And in the moment they'd all followed the knife's trajectory, the ops guy had his gun out, shooting, winging Mollie, and everyone scrambled. Aiden popped a few shots the couple's direction, but he couldn't get a bead on the asshole ops guy without killing the woman, and Sean didn't want her dead.

Yet.

The woman had a SIG from heaven knows where as she and the ops guy shot back—the ops guy managing to nick Aiden in his side and leg. They hurt like a sonofabitch, but it wasn't fatal, and at least the injuries weren't to the point of leaving him lame, because the last thing he wanted was to be a drag on the team and hear Sean humming "There's a Hole in My Bucket."

The gunfire drew one of the news helicopter's attention and it flew toward them. They didn't have time to stay and grab the woman here.

"Regroup," Sean commanded, seething.

Cam scrutinized the chaos at the mill, knowing there was nothing useful for him to do. One of the first responding officers jogged over to him—Luke James, good kid, fresh out of the academy.

"Sir, no one seems to know where Miss Bobbie Faye is. But they seem . . . odd."

"Odd, how?"

"Well, I can't say exactly, but when I asked if they thought she had died in there, most of them avoided looking directly at me and were too nonchalant in their answers. The really bad actor guy—the one in those commercials?" Cam nodded. Donny. "He started to act all sad, like she'd died, and he was totally overselling it."

"Which sounds like . . ." he couldn't say it. He took a deep breath and pinched the bridge of his nose, willing the headache away. "Good job, Luke. You get anything out of the other guys?"

"Nope. They clammed up. They're supposed to be bikers but there's something weird about them."

"Put everyone in a squad car and haul them in. Call the captain and tell him we're going to need several rooms cleared for questioning."

As Luke headed back for the cousins and the bikers clustered in the broiling sun near one of the squad cars, Cam spied Reggie near one of the fire trucks, bugging the hell out of Jordan, from the grimace Jordan sported. She was smiling—always a bad sign. He strode toward her. There was a decent possibility she'd gotten footage of Bobbie Faye going into, and maybe coming out of—

"Sir," another patrolman called out, jogging over to Cam. "Overheard one of the newscasters say there was some shooting out in the trees way in the back of the property just a minute ago—one of the stations tried to get some footage, but it's all trees back there and they had no real visibility. Something about a motorcycle racing away, maybe had a couple riding it?"

Cam's gaze immediately went back to the motorcycle parked in front of the house. One Harley. He glanced over where Luke corralled the cousins and the two extra men. Two. One bike. Both guys looked like bikers, and he doubted one of them was riding bitch. There was a GTO with tires shot out, someone who fit Trevor's description had driven over the bridge and forced her to ride, and rumor had it that Bobbie Faye had been seen on the back of a bike when leaving Marie's.

He looked back at that single bike again. Two minutes later, he'd commandeered the keys.

From: JT
To: Simone

What do you mean, lost her? Like lose lose? As in dead? Or just misplaced? Please God, tell me you just misplaced her. Go look in the silo. Maybe she's only singed a little around the edges.

(sent via cell)

Bobbie Faye and Trevor raced away from the mill on the Harley. Blackened smoke from the burning silos and house billowed upward, inking the clear blue sky with an ugly scrawl. They sped along an old dirt road, packed hard over the years with a smattering of gravel lining the ditches that ran alongside it. Big live oaks and pecan trees shaded them, protecting them from the notice of the helicopters as they passed farms and the occasional rural business. A tractor distributor, a tiny convenience store, and a farm supply warehouse were scattered among the small farm homes.

She rode behind Trevor and for once, she didn't care where they were going, just that they were getting out of there and leaving the would-be assassins and kidnappers and deranged cousins behind. She hugged herself closer to Trevor to avoid the brunt of the wind (well, hell, that was her story and she was sticking to it), and she laid her face against the center of his back, careful of where he was scraped and burned from the fall, and she snaked her arms around his waist to hang on. He laced one hand into hers. Then he lifted it and kissed the palm and then held her hand back at his waist and her heart raced with pure Fear.

It scared the living hell out of her. Not really the kiss. The look he'd given her. The connection she'd felt going over that rail and looking into his eyes. How could she trust her instincts when she had such a crappy track-record in the past? He'd killed people in front of her and she should have been afraid of him then, but she hadn't been. He'd stepped in front of bullets, and she'd taken that in stride. They'd dangled over death, and he'd nearly sacrificed himself for her—and her for him—and she hadn't questioned *why*. It was some sort of normal for them, this way of working dangerously in sync. Could she trust it?

Gunshots. Not far behind. She chanced a look over her shoulder and damned if it wasn't the merry crew of psychos belonging to the Irish guy. She wondered just when she'd been reincarnated as the mad leader of this deranged, never-ending Conga line? Two of them were shooting out of the back passenger windows of a souped-up Subaru, aiming wide to get their attention.

The Subaru tried to pass them (and they had better traction on the gravelly road than the bike). They shot again, trying to force Trevor to the right. Trevor moved her hand to his gun. As she grabbed it and pivoted enough to squeeze off a couple of shots, he reached back, holding onto her so she wouldn't fall. The Subaru backed off as she unloaded a few rounds—putting bullets into the car but not doing enough damage to stop them. She couldn't bring herself to shoot the driver or the passengers. They must have realized her hesitancy, and the car inched closer.

Close enough to see the deadly expression on Sean MacGreggor's face and—seriously? They could use his image for *Scared Straight!* posters and every delinquent kid in the country would line up for devotionals and charity work.

She tried shooting out a tire, and the gun clicked. Empty. "Do you have another magazine?" she shouted above the engine and Trevor shook his head. Instead, he reached down beneath his left leg to some sort of saddlebag and she peered over his arm in time to see him retrieve a grenade the same casual way Lori Ann would have reached for another beer. She wasn't sure whether to be relieved or horrified that she'd lusted (*past tense!* this time she *swore!*) after a guy who actually thought to carry around *grenades* for a day's outing with her. Now there was a personal ad just waiting to happen:

> **SWF looking for sexy, strong, and muttering type, must dangle well from burning buildings. Able to kill people and have your own grenade stash a plus.**

"Hang on tight," he shouted, and he pulled the pin with his teeth and dropped the grenade into the middle of the road. Two seconds later, the grenade exploded a few feet shy of the mark of Sean MacGreggor's car and shrapnel from the grenade blew the tire. The Subaru spun off the road, going nose-down in the ditch.

Trevor gunned the bike around a curve and when they came to a crossroads, he turned to the right even before Bobbie Faye could make the suggestion. She wondered where they were headed, because surely, the fact that Roy had a camp this direction . . . a camp no one knew about . . . was a coincidence.

Cam realized he'd taken the wrong road as soon as he heard gunshots and then, God help him, what sounded distinctly like a grenade on Old Mill Road. There were two roads which ran perpendicular to Landry's property—he was on one, and the grenade had come from the other. He turned his bike around, heading back to the Mill Road, "road" being an euphemism for the compacted ruts with loose gravel that ran for miles before it joined up anything resembling a paved highway. On the Harley, it was not an easy ride. He couldn't imagine why Trevor would choose that direction, because it wound southeast and . . .

He knew where they were going. Assuming they survived the grenade blast.

Up ahead, he saw a crater in the center of the road and a Subaru in a ditch—with a couple of suits milling around. A black SUV had parked to block the road and a tall redhead, ugly haircut, like she was trying too hard to not look feminine in the workplace, put her hand up to stop him. She flashed a Homeland Security badge . . . a Simone someone . . . and he pulled out his own detective shield badge and ID, which she read carefully.

"We're working a crime scene, here, Detective," the woman said, her silky voice floating on the summer air, a timbre much lighter and sweeter than her sour expression would have led him to believe possible.

He nodded toward the car—there didn't appear to be a bike mangled beneath it. "Any fatalities?"

"No," she said, "but you'll need to answer some questions. We want to know the whereabouts of a Bobbie Faye Sumrall."

He revved up his bike. "You and half the country. Good luck with that."

"You can't leave," she yelled, and two of her cohorts were headed his way as he fishtailed the bike out of there. The crater in the road had prevented the SUV from going forward—and they couldn't get back to their vehicle fast enough to follow him. He had one chance of overtaking Bobbie Faye and Trevor and finding out just what in the hell was going on.

Aiden followed the old dirt road in a car stolen from a farm supply place—an old Crown Victoria some farmhand had parked with the keys inside. It was like driving a boat in choppy water as the car bounced over every little rut and bump in the road. He'd taken over driving from Sean as Mollie tore part of his t-shirt into bandages to deal with the cuts from the shrapnel that had flown in the window of the Subaru. She seethed in fine form, something to admire, Aiden thought, though he wasn't stupid enough to say so, especially not with Sean stewing violently next to her. Robbie's knife wound leaked blood onto a makeshift bandage Mollie had already tied, and Aiden wasn't sure if his features were drawn into a stark frown from pain or embarrassment.

They wound through a couple of towns that weren't large enough to be dots on the most detailed maps, and then they followed a river until they rounded a bend, and Aiden had to stop the car as they all gaped. In front of them was a drawbridge, but instead of splitting in an inverted V, the part suspended over the water lifted straight up by two large hydraulic pistons on either end. It hovered twenty or so feet in the air, which wasn't the surprising thing. No, *that* was the woman, jumping down from the drawbridge's control tower, onto the bridge, then running across and leaping from the bridge onto the muddy shoulder of the road on the bank opposite from where they sat. She jumped on the back of the waiting motorcycle with the ops guy and as they sped off, she glanced back at them, staring at the unmoving bridge . . . and waved.

Aiden braced for a tirade of wrath from Sean, but instead, his boss smiled.

"Are ye legs broke?" Sean asked Robbie, who—in spite of having a shoulder sliced through—didn't complain as he bailed out of the car and climbed up the ladder to the control tower.

"Well," Aiden said, to break the silence. "She sure isn't bashful much, is she?"

"Aye, she'll be a handful, I imagine, but useful when I have 'er."

"You mean useful to get the diamonds, right?" Mollie asked in that half-annoyed way women have of not-quite-stating that you've lost your marbles.

"No, I meant exactly what I said. I'll have the diamonds, too, o'course, but that sort of initiative is a fucking handy thing t' have."

Mollie rolled her pretty blue eyes as Robbie was heaving back from the control booth.

"It's no' comin' down," he said when he returned to the car, panting from the exertion, and his wound bleeding even more. Mollie grunted, annoyed, and set to rebandaging it as Robbie explained, "She's jigged somethin' or stolen somethin'. I canna tell."

They could watch the small GPS tracking unit signal that was still emanating from her purse where Mollie had put it, but Sean wanted her—wanted to intercept her and be there when the diamonds were found. Aiden suspected his boss was cursing himself for keeping this operation as small as he had. "How much trouble can one woman be?" Sean had said at the time.

"How are we goin' t' follow her?" Aiden asked.

"It's time," Sean said, "for Mollie m'girl to find out what her 'long lost' American cousin might be doin' headin' this direction. Someone's bound t' know. Let's go make friends."

John hid in the field behind the burning house. The top of the silo blew just before he'd arrived at the field, and he'd run for cover. He was down three men so far. Including his best sniper. Another one of his men had acted as lookout, and had seen the freaking woman get clear of the silos and disappear with the asshole Fed on the back of a bike. She was still running. He couldn't get his payday if she were alive, and after what this fiasco cost him, he wasn't about to give up on that—or those diamonds. She owed him.

He limped off, heading for his car, knowing he had two possibilities of locating her. She might not check in with many people, but she did check in with her brother and sister. After something like this, she'd call. He just had to be persuasive enough to get one of them to talk. In Lori Ann's case, a fifth of Jack ought to do the trick.

Bobbie Faye and Trevor stopped several cabins away from Roy's fishing camp—well, it was technically Roy's; it was listed under a friend's name and Roy didn't tell many people he owned it—

too many pissed off husbands had shown up to kill him at his previous camp. Even Roy's anti-intuitive survival instinct could comprehend "impending death" after a few dozen attempts on his life.
The rundown camp looked empty, unlike those near it, where
smells of frying catfish and a crawfish boil or two permeated the
heavy afternoon air.

The cabin was set on poles out over the lake itself—tall poles,
which allowed a good twenty feet clearance when the lake was
swollen from heavy rains. Someone would have a hell of a time
ambushing them from the perimeter. The wraparound porch connected to the land by a pier—wide enough for a motorcycle, but
not wide enough for a car.

"Your brother's off-shore, right?" Trevor asked as he cut the
engine. Just one more reminder that he'd surveilled her enough to
know every freaking detail about her life. Jesus, he probably even
knew about the chocolate she hid in the freezer. Was she a job to
him? Were those expressions of outright horror over her nearly
dying due to feelings or because the government might lose some
expensive baubles?

"He's supposed to be, but you never know with Roy," she
snapped, harsher than she'd meant to. Her Poker Face was seriously
in need of a rehab from the bemused expression on Trevor's bruised
face. "He could be in there with the governor's wife, for all I know."

"I'll go check it out." They hopped off the bike and he knocked
the kickstand in place. "Alone. Unless you're in the mood to see
your brother having sex?"

"Okay, ewww, scarred for life, thank you."

"Glad to help. I'll be right back."

He stepped away and she looked down for one second, then
back up, and he'd melted from view into the swamp that sur-
rounded Roy's place. He was just . . . gone. He was very good at
that. At his job. Being able to blend, to disappear. *To go undercover.*
He'd fooled a lot of people when he'd helped her with Roy—
everyone had believed him to be a completely amoral renegade

FBI agent on the take. Someone who'd kill for money. He'd convinced Emile in believing he was still that guy, and Emile—a man who wouldn't have trusted his own mother to bake him poison-free homemade cookies—had hired him. So who was to say this wasn't a role?

She shook herself free of the thoughts and pulled out the photos, which were practically burning a hole in her back pocket. When she held them side by side, they were very similar. They each were taken in V'rai's living room, with family gathered on the sofa. Everyone was older in the second photo, which was the only one to include Bobbie Faye and Francesca as toddlers—maybe they were three years old? Bobbie Faye had on threadbare shorts, a shirt with a juice stain, and peanut butter in her hair. Francesca was the one wearing the pink dress, the pink shoes, the pink purse, and the pink hat over her curls.

Poor Francesca. She never had a shot at being anything other than a princess.

"Let's get you inside," Trevor said in her ear, and she jumped and yelped and he caught her before she plastered her face in the gravel road.

"Holy fucking *geez*, make a noise next time."

"Why would I want to do that?" He grinned as he set her down and hopped back on the motorcycle to ride it the rest of the way to Roy's.

Reggie and DJ waited a short block from the police station, keeping the front door in sight. Donny finally ambled out with that half-hopeful expression she'd seen some actors get when they wear huge sunglasses and big floppy hats and wildly ugly "stylish" clothes while they were supposedly incognito, but which screamed *recognize me!* His expression fell when absolutely no one paid him the least bit of attention. He scanned around, saw her wave, hurried over, and climbed into her car.

"You're not going to regret this," she told him as he peered around, apprehensive. She'd worked too hard and put too much of her future on the line for him to chicken out now.

"Just go. I don't know where Francesca went and if she sees that we formed a secret liaison, she'll be really mad at me."

"Sure thing," Reggie snorted. "Because the last thing I'd want is for the makeup queen to force me to buy that extra concealer she babbles about every time I see her. Woooo, scary."

Benoit had kept up with the silo disaster while he finished canvassing Bobbie Faye's neighbors. He'd been avoiding the captain by being conveniently out of his vehicle. The rumor mill worked overtime with any Bobbie Faye–related gossip, particularly on days like today, and so many people knew he had a copy of the surveillance video, he was surprised he hadn't been offered bribes for it. Reggie would have had a heart attack trying to get her hands on it. The only thing preventing the captain from finding him personally and reaming him out for not logging the security footage into evidence was the minor detail of having to organize the police effort at the silo plus the questioning effort when Cam had everyone rounded up and sent to the PD. Cam was a genius.

His personal cell phone buzzed with a voice mail message. Oddly, it hadn't rung through with a call, but he'd been in a bad reception area of the town out where Bobbie Faye lived. He dialed in to pick up the message and heard a woman, vaguely familiar, though she sounded like she was running and out of breath.

"Benoit, it's Bobbie Faye. I've got something for you. It's important. I can't call Cam and I don't know who else to trust. Remember where we hid the mascot senior year? Meet me there. Fast, okay?"

The message ended and the callback number was blocked.

That was odd. But then, she'd already been nearly killed on a bridge, in a house and now, if the news was correct, at the silos. Anyone would get a pass for being a little twitchy at that point. They'd been friends too long for him not to hear her out. It was a helluva drive to meet her, and he couldn't fathom why she'd gone all the way to Baton Rouge after the silos that morning, but he owed it to her to go. Maybe he could talk her into turning herself in. It was the only way she was going to have a chance in hell of getting out of this without life in prison.

From: JT
To: Simone

Her phone is still receiving calls, one from Italy—possibly the buyer. SAT position coming in . . . now. Sending coordinates. Find her. Soon. Or you'll end up answering to Brownie.

(sent via cell)

From: Simone
To: JT

Holy shit, no. I'll find her.

(sent via cell)

Bobbie Faye ignored her phone, buzzing with messages—they'd have to wait. She knew one was Lori Ann, who'd probably just called to bitch about not being able to hang up on her that morning. One was Nina, but she'd texted Nina back from Trevor's phone, keeping her updated. Trevor had parked the bike and gone through the cabin once—but Bobbie Faye knew how wily her brother could be when he was hiding from the husbands or boyfriends of his "dates." While Trevor reloaded his gun from the ample ammo supply Roy kept on top of the refrigerator (Roy's theory of the universe apparently only contained short thieves), Bobbie Faye re-checked the rooms. Everything in the ramshackle, cluttered camp was pretty much as she remembered it: a dark paneled "great" room with a kitchen/living area, with bedrooms and bathrooms protruding from that central location like spokes. Roy's tastes were all bachelor, all the time; he worked off-shore (when he worked) and probably still did some lucrative shady work for Alex, so he blew his money on junk: big screen TVs, loads of fishing gear, hunting gear, sports gear, DVDs, games. At least she *hoped* it was his money he was blowing, because if he was involved in anything else quasi illegal, he was going to have a long stint at the hospital for two broken legs. She circled through the rooms and, satisfied that Roy hadn't climbed in a closet, buried himself in a floor space, or sat hunched on top of the hot-water heater, Bobbie Faye returned to the kitchen.

Where *whoa*.

Trevor had taken off his ripped, bloody shirt and as he set down the now-loaded gun on the peninsula counter and walked toward her, Lust was doing backflips.

She had to focus. And not on him. "We should keep moving. Diamonds to find, things to destroy."

"I've checked—the bridge is out, and they expect it to take hours to repair. Nearest bridge is more than two hours away, and I've already got roadblocks there, checking for Sean's team and anyone else who looks suspicious." He tapped his spiffy cell phone. "And Emile thinks we're on our way to New Orleans with information, so he'll wait there—which means, we have some time. You need to decompress."

He was half-naked and several regions of her body were voting for him to be all-naked and *what in the hell was wrong with her?* Not three seconds ago, she was worrying about motives and all it took was his abs and the chest and the shoulders and holy fucking geez, the smile, and she was a blathering idiot. He backed her up to the overloaded kitchen counter, the chipped yellow Formica barely peeking out from beneath stacks of garage-sale dishes. She knocked over three pots just trying to sidle away from him; he boxed her in, arms on each side of her, palming the counter.

"Are you okay?" he asked.

"Just *peachy*. Now let me by."

"Nope." He moved a set of knives just out of her reach. "I'm an idiot." He looked away, his jaw clenching, shoulders tense. "Kissing you like that."

Her Hormones squealed as they screeched to a halt, toppling over each other. There was major internal pouting going on, which was just stupid. He didn't want a relationship, and she'd suspected that, so, she shouldn't be so freaking surprised.

"Let me rephrase," he said, and she realized he'd been watching her reaction. "It was a stupid rank amateur mistake. I was being selfish. I'm sorry my kissing you at the silo put you in more jeopardy."

The low-grade hum she'd felt since she'd first seen him yesterday hadn't abated, but now the way he looked at her made her feel as if she'd been plugged into an amp and the wattage was going to overload her system. Kissing him *anywhere* put her in more jeopardy, and she wrapped her arms tightly across her chest. Then her eyes—on their own freaking accord and without getting their permission slip signed—*looked* at the abs just inches away . . . and then the biceps (Good freaking Lord, You did a good job there, *thank You*) and then the jawline, and she veered her gaze away, trying to maintain some semblance of stoicism, and ended up back at the abs. She may have whimpered a little, because he grinned.

"You're having an entire argument in your head right now, aren't you?"

"Just admiring how really good you are at—" she swallowed hard as his muscles in his arms tensed "—your job. You know, this whole fake relationship thing—kudos. Impressive marksmanship."

"Job?" He frowned. "I thought I made that clear this morning."

She pointed to herself. "How in the hell am I supposed to

know that this *isn't* just a job to you? You know, seduce the crazy lady, keep her on your side."

"Are you out of your flipping mind?"

"According to the bookies, that would be a *yes*."

He resonated anger. Tamped down, forced under control. "I get it—I've worked undercover and you don't yet know me well enough outside of work to trust what we have. I may fuck up in a hundred different ways, but being clear with you isn't going to be one of them. Think about it: would the Agency spend the money and the manpower to romance a woman everyone knows is already the kind of person who'd help us if we *just asked*? Or, worst case scenario, if we threatened her family?" His expression softened as he waited while that sank in a moment, and Epiphany did a mamba up her spine as he added, "I'm telling you straight up, right now: I want you. So either I'm a lying bastard you can't trust, that you wouldn't want to have at your back with a gun, or you're scared."

"There's a helluva lot of difference between knowing you'd have my back in a gunfight and having—" she pointed between them "—this."

"Completely scared."

"And," she added, ignoring him, "it's not exactly like I haven't cornered the market on the Lying Bastard Collection."

"Totally chicken."

"And!" she said, thumping him in the arm. "Lying Bastards always make a great case for why they're telling the truth!"

"You're practically growing feathers here, Sundance."

He cupped the back of her neck, pressing into her, brushing his lips just barely across her own as she braced her hands against his chest, trying to hold onto her control as her Hormones were all *hell, yeah!* and fighting their way to the accelerator. He shifted against her just enough to let her feel the length of his body and her every single solitary nerve ending said *hello, Sailor* in their best Mae West voice and she may have wiggled against him. A lot.

He smiled against her lips. "You're going to have to pick which side you want to be on. Either you want me, or you don't, but I didn't come to play." His eyes grew dark and serious.

Oh, holy shit. Her pulse went up to a thousand, her Hormones threw a party and invited in the Emotions and her senses saturated with heat, overwhelmed by how close he was standing . . . and then she heard the front door open. Trevor was already reaching for his gun when she glanced up for that one split second and she yelled, "Down!"

They hit the floor in unison, Trevor landing on top of Bobbie Faye, his gun ready as a butcher knife thwanged in the kitchen wall right behind where they had been standing.

Chapter Twenty-three

"You're not Roy," a female voice said as Bobbie Faye tilted her head backward to see an upside-down view of Crazy Carmen, the butcher's daughter who'd tried to cleave Roy in half not all that long ago. The woman was barefoot, which explained why they hadn't heard her approach.

"Carmen," Bobbie Faye said as matter-of-factly as she could to a raving loon, "you're looking good. Been out of jail long?"

"Where's Roy? I've been watching this place for weeks and he always sneaks past me."

Crazy Carmen—sultry hot, tanned body with curves that would make Marilyn Monroe weep with envy—did not pay attention to the gun Trevor had drawn on her; she did, however, adjust her too-tight knit red dress and then her ample bosom for Trevor's benefit as he stood and then helped Bobbie Faye up. The loss of the weight of his body, his heat, was sudden, and so tangible Bobbie Faye had to blink a moment to process why she felt immediately bereft.

"Roy's moved," she said, stumbling over the words, kick-starting her brain again. "Got a job in—" she searched her memory for a distant locale.

"Guam," Trevor supplied.

"He won't be back for a couple of years," Bobbie Faye added.

Carmen's gaze swept Trevor's body from top to bottom and Bobbie Faye found herself suddenly loathing Carmen. Irrationally, vehemently, *loathing.*

"Who's the hunk belong to?" Carmen asked her, with that bright smile against that dark Cajun complexion.

"We were just working that out," Trevor said from behind Bobbie Faye.

"Go away, Carmen."

"So he's yours, huh?"

Yeah, something inside Bobbie Faye said, and something that controlled her muscles—it sure as hell wasn't Survival Instinct—made her head nod.

"Lucky girl," Carmen said, reluctantly backing away. "I'm all about respecting relationships—something your brother needs to learn, by the way." She gave Trevor the once-over one last time before sashaying out the door.

Bobbie Faye could practically hear Trevor smiling behind her. "Shut up."

It had taken Cam too fucking long to make the phone calls from the sabotaged bridge area in order to track down Brian Thibodeaux in a bar, drunk off his ass, instead of where he was supposed to be: running his barge back and forth across the river. The same river now blocking him from getting to Roy's camp, where he believed Bobbie Faye may have headed. She, of course, wasn't answering her phone, and Brian had slurred so badly, Cam wasn't a hundred percent sure he understood Cam's instructions. If Brian was completely sober, it would still take him thirty minutes to cross the river, and then another thirty to pick Cam up and cross back. It galled Cam to wait, but it was the barge or drive two hours away, only to have to ride two hours back this direction—and who knew if Bobbie Faye would have moved on to destroy something else in that span of time.

• • •

obbie Faye faced Trevor's pleased-with-himself expression. His deep blue eyes were oh so amused. Ha. Damned man. "What happened to you being the guy who pretty much hated all women—who said that after meeting me, your opinion of them was just getting worse?"

"I believe *some*one—" he leaned toward her "—pointed out to me that I had been dating the wrong women." He took her hand, grabbed one of his SIGs, and led her into the bathroom.

"So you had a complete turnaround in one day when we met? I know you got smacked around pretty bad in a couple of those explosions that day, but I didn't think it jostled your brains that much." He spun her to face the mirror, and she flinched at her disheveled, bloody, and blue image, taking in how well they matched with their scrapes and grime. He grabbed a comb from a cabinet and set to work on the tangles in her hair, pulling the comb through a bottom section, working higher and higher with each pass.

"You're really good at that."

"Three sisters, remember?" He hesitated, pulling the comb through another section. "And the turnaround wasn't in a day."

She thought about that, watching Trevor's intent expression, remembering their argument from that morning, remembering, too, what he'd said to the other agent about giving notification of his intent to date her. Then it hit her. "From the surveillance?" She'd been having a particularly bad streak of luck at the time they'd met, and an equally foul disposition to go with it. "You liked me enough from that? Are you insane?"

"Apparently." He chuckled when she made a face at him in the mirror. She watched him, and he was deep in thought, but not hiding his internal battle from her. He could have. She knew that about him now. Finally, he said, "I was never going to have that one someone special in my life and I was okay with that."

"But you had it before." She interrupted, referring to the divorce he'd mentioned only once.

"No." His grim expression underlined his point. "Not even close. And it taught me: never again. And that was best, in my line of work. *You* intrigued the hell out of me, but there was no expectation. You were supposed to get the tiara, hand it to me in the parking lot, and I'd have left."

"So I held a gun on you instead, shot your truck, and you decided, gee, *this* is the person I'd like to date? I'm a little worried about your standards there Trevor."

He grinned, wicked. "Yeah, well, I really did like the shirt you had on."

Then he held her gaze and lightly traced the lines of her face.

He was referring to the SHUCK ME, SUCK ME, EAT ME RAW t-shirt, and she blushed three kinds of red.

In her purse in the kitchen, her cell phone blasted the tone she'd programmed in for Cam. She grimaced and ignored it—if it was a Stacey emergency, Cam's mom or sister would call. Trevor turned her around, lifted her and set her on the big white faux marble top of the bathroom vanity. He stepped between her legs and she was damned glad she wasn't actually having to use them to stand up because they'd just sent a resignation letter to her brain: *quitting now.* Especially since he'd pulled her hips so that she scooted forward and pressed into his hard body. A very toned, *half-naked* body. (*Yes,* said Lust. *Let's focus on the important things here.*) His hands slid gently up her arms, caressing the curves of her shoulders and then down again as she moved her own hands around to hold his waist, but detoured, mmmmmmmmmmmmm, to his abs. Her fingers drifted lightly, and Dear God, he got all tense and hot and then his hands were beneath her shirt and her brain hung a "not operational" sign up.

Somewhere far far away, probably on another planet even, she heard the dim racket of her phone ringing once more with Cam's designated chime. Trevor reached over and slapped the bathroom door shut, muffling the sound. "I'm going to say this one time." His tone was not without a hint of frustration. "Cam is a *good* man."

It took her brain a moment to fight through the lust. "Huh? What?" And then she registered what he was saying, which was in direct juxtaposition of just how intimate his caresses were becoming. "Okay, that's about the dumbest wooing strategy I've ever heard of."

"I'm serious. He's in love with you," he said, softly, "and you're a fool if you don't see it."

They both stopped the caressing as she stared at him, trying to form a sentence, stopping and starting over twice before she could think of something coherent to say. He was wrong about Cam, but there was no point in arguing about it. "I'm beginning to see why you got divorced. You suck at this whole 'wooing' thing."

"Oh, there will be wooing." (And her Hormones did the Wave.) "But this is the only time I'm going to say this: you know him, you have a background in common, and he could provide you with a good future, as soon as he gets his head out of his ass—and he will."

"We really need to get you a manual. Wooing 101." His hands slid through her hair, his touch setting every single nerve ending she had on vibrate.

"I've been around longer, I'm hell to live with." She eased him away and hopped down as he talked. "My job has been to manipulate, infiltrate, and, on occasion, kill. I'm good at it, Sundance. All of it. In fact, very damned good. That's not ever going to change."

"Are you under the impression that I hadn't figured this out?" She cranked the shower knob on and water spewed out, hitting the chipped tile. She faced him again.

"I'm just warning you—I don't care if he's in the way. Emotionally or physically. Unless you tell me right now that you're in love—" she lifted her arms up "—with him—what are you doing?"

"I wonder if there are wooing instructions on the Internet?" He frowned, and she loved that completely confused expression.

She so rarely saw it on him. She leaned in a little, letting him in on the plan. "We're getting naked now."

He watched her, with her arms in the air, waiting for him, and the slow, sizzling grin that spread across his face melted her bones. "I can work with naked." He reached for the hem of her shirt and began sliding it upward and then stopped a second. "But I want more than that."

"Then you better get busy."

"Are you always going to be this bossy?" he asked, tugging the shirt off and tossing it to the floor.

"Yep." She worked the button on his jeans.

"Good to know."

She felt her breath hitch at that and she stilled—he *got* her. He framed her face with his hands and kissed her and she'd never been kissed like that before, had never known that sort of possession, searing heat and tenderness all at the same time. She worked her hands into his now-loose jeans (Hormones: Score!) and cupped his ass as he reached between them, undoing her own jeans, and the feel of him in her palms? Well, she was writing a letter when this was over:

Dear Sister Mary Margaret:
 Hell is soooooooooooo worth this. I promise.
You have no idea.

Then he shucked her jeans, impatient, and she tugged his off, just as determined, and within seconds, gone was the bra and everything else and he took a minute to scan her, head to toe, and said, "Dear God, *thank you.*" She nodded at him, in awe; she didn't think it was entirely right to say *holy fucking Jesus he's gorgeous*—it might seem sacrilegious or something, and if she got struck by lightning right now, she was going to be *completely* pissed off.

He pulled her to him, kissing her, pressing against her and *wow.* She ran her hands over him as he devoured every inch of her body, spending an inordinate amount of time on the inside of her left thigh and then at her center; his mouth was hot and talented and that's pretty much when she lost her entire mind.

Somewhere in there, she slapped off the water and managed to breathe out "floor." She wasn't entirely sure which one of them had opened the bathroom door (there was soooo not enough floor space in there) and how they'd managed to get to the plush living room rug (and when did they turn over that coffee table?) or how they knocked the fishing poles down (all thirty or so of them) or when the fish mounted on the wall fell and broke the lamp—these things skimmed around the edges of her awareness only as Trevor moved them to safety each time while they kissed each other crazy.

And then they were on the rug, tangled and rolling (and there went the DVD tower, oops) (and holy crap, all the knickknacks on the book shelf were toast) and there was nothing in the world that she wanted more than this. *Need* pulsed from her core, radiating outward, hungry for him. All of him. He worked his way back up her body and he paused there as she moved to take him in; she gazed at him watching her, and saw him *wanting, needing* in return, and realized *that's what that expression was that he'd had when she fell over the railing.* She knew he could see a reflection of that same feeling in her, and he skimmed a finger along her lips, drawing out the suspense until she thought she'd snap in half from the tension.

"I will beat you senseless if you make me wait," she said, wiggling beneath him

"I think that's the same thing you said when we were waiting for the chili cheese dogs," he teased, smiling against her lips as he moved just enough to taunt her into madness. She squirmed, and he touched her, bracing on one elbow as he skimmed his other hand between them.

"Trevor?"

"Hmmm?" His lazy growl belied by his own taut body.

"Need," she ground out as his fingers pressed into her.

"This?"

"You." She tangled her fingers in his hair. "Just you."

"It's about damned time," he said, and then he kissed her, rough and hard, as he thrust inside her and she arched, shocked, filled with him, with mind-bendy goodness. He moved then, and took her with him over the edge and the world stopped; there was just him, just the feel of him and his blue eyes on her as everything else simply ceased to exist.

A iden watched Mollie saunter back to the car, a feline grin lighting up her face and he knew she'd scored.

"So?" Sean asked as she climbed in the back seat. "Are ye gonna make me wait all day?"

"They're right friendly here," Mollie answered. "Seems there's a cabin down a bit, b'longs to the brother, tho' he don' let on."

"No' real helpful, with a bridge out."

"Sure," she said, the smile evident in her voice. "But there is a barge that'll ferry us, for the right price."

T revor carried her into the shower, which was probably a necessity since she could barely walk. The fact that he was fairly proud of that fact made her want to smack him, except that might be counterproductive because then he might not be as . . . vigorous next time. Except she discovered he had an entire arsenal of *vigorous,* including the slow, delicious, suspend-Bobbie-Faye-against-the-shower-wall version, which blew her mind. *Vigorous* was her new favorite word. She sort of came back from nirvana a while later when he had her leaning against him, her back to his chest, and he worked the shampoo through her hair.

"Um, hi," she said, sheepish.

"Welcome back."

"How long have I been . . . drifting?"

"Oh, not long. Couple of stars imploded, they changed the name of the continents, nothing big."

She faced him as he helped rinse her hair. "Proud of yourself, aren't you?"

"Hey," he held his hands up, all *you asked for it,* and said, "you mocked the wooing."

"Are you always going to be this smug?"

"Every. Single. Chance. I. Get."

"I'd complain, but I'm thinking this is going to work in my favor."

"Very smart woman."

She relaxed into him, the warm shower water washing over them both, and she was a little stunned that she was happy he understood her so well, when just that morning, it had freaked her out. But he did know her well—something he'd gotten from more than mere observation—because God knows other people in her life, who'd known her for years, didn't get her. She wished she was as up-to-speed on his past, though. A frame of reference, a—wait.

She stiffened. The photos. Point of reference. She thought she knew what V'rai had wanted her to see.

Chapter Twenty-four

Roy had experience in sweet-talking nurses, so he felt pretty confident about being able to break Lori Ann out of rehab. The trick was finding the right-aged nurse. Someone too young would be too nervous if she were questioned later, and someone too old wasn't going to buy that he was "security" sent by a judge who wanted to put Lori Ann into protective custody until this Bobbie Faye thing blew over. He'd planned out everything he'd say, how he'd say it, how he'd smile. It seemed that, dimples were a big deal, and while he had no idea why, he had two and knew how to put 'em to good use. If that failed, he'd do the stretch and muscle flex thing—that usually wore down any resistance.

He looked at the seat next to him at the security badge he'd purchased at the local cop shop on his way to the rehab hospital. It had cost him a few extra minutes, but he'd flash it, and the nurse (assuming he got lucky on the age), would barely glance at the badge; she would probably be checking out his ring finger (he would hold the badge with his left hand) and realize there was no ring, no mark of there ever having been a ring, and for some reason, women seemed to think that meant he was a "catch" and they'd be thinking more about getting him into bed than whether or not he was legitimately a security guard.

So when he pulled up to the rehab center to find Lori Ann casually sitting on the curb, waiting for him, (annoyed, as usual), he was actively disappointed. No reason to hit on the nurses now. Damn, but his sisters worked hard at making his life miserable.

Lori Ann was a tiny sprite of a thing, barely came up to his shoulders, and her blond hair was fixed perfectly. She looked every bit the former cheerleader she'd been, except for the annoyed part—that part looked like she was going to do a back-flip on someone's head any moment now. He liked her better when she was drinking. She climbed into his car, slamming the door a little too hard.

"How'd you get out?"

She turned and plastered on that *you want to do something for me* smile that all three siblings shared. "Easy. I told my counselor that if I didn't get a furlough, I'd have to explain to Bobbie Faye why I wasn't able to help her, and I would then give her his home address so that she could pay him a visit. I've never seen a man race through paperwork so fast."

"Wow. I'm gonna have to use that one."

"Get your own, that one's mine."

"So what makes you so hot and bothered to help her? You're still not speaking to her."

"I tried calling her back and she didn't answer. The only time that happens is when she's being almost-killed. And nobody kills my sister except me."

Bobbie Faye wrapped a towel around her and hurried to her jeans crumpled on the floor. Trevor stepped out of the shower behind her as she retrieved the photos. She glanced over at him and her brain shifted into neutral.

After a minute, he tapped her on the forehead and she met his gaze.

"Huh?"

"Photos?"

"Oh. Oh! Right. Can't think when you're naked."

"Good to know," he said, smiling. "And should I be insulted that you are already over the aftereffects?"

"I think I really like that whole overachiever thing you've got going on," she said absently, focusing back on what she was seeing. "I think better when I'm—" she suddenly paid attention to what she was saying and looked up to where he waited.

"Satisfied?" he asked. There was a shadow of something behind his poker expression that pulled her to him, and she put her arms around him.

"Happy," she said, and she kissed him. He held her, lingering on that kiss, which trailed to her shoulder. She waved the photos at him. "Hold that thought."

He glared at the photos as if they were his enemy. "Damn," he muttered, "you managed to make me forget all about work. That never happens."

She beamed. "Maybe that's my superpower."

"I thought blowing things up was your superpower."

"Hey! A girl can have two superpowers." She thwacked him on his bare and oh-so-fine ass.

"I'm just glad I get the naked one."

Bobbie Faye had clothes stored at the camp from various trips there in the past. Digging through Roy's stuff to find jeans to fit Trevor was a challenge—Trevor was Roy's height, but a lot more muscle—still, they found a pair. The whole domesticity of the action made her smile. Which is when they heard someone pound on the front door . . . and then the door started opening.

Benoit parked behind the Capitol Lakes near the Governor's Mansion; the heat of the day had chased most of the tourists inside their hotels. Only a tiny smattering of hardy souls dotted the banks of the lake, picnicking a late afternoon meal under the pines and the oaks. The white Greek Revival-styled mansion shone in the sun, the reflection nearly blinding him where its back antebellum verandas faced the lake on the bank opposite him.

Why in the hell would Bobbie Faye choose this spot? Sure, as seniors, it was revered. Several of them had swiped Catholic High's bear mascot ahead of one particularly vehement rivalry game and tied it up to . . . he looked around . . . that sculpture. And had gotten in huge trouble for it, now that he thought about it. Cam and he got put on probation with the football team for that game (and they lost), Francesca was sent back to live with her dad, Jordan and Jeremiah were grounded so long, they practically needed introductions once they were free again, and Bobbie Faye, whose idea it was, had gotten a week of suspension from school and her trailer was rolled with TP every night for a month. Of course, after a couple of years had passed, the myth had grown—and the way he heard it, they'd stolen a live bear mascot and Bobbie Faye had wrestled it, had lost an arm (which was reattached), but then scared the bear so much, it would only curl up in a fetal position and whimper.

He saw a flash of movement and recognized her. She moved across the clearing, keeping to a more protected area. Was there some other danger here? What was she being wary of? Surely not him, unless she, too, had heard the rumors of the surveillance footage, but she had to know he'd have talked to her before hauling her in, right?. He slowly canvassed the area, and then radioed ten-oh-seven to dispatch, giving his location, and then climbed out of his air-conditioned truck. An . . . oddness, something wrong . . . pricked at the back of his neck.

"Bobbie Faye?" he called as he eased toward the sculpture and remembered that was one of Marie's. There had been a huge controversy back when it was first installed. The governor had been a state senator then and had pushed it through Congress as "support for a local artist" while neglecting to mention it depicted a couple having sex. It was an instant hit with every high schooler and still offended all of the church crowd, who tried every four years to have it removed.

"Bobbie Faye?" he called again. "I'm here to talk, like you asked. No need to hide, *chère*."

"You didn't bring anybody, right?"

"No, *chère,* just me. I need to talk to you. I think someone is trying to frame you."

"Someone is," she said from almost right behind him, and it struck him the instant the bullet did that he'd been had. He slammed forward to the ground, cursing himself for such a stupid mistake. He should have known. He needed to shoot, he needed to stop her, and he tried to lift his gun, but his arm wasn't working right and then the second bullet hit. She leaned over and peered into his eyes as the world drifted down into blackness.

Bobbie Faye and Trevor sprinted toward the kitchen—each grabbed a gun off the counter—only to see the front door opening and Cam filling it with six-foot-four-inches worth of pure annoyance. He tossed Bobbie Faye his spare key when she made muffled "how?" and "locked" noises.

"Twice in one day, Detective," Trevor said, his voice like finely edged steel. As Cam took a moment to glare at Trevor (only in jeans) and then gaze at her (jeans and a very lacy bra—she hadn't quite gotten to the shirt yet), Trevor added, "Maybe next time, we'll have some hors d'oeuvres set out for you. Were you followed?" He went to the front window, edged the curtain over, and peered out.

"No. But if I can track you, someone else could, too," Cam answered without looking at Trevor. Bobbie Faye could see how he catalogued her appearance—the bruises, the cuts, the way she probably looked thoroughly kissed . . . and oh, Lord, there were probably hickeys, though really, at this point, she was one big bruise so how would he know? She shook herself—didn't matter. If she didn't know better, didn't know that he hadn't wanted to be with her, she would have sworn he looked gut-kicked, but then he rubbed the back of his neck and pinched the bridge of his nose and she knew he was, instead, still fighting a headache. "Get dressed," Cam snapped, and then realizing how he'd barked it out as an order, he amended, "please."

She still clutched the camisole in her left hand—she must have picked it up before they'd run for the kitchen—and she set the gun down to put it on. She moved to Roy's kitchen cabinets and dug out the headache meds she'd once kept there.

"What are you doing here?" Trevor asked. She looked back at him and knew he was livid, though the only thing that gave it away was the tiniest tick in a muscle in his jaw. Anyone else would have only noticed the nonchalant, unworried stance as he leaned casually against the wall at that window, his arms crossed at his chest. She noted he still held his gun.

"That's what I came to ask you," Cam said to her, ignoring Trevor. "The silos? Shooting? And now the drawbridge—which fucked up traffic for hours. Was that really necessary?"

"If we wanted to live, it was," Trevor said.

She grabbed a glass, filled it with water.

"I knew I should have locked you up earlier," Cam griped, "for your own damned good. You don't have sense enough to stop, and you're going to get yourself killed."

She held out the meds and the water to him. "Do you want to take these orally, or should I just shove the bottle up your ass? And I have sense, you jerk. I just don't have a choice."

He gulped down the medicine and handed her back the glass. "You *do* have a choice. You could have turned this over to me. Or the Feds," and he said that last word like someone else would say *maggots*, "and we would have investigated. Instead, you damned near got yourself killed *three times*—it's only a matter of time before you end up in the morgue."

"Gee, thanks for the vote of confidence."

He ignored her, speaking to Trevor. "This is *your* fucking job, not hers."

She thumped Cam in the chest with her index finger. "If you

don't stop talking about me like I'm not in the room, I'm going to drop-kick your ass into tomorrow, with or without that badge, and I don't care if you have a headache. This wasn't just a job—people in *my family* are going to be killed. I have to find those diamonds."

"Yeah? Well, you're not trained for this," he seethed.

"Whose fault is that?" Trevor asked, deadly calm. Too calm. She cast him a worried frown and he met her gaze, settling down a fraction. "You could have made sure she was trained."

"And I suppose that's what you'll do now," Cam said, and she knew they were talking about way more than her knowing how to throw a punch.

"Yes."

Although knowing how to really throw a punch—a knockout kind of punch—would come in freaking handy right about now.

"They're just fucking *diamonds*," Cam said to her, "and he—" he jabbed his finger toward Trevor "—if he cared about you at all, he would know better than to let you put your life on the line for some stupid rocks. I don't care *how* valuable they are."

Bobbie Faye leapt into rant mode, all set to tell Cam how she wasn't some pet whose actions could be dictated, when she felt Trevor's palm on the back of her neck, beneath her hair, stroking his thumb there. She wasn't sure if he did it to calm her, or himself, and he'd moved so fast, she hadn't heard or felt the motion until he was there.

"You have no idea how much I care about Bobbie Faye," Trevor warned, and Cam's eyes slitted downed to hatred.

"Why don't you tell me what it is I don't know, Cam," she said, "because you didn't come all this way to yell at me."

When he looked at her, there was so much pain behind his eyes, she wondered just what could be so bad . . . because this pain? This was more than a headache.

"First, you're going to tell me why the Feds are so hot over some stones," Cam said to Trevor, "or else I haul her in right now."

"No," Trevor said, very quietly, "you won't."

The two men glared at each other and Bobbie Faye was certain that if testosterone poisoning was tracked by the CDC, it would throw up its hands and run around like a freaked-out Chicken Little at the epidemic proportions of the disease. She plopped down on a dining chair and before she'd even exhaled, Trevor had taken the chair next to her, forcing Cam to sit opposite.

"Start with the diamonds," Cam said, and both he and Bobbie Faye looked expectantly at Trevor.

"They're fakes," Trevor said, and she felt a little woozy. She was putting her life on the line for a bunch of fakes? Was he crazy? "They're so well done, they can only be detected one of two ways—by a specially rigged Geiger counter or under an electron microscope. At least one of them has the formula etched inside it on a microscopic level, and since they can be duplicated, they're worth at least a half a billion—and more if they're mass produced." *Oh, okay, something every terrorist would want. That was much* better.

"Holy fucking *geez,*" she said, and she pressed her forehead against the cool tabletop.

"Your turn," Trevor said to Cam, though he put a reassuring hand on her shoulder, which was hunched so high from the stress, she probably looked like a turtle.

"We have surveillance footage with Bobbie Faye on it, shooting the jeweler."

She sat up so fast, she nearly toppled over.

Cam watched Bobbie Faye's reaction and he knew she was stunned. She'd never been that good at a poker face and she never lied, even when she was pulling a prank, like lowering all of the furniture in the principal's office every other week—then raising it back up each time—to confuse the new asshole principal. (He made her clean chairs for a week, until everyone kept sliding off them and the principal realized he'd neglected to specify what she had to use to clean everything *with*, so he couldn't suspend her for the heavy use of WD-40.) Right then, though, she'd gone so pale, Cam wished he could take back the announcement of the video, give her the blow softer—but he'd needed to see her reaction.

"I . . . what?"

He detailed the evidence piling up, and with each additional layer, she looked more and more bewildered and devastated. When he got to the part about the casings, he knew she was going to be furious. He pulled out the plastic bag he'd kept with him in his back pocket and set them on the table. She recoiled as if he'd set a bag of water moccasins in front of her.

"So that's what you were after in my trailer?"

"No, I wanted DNA to prove that wasn't your hair at the murder site. I saw these by accident—someone had shoved them behind the sink. I thought it was jewelry—I was going to fish it out and leave it for you on the counter."

She blinked. He'd always done little things like that—fixed things, built her shelves—well, in the last trailer—made sure she hadn't left stuff in her jeans before she washed them.

"Why aren't these in evidence?" she asked.

"I didn't turn them in." He met her gaze and saw that she grasped the enormity of what he'd done. They'd lived together for nearly a year—you didn't live with a cop and not learn the procedure.

"He didn't have a warrant," Trevor added, and Cam hated the man right then. "It wouldn't hold up in court."

"I have Stacey at my mom's," Cam said evenly, "and there are any number of things she could have needed from the trailer, which would have been a justifiable excuse, if I'd wanted to manufacture one and if I'd wanted to turn these in." He looked at Bobbie Faye. "I hate to ask who you've pissed off lately, but is there anyone specific who would hate you enough to go to this trouble?"

"There are too many to count."

"That's not the question we should be asking," Trevor said, and Cam looked at the man. He didn't know if the agent realized he was holding Bobbie Faye's hand, but odds were, it was a premeditated choice. "We should be asking: how does implicating Bobbie Faye in the jeweler murder benefit anyone looking for the diamonds?"

"How is Sal connected?" Cam asked.

"We knew Marie had the diamonds because she'd paid him with one just a few days before he was murdered. When he sold it on the black market, we traced it back to him and we learned Marie was the source. I believe the Agency was closing in on her when she realized what was happening and disappeared—setting up a sale for the rest of the diamonds with an unknown buyer from Italy."

"He made fakes for Marie," Bobbie Faye muttered. When both men looked at her, she shrugged. "It's what I would have done in her place. Have Sal make a bunch of fakes, and no one would know which were the real diamonds unless they had the right equipment."

"We don't believe even Sal realized what he had," Trevor said. "He'd have charged way more for it on the black market."

"Still, the fakes would work for Marie. Scatter 'em around to a bunch of places, make it look like she was putting some in her textiles that she was shipping overseas—have everyone running around in so many directions, finding stuff, no one would see the real ones. So someone probably wanted him to tell them how many fakes he made—process of elimination . . . even if they didn't know which ones were the real deal, they would know if they had all of them."

"This is why you have to stop looking for the diamonds," Cam said, thumping his fist on the table. When she looked confused, he explained, "because every step you take toward finding them just gives you a stronger and stronger motivation for murdering Sal."

"If I stop now," she said, furious, "then someone gets away with this. And no fucking way in hell am I letting that happen."

Reggie and DJ and Donny were stationed in the Capitol Lakes park when Benoit drove up. Ever since Donny had let it slip that everyone was running after diamonds, Reggie had one goal: catch Bobbie Faye in the act. That story would at least give her a segment on the national news—and that was the sort of thing a reel was made of—great stories to show producers to move up the news ladder.

For Donny, this was a chance to be on camera, babbling on and on about how he'd been forced to help, how he was an upstanding citizen, and by the way, if there were any acting agents interested, here was his number. Reggie had met quite a few Kato Kaelins in her time, but she'd never seen someone like Donny who'd viewed the O. J. Simpson hanger-on to be a personal hero.

"Are you sure the diamonds are here?" she asked Donny.

He posed for the camera before affecting a deeper voice and said, "Why yes, Reggie, I have it on good authority that the diamonds . . . and Bobbie Faye . . . are going to be here."

"Doofus, the camera is off if the light isn't on."

"And when I'm pointing it at the ground," DJ said helpfully.

Donny deflated, and Reggie shushed them both when Benoit came into view, calling for Bobbie Faye. DJ started rolling, using the zoom lens from their position a few yards away in the thickest batch of shrubs. Bobbie Faye appeared, and in a blink, Reggie heard a pop and the cop fell. Then another pop and Reggie realized *Bobbie Faye just killed her friend* and Reggie must've made some noise, some gasp at having gotten that on tape, because when she looked up into the woman's eyes, she realized two things: she'd been seen and it was the biggest mistake of her life.

A bullet sliced through DJ's chest before he had a chance to know what happened. He dropped to the ground and the camera bounced and rolled.

"Donny, you're an idiot," the woman said, and then there was a pop and Donny clutched his stomach and fell to his knees.

"Bye, Reg," was the last thing Reggie heard, and she felt herself go white hot and then cold, and realized she was on the ground, bleeding out. She thought, stupidly, about how pissed she was that she finally had the kind of exclusive that would have gotten her on every morning talk show in America, and she wasn't going to live to use it. And then she thought of her son, Nathan, how he looked holding that big fish, his smile practically as big as his body, and then he was waving at her.

Chapter Twenty-five

Bobbie Faye spread the two photos on the table and said to Trevor, "This is what I was rushing to show you earlier." She tapped on the right-hand side of each photo. The time elapsed from the first to the second was probably about ten years, from the changes she could see in her aunts' appearances and clothing styles. Marie sat in the center of the sofa in both photos. There was a young man roughly her age to her left in each picture, but not the same man.

"I remember this one," she tapped the later one where she and Francesca huddled on the floor in front of the sofa. "And that's Emile." She tapped the deeply tanned man in the latest photo. "That, isn't." She tapped the man in the other photo. "Familiar?" she asked the men, and while she wasn't entirely sure Trevor would recognize the man, she knew Cam would.

"Holy shit," Cam said, once he pulled it closer. "I didn't know Marie dated the governor."

"I don't know the details, but they broke up in college and that's when she met Emile."

"She doesn't look as much like you as V'rai does," Trevor said, scrutinizing one of the photos. He was right—it was eerie how much V'rai looked like her; Bobbie Faye had never noticed because, well, duh, the family had never included her from her preteens forward. Even when she first glanced at the photo, the hair and clothes of a different era distracted her from seeing the similarities.

"What I really don't get," she said, "more, even, than the whole 'frame-me-for-murder'—"

"That should tell you something right there," Cam muttered, and when she glared at him, he said, "that you live in such a way where 'framing you for murder' can somehow not be the biggest thing that confuses you."

"Bite me," she said. "What I was saying, though, is why would Marie have put that note in her day planner, indicating me?" She had to explain to Cam what that was.

"Cute. You didn't mention that this morning."

"You were being the King of Annoying this morning. And I haven't talked to Marie in . . . well, I think since Francesca was a senior."

Cam's phone rang and he stepped away from the table to answer. She brainstormed over all of those threads tangling, and as she started unraveling them, she had an idea—and then Cam doubled over, leaning against the peninsula as if he'd been kicked, hard, and he said, "Dear, God, no. Is he—" and he shook as the caller answered. His skin took on a clammy sheen. "No fucking way. No, I'll tell you later. I'll be there."

"What?" she asked when he turned to her, and oh, God, "Stacey?"

"No, Benoit." She froze, because she knew he'd only be reeling if it was terrible. "He's been shot." She couldn't even form the words to ask him the next question and he shook his head. "He's breathing, but he's lost a lot of blood. He's on his way to surgery now."

She'd moved before she realized what she was doing, going to Cam, wrapping her arms around him in comfort as he continued. "She shot him in the back," he said, enveloping her, his voice cracking. "Fucking shot him in the back. They don't know if he's going to make it. And that's not all," he said, leaning her so that she tilted up to see his face. "Reggie and her cameraman are dead.

Your cousin, Donny, shot in the stomach. They think Donny's going to live, but he's also going into surgery."

"Who?" she gasped and then realized that Trevor was on his phone behind her. She turned to him as she heard him curse and hang up.

"According to a preliminary view of the cameraman's tape," Trevor said, his expression grim, "the killer . . . is you."

The world tipped on its axis, then. Just fucking flipped over, *Hi there floor, how'ya' doin'? Think I'll splat down here for a while.* Except she never hit the floor—and she thought maybe Cam had caught her, but she opened her eyes and realized Trevor cradled her, and he carried her to the sofa. As she tried to wrap her mind around the news (which it determinedly stamped "return to sender" each and every single time), Cam handed her a glass of juice. Orange juice.

Benoit had been shot.

Orange juice. Shooting. Orange juice. *Shooting.*

She stared at that glass, locked on the color, lost in the memories of drinking juice Saturday night, the night the jeweler was murdered. Drinking the juice and then feeling strange, and having such terrible dreams about shooting . . . Sal. Odd voices piped into her memory, voices she recognized, but had thought they were a part of her warped imagination, until now. When she looked up, she realized Cam had said, "She needs to eat, god*damn*it, she's never done this."

"She *has* eaten," Trevor said, words which might as well have had a big comic strip bubble above them with "back the fuck off" in all caps.

She stared at the orange color of the juice and pieces of memory fell back into chronological order; it hadn't been a dream. She should have suspected the next morning when she had a gun in her hand, should have wondered a little more about the cotton mouth. She'd been roofied: the date-rape drug. She'd been given just enough of a dose to make her compliant. Enough to fuck with her memory, so that she'd think it was all a dream. Bobbie Faye hadn't read the details of the jeweler murder in the paper. She had thought she'd been coming down with the crazy, the way her Aunt V'rai had, able to see things ahead of time.

"I'm okay, Cam. Benoit's in Baton Rouge?" He nodded. "You go see him. See how he's doing. We'll be headed that direction as soon as I can arrange stuff."

"What?" Cam asked.

"You know where the diamonds are," Trevor said, seeing her determined expression.

"You damned well better not go after them yourself," Cam said, and there was more than just cop bossiness going on. There was fear. "Benoit's been *shot*. They think you shot a *cop*. You'll be dead before you can explain anything."

"But . . . you and Trevor *both* know I couldn't have shot him! I've been here."

"They're not going to believe me," Cam said, pissed off and slamming his hands through his hair. "They'll assume I'm covering for you."

"They don't know about the casings. You have never covered for me in the past. Why would they assume that now?"

He cut her a look, a *get real* expression. *Oh.* Hmmm. Maybe he had done more than she realized.

"They won't believe me, either," Trevor said and she caught his apologetic grimace. "They'll assume I'm compromised, since we're dating."

Cam seemed to flinch, but Bobbie Faye wasn't looking at him directly, so she wasn't entirely sure. "See?" he said, "You'll be *killed*. Don't do anything stupid."

"I could tell you that I'm going to hand everything over to Trevor and let the Feds handle it."

"You've never lied before, so don't start now. Tell me who you think it is." He choked up, devastated.

"Go see Benoit, Cam."

"*Tell* me."

"I've got to figure some things out. You've got enough to deal with."

Cam glared at Trevor. "If she gets hurt, I'm coming after you."

Dear God, just this once, just this one time, please please please let her be the planny type.

Cam walked onto the back part of the wraparound porch of the cabin with Bobbie Faye, and he knew he should just leave, climb on that motorcycle and go see his partner. In the late evening light, he noticed something blue at her hairline and without thinking, he held her chin in one hand and lightly rubbed his thumb over the smudge. Whatever it was, it was gone, but he lingered there a moment, and she stared at him with those big green eyes, and Cam knew what she was thinking: this change in him was about Benoit, and how upset he was, because Benoit could very easily die. His grief swallowed him, and yet, he'd realized something: at the precise minute she'd rushed to comfort him, at the second that had been her instinct, his headache had simply evaporated. He'd breathed again, without the pain throbbing deep into his shoulders, and he didn't quite know what that meant.

He hadn't realized he still held her chin in his hand; the moment grew awkward and she backed away.

"You stay safe," he said, wishing he had used a different tone, less antagonistic. Why in the hell couldn't he just *talk* to her— they used to do that so well.

"I promise. Completely safe."

He looked her over as she attempted something that might have been called "completely innocent" on someone else. Now he knew why she never lied.

"Do me a favor, Baby. Don't take up poker."

•　　•　　•

Lori Ann was about to beat the crap out of Roy; they had stopped for gas and he was flirting with the manager's wife, which was making the manager extremely unhappy (and the poor man was going to give himself a heart attack sucking in his gut for as long as Roy had been standing at the counter). She marveled at just how very little survival instincts her brother possessed.

"Oh, the bridge is out, sweetie," the wife said. "Your sister's been at it again. I hear it might be another hour before they get it fixed. The police are checking everybody who tries to take a boat over. Unless you can do that flying squirrel thing, you might have a long wait."

Lori Ann stood there with her big fountain drink (and Roy had watched her like a hawk around the liquor aisle. "I am not saving Bobbie Faye's ass so she can kill me over you drinking," he whined. Wimp.). She had a pile of candy bars she set on the counter.

"And who's this cute little thing?" the husband asked, beaming.

"Oh, that? That's my little sister."

"Bobbie Faye has a baby sister!" the man said. "Wow, that is so nice." He leaned toward her. "Can you get me her autograph?"

"Oh, Jesus," Roy said, flinching, and the man immediately looked wary, caged as he was by his wife and the counter, so that he was within striking distance of Lori Ann. Roy grabbed her shoulders, steering her out as she yanked the bag of candy bars from the wife, who was giving her husband that *if you only had a brain* glare. "She's a little touchy about that," Roy explained as they left.

Just what she needed, on top of having to be Bobbie Faye's sister: being invisible.

When Bobbie Faye re-entered the cabin, Trevor stood facing the back windows, which overlooked the lake. She took a couple of steps inside and it hit her: *people were dead.* Her friend was fighting for his life in surgery. Trevor walked toward where she stood still, doing that whole pillar-of-salt imitation, shock putting her body into lockdown. She'd thought she'd known *bad* before, but this was the capitol city of Bad, the entire empire of Bad. And now she knew the killer had been right in front of her the entire time.

She started shivering. Volcanic, *hi, let's have an earthquake,* shaking. Trevor folded his arms around her, holding her, and swayed a little, almost rocking her. Everything that had transpired over the last two days slammed into her thoughts, a head-on collision she couldn't veer away from.

"Couldn't compartmentalize."

"Couldn't escape."

Her throat burned and her eyes stung and the ache in her chest weighed a million pounds. It seared like hot metal, too big to fight, too harsh to ignore.

Everything she'd ignored, all the screaming, raging pain, and heartbreak.

She leaned into Trevor as he stroked her back and kissed her temple. She didn't miss the irony that this man, this former assassin, this agent, was refuge. She hid her face against his shoulder because if he didn't see her cry, then technically, she didn't have to admit to it. She wasn't entirely sure how long they'd stood there, but after a while, she finally felt calm.

"Calm" of course being a euphemism for fucking *furious.*

"Cam was right," Trevor said, and she could see he wasn't happy admitting it. "If he could get across the river and find us, we have to assume others can, too. We should have kept moving."

"Don't." She put a hand on his chest. She'd lost too much today. She wasn't going to let regret steal something so important. "We're not Super Heroes."

"Do I need to remind you about the shower already?"

"Damn, you're going to be hard to live with." Oh, hell. She blushed. "Shut up," she said, fingertips against his lips to stop him from building on the pun. "Besides, who's to say we couldn't have been tracked to any hotel or any other place we'd have holed up in?"

He seemed reluctant to accept that, but finally nodded. "Ready to kick some ass?"

"Oh, *fuck,* yeah."

"And would this be Francesca's ass we're kicking?"

"I just put it together. How did you—"

"The double image Cam described. Whoever killed Sal would have to look enough like you to expect to fool the surveillance cameras, and she obviously planned on being caught on video, given where she lured Sal to stand."

"Why drag me out there, why not just plant my DNA? Oh!" she said, before he answered. "The eyewitnesses. She knew my trailer park manager and Mrs. Oubillard would recognize a fake. She needed at least one of them to confirm I wasn't home or was near the crime scene."

"But the double image on the footage Benoit had gives away the game."

"So she went after Benoit to get it. But she's reacting there. Sal was planned. Why?"

They hunted for their shoes so they could leave.

"It's classic misdirection. Too many people after the diamonds means—"

"She needs everyone to believe someone else has them while she gets away. So I'm the fall guy." The more the shock subsided, the angrier she felt. *Furious* wasn't even beginning to describe the white-hot searing rage boiling through her. "I'll bet she found a second set of the diamonds and needed to know which ones were real. That's the only thing that makes sense—why go to Sal in the first place? She knew as soon as she asked him questions about the diamonds, he'd tell her mom. So she plans to kill him as soon as she's asked him, so he can't talk to Marie. And if she were to suddenly disappear, everyone—"

"Including MacGreggor—"

"Would immediately try to track her down. But if I'm the suspect, she's bought herself some time. That explains the babbling."

"The what?"

Oh, shit. She hadn't told him. She explained the drugged orange juice and the dream-that-wasn't-a-dream. "And Sal was babbling when he died about there being fakes. I was so out of it, I thought he meant my boobs. I mean *her* boobs." Trevor looked amused. "Hey, hers are smaller and she was wearing falsies. They were crooked! It was a logical conclusion for a drugged woman, give me a break. But he was telling her there were more fakes."

"So now we know why she didn't just leave town after she framed you."

"You realize she's been playing the complete ditz for so many years, everyone has bought it."

"I know. And we have absolutely no proof you didn't commit Sal's murder, but we can probably put you here for Benoit's shooting and the new murders."

"How? With Crazy Carmen as my stellar corroboration? You and Cam are suspect and no one else has seen me here."

"I'll get you out of the country."

She blinked. He was serious.

"I'm not going to let you sit in jail."

She grinned at him, and he began to look wary.

"You have that 'I have a plan' look," he said.

"I *do* have a plan."

"Okay, now you're scaring me."

Back in Ce Ce's office, as the sound of construction repairs echoed around them, Ce Ce and Monique frowned at the plastic container of blue gel. Monique poked at it, but the gel simply lay there. Completely still.

"I think it's broken.

Ce Ce sank her face in her hands. "She must not have heard

the part about not washing it off for twenty-four hours. It's got to stay on that long for the spell to last."

"Ce Ce!" one of the twins shouted from the store front. "Quick, come see!"

Monique just barely beat her out of the office doorway, using her short, squatty linebacker build to elbow Ce Ce out of the way. They ran into the main store and found the twins and a couple of construction workers gaping up at the TV above the little dinette area. The slick young woman anchor had a very practiced somber expression.

"As we reported, we do not yet have the details, but it is confirmed that our own Reggie O'Connor and cameraman DJ Millerville have been shot and killed while on location. We believe there are two other shooting victims, both in critical condition. The state police have put out an APB for our own Contraband Days Queen, citing her as a 'suspect' and not just a 'person of interest' in this case. If you see Miss Sumrall, you are encouraged not to try to bring her in yourself, but to call the state police, as it is assumed she may be armed and dangerous. We have the state police hotline number listed at the bottom of our screen."

The anchor moved on to the next story and Ce Ce reached for the remote and turned off the TV.

"Man, the Bad Ju Ju has really got it in for that girl," Monique said as they all stared at one another, construction workers included.

"Kinda like global warming," one of the construction workers said. When they all looked at him like he was crazy, he explained, "They warn you about it and you think you're doing stuff to help, and no matter what you do, the universe is gonna fry your ass anyway."

"Hmph," Ce Ce muttered, "we'll just see about that."

Bobbie Faye dug through her purse as she made the phone calls she needed to make, and she pulled out the cards and miscellaneous junk she'd been packing around since Marie's. As she shook it all onto Roy's little kitchen table, a small round disk fell out and rolled half-way across the enamel finish like a penny, only it was black and a little thicker.

"Sonofabitch," Trevor muttered, and grabbed it up and turned it over. It looked like a very expensive high-tech gizmo, and from Trevor's expression, she was going to go with the wild-ass guess of "tracking device." "We dumped everything out of your purse earlier." She nodded. "When in the hell?"

Bobbie Faye thought over the morning. "Fuck. The blonde in the gas station—asked me for a light. I think she might have been the same woman as the redhead that was with MacGreggor later at the silo."

They heard footsteps on the pier out front and Trevor had his SIG ready, flanked the door, and peered out the window beside it. "Goddamnit."

"MacGreggor?"

"Worse." He opened the door as Roy was reaching for it, and a very sour Lori Ann fumed behind him.

"How did you get across the river?" Trevor asked, scanning out the window for other movement.

"I've got lots of escape routes and contingency plans," Roy explained. "Hidden cars, couple of boats, places I know I can land that no one knows about."

"You need a safer dating life," Bobbie Faye told her brother.

"Yeah, like you're the big expert there."

Trevor grew unhappier by the second. "We need to get out of here. Now."

"What the hell are y'all doing here?" Bobbie Faye asked her siblings, and then to Lori Ann, "Please tell me you did not just walk out of there without permission."

Lori Ann's little pert bow-shaped lips formed a line so thin, they almost disappeared.

"I don't think she's speaking to you, yet," Roy said. "But she made me come so we could—oof." He doubled over, as Lori Ann elbowed him. "We came to help."

"You turn around and take her back. She's got to finish this stint or they won't let her out at the end of the month."

"You're my sister," Lori Ann said evenly. "Not my boss, not my jailer, not my conscience." She stomped up to Bobbie Faye, so short that she barely came to Bobbie Faye's chin. "So just *shut up* and listen."

"We don't have long," Trevor interrupted, bouncing the GPS unit in his palm.

"He's the agent guy?" Lori Ann asked Roy, and Roy nodded. "You," she said to Trevor, pointing at him, "stay out of this."

"I," he said, gently, to Bobbie Faye's surprise, "care too damned much for your sister—I am trying to keep her from getting killed."

"Well, okay, then, good plan. I'll speed this up." She turned to Bobbie Faye. "You don't get to keep bossing me around, telling me that I should have come to you for help with the drinking and with Stacey and then you just go run around, blowing up half the state!" When Bobbie Faye started to interrupt, Lori Ann held up her palm. "And then you were *blue*! And being *shot at*! And then the silo! And the fire! I'm not completely incompetent, you know. I *could help*."

"I don't want you to get hurt!"

"So it's okay for *you* to get hurt? It's okay for the Great Almighty Bobbie Faye to never have to ask anyone for anything?"

"I . . ." Fuck. She wanted to be angry. Hell, she was an expert in Angry, and probably could get certified in Immature, too, but she saw the tiny tremble of Lori Ann's lips, and realized, holy shit, she mattered to Lori Ann. Really mattered. And her sister was afraid of losing her. She pulled Lori Ann into a hug, and her little sister hugged her back . . . hard.

"I hate to break this up," Trevor said, and walked to the back door, about to toss the GPS unit into the lake; Bobbie Faye stopped him, grinning. She had an idea, and he gave her his sternest FBI worried look.

"Trust me," she said, and she held out her palm.

"Trusting you doesn't mean I think you're sane," he groused, but he dropped the unit into her hand. "We have to get moving. You have everything set?"

She turned to hand the GPS unit to Lori Ann, about to fill her siblings in on where to go and what to do, when she suddenly wondered aloud, "Wait—how'd you know I was here?"

Roy turned a deep red and pointed to the mounted fish that had fallen to the floor earlier and said, "Um, I like to be able to check and see if anyone's been here while I'm gone, because, um, you know—some guys get a little bent—and I had one of those little cameras installed in Henry over there . . . I can pick up the images on my cell phone."

"Oh. My. God," she said, when she realized what he had seen of her and Trevor earlier.

"Yeah. I gotta go dig my eyes out with a spoon now."

"I'll help."

Cam rushed into the antiseptic corridors of the hospital, sprinting past chiding nurses, hurdling over carts, and dodging around wheelchaired patients until he rounded the corner where a large number of fellow cops milled about, drinking bad coffee and looking glum, but stoic.

"Any word?"

"No, not really," one of the officers, an older, tired cop named Amon said. "They're working on stabilizing him and there's a neurosurgeon that came out a few minutes ago just to tell us that they're going to be operating soon. He's got one bullet very near his spine and one in his shoulder."

Cam didn't think it was possible to grow colder, but his hands went icy. "Spine?"

"That Bobbie Faye bitch shot him in the back," the man said. Then realizing who he was speaking to, "Sir. Sorry."

"She didn't do this." Nearly all of the cops shook their heads, disgusted.

"You gotta be kidding," Amon said, losing all pretense of respecting Cam's rank. "Even *you've* got to see she's out of control."

"No." He needed them to know, to believe, so they wouldn't be gunning for her. "She wasn't there. This is a mistake—she—"

"Seriously?" a young big cop, Eric, snapped. He was the kind of man whose idea of "subtle" was refraining from shooting someone, and he unraveled as he stepped between Amon and Cam, getting into Cam's face, actually looking down into Cam's eyes, which put his height over six-four. He outweighed Cam by at least seventy-five pounds. "I think you're too damned close."

"Back down," Cam instructed, but the man—who had been mentored by Benoit—made no sign of hearing him.

"That's your friend in there," the big man gestured toward the surgery wing, "and you're still defending her! You're blind, man. You always help her get out of trouble and now you can't see that she's completely played you."

"First, you don't know what you're talking about. She *wasn't there*. She was—"

"I think she's twisted you nine ways to Sunday. We have her *on the cameraman's tape*. How much more is it going to take? You let her run around, blowing things up, and now *murdering* people and *shooting cops*. Someone needs to take her down. If you're too whipped—"

Cam wasn't even aware he'd clenched his fist and thrown a punch until Eric landed on the floor, out cold. Cam stood over his fellow officer, both satisfied and horrified. Several of the other cops knelt, helping Eric as the captain huffed out of the triage area, his ruddy complexion especially florid and a sweaty sheen glistening on his receding hairline. He took in the situation with one sweeping glance.

"Moreau, get your ass in here," he said, indicating a waiting room.

Cam followed him to the partially secluded waiting area, aware that his fellow officers were being particularly quiet in order to hear what the captain said.

"I don't know what the hell has gotten into you lately, but you're just not yourself. You're usually the most levelheaded cop I've got and look at you. You punch a hole in the wall, you go missing for half the day, you don't call in, and now you knock out a fellow officer. I think you've got to take time."

"No, Sir," Cam argued, vehemently. "I've got a break on this case. Bobbie Faye wasn't there. I can prove it."

"Then turn all your notes over to Fordoche."

"Sir, I'm fine. She didn't—"

"Turn it over, Detective. Period. If she didn't shoot Benoit, fine, but if she shot a cop, I don't want her in a position to talk her way out of this one. She's going to have to deal with *me*. Not you. As of right now, you're on leave until this case is solved." Cam started to argue and the captain put his hand up. "No. Go somewhere, cool off. We'll call your cell phone as soon as Benoit comes out of surgery and I'll let you see him, as his friend, but not as a cop. Now go."

Cam struggled with what to say. He'd lost the woman he loved, he was in danger of losing his best friend, and now his job, since it was clear the captain didn't believe a word he said. Maybe someone else saw them go into the camp and could place Bobbie Faye away from the scene of the crime.

"You'll be back on duty when this is over and you'll thank me for it," the captain said, dismissing him. Cam nodded, knowing that nothing he said was going to make any difference.

As the captain walked away, he turned, pausing as if this were an afterthought. "You know anything about that surveillance footage Benoit was supposed to have had in his truck?"

"I've heard the rumors. Why?"

"It went missing. Damn fool girl went to all that trouble to get that footage back, and then she forgets the cameraman's camera.

She's losing it, Cam. You stay away from her. If she'll shoot Benoit, she'll shoot you."

The captain stalked back to the area where the other cops were murmuring and Cam knew their minds were made up. He saw a TV mounted in the waiting area—silent, though the picture was on—showing a terrible old photo of Bobbie Faye with an "armed and dangerous" banner slapped above it and "wanted by the police" below. She was going to be in every yahoo-with-a-gun's crosshairs. His phone rang as he left the hospital; he hadn't even been sure where to go, how to help, until that call.

Chapter Twenty-six

Zooming up and over the Mississippi River bridge—
particularly on the Harley—reintroduced Bobbie Faye to
her old friend Fear of Heights and his best buddy, Panic Attack. It did not help that her brother followed too closely. He was
probably going to run over her while he argued with Lori Ann.

The wide black river rolled lazily beneath her and as they
reached the peak of the bridge arch, she could see Baton Rouge's
Old State Capitol off to her left, just beyond one of the riverboat
casinos and the downtown USS *Kidd* museum. The Old State Capitol stood out from the rest of the normal French and Spanish archi-
tecture, with its unusual castle construction: four stories, with
towers flanking the front and back entrances. It had been built in
the early 1800s on a natural levee that overlooked the expansive
lawn that sloped down to the Mississippi River, and had been saved
(and burned and salvaged) over the years.

One of the postcards from Marie's had indicated that she
would have several pieces at the Art Show benefit hosted by the
governor in the old building tonight. The FBI had assured Trevor
that all of those pieces had been thoroughly inspected and there
were no diamonds to be found.

Bobbie Faye knew Marie was wilier than that.

Worse, now she knew Francesca was wilier than that.

The reality flooded in. . . .

People are dead.

People are *dead.*

Benoit's been *shot*

Don't think about it. How do you put that into a compartment and shut it away and deal with it after a disaster is over? *Don't think about it.* How does the horror not claw against its confines? *Don't think about it.* How could she keep putting one foot in front of another, keep moving forward, find a way to end the nightmare? *Don't think about it.*

The black river pushed the dark banks wide apart, and she felt as if she and Trevor hung there over the enormous void of the mirrored water. They were suspened in the darkness, the hum of the bike the only thing that riveted her to this world, the rhythm of the tires slapping against the bridge's construction joints like a staccato drum line underneath a bluesy song. It was one of the few places in Louisiana where the inky horizon felt big and open and not crowded with trees, and even though there were lights to the city and even though there were lights on the bridge and even though there were headlights and taillights from the cars speeding nearby, Bobbie Faye felt swallowed up by the great big darkness of the night.

She fucking hated the dark.

It was hard not to *think* in the dark.

So, as she and Trevor raced down the bridge, Adrenaline was talking about unionizing Fear and Flight because they were seriously overworked and underpaid. She just could not give in. She *would* not give in.

They exited the off-ramp, speeding past the large River Center entertainment complex and then up the natural bluff and parked at the building next to the Old State Capitol. The all-glass Manship Theater was stunning in its minimalist lines and with its proximity to the castle next door, it seemed as if its owners were intent on showing the juxtaposition of the passing centuries . . .

and Bobbie Faye hoped it would make it to the next decade, because her first thought when she saw all of the glass: *fuck*. This was *asking* for Trouble to show up with a torpedo and a bad attitude.

Everything for the big televised Art Benefit that evening was being set up inside the Capitol. Floodlights washed over the sides of the castle while wait staff and valets for parking milled about; caterers scurried, carrying in trays and tables and scads of linens from the big catering vans parked a block away. Trevor climbed off the bike after Bobbie Faye, and they watched as Roy parked his car, unfolded himself lazily and sauntered up to one of the vans; she thought at least four of the waitresses were going to collectively bean him in the head with their trays—apparently, his womanizing reputation extended beyond Lake Charles—but they pointed him toward the woman who appeared to be in charge. When that big, bosomy woman gave him a backbreaking hug, Bobbie Faye figured Roy and Lori Ann would be able to carry out their part of the plan. Of course, that's when she saw Lori Ann eyeing the liquor part of the catering supplies with the same expression Stacey got when she gazed upon the candy aisle: pure nirvana was almost within her grasp. Yep. Trouble. Torpedo. And Bobbie Faye had a target painted on her back.

"You're sure you want to do this?" Trevor asked. "I could have the whole place in lockdown, and we'd find the diamonds."

"But with no evidence for the murders." No, there was *no way* that was going to happen. "Just show me the stupid dress I have to wear. I can't believe I let you talk me into this."

He grinned, and she knew she was going to regret trying to be the planny type. "Hey," he shrugged a little too innocently, "it was the contact I happened to have, and the quickest way to get you inside the benefit."

She followed him through the double glass doors of the theater building into a massive, high-ceilinged glass entrance. He greeted and seemed completely at one with the quintet of well-dressed men who, in spite of the spiffy rental tuxes, looked like they had a thousand years of wear on their faces and could personally attest to every line of every blues song written. Trevor slapped a handshake on the oldest—a guy in his sixties who cradled his saxophone like a beloved child; the man turned and handed the wad of cash Trevor had just given him to the next man, who peeled off hundreds and passed them out. Each man got at least three.

"Holy geez," Bobbie Faye muttered, aware of her voice echoing in the cavernous room. "Since when did you turn into an ATM machine?"

"When I started traveling with a woman who's destroyed half of the state and the other half doesn't take the Universal Platinum Card."

One of the band members grabbed a bag that was lying over an instrument case and hauled out the tiny red kerchief. "This was Della's, but Trev here paid her to go home. I think she's about your size." He handed her the "dress" and the shoes.

"Where's the rest of it?" When they all grinned, she said, "Oh, no fucking way. You'll have to shoot me, first."

"Hey, you wanted to be able to get into the benefit without anyone realizing who you were. Best way to do that is for them to think they recognize you because you're in the band."

"Or the local hooker," she griped, but that apparently wasn't a negative argument for the men.

Just as Bobbie Faye pushed her way into the restroom to change into the dress, she could hear Francesca griping as she came barreling into the lobby area. Her high heels clicked on the tile floor, the sound reverberating off the glass windows; Mitch and Kit trailed behind. From what Bobbie Faye could hear of the conversation, Francesca pulled a serious amount of diva for not being included in any plans except where to show up. Bobbie Faye gritted her teeth and tried to ignore her cousin as she attempted to change into the dress.

There was just no way this scrap of material was an actual item of clothing, and she turned it several directions before figuring out which part was the top, which just did not bode well. After six tries, wherein she discovered that the part she thought was the top was the sleeve, she was pretty sure she finally had it on correctly. She took a look in the bathroom mirror and knew that if she made it through the night without flashing the world, it was going to be a miracle on the level of the second coming. She could have spray-painted her body and gotten more coverage than this thing, and she tugged and tried to squeeze the boobs better into the bodice of the dress and it just was hopeless. She was going to kill Trevor for this one.

"This is a good room—plenty big enough to shoot someone," Mitch's voice rumbled, carrying back to where Bobbie Faye gathered up her own clothes, and there were many simultaneous exclamations from the band members along the lines of *what the hell did he say* and *dude, chill*.

"Don't worry," Kit answered the other's concerns, "he's not loaded." And then she proceeded to grill the band as to whether or not they had any prior convictions and just what area of illegal activities did they want to concentrate on, and it sounded like Kit was handing out her business card. Great.

As Bobbie Faye screwed up her courage to walk out of the bathroom, she heard Francesca ask Trevor, "Why are you helping Bobbie Faye? I didn't think Daddy paid anyone enough to get almost blown up this much."

Bobbie Faye walked into the lobby in time to hear him say, "I'm not working for your dad anymore." His voice resonated, deep and warm like a strong bourbon, sending a shiver up Bobbie Faye's spine. It stunned her to see the other new arrivals: her dad, V'rai, and her Uncle Antoine—none of whom seemed to faze Trevor. "Bobbie Faye's my . . ." he looked up just as she stepped into the room and she instantly knew that there was not enough *dress* to the dress because his eyes went completely dark and his smile, predatory ". . . fiancée," he finished, striding over to put an arm around her.

"Oh, yeah?" she asked him, laughing, knowing he was joking just to rattle Francesca.

"Yeah," he said, openly admiring that dress. "I know, Wooing 101. I bought the CliffsNotes version."

Francesca looked harried and unpolished; her clothes had that thrown-together-in-the-dark look: nothing matched, particularly the still-bright-flamingo pink-feathered purse, which clashed so mightily with the yellow top that Bobbie Faye thought she might be temporarily blinded. For Francesca, this was the equivalent of a complete psychotic meltdown, and her cousin sputtered, "Fiancée? She's not wearing a ring!"

"She will be," Trevor said.

"Does Cam know about this, Bobbie Faye? Because everybody knows he's your boyfriend and it's just really not fair for you to get Cam and this guy, too. I don't think Cam's gonna be too happy about this."

Trevor clasped her hand and looked Bobbie Faye in the eye— he was studiously, purposefully not rising to the bait.

"Daddy's gonna have a cow," Francesca said when Trevor ignored her. She turned on Bobbie Faye, tapping her toe, "And you! You left me at Aunt V'rai's! You're supposed to stay with us, and help me keep Mamma from getting killed. And I don't think marrying the help is exactly what we talked about!"

"I *am* helping you, Frannie. That's why I called and told you to meet me here. I know something about how to find the diamonds that no one else knows—and I have a way to make sure they're the real ones."

"What are you talking about?"

"Where's the rest of your dress?" her dad interrupted.

"Don't even start with criticizing me," Bobbie Faye warned him. "You weren't invited. Just Uncle Antoine."

"Yes, I was," her dad said.

"Who invited you?" She looked at Trevor and he shook his head, which left only one other suspect, yet to arrive. "I'm going to kill someone," she mumbled.

"Wouldn't try it in that dress," her dad said, "unless you're planning on flashin' 'em to death."

"Etienne, be nice," V'rai coaxed. "I bet she's *une beaute fillé, mais non?*"

"And you, Aunt V'rai, don't even try to make good now. You could have warned me a little more clearly about the whole silo blowing up thing!"

"No she couldn't, *chère,*" Antoine said, and it was the first time in years that she'd heard him speak. She was startled to hear how much like her dad he sounded—they looked so much alike, it shouldn't surprise her, but it always had. "Any time she ever tried to help, it only made things worse."

"And we didn't think you'd live through anything made worse," V'rai said.

"Especially when you don't even have sense enough to wear shoes," Etienne added.

Everyone looked down at her bare feet and she glared at him.

"I'm beginning to see why you shot him last time," Trevor offered.

"You have no idea." Bobbie Faye held up the stiletto heels to him and said, "These straps hurt. Can you—" Trevor dug out his pocketknife, cutting off the back straps, turning them into slides, and Francesca nearly fainted.

"Ohmygod," Francesca gasped, "you just desecrated the Power of Cute Shoes!"

"And they look great on her," Cam said, standing in the open doorway of the entrance. Then his gaze trailed up her body and over the snug, too-tight dress and his eyes dilated and he appeared to be very appreciative, and she immediately felt self-conscious. She glanced down at her cleavage and realized everything was almost spilling out again.

"Damnit, this dress is too small," she muttered and Cam coughed, hard.

"No, Baby, I'd say—" and he caught Trevor's glare "—you're fine," he finished, looking back at her.

"Bobbie Faye," Francesca snapped, "this is not a fashion show, though you really need to let me fix your foundation. You're supposed to help me find—"

"And Benoit?" Bobbie Faye asked, interrupting her cousin.

"Still in surgery," Cam answered, and Bobbie Faye felt the knot in her chest. Dear God, just let him be okay.

"You're not here to arrest her," Trevor stated, not being all that subtle about putting himself between her and Cam, and why in the hell did she think she could have a *plan* without it spiraling out of control?

"No," Cam said, and then added, looking directly into Bobbie Faye's eyes, "you don't have to protect her from me."

"Wait—how'd you know I was here?" This was so not going the way she expected, and if the cops were coming to the party, she was dead. She really didn't want to die in a red dress that was probably featured on the Whore's Uniform Daily Web site. Cam made a phone call motion with his hand and Bobbie Faye was going to kill a certain little Bluebird of Telephonitis when she got the chance.

"By the way," he asked, "how in the hell, did you manage to have dispatch convinced you were running through the swamps, heading for Texas?"

"Nina—she landed in New York and she's been 'talking' to me ever since." Bobbie Faye smiled, thinking about how frustrated that had made Nina, who wanted to get back to Baton Rouge instead of waiting there, misdirecting the cops. "You remember Old Trapper Crowe?" Cam grinned—and she knew he remembered the old Chickasaw Indian who was older than God, who still tooled around the swamps, trading furs and whatever he could. No one knew where he lived, but he had a deep affection for Bobbie Faye and brought her candy every spring equinox. "He did me a favor, took the phone with his dog and a bateau. He could be halfway to Galveston by now."

"You should stay away from that old *coo-yôn*," her dad snapped. "He ain't nothin' but crazy."

"Not half as crazy as her own family," Cam said, his arms crossed, his cop glare hard—and every muscle she had lockstepped into attention.

"You . . . *knew?*" She'd always assumed he believed her dad had died. How had there been so much they had never talked about?

He shrugged. "I suspected, and you look just like V'rai. You didn't want to talk about it," he said to her obvious surprise, "so we didn't talk about it. One of several mistakes I'm not going to repeat." He gave Trevor a look. One of those male, *you have been warned,* stares.

Trevor returned the favor. Tension swamped the room, as aggressive as gang members breathing on their necks, thugs brushing by and hovering too close. She so wanted to get the hell out of there. *Jesus, where was spontaneous combustion when you needed it?*

"Bobbie Faye—" Francesca tried again, growing even more upset, but the double doors burst open and everyone spun, with Trevor and Cam and her dad and her uncle and every single member of the band coming up with guns, aimed at the door. Monique squeaked and threw her hands up in the air as she and Ce Ce stumbled into the room.

"Sorry, sorry," Monique babbled, "but we were in a hurry." She turned to Ce Ce, who looked scared half out of her wits. "See? I told you we'd make it in time if we broke one-twenty."

"You let her drive?" Bobbie Faye asked, incredulous. Ce Ce nodded, her massive chest heaving from overwhelming adrenaline, not having yet caught her breath. "And she did one-twenty?" Ce Ce held up three fingers. "One-thirty? Good grief, Ce Ce, how much has she been drinking?"

"Honey, I quit asking after she hit a hundred. I didn't want to distract her."

"Bobbie Faye!" Francesca snapped, stomping her foot on the tile, and it echoed. "What's going on? I thought you were going to find the diamonds!"

"I am," she said, smiling. "And Ce Ce's going to do a special locator spell to help."

John had followed the idiot brother and the drunk of a sister all the way from Lake Charles out to the camp, and just before he could get completely set up with his rifle and scope, they had all come out of the camp and were leaving. He couldn't fucking *believe* it. They were gone before he climbed back in his car, and he had to follow them again—keeping a safe distance. He'd hoped to kill everyone else and wound her, and then force the bitch to tell him where the diamonds were. Now, he didn't know what their plan was, and he had a hard time staying in sight of the brother's car, especially since the Fed on the bike drove like he was God and owned all of the speeding laws.

It pissed him the hell off that they'd driven all the way to Baton Rouge, but he kept reminding himself: diamonds. He'd kill Bobbie Faye after she gave them to him, just for the sheer pleasure of getting to rub her nose in it—that he'd tried to ask her out, tried to be a boyfriend, and what does she go and do? Get a fucking restraining order on him.

He'd tried to make her see reason. They put him in jail for that. Fucking *jail*. She had no idea what they did to him in jail, but she was going to learn. He'd been waiting for this chance for *years*. When the word went out from a fence that a buyer needed her stopped? He jumped at the job. Hell, he'd have taken it for free.

When they got to the Old State Capitol, though, he worried that his quarry might slip from his grasp—there were so many people, he couldn't see where she'd gone. There was obviously some gala being set up, and lots of press there, so it wasn't like he could just pop her asshole Fed escort in the street and then force her to hand him the diamonds.

He had to think. There had to be a good contingency . . . ah. He saw it. He knew where he'd set up and there was no fucking way she'd ever get out of his sight.

T his is insane," Lori Ann griped as she pulled on the waitress uniform. Roy was dressed in a waiter's uniform already and had his back turned to her; he peered out the door, acting as a lookout.

"Yep," he said. "Hurry up."

"Why in the hell did we agree to do this?"

"You're the idiot that wanted to help."

"I'm the family drunk! Since when do you listen to me?"

"Since you threatened to e-mail every woman I've ever dated with my new home address."

"Oh. Right. Wimp."

"C'mon, we have to go plant that thing." He nodded toward the little GPS unit Bobbie Faye had given them. "Are you ready to go do something stupid?"

"I think that's the family motto."

From: Simone
To: JT

Followed the coordinates of the phone. Unless she grew a beard and turned into a 90-year-old Native American, I think we've lost her.

(sent via cell)

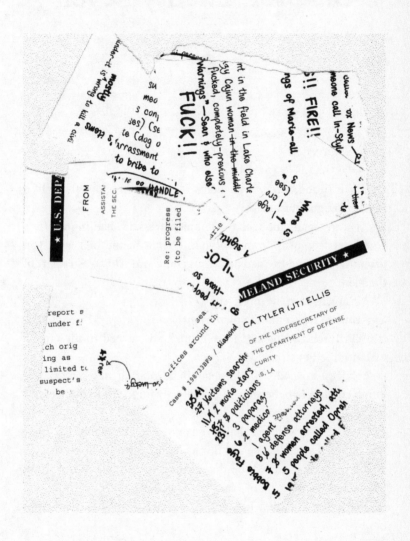

Chapter Twenty-seven

O h, good, everyone's here," Ce Ce said, now that she'd
caught her breath.

"Yeah, about that," Bobbie Faye said, hauling Ce Ce a
couple of feet away from everyone. "What in the hell were you
thinking, inviting my dad and V'rai and Cam? This wasn't part of
the plan."

"It's okay, Hon, we need 'em."

"You are following the plan, right?"

"Oh, sure, completely. Except not." She turned to the crowd.
"We need to get started."

Francesca paced. "You have got to be kidding me! You can't be
dumb enough to believe in all of that silly junk! All that blue stuff
did was give you a bad complexion."

"I don't know about that," Trevor said. "The whole silo blew
and Bobbie Faye's still here. I think Ce Ce's got a lot of power."

As Francesca started to argue, Ce Ce said to her, "Keep it up,
Sugar, and I'll make all of your hair falls out."

Francesca clamped her lips closed, but she was clearly unhappy.

"Now, Bobbie Faye, come on over here." Ce Ce led Bobbie Faye
to a set of three concentric rings Monique was setting up: a dozen
candles formed an outer ring and a dozen little jars of some sort of

liquid Bobbie Faye wasn't about to question too closely formed an inner ring, with sand between the two. "Careful when you step over," Ce Ce instructed. "Don't break the circle."

"What's this?" Bobbie Faye asked. She'd seen Ce Ce do locator spells for people who'd misplaced their cell phones or keys or laptops and even one time when a woman lost a baby grand piano. The woman never did explain how she managed to lose something the size of a cow, but Ce Ce helped her find it. The locator spells were usually made up of a little bit of spice tossed over the client's shoulders, and then the person had to turn around a few times while saying something stupid in another language which could very possibly mean "I now humiliate myself." Bobbie Faye had expected Ce Ce to come up with something a little flashier because the goal was to completely agitate Francesca, but she still expected the spell to be a real locator spell. This? Something completely different.

"You need to know that this," Ce Ce said, holding her hand as Bobbie Faye stepped over the candles, "is the most powerful spell I've ever done. But it's one-time only—we won't get another chance."

"I am not here to watch *The Bobbie Faye Show*," Francesca huffed, pacing off to the side.

"You're not going to turn me into a chicken or anything, are you?"

"That would be fun," Francesca said, cheering a bit.

"No," Ce Ce answered, but she didn't look Bobbie Faye in the eye.

"We don't think so, anyway," Monique added. Ce Ce frowned at her. "What? You were worried, is all I'm sayin'."

"If you want to keep being my apprentice, you gotta learn when not to tell that part." Ce Ce turned to Bobbie Faye and said, "You'll be fine. There are just a lot of ingredients and everything has to be just right to pull it off."

Bobbie Faye leaned close and whispered, "What happened to the simple locator spell we talked about?"

"You gotta have touched the thing at least once. You didn't touch the diamonds, so I have to do something stronger."

"How strong?" This was starting to worry her. The last time Ce Ce did something strong, Bobbie Faye looked like a giant blue jellyfish.

"It's a love protection spell," Monique volunteered and then slapped her hands over her mouth when Ce Ce threw her a withering glare.

"A love protection spell? Like to protect me from love? Where in the hell was *that* a couple of years ago?"

"Hey, still standing here," Cam said, and Bobbie Faye blushed. "Sorry."

"No, I deserved that."

She frowned at him—he was just being so freaking confusing. Accommodating. Cam was *never* accommodating. Benoit's being shot and in surgery had clearly unsettled him, because he wasn't being himself.

"How is this supposed to work for what I need?"

"It's a combination spell—it gives you the protection of the strength of the people who love you and that gives you the purity of sight—you'll know the real thing when you see it."

"The diamonds?"

"Um," Ce Ce said, looking away, "them, too. Now, I just need you to stand really still while I do this."

"Wait—people who love me?" This was so fucking not what Bobbie Faye had in mind. She wanted to annoy and upset Francesca by looking super-empowered, and that wasn't going to work by having the most humiliating moment of her entire life played out in front of Trevor, or for that matter, Cam. And her family. And those band guys who were gaping at this whole thing. (If that one guy made the sign of the cross any harder, he was going to dent his forehead.)

"Yes," Ce Ce answered, "five people who love you. Enough to die for you. And the spell will know if they're lying." She sprinkled something purple around Bobbie Faye's feet. "Which is why, a lot of times, it doesn't work. . . ."

Bobbie Faye didn't like the way Ce Ce's voice sort of trailed off there at the end. "What happens if it doesn't work?" she whispered, as if the spell would somehow hear her and start paying closer attention. Monique kept one hand plastered over her mouth, but started waving the other in the classic, "I know, I know, call on me," maneuver.

"We don't want to think about that," Ce Ce said, and then when Bobbie Faye stopped her from moving to the next ingredient, she caved. "Well, the person in the circle usually dies."

Bobbie Faye leapt out of the circle.

"No fucking way. Where's the back-up spell?" Ce Ce gave her a blank look. "Please tell me you didn't put everything into this one spell?" She didn't even know how to process that. Everything she'd hoped to accomplish with this little insanity had just boomeranged on her. Maybe if she went and found Lori Ann, that might give her one person for the spell, and on his most desperate day, Roy would count for two. "I am sooooo not getting in that circle, Ceece. You're five people short, so we're just gonna—" and the next thing she knew, Trevor had picked her up and lifted her over the candles, setting her down into the center of the circle again, the heat of his hands pressing through her thin dress at her waist.

"She's only four people short."

She gaped at him, and felt a sudden presence behind her as Cam stepped up to the circle.

"She's only three people short," Cam said. The shock that slammed to her brain nearly switched off the part that told her legs how to work.

"What are you doing?" she asked him.

"What I should have done a long time ago."

"See, I told you," Francesca piped up, "that Cam wasn't going to like it that you got engaged to someone else."

Glaciers cracked and melted at the North Pole, millennia

passed, spaceships landed, the world ended and began again before there was a single sound in the room. Bobbie Faye was absolutely certain her head had exploded and no one had bothered to tell her. Cam looked at her left hand, then looked past her to Trevor and said, a little too casually, "She's not wearing a ring."

"She will be," Trevor said for the second time that day, and Bobbie Faye wondered if he'd lost his mind, because it was one thing to make Francesca annoyed that Bobbie Faye was getting all of this good attention, but there was no way in hell Cam was going to swallow that as easily.

Francesca leaned in to where Cam stood in the circle, a wicked little smile playing in her eyes and she said to him, "I'll bet you wish you hadn't thrown Bobbie Faye's engagement ring into the lake now, don't you."

"Ring?" Bobbie Faye asked, the word rough as razor blades in her throat.

Cam glared at Francesca, and for Bobbie Faye, the final piece of the puzzle clicked. It hadn't just been the usefulness of having someone like Bobbie Faye as a scapegoat for the diamonds. Bobbie Faye had what Francesa wanted: attention. And, from the expression on Fluffy Head's face, it galled her that Bobbie Faye had *Cam's* attention. No, framing Bobbie Faye wasn't enough. Francesca hadn't been able to resist the symmetry: take everything away from Cam, and make it look like the woman Cam had chosen instead of her had shot and (maybe killed) his best friend. Hell, Francesca probably hoped Cam would have to be the arresting officer.

"I didn't mean for you to find out this way," Cam said, referring to the ring, and Bobbie Faye came back to the present; Trevor was searching her expression, frowning, since she hadn't responded, not even with a smart-ass answer.

"Only two short," Ce Ce said, stepping into the circle and bringing them back to the task.

"Only one short," her uncle said, joining them, and Bobbie

Faye glanced over at him: tears in his eyes. She knew he'd cared about her—her mom always took her to visit him when she was a kid—but this much? This wasn't poss—

"None short," her dad said.

Of all of the people Bobbie Faye thought would have stepped up to fill that spot, her dad wouldn't have even made the list. Rage rushed her body, a heat-seeking missile wanting to detonate on someone, and she couldn't tell if she was livid that he had never said anything about caring for her before, or angry because he was probably lying right now.

"You realize if I die, I am coming back to haunt your ass."

Her dad chuckled. "Girl, there's a lot you don't know about. Now hush and let Ce Ce do her thing."

Bobbie Faye wished she understood, she really did. How could he love her at all? How could he stand there as if he did, when he'd never been in her life? When they'd been so hungry after her mom had died, and she'd volunteered to clean up two restaurants after hours just so she could bring home leftovers to Roy and Lori Ann. Where was he then?

"Let it go," Ce Ce instructed, "and look for peace. Face true north—that would be Trevor."

Bobbie Faye faced him, brushing away the traitorous tears running down her cheeks.

"If I croak, you'd better kill somebody," she told him.

"Deal."

"Hush," Ce Ce said. "Now put your hand on Trevor's heart and Trevor, you put yours on Bobbie Faye's. Everyone else, place their right hand on Bobbie Faye. No cell phones, no talking through the spell. No moving away, either, no matter what happens. If you do, I can't promise you'll be safe."

Bobbie Faye placed her palm on Trevor's chest and she would have sworn electricity jumped from his to hers as her own heartbeat accelerated. Ce Ce's words sifted back to her from a few minutes ago: *People who love you. Enough to die for you.* Trevor had stepped up, immediately, no hesitating. She gasped and looked up into Trevor's eyes and knew he saw her finally understand.

At the same time, she felt Cam's hand at the base of her neck as he stood directly behind her, his fingers threaded through her hair. He'd wanted her out of his life. He'd been glad she was gone, and he'd made it crystal clear that she should stay gone. She'd have never guessed he'd been contemplating getting married.

Or that there had been an engagement ring.

In a lake, no less . . . and yet . . . he was standing in this circle. Along with her uncle and dad, and the whole world made absolutely no sense.

Ce Ce had begun the spell. There was smoke (Bobbie Faye didn't know how or where it started, but it filled the room) and a whirlwind of pressure and movement around the circle, but the wind didn't knock the art from the interior displays. The candles flickered, and a roar echoed off the tall glass walls, and then the musicians' instruments started playing. . . . Bobbie Faye wasn't sure who was more shocked—her, Francesca, or the musicians who weren't actually *playing* their instruments. Suddenly there was the brightest white light she'd ever seen, and it was emanating from . . .

Her.

Oh, wow.

She couldn't look away from Trevor's eyes, and his hand over her heart was warm and powerful and molten and she felt like they'd interconnected somehow. Then energy flowed from everyone's hands, and it felt like . . . love streaming through her . . . from her uncle and her dad. And such a flood of feeling from Cam. She didn't understand, and her gaze never left Trevor's, but Ce Ce's words tugged her somewhere else . . . words about listening to her heart, listening to her instincts, sharpening her senses for her own protection. The noises roaring around them increased and the lights snapped out and there were bizarre crashes going on somewhere beyond the circle, but inside there, she felt safe. If this was dying, then that was okay.

She saw the night sky above them, which was really weird when you think about it, because she was inside and she didn't remember this building having skylights. But there it was, filled with stars, and she floated somewhere above the city. Maybe she *had* died back there, but she didn't feel like haunting anyone just yet. She felt like floating there, watching the stars, until from somewhere far away she heard Ce Ce say, "Now call her back, Trevor."

When she opened her eyes, Trevor breathed a haggard sigh, his face drawn and worried. She was cradled in his arms in the center of the circle, Cam kneeling just inches away, a sick expression in his eyes. Bobbie Faye looked back and forth between them, and Trevor said, "I've been calling your name for five minutes."

She looked around and saw Ce Ce, who was handing out her card to the musicians. "Ceece, did it work?"

"Honey, it worked, or you wouldn't still be here."

"Are you okay?" Cam asked as Trevor helped her up, and she didn't know how to answer that. In a way, yes. There was a peace she felt that she hadn't expected, and maybe that was because of the outcome of the spell—hell, she was still alive, score that one in the win column—but the how and the love amidst the loneliness in her life? Nothing made sense. "You're kinda," Cam looked her up and down, "glowy."

She looked down and sure enough, there was almost the impression of a halo effect around her, and she lifted her arms and examined them. "Well, it beats the hell outta being blue."

"Now that we know," Francesca bit out, not hiding the seething all that well, "that everyone in the universe luuuuuuuuuvvvvvvs our precious Bobbie Faye, what is the deal with the diamonds? Do you know where they are, or not?"

Bobbie Faye beamed at her cousin. "Oh, Frannie, wouldn't you like to know. I think I'm going to take my new fangled power and get me some diamonds."

"But . . . you can't do that!" her cousin sputtered. "Those belong to M . . . Mamma."

"Sure I can. I'll give some of them to the police—" she turned to Cam "—and you can get the credit for finding them. All I need is one—then I can afford to get out of the country 'til I get a good attorney."

"She . . . you . . . She can't do that!" Francesca snapped. "You're a cop," she said to Cam. "You can't let her do that."

Cam smiled at Bobbie Faye. "Oh, yes I can."

Benoit blinked and a ceiling came into focus. It wasn't the ceiling in his house. There was a dark armoire with a TV on it to the left across from the foot of his bed, but the TV was off and everything around him sounded hushed, like his ears had been stuffed with cotton. A monitor beeped rhythmically to his right and when he finally managed to turn his head, he saw an IV stand and clear something-or-other dripping down into a tube.

A cute blond nurse hovered over him just then, and he blinked again, trying to decide if she was real or a very nice dream, and he decided he very much liked whatever it was dripping down into the tube if this was the result. She smiled, extremely pretty, and she looked excited for a moment, then disappeared—only to be replaced by his red-faced captain, whose worn and exhausted face bent too close. Benoit thought the man was going to kiss him. He was radically changing his opinion about the clear dippy stuff if dreams of pretty nurses could morph this fast.

"Benoit," the dream-captain said, "you're in the hospital. Do you know who shot you?"

Oh, that's right. He'd been shot. People sometimes said being shot didn't hurt. People were full of shit.

"Was it Bobbie Faye?" the captain asked, and images spiraled in Benoit's mind. Someone shooting him, and he saw a face; it floated there a moment, then he saw Reggie on the ground, bleeding, and he knew he was supposed to remember something about Bobbie Faye, something important, but it slid away from him.

"Did you see Bobbie Faye there?" the captain asked again, trying to make it easy for him to answer, and he nodded. Then shook his head, because no, there was something wrong with that image, but he couldn't speak and the captain wasn't looking at him. "That's it—he's confirmed she's the shooter. I want her, *now.*"

"What are you doing in here?" some deep male voice asked from the doorway, and Benoit looked over to see blue scrubs. "I told you he'd be out of it for hours—he's still critical."

"That's okay, doc, we got a confirmation on the shooter that we needed."

Shooter, Benoit thought, mulling over the word. He had the distinct impression that something was wrong with what just happened, but he couldn't remember what it was. He felt a warm lethargy creeping up on him again, and he slid away into a welcoming darkness.

L ori Ann mingled among the guests, heaving a fucking heavy tray of hors d'oeuvres around to snotty people who all towered over her in their shiny, happy clothes. She kept trying to ignore the trays upon trays of champagne as they passed by her, and if it wasn't for the fact that she knew Bobbie Faye was somewhere in the building in ass-kicking mode, she'd have been very very tempted.

Roy circled around a group of people with an empty tray of his own. "Have you seen anybody matching the description of the people we're supposed to be watching for?"

"I can't see anything but cleavage and bow ties."

"Well, I planted that thing where Bobbie Faye told me to, and I think those are Trevor's guys waiting over there," Roy sort of nodded toward a corner near a big display of Marie's bizarre artwork, "but so far, I haven't seen anyone like the guys she described."

"Do you think the GPS thingie is broken?"

"Fuck if I know. Bobbie Faye was holding it earlier. It's probably a miracle it didn't melt down in fear."

Trevor carried the small contraption that Bobbie Faye requested from her uncle as they entered the Old State Capitol through the servants' entrance at the basement level. Bobbie Faye knew it grated on Trevor not to just end it all now, throw a net over Francesca and then whisk Bobbie Faye away to safety. She could sense his growing unease—she was putting herself at risk, and he knew it, opposed it, and yet, agreed to help her do this her way. Every single time he touched her—a palm at the base of her spine to balance her as she teetered down the stairs in those heels, the brush of his hand at her hip as they turned a corner into a dark corridor, tucking a strand of hair behind her ear—sent jolts of light through her, and she half-expected to short-circuit the building with her energy surge. Instead of making it difficult to focus, as she would have expected, it made her hyper-aware of all of their troupe trampling through the underbelly of the building.

Trevor had demonstrated his slick ability to con anyone when he convinced the governor's office manager, Michele, that the governor really wanted to meet the singer of the band. Michele lead the way. Cam—who'd worked construction in his summers during high school and had worked the renovation of this old building—followed, and then Francesca. (Kit and Mitch were made to wait outside, as were her uncle and dad.) Bobbie Faye walked behind Francesca while Trevor watched their backs.

They stopped at a dark brown wooden door and Michele turned to Bobbie Faye and said for the third time in the last ten minutes, "You know, you really do just look so familiar. Are you *sure* we haven't met?" Cam had to look away to not smile.

"I'm sure I would have remembered," Bobbie Faye answered, and she was certain the only reason Francesca hadn't ratted her out (and had her arrested just for the joy of it) was because her cousin was waiting to see where the real diamonds were.

Michele shrugged and unlocked the door. They wound their way through an outer storage space filled with empty desks and open shelves, and she knocked on another inner door. Laughter and boisterous voices vibrated from inside, and when no one objected, she opened it and ushered them in. Two state police guards sat off to the side in easy chairs while the governor and several buddies sat at a round walnut table and shuffled cards and dealt another hand. Cam nodded to the fellow cops as he stepped inside the room—halfway blocking her view.

"The singer's here, Governor," Michele announced.

"She needs a shave," the governor quipped when he glanced up and saw Cam at first, and his friends laughed a little too loudly. "But I didn't—"

Cam turned and let Bobbie Faye move past him.

Trevor could not believe how she worked that dress. He was going to have to figure out how to get her into dresses more often. Well, privately. Because, *damn.*

He should not have been surprised—even when she hated doing something, she didn't quit, didn't give in—but he had never seen her dressed up in all of the time he'd surveilled her. He hadn't known what to expect, though he had convinced her he was going to need her in a dress to distract, and dear God, did it work.

The two state cops had yet to scrape their chins off the floor. He was ignoring Cam's reaction (for now), but when she placed one long, tanned, high-heeled leg around Cam and walked through that doorway, every man in the room had stopped, mid-motion. He had both cops disarmed and very disgruntled, though they probably would have been much more trouble if he hadn't flashed his badge. They were still distracted . . . and while he had the cops sit, he watched the expression on the governor's face: first, utter appreciation of what a stunning woman she was, then slight puzzlement as to why she looked so familiar, then growing confusion as she got nearer, and finally, when she stood next to the table and said, "Hiya, Delano, how are ya?" the governor screamed, tossed his cards in the air, and dove under the table.

"Oh, you have got to be kidding," Michele said. "It's the Contraband Days Queen. That's why she looked so familiar. I didn't recognize her all decked out." She turned, angrily facing Cam. "It took me all damned day to coax him out of his bedroom because I *promised* him she was on the other side of the state."

"Oops," Cam said, and Trevor had to laugh.

"Delano, come out from under there and fight like a man," Bobbie Faye said, motioning the governor's buddies to back away from the table. They took one look at her expression and moved.

"It's not as bad as when she accidentally blew up your limo," Cam said, and there was a distinct sobbing sound coming from beneath the table.

"Or the time she accidentally set fire to your vacation home," Trevor added, and Bobbie Faye pulled an exasperated glare at him and Cam arched a brow in surprise—not many people knew about that one, but then, he'd done his homework.

"Or that time you were hiding in the—"

"Will you two quit helping?" she interrupted Cam. "Thank you." She turned and tapped the poker table, which quivered. "I have one word for you, Delano, if you don't come out from under there. *Pictures*."

"You wouldn't," he sniffed.

"Ya think?"

"I want 'em back if I help you."

"If you want them back, you'll have to deal with Nina. But if you don't help me, they'll be in the news by tomorrow."

"I'm not breaking any laws. Not with all of these witnesses!"

"Nice to see your moral ambiguity's still intact."

Chapter Twenty-eight

Bobbie Faye sat on the corner of the table where she could accomplish two tasks: give Delano an ample cleavage shot and keep her eye on Francesca, who was fuming. The governor reluctantly crawled out from underneath the table, making it a point to stand on the other side, putting ten feet of mahogany between him and Bobbie Faye. He was nearing sixty, his silver hair and suave looks had clearly gotten him elected—it certainly hadn't been his platform, which would have been entirely comprised of "huh?" if his staff hadn't micromanaged him.

"What do you want?" he asked her, though he couldn't lift his eyes from her chest to her face.

"I want to see Marie's art." He looked blank, and then guilty, and then tried to go back to blank. She noticed he had the fewest poker chips in front of the chair where he'd been sitting.

"It's all upstairs on display," he said, motioning her away like he would a fly. "Go on up there and have a gander."

"No, Delano, I want to see the stuff you have in your safe."

"I don't have anything in my *safe*."

Bobbie Faye held out her hand and Trevor pulled his cell phone from his pocket. "I think Nina's landed by now, probably wouldn't take her long to log onto her computer files and—"

"Fine!" the governor said. "Here." He went over to a side door that had two combination locks on it and he spun them. "But I don't know what you're so fired up about."

"Delano, this thing you have for lying is going to get you killed. Because Francesca over there—you remember Marie's daughter, right? The one she got pregnant with by Emile when she was supposed to be engaged to you? Yeah, I called a few people and got the specifics of that little history. Or . . . are we absolutely sure she belongs to Emile?" she asked when Delano looked suddenly very awkward. "Hmmmm . . . Now that could explain a lot, too. Anyway, Francesca ran around telling everyone I could find the diamonds."

"That has nothing to do with me," he huffed, then sat down.

"Isn't it interesting how the word 'diamonds' doesn't surprise you? Diamonds. Worth at least a half a billion." Both Delano and Francesca gasped at the real value. "Marie had them and needed to get them out of the country. And wow, her old boyfriend is the governor, and guess what he's going to be doing?"

"Shipping the whole Louisiana Folk Art Show to France . . . and then Italy," Trevor explained. "Anything with the governor's seal on it wouldn't be opened when it goes through Homeland Security checks."

"What does me shipping some art have to do with an ex-girlfriend and some diamonds?"

"Well, you see, Marie is kinda obsessive about leaving little notes. Everywhere. And she left one that our dear Francesca over there found and deciphered:

d's safe check copies check b.f. knows where

"I thought at first it meant that the diamonds were safe, and the word 'check' was as if she was checking off a list. Then 'copies check' meant she'd checked off her list that she'd had copies made. It was the 'b.f. knows where' which got me. The FBI and a whole host of people thought that meant I knew where they were."

Francesca piped up, "I didn't find any note."

"Sure you did, Frannie. Your dad told me you had, and you said, yourself, that you and the cousins had been all over your mom's house, looking for the diamonds. You couldn't have missed the note in the day planner. It was real cute of you to add the 'knows where' to the end of that sentence." Bobbie Faye turned back to the governor. "See, it originally read: d's safe . . . as in, 'delano's safe' . . . and then 'check copies' which confirmed to Francesca the fact that there was more than one set of copies of the diamonds. And finally, 'check b.f.' was 'check before Friday'. Marie had abbreviated days of the week all through that day planner. But you know how sometimes you look at something and you think it's one thing and it gets locked that way in your brain? We all only saw that last part as 'b.f. knows where' and assumed it was a part of the original note. But Frannie knew she wasn't going to get access to anything over here in your safe—not with the bad blood between you and her dad, so I don't think it's a stretch to say Frannie was in desperate need for a way to get in here to find the diamonds. Or should I say . . . the *real* diamonds. How's that purse working out for you, Frannie?"

Francesca gasped and gaped at Bobbie Faye and then looked down at the flamingo pink-feathered purse.

"You have never carried the same accessories twice, Frannie. And yet, I have seen this butt-ugly purse two days in a row. And all of those posters for your mom's art? Featured a weird sculptural installment with a dozen purses like that."

"I like this purse. It was designed for me," she pouted. "And it was featured in *InStyle*."

Bobbie Faye grabbed the Geiger counter Trevor had carried in and turned it on as she walked into the small safe room—though everyone could still see her since it wasn't more than a glorified walk-in closet. "Oh, Frannie, you wanna know where you slipped up?"

"I did not slip up."

Bobbie Faye beamed at her. And Francesca looked murderous.

"Um, yeah, gotcha. It's called 'excess' Frannie. You should look it up. You'd found a couple sets of diamonds and you probably tried to fence them. Maybe you thought they were all real, just hidden in two spots, or maybe you thought one was real. But which one? So you go to Sal. He'd worked with your mom. Maybe even fenced other jewels for her in the past. Except Sal wouldn't tell you how many fakes there were, and even though you're listed as your mom's assistant in her business—the FBI is a really handy friend to have—there was only one place your mom would have access to that you didn't: here."

"How do you know she didn't just ship them somewhere already?" Francesca asked.

"She's too much like you, Frannie—Marie is a strategist. She was always good at games and hell, she dated a politician and an organized crime leader at the same time—there's no way she'd let those diamonds, worth that many millions, out of close sight. You knew that. This was the one and only place those diamonds were safe against what your mom thought was her biggest threat: *you*.

"You needed access to this location and there wasn't a single soul you could con to get past Delano. Except me. You overplayed that, Frannie—bringing in the cousins. Although using the sniper to convince me you were in danger back at Ce Ce's—nice touch. I might not have been convinced without the sniper and might have just left you to the authorities. But you couldn't trust that. You definitely didn't trust me to stick by you, even though you were family, and you knew if you changed that day planner entry to make it look like I was a part of Marie's plan to hide the diamonds, the Feds would probably force me to help. Or you could blackmail me, I guess, if they hadn't stepped in. You should have settled for one or the other strategy—you didn't need both."

Bobbie Faye turned on the palm-sized Geiger counter and slowly waved it over the pieces of art stacked in the safe.

"What is she doing?" Francesca said.

"Figuring out which of the diamonds are real. The originals have a slight radioactive signature that a Geiger counter will pick up."

"Your mom had a bunch of copies made. I think she knew she couldn't trust you."

The Geiger counter's meter pinged to the right as she moved the unit over a stack of gorgeous chocolate brown alligator handbags. Polymer handles embedded with stunning jewels sparkled, even in the light from the safe, and Bobbie Faye knew everyone was watching as she paused there. She clicked the meter's button and the static of the counter crackled through the room, and she picked up the bag she needed.

"Bingo." She smiled at Francesca.

"So," Cam said, "she killed Sal."

"I did not! Bobbie Faye did that!" When everyone looked at her like, *duh,* she stomped her foot. "Everybody's heard about that surveillance footage by now. I'm not the only one who thinks she did it!"

"You probably should've used a little more of the roofie drug, Frannie." Bobbie Faye saw an almost imperceptible change in Francesca's expression. Jesus, the woman was good at self-control. All of those years living with Emile had trained her well. "Yeah, I *remember.* You were good, Frannie. But really, not good enough. And pretty soon, everyone's going to know it was you."

"You're making up stupid stuff, Bobbie Faye, and that's just mean, especially when I tried to help you with your makeup and hair. Which really needs help, by the way."

Just as Cam turned to Francesca—and Bobbie Faye wasn't entirely sure it wasn't to kill her, because he'd realized she'd shot Benoit—one of the cop's radios blared out a notice that Bobbie Faye had been spotted at the Old State Capitol and was considered armed and dangerous.

Bobbie Faye held up the gorgeous alligator purse and wagged it toward Francesca. "You lose."

"The state police are gonna fry you, Bobbie Faye," Francesca said, waving her phone back at them all. She must have tipped off the police.

"They're not going to find me. The cops certainly aren't going to check the governor's car as he drives me out of town and then Trevor will take over from there."

"What? Me?" the governor said, and he pushed away from the table so fast, his chair fell. "I am not getting in a car with you."

"Fine. Then you can explain to the federal government just how you came to have all of these stolen diamonds in your safe," Bobbie Faye said, smiling sweetly, holding up the purse.

"I hate you," the governor said.

"Yeah, the six memos you sent out to the newspapers last year pretty much covered that."

Cam was pretty sure Bobbie Faye had lost her mind, but then, he might not be thinking all that clearly himself. Between Benoit being shot, learning the details on Francesca, knowing he'd been near the person who had shot his partner and he hadn't been able to snap her into cuffs had frayed the last tiny bit of logic he had left. It did not help one bit that the governor was leading them to his limo by way of a tiny, cramped secret staircase that Cam couldn't defend and couldn't maneuver in.

"Do you think you can get her to crack under interrogation?" Bobbie Faye asked, and he wasn't sure if she was asking him or Trevor. They'd left Francesca in the custody of the two state troopers. It had been hell to convince the men to hold Francesca instead of Bobbie Faye, and Cam grudgingly acknowledged that Trevor had helped. He wasn't sure what the agent had said to the troopers, but it had worked. For now, though, they had to get Bobbie Faye to safety before someone got trigger happy, avenging Benoit.

"When she knows you've gotten away with the diamonds, I think she'll be so livid, she'll trip herself up," Trevor answered.

Cam knew Trevor was going to call for backup as soon as they got out of the stairwell and he had cell reception. They exited the top of the staircase, which opened into the main Senate room. The large space had a soaring ceiling and stained glass windows, and it was located opposite from the other large House Chamber, where the gala was in full swing.

Aiden and Sean moved to the rotunda in the old castle building, the black and white checkerboard floor polished to gleam. They saw Bobbie Faye when she and the other men exited the stairwell and they both did a double take—the woman, the dress, the general glowing quality—stunned them for a moment.

"Got her," Aiden whispered into his Bluetooth earpiece.

"I told ye it would help to track the cousins, too," Robbie answered. There was going to be no living with him now.

Ignoring the guns the special ops guy and cop had, Aiden and Sean moved as a unit. As quick as the special ops guy was, he couldn't hurdle the governor, who'd accidentally blocked him in the same moment that Sean had a knife to the woman's throat. The cop was at a disadvantage taking up the rear; he moved a step and Sean tightened his hold and a thin line of blood appeared at the knife's edge.

Everyone stopped.

"I'll be takin' the diamonds, darlin'," Sean said, and as the ops guy eased just a hair to his left to get a better shot at Sean's forehead, Sean grinned. "I wouldna' be doin' that, unless ye want to have my people blow the other room." He nodded toward the big gala just on the other side of the double doors. "I don' get the diamonds, ye'll get a lot o' people killed, including 'er."

"He's bluffing," the cop said to the ops guy.

"He took out an entire restaurant in Lisbon last year," the ops guy said.

"I'd like to vote we believe him," Bobbie Faye said, and Sean chuckled.

A lanky lad bobbed around a corner and came to a complete dead stop. "Sonofabitch, I was trying to find you to tell you we never saw the guys you were looking for."

"Found 'em," Bobbie Faye answered. "Sean, I've got to move to hand you the stuff."

Sean relaxed the knife a fraction so that she could slowly turn to face him, and instead of looking afraid, like any sane woman would, she *smiled*. She not only smiled, she beamed such a high-wattage, come-hither attitude, even Sean was taken aback. She was radiant. That was the only word Aiden could think of, and he could tell she floored Sean's senses—tough, thug, kill-or-be-killed Sean, *who smiled back at her*.

Bobbie Faye draped her left hand over Sean's shoulder, and dropped her right hand to her thigh. She wasn't sure where her courage came from, but her instincts said to run with it. One another, She eased up the short, swingy skirt a half an inch at a time, drawing it out, implying the diamonds were beneath the skirt, and then two things happened: Lori Ann burst through the double doors, thoroughly confounded by the site of people with guns all aimed at one another, and Francesca stepped out of the stairwell, having somehow gotten away from the two cops.

There was a moment where everything suspended—the entire gala paused on the other side of those open doors behind Lori Ann, and though they couldn't see Sean's knife at Bobbie Faye's throat, they could see the guns. News cameras swung their direction, the band stopped, Francesca cursed, and the governor fainted, all as Bobbie Faye leaned forward a bit and said, "Welcome to my world, Sean," and pulled the small knife she'd strapped at her thigh out and threw it, nailing the fire alarm a few feet away.

The alarm blared and the gala audience ran screaming out every doorway. Francesca sprinted toward Bobbie Faye (leave it to her to be able to sprint in heels), which is when a sniper round crashed through one of the gothic arched windows of the ball-room. It angled down just right and sliced through the tiny skirt of Bobbie Faye's dress—she'd be dead if Sean hadn't yanked her to his chest when he had.

The gunshot elicited more screams and panic from the crowd, more running, and Trevor and Cam tried to break through the rushing sea of people to get to Bobbie Faye, but they had no shot. Mitch and Kit arrived, Mitch asking, "Now?" and Francesca nod-ded. Mitch fired on Trevor and Cam, laying down a hailstorm of bullets, ratcheting up the panic and like a tidal wave in reverse, the crowd changed directions, cutting Trevor and Cam off from following. Sean and his good-looking cohort rerouted out the front door of the building and onto the spreading, sloping lawn.

A helicopter hovered, down the steep hill, and Sean, his good-looking accomplice, and Bobbie Faye started toward it on a dead run until sniper bullets ripped up the lawn next to them and Sean pulled her behind a tree.

"You are out of your mind," Bobbie Faye said as she saw Sean try to calculate the best angle to get from the tree to the helicopter with the least amount of exposure to the sniper. "I'm not going out there. He's shooting at me."

"Love, have ya noticed that pretty fucking much everybody's shootin' at ya?"

"It's a talent," she said. A sniper bullet cut close to the tree and they squeezed together a little bit, each of them craning to see where the sniper was. They could see the rifle barrel silhouetted against a turret in one of the towers. "You know, if you give me a gun, I could make that shot."

"I know," Sean said, grinning, "which is why I'm no' gonna give you a fuckin' gun. It's no' like you'd give it back, lass, now would ya?"

His grin was, as Trevor had said, extremely charming. It lit up his otherwise deadly amber eyes, and she found herself smiling back at him.

"Probably not."

Then she heard him laugh and say something in Gaelic that made his henchman guy with the Hollywood looks gape a bit, then study Bobbie Faye like she'd just wrought a miracle. The guy looked to Sean for permission and then translated: "He said you're his kind of woman and he thinks he'll keep ya." When she blanched as Sean dialed someone on his cell phone, tall-dark-and-clearly-worried suggested, "It's better than a hole in the head."

Bobbie Faye wasn't so sure of that.

Trevor and Cam took a moment to assess the situation: everything was fucked six ways to Sunday. No sign of Homeland Security, and the state police had their hands full with the madhouse of screaming people trampling one another (and the cops) in an effort to leave the gala. Sean's other two cohorts were moving along the perimeter of the lawn, trying for a shot at the sniper, who forced them to take cover. An older woman, slipped out from behind an enormous fountain located on the outer edge of the lawn, stepping out right behind the little rat-faced weasel of Sean's. She pulled a huge Bible out of her enormous purse and smacked the living hell out of the man. She beat him several times, then walked off. The rat-faced guy was on the ground, shaking his head, dazed.

Sean, however, looked adamant about getting to the helicopter, with his men covering him and an unarmed Bobbie Faye. However they were too far away for a clear shot.

"I can stop the sniper," Cam shouted above the wail of the sirens, "but that'll give them freedom to get to the helicopter."

"You can't get a shot from here," Trevor shouted back, studying the angle up to the tower. They were hunkered down just inside the front doorway.

"I'm not going to shoot him. Just don't fucking let that asshole get her on the helicopter."

They looked out at Bobbie Faye and both men froze. Sean had

thrown his head back, laughing at something she said . . . and then grabbed her and kissed her. Thoroughly. She pushed away, but he didn't let her go and she was directly between them and him.

"He dies," Cam said.

"Oh, yes, *he dies*," Trevor agreed, and they split up.

Chapter Twenty-nine

John almost had her. He could see just the slightest bit of red that had to be the outer edge of her skirt, but the oak tree trunk was so fucking big, he couldn't get an angle.

They couldn't stay there forever, though. Not with the cops getting the crowd under control, and more sirens blaring toward them from the city streets—oh, yeah, he had a good view of that. It was going to be a fucking cop convention in a minute, and she'd move to get the hell out of there. Then she'd be dead, everyone would fucking *boo hoo* and freak out, and he'd be out of there, collecting his fee. He'd have to let go of getting those diamonds, but really, when he thought about it, killing her like this was much *much* better.

Cam made it to the fourth floor in record time, taking some of the back cypress stairs. He had to shoot the lock to get past the heavy cypress door and into the office space, then another to get into the specific office he needed, the one that faced the front towers, and he looked out. He couldn't see the sniper in the dark . . . but he could see the gun barrel where it rested on the turret of the tower.

At best, he only had a minute. Maybe less. Sean wasn't going to wait long to make his move toward his helicoptor. Cam's heart beat in his ears. He yanked the extension cord off the printer and out of the wall; with his pocket knife, he sliced off the "outlet" end, separated the wires, and peeled the ground back out of the way.

Two more shots spit out from the sniper rifle, and Cam cursed. He eased over to the exterior door and slid out quietly—but it was noisier outside, with other gunfire down below.

Please, God, let Bobbie Faye be okay.

Cam slipped out onto a catwalk that spanned the roof and found the cabled wire that ran around the perimeter of the towers to the main building. This was the ground for the building's lightning rods. He shot it, splitting it apart. He then hooked his extension cord's exposed wire to one section, and sprinted. Back inside he plugged the extension cord into the wall. The electricity ran around the cable, needing a way to go to ground. As the sniper leaned forward to aim, the jolt went straight through the sniper . . . and he screamed as blue electricity jumped through him and lit up the turret.

Cam thought for a brief moment that he recognized the shooter—the guy reminded him of that creepy bastard Bobbie Faye had gotten a restraining order against years ago. He didn't have time to confirm it—the helicopter below had swooped lower, heading for what he'd known Bobbie Faye's last position to be.

When the electricity spiked on top of the Old State Capitol's turret, Bobbie Faye thought, for a split second, that she saw Cam's face in the opposite office window, and dear God, please let him and Trevor be safe. The bright blue-white flare dimmed the klieg lights washing over the castle wall, and then dissipated as quickly as it began. What the hell?

She didn't have time to figure it out as Mitch picked that moment to pop up from behind an oak tree and shoot at them, not looking the least bit befuddled and confused, and the little smidgeon of her brain still operating realized *she'd been had*. Yet again. So much for Mitch having short-term memory problems— he seemed more than fine now. Determined, and alert. It had all been a fucking act. And then she flashed back to Sal's murder and finally remembered who'd helped Francesca. The man who seemed to know her, but she hadn't been able to place why.

Sonofa*fucking*bitch.

Mitch fired on Sean's crew as they dragged her over damp grass toward the helicopter hovering down the lawn.

Cop cars blared in from every direction. The news crews who'd been inside the gala crowded around the perimeter, getting every single fucking thing on tape.

Holy fuck. So much for being the planny type. It had all gone to hell, so fast, she had to have broken some kind of fuck-everything-up land-speed record.

She did her dead level best to "fall" and slow Sean and his crew down, but for the record? She was never ever wearing a stupid fucking dress, ever again, no matter how Trevor looked at her. Sean kept a gun in her side, so falling was trickier, but she managed to slip and he adjusted, pulling back just enough not to actually shoot her (yay) but he recovered way faster than she'd expected and yanked her back up (bastard).

"I might wan' t' keep ye alive, darlin', but that don' mean ye can't 'ave a few holes in ye. Stay on yer feet."

A new barrage of bullets erupted and Bobbie Faye could see Francesca's group shooting at Lori Ann, who'd ducked down behind a big-ass column, and Sean's redhead taking dead aim at Roy, who was such a crappy shot, he couldn't hit a target if it stood perfectly still two feet in front of him. Luckily, he learned to drop and roll in kindergarten, and now he tumbled toward a big stone planter. The redhead moved steadily on, determined to nail Roy, and not in his preferred way, and it was all too damned fucking much, to hell with Sean and his gun in her side, she just couldn't get dragged around like a fucking ragdoll.

She slid off the heels on the pretense of being better able to run and instead, spun, heels out in each palm, using the stilettos as a weapon and clocked Sean and his movie-star-looking thug. The Power of Cute Shoes, indeed.

Both men staggered back from her at the same time the redhead went spastic, blood mushrooming from her back and leg; she dropped onto the hilly lawn as Sean and tall-dark-and-angry gaped.

"Mollie!" the good-looking guy shouted, anguished, but the woman didn't move.

Kit had made the shot from the opposite side of the building from Mitch, who nodded to her, a plan in motion. They both took aim at Bobbie Faye and Sean, and in that second, Bobbie Faye heard, "Sundance."

She saw the glint of metal in the air as Trevor tossed her one of his SIGs and he was already moving, already a blur, and bam, Kit was down, Trevor having caught her center mass, but he had no shot at Mitch. The SIG flew and she wasn't sure how she snagged it out of the air, but she felt the weight hit the palm of her hand and as she landed, she dropped Mitch, blink, to the ground.

"Mitch!" Francesca screamed, running from behind a tree over to their fallen cousins. "You *bitch*," she yelled as Sean clobbered Bobbie Faye on the back of her head with his own gun.

"Ow!" She stumbled forward and fell to her knees.

"Put the gun fucking *down*, lass, or I'll cut me losses now."

"So . . . we're not gonna hold hands and skip anymore?"

Sean's man grabbed the gun and tossed it away from her before she could move, and then pulled her toward the helicopter, just fifty feet away.

"Robbie, *now*," Sean shouted, and the rat-faced man jumped out from behind a bush and rushed their direction, then stopped, arching his chest forward, a permanent question mark, and Bobbie Faye saw Cam standing, grim, at the front door, gun drawn, aimed at where the little man had fallen.

The smell of cordite choked the air.

"You stupid fucking *bitch*," Francesca continued to yell, moving slowly away from Mitch and focusing on Bobbie Faye.

Sean's redhead raised herself back upright, dazed, her eyes unfocused, her bloody hand holding up a gun, aiming at Bobbie Faye.

"Ye ruined ev'r'thin'," she slurred.

Her gun wobbled, her shot just as likely to wing Sean, and he shouted, "Mollie, *no*," but the determination on her face said she didn't have the slightest intention of stopping. Her hand wavered and one shot from Trevor took her out as another from Sean spun her as she fell to the ground.

"No!" Sean's accomplice shouted, clearly devastated, and he looked wildly around for who'd made the shot, and saw Sean lower his gun. "Fucking *no*, Sean."

"She was already dead, Aiden. Keep moving. We'll get even later."

Cam ducked behind the tree where Bobbie Faye had originally started out this whole disaster. Between them, Francesca walked toward the helicopter, looking wholly deranged, but using the trees for cover. Bobbie Faye's vision blurred from the hit Sean had given her and there were three Cams and three trees. She blinked and felt the back of her head, where blood oozed into her hair. Along with never wearing a dress again, she was never, ever, using the word "plan." Apparently, the word "plan" was code for the Universe to strap on its tights and go all World Wide Wrestling on her.

Sean nodded at her cousin. "Stop that one," he said to Aiden. But Aiden was still rattled from Mollie, and Bobbie Faye thought he was too shell-shocked to comply. Sean didn't seem concerned, and he turned to Bobbie Faye. "If ye wan' me t' let ye live, ye better have those bloody diamonds, or I'll toss yer sorry ass out when we're over the Gulf."

"Goddamn you, Bobbie Faye," Francesca shouted, nearer now,

and Bobbie Faye heard a sickening *thunk* as Sean's cohort beside them took a round in the chest. He slid to the ground, and Bobbie Faye could have sworn he was humming "There's a Hole in My Bucket."

"You are not leaving! Everybody's always leaving. Mamma and her stupid art and Daddy and his stupid hootchie fling, and I out-smarted the great Bobbie Faye. I did not do all of this work for you to get away with it *and* the diamonds, too," Francesca seethed.

"They're gonna know it was you, Frannie, especially if you shoot me now."

"No, they're gonna think I was trying to help them keep a mur-der from killing the rest of my family. Totally self-defense."

Bobbie Faye wasn't sure where Cam or Trevor had gone, but clearly, neither of them had a shot at ol' Fluffy head. Great. Sean tried to shove Bobbie Faye into the helicopter and Francesca closed in on them, her gun aimed firmly at Bobbie Faye's cleavage. Bobbie Faye was seriously considering the helicopter to be the better of the two choices when Lori Ann broke and ran, getting closer to try to get a shot (God *damn* Roy for having an arsenal with him everywhere he went—Lori Ann was a worse shot than Roy, if that was statistically possible). Francesca saw the move-ment and spun, firing, and if it was possible to die three billion times per second, Bobbie Faye did.

Cam perfected the flying tackle, taking Lori Ann down to safety behind another tree, but not before Bobbie Faye saw the bul-let rip into his thigh. Bobbie Faye started to move toward them to make sure her sister was okay when Sean pushed the barrel of his gun to her temple and shouted, "Get in, love," in the least loving voice Bobbie Faye had ever heard.

"I don't think so," Trevor said from about thirty feet behind them, and there was no mistaking his fury. Sean turned and time crawled for her as she felt the cold horror of watching the barrel of his gun slowly swing away and aim at Trevor . . .

. . . who moved toward them like thunder, hellbent and fast, gun up, storming forward like an angry God, fire spitting from his fingertips, unloading rounds, dropping and switching magazines in a lightning move. Sean slammed backward into the open door of the helicopter, several rounds shredding the shirt at his chest, and as he fell, he tried to pull Bobbie Faye with him, and Trevor just kept coming, kept firing, nailing Sean's arm, forcing the man to let go, but not before Sean grabbed the alligator purse and reached with the other hand for Bobbie Faye . . .

And Trevor moved forward, utter vengeance in his eyes as he kept firing kept firing . . .

Francesca was suddenly up, oh *fuck* no; Bobbie Faye grabbed Aiden's gun, spun and loaded a round into Francesca's shoulder, and Trevor kept moving forward.

Sean rolled and used the protection of the helicopter door as he aimed at Trevor, at the same time that Francesca switched the gun into her left hand.

Aiden's gun clicked. Empty.

Francesca didn't aim at Bobbie Faye. She smiled, aiming at Trevor's back, and he kept moving forward, never knowing that Francesca's hand moved up, up, up, behind him, level.

Without really thinking, the moment she saw Francesca take dead aim, she knew Trevor wouldn't live, and Bobbie Faye leapt in front of him—all she knew was, *no, not when I've found him.* Three rounds drilled into her as Trevor registered what she'd done and he yelled *noooo* when a bullet from the helicopter sliced through the spot where she'd just been standing.

Bobbie Faye crashed into the lawn and the slow-motion world stuttered and jerked, all intermittent flashes of images and splashes of black and bursts of noise, as if the pictures and sounds were out of synch. She saw Cam take Francesca down, hard, disarming her and cuffing her the next second; she'd never seen him move so fast, in spite of the blood pouring from his leg. People shouted her name and the helicopter lifted off. She could have sworn she saw Sean, bloody inside the craft, looking at the stupid alligator purse he'd managed to grab, but maybe she was dreaming. She felt all floaty, golden, and fuzzy; she thought she heard Cam call her Baby and Trevor, closer, growled out, *Sundance, stay with me,* and it got quieter as the sound of the helicopter's rotors dimmed and then disappeared, though the sirens were still there. It all seemed so very fuzzy now.

Cam cradled her head as Trevor pressed on the wound and she thought for a moment she heard the distinct silky voice of the woman who'd threatened her in the SUV. Bobbie Faye reached down to feel her right abdomen and touched Trevor's hands and everything oozed, slick . . . sticky and warm when she had grown colder and colder, and she knew that really wasn't a good thing. She saw the absolute terror and love in Trevor's eyes. She didn't know he could look so afraid.

Then the last stupid thought she had was that at least her boobs hadn't popped out of the dress on national TV. Then everything was gone.

FROM THE DESK OF JESSICA TYLER (JT) ELLIS

ASSISTANT TO THE UNDERSECRETARY OF THE UNDERSECRETARY OF
THE SECRETARY OF THE ASSISTANT TO THE DEPARTMENT OF DEFENSE
HOMELAND SECURITY
NEW ORLEANS, LA

Re: progress report stats
(to be filed under field notes, personal, **only**)

Case # 198733BFS / diamond search

notes:

A few mild glitches—some civilians searched, items not found.
Minor injuries (sent to legal) and PR snafus (also to legal),
but all worked out fine.

Some expenses incurred by Sumrall woman.
        -must be paid
        -emphasize to superiors the amount recovered
        -cannot jail Sumrall woman or press will swarm
        -security demands prohibit (unfortunately)

Diamonds recovered.

Sean MacGregor jailed, high-security risk.

Case closed.

Chapter Thirty

appy birthday, sleepyhead. You'll be happy to know," Nina
said to her as she rested in the hospital room, "that you're
quite the celebrity again."

"Hey, you're not supposed to taunt the wounded."

"Wimp."

"Damned straight. Did I hear two women arguing over some
sort of jurisdiction over me?"

Nina nodded, fluffed her pillow and handed Bobbie Faye some
water to sip. "Yeah, apparently one of the three people who'd hi-
jacked you in the middle of the street was actually Homeland Security, who hadn't bothered to check in with the FBI over just who
you were; they assumed you were really going to give the diamonds
to Sean. Trevor set them straight and his boss and the SUV woman
were not pleased with each other. I think this is the first time both
sets are actually trying to *claim* you, B."

"Oh, dear God." Bobbie Faye tried not to move too much—the
crater and two flesh-wounds on her side where her appendix used
to be hurt like hell, and she hated morphine, so she was trying to
avoid using the stupid drip. She was quite proud of herself for not
needing the medicine yet, for the whopping forty-five minutes
she'd been awake. Given the slack-ass way her willpower usually
worked, this was actually promising.

"Although they are somewhat distracted from you because they are also fighting over Emile and Sean—yeah, the state police helicoptors stopped Sean from getting away—and they're still looking for Marie. Oh, and you're gonna love this one . . . the governor claims he helped you in your undercover sting operation and he's assured the public that you are completely innocent of any possible wrongdoing."

"Are you going to give him back the pictures?"

"Ha. No way. Those puppies are mine." Nina smiled at her and fussed a bit, brushing Bobbie Faye's hair as she sat on the side of the bed. "You've been busy," she said, and Bobbie Faye tried not to laugh, because laughing hurt. Hell, everything hurt, including thinking.

"Benoit?"

"Waking up as we speak," Nina said. "He's kinda gone in and out of consciousness, but he seems to be stabilizing, so they think he's going to make it."

Bobbie Faye relaxed back into the pillow, so relieved she didn't even bother to hide the tears flowing down her cheeks. Nina sat with her a minute, handing her a Kleenex without mockage.

"There are two guys out there holding a barely controlled truce," Nina said. "I don't know what the hell you've been up to, but they both look incredibly haggard, and Cam acts like he's . . . come to his senses or something?"

"I have no clue. He certainly was . . . confusing, yesterday. From one extreme to the other."

"You had to go pick the two alpha-est males on the planet, didn't you?"

"Apparently, I'm very talented in 'stupid.' And hey—you didn't have to rush home. I know you have a life—you can't always drop everything when I'm blowing things up."

"Well, fine, then I'll just come for every *other* time you take out the entire political structure of the state, along with a couple of landmarks. But get used to me—I'm going to be here until you're okay." When she started to argue, Nina shushed her. "No, sorry, but you don't get a vote, B. That Irish guy? He's apparently unhappy."

"I thought Trevor shot him. A lot." She knew she must be groggy from some form of pain meds when she only felt like throwing up in panic, not completely wigging out.

"He did. But the bastard lived and it should have been a fatal. He had on body armor underneath his clothes because Trevor shot him multiple times, though he grazed Sean's head twice, once pretty badly. And Sean won't be running or using his arms anytime soon—Trevor put several shots in each appendage."

"Wow."

"Exactly. And this came for you today from Sean." She showed Bobbie Faye a note, sealed in plastic. "They were going to take it in, but I convinced them you had a right to see it."

Bobbie Faye looked at it, but it was in Gaelic, and she glanced up to Nina, puzzled.

"Apparently it says that 'you're his'—in a way that's strongly emphatic. Like, he owns you. So we're being extra careful until he's transferred into a maximum security prison."

"Lovely."

"Meanwhile, there are two guys out there, and I don't know how long that truce will hold. The question to you is . . . who do I send in first?"

Cam loomed in front of the doorway, favoring his bandaged leg. Thank God he'd been reinstated. She'd never seen him this ragged before. That he cared about her hadn't totally surprised her—even when they had fought bitterly and regularly, she knew he cared, at least as a friend.

But this was the first time in a year she could see more . . . the way he used to look at her. *Damn,* she really was regretting the no-morphine decision.

Instead of taking the chair next to the bed, Cam sat on the bed itself like he would if they had been together. The electrical jolt to her heart made her blush and she knew he saw it. He brushed her hair out of her eyes a little, and she waited, wondering just what in the hell he was thinking.

He stared for a long, long moment.

"If you're going to yell at me, could you get it over with? The suspense is killing me."

"I'm not going to yell. I'm going to tell you that when I saw how much control you had with that guy—how you didn't show any fear, though I know you, I know you were feeling it, and you thought so fast under pressure, I was really proud of you. Scared to death, but proud of you."

She blinked. *Holy shit.* She couldn't think of a single sensible thing to say. He was *proud* of her?

"I see my plan to confuse you has worked," he said, grinning.

"There aren't a lot of coherent brain cells left here—play fair."

"Look, we've got to talk. I know you've started seeing this guy, and as far as I'm concerned, that's completely my fault. I thought I had good reasons for what I did, but I went about everything all wrong. Completely, stupidly, wrong."

She was groggy and tired and her brain must not be working because *what the hell?* "Well if you'd wanted to break up with me, all you had to do was—"

"What? What are you talking about?"

He was back to being daft again. She sighed. "Before you arrested Lori Ann. I mean, I could tell you were unhappy, and for several months you were distant and weird and kept pushing me away. I knew something was wrong. If you'd just said—"

"Stop. Just . . . holy . . . Baby, is that what you think?"

She stared at him, and her head hurt with the noise from her careening thoughts. Because *of course* that's what she thought. And their stellar argument after he'd arrested her sister and him yelling *get the fuck out of my life with this shit* pretty much sealed it.

"I was nervous because I had bought you a ring and wanted to ask you, but things kept happening and the timing was never calm or right or happy. I was more nervous than before a game. I couldn't figure out a good, romantic way to do it."

"You're kidding me." She must be dying. She had a terminal illness. They found it when they went in after the bullets. That was the only reason he was being so nice.

"No. *You* better than anybody know how all kinds of stupid I can be. I'm asking you to forgive me. Please. You were so worried and upset over your sister. It killed me to see you in knots. I thought if I just solved the Lori Ann problem, you'd be able to breathe peacefully a little while, and when you went ballistic . . . I went to the moron end of the scale. And those arguments—they were bad. We both said things we didn't mean."

They had. *She* had. It had been bloody and merciless and somehow, she had lost sight of the fact that as best friends, they had always known that they would be there for each other—no matter what. Even through a fight. And yet, they had taken that for granted, and had thrown it away. He entwined his fingers into hers, brushing away tears she didn't know she was shedding.

"I'm not going to force you into a decision. I know I pushed you away, I know this guy has stepped up, but we have something permanent, and you know it. We have always had it, even when I was too stupid to know. That doesn't ever go away—not if it's real, and ours was. *Is.* If I hurt you half as much as I'm hurting now, I don't know how you can forgive me, but I'm asking you to try.

"But I'm done being stupid, Baby. I want you to think about that, before you commit to this guy."

She just did not know what to say, and she knew he saw that. It broke his heart, she could tell, that she didn't automatically leap into his arms, picking up where they left off . . .

. . . because she honestly didn't know what she felt.

And it was killing her.

Nina stood outside Bobbie Faye's room where Trevor had not-so-subtly parked himself so that he could see into the small window on the hospital door. She had to give it to her best friend—she sure as hell knew how to pick the good-looking ones. Extreme alpha, knocking against the top rating on the damned-gorgeous sex-ometer.

The man stood quietly, his arms crossed. She finally decided to cut him a little slack.

"She asked me to remind you that you had a manual you should be studying." She looked at him for a response, and he allowed the smallest indication of a smile, his gaze never wavering from that window.

They fell silent again for a minute, until he finally said, "He's going to be a real problem for me, isn't he?"

She looked into the window, saw that Bobbie Faye had tears on her cheeks, though they couldn't see Cam's face.

"Probably." Then after a moment, she said, "I'm not entirely sure that he's not the best choice for her, you know." She looked pointedly at him. "The safest." When he didn't answer, she said, "But you're not backing away, are you?"

He shook his head slightly. "I'd have to stop breathing, first."

She hmphed, and they went back to staring at that door. Then she said, "I'd have never believed it, with someone with your reputation." That got her the arched eyebrow, but he didn't waiver from his watch. "Have you told her all about your past?"

Their gazes met. "Have you told her about yours?"

She thought about that and shook her head. He had a point. "I don't think she has to know."

"Eventually, she will, you realize. And I'm not hiding my past from her."

"That's a big risk."

"She's worth it." He waited a moment. "So how was Italy?"

It was her turn to look at him with an arched eyebrow. That meant he had as high a security clearance as she did, if he knew to ask.

"It was sad really. Unfortunately, a wealthy businessman there had a tragic ending." She smiled. He smiled back. She let the moment linger, then they both grew serious. "You understand," she said, quietly, "if you hurt her, I will kill you." It was not an idle threat.

He went back to watching that door. "If I hurt her, I will let you."

Cam came out of Bobbie Faye's room, gently closing the door, giving Trevor the hard, take-no-prisoner's stare that cops seemed to perfect after a few days on the job. There were about fourteen-thousand threats that passed silently back and forth between the men. Nina half-wondered if she was going to have to step between them, when Cam said, "I'll be back to see her in a couple of hours. Enjoy the very limited time you have."

"I will," Trevor said, as Cam left the waiting area.

When Trevor walked into the room, Bobbie Faye pulsed with the hum in her skin the way she always did when he was around, and she felt happy and guilty about that at the same time. Guilty because Cam had stirred up so many memories . . . feelings? Or just memories of feelings?

Her brain sent up a white flag, begging for mercy.

Trevor stepped to her bedside, and asked, all impersonal sounding, no sexy growling, "Did Nina tell you that the judge put Lori Ann in a very nice work-training program with day care?"

"She said you were instrumental in setting that up. In one day, no less. And an apartment for her."

"Do you mind?"

Bobbie Faye shook her head. She was relieved, actually. "Does she know you did this?" Lori Ann was about as enthusiastic over people interfering in her life as Bobbie Faye was.

"No, she thinks the judge looked at what happened with you and decided her sentence was out of proportion. She thinks it's all court-ordered. And, Roy, of course, has four dates lined up with the nursing staff. At last count."

She smiled. "Thank you." He nodded. At least this meant Lori Ann could help with the expenses of raising Stacey. Well, technically, it was Lori Ann's responsibility, but Bobbie Faye wasn't about to dump that whole burden back on her sister. They'd share it, share the expenses. But at least Bobbie Faye could quit worrying about trying to start a second job, like the swamp tour business.

Jesus, *swamp tours*. With her, leading people through the water with the alligators and the spiders and mosquitoes and . . . ohmygod, she'd been insane. She was already zooming off the Cranky charts—she'd have gone completely into Psychotically Grouchy.

There must have been Divine Intervention going on when she couldn't buy insurance.

And thinking of *psychotic* reminded her of Francesca all over again, which reminded her what she'd forgotten to ask. "Did you find the diamonds?"

"In the safe, where you said. Good job on faking the Geiger counter. When you made it ping on that specific purse, for a moment there, even *I* believed you. You heard, Francesca's going to live?" Bobbie Faye nodded. "She won't ever get out, though. If she hadn't cracked emotionally, I'm not sure we could have nailed her. The forensic evidence against you would have given any jury reasonable doubt. Smart move to do that spell."

She'd made Francesca break. Made her so jealous, that calculating reserve she'd had came crumbling down. She didn't feel victory in that. Bobbie Faye had underscored how alone Francesca was—her mother abandoned her, an indifferent dad. Their lives hadn't been all that different after all. Bobbie Faye leaned back into the pillow. Grief overwhelmed her. So much loss, for nothing. She couldn't even wrap her mind around the deaths, the mill burning, the chaos that was supposed to be her family.

Trevor stood there, very businesslike, an abyss of two feet between them, and she couldn't stand it. She wanted to touch him, but at the same time, maybe he'd come to his senses and decided that dating a one-woman-demolition-disaster was possibly a bad idea. Especially for a Fed. Maybe this was his polite way of saying good-bye, no thanks, see ya. Maybe she needed to let him know he didn't have to stay out of guilt.

"I didn't know that was the kind of spell Ce Ce was going to do, by the way. I thought she'd just do something simple that would still make Francesca jealous. I didn't mean to put you on the spot, or make you have to fake . . ." She let it drift off and studied her hands.

"You didn't," he said, and that growl was back and he kissed her, *claiming,* and she wrapped her arms around him, relieved to sink into that kiss. Not just relieved, she realized, but dizzy with him next to her. He looked down at her bandages peeking out from beneath her gown, and he traced the outer edge where the tape pulled at her skin. His breathing grew more ragged, and she understood, now, he was fighting to hold onto his control, that he was deeply upset that she'd been hurt. She laid a hand on his, stilling it until he raised his head, heartbreak in his eyes.

"My God, Sundance, don't put yourself in danger again."

"Don't get shot at and we have a deal."

They held each other's gaze, and she wasn't even sure if minutes had passed, or hours. Then she buried her face in his shoulder. She didn't think she could hold it together any longer. Her heart ached, blistered, and all she wanted to do was lose herself in him, and it was like finding herself as well. She did not understand and the pain Cam had raised slashed the edge of her heart. Trevor held her, and her body hummed, her soul sang, and she cried.

Nina sat in the lounge area where she had a good view of Bobbie Faye's door. It didn't surprise her that Old Man Landry stood there, looking in the window. It also didn't surprise her that he turned to leave without knocking.

"You want me to tell her you came by?" she asked.

"No," he said, and walked away.

Trevor leaned back from Bobbie Faye a little, and she knew he was going to be direct. It was something of a relief to know that about him.

"I meant what I said, yesterday. I want to marry you. I know Cam wants you back, but I'm not letting you go. That's going to be real hell for you, because of who you are. The guilt he'll make you feel. I get that. And I'm still not letting you go."

She felt so much it scared the hell out of her. She wanted *so much*, she almost couldn't breathe, like all the emotion would rip her apart. She didn't know what to say . . . all articulate thought had gone on strike, apparently, so she did the only thing she knew to do—she scooted over to give him room in the bed. He carefully climbed in and adjusted the covers as she snuggled into his arms, her head on his shoulder.

"Can you stay for a while?"

"I'm not going anywhere. Besides, I found that Wooing Manual."

She angled her head back where she could see his mischievous grin. "Oh yeah?"

"Yeah," he said, his voice a low, wicked rumble. "It's got *pictures.*"

"Oh my."

"And I'm *very good* with pictures."

Acknowledgments

The thing I've come to realize as an author is that there is no way possible to adequately thank everyone for the help they've given me for these books. If I tried to convey just how much I feel, and how appreciative I am, I'd have to go on and on and someone would need to smack me with the schmoopy stick. I mean, seriously, how do you express the feeling you get when you have a letter from someone who was enjoying the book so much that she took it into the shower with her, holding it just out of reach of the water? Or the reader who wrote that during an incredibly difficult time, while her mom was undergoing treatment for cancer, the craziness of the book made her laugh? How do you tell the librarians and the booksellers a simple "thank you" and impress upon them that they have rocked your world with their recommendations and handselling? I'm not sure, honestly.

Still, I'd like to include at least this short list, knowing I'm going to be horrified later that I've left off too many people.

On the technical side of things, many thanks go to: Luke Causey, a police officer, for not having your mom committed for all of the random "so, this gun, how does it work again?" e-mails. To Jake Causey, thank you for all of the car and motorcycle information. If there are mistakes, they are mine alone because, believe me, they tried to make the information clear. To A. S. King, for all your help with the Irish (Gaelic), your time and teaching are greatly appreciated. Rae Monet, who helps me keep the FBI information plausible . . . er, in the Bobbie Faye world—you rock.

Sergeant Marcus Smith, of the Louisiana State Police, thank you for taking time to patiently answer the most outlandish questions, without sending someone to haul me in. Nancy Chesson—thank you for the incredible tour of Louisiana's Old State Capitol and the look into the areas featured in the book; the staff there and the beauty you all have worked hard to preserve do our state justice. To the fine people who run both the Weapons_Info and Crimescenewriter sites, thank you for providing such a much-needed and incredibly useful service (and archives).

The city of Lake Charles, LA—thank you for your support and for not minding too much that I moved things around in the last book. I sort of did it again, though I think you won't mind so much since I blew up most of those things.

The readers: *Thank you.* If I have in some small way made you laugh or enjoy a distraction from the tension or hectic life we all face, then I am incredibly lucky and I am very grateful that you invited Bobbie Faye into your world.

The booksellers and librarians: I am in awe of your generosity in giving a new author a chance, and in the wonderful support you've shown me.

Allison Brennan, for all the belief and encouragement—you have been a rock (a five-carat flawless gem) and an amazing friend.

Kim Whalen, my agent—your sense of humor and support have kept me sane. (Well, more than anyone would have thought possible; I'm not guaranteeing I was entirely wrapped to start with.)

Nichole Argyres, my extraordinary editor—thank you for all your hard work and for seeing the potential even when I wasn't so certain. And to Kylah McNeill, for so much help with all of my annoying questions, thank you.

Matthew Shear, Anne Marie Tallberg, John Karle, Michael Storrings, Joe Goldschein, Kathryn Parise, Gretchen Achilles, David Cain, Elizabeth Curione, and the rest of the staff at St. Martin's

Press: You are amazing. There are so many things each of you talented people did to make the first book a success, it would take ten more pages just to list them all. Thank you for all of your terrific support and enthusiasm.

Pamela Dumond and Christina Donatelli and Julie Burton and Michelle Montgomery—you were amazing in your belief in the book and seriously, I think you bought half the books sold. And to Emilie Staat, who got me through that first signing without letting me spontaneously combust, thank you. (I am amazed you survived.)

To my friend and mentor at LSU and extraordinary writer, David Madden: You paved the way. Thank you.

Beta readers (in the order that they were subjected to my constant crankiness . . .) CJ Lyons, Lori Armstrong, Patricia Burroughs, Emilie Staat, Tamar Bihari, Diane Patterson—thank you for reading and letting me bounce "what if?" questions off you. In all of the many times I bugged you, none of you tried to have me killed. That I know of. Which is kinda amazing, really.

My relatives have been flat-out awesome, including many of my extended family. I am, frankly, relieved and not just because several of my aunts (both sides) took me aside to let me know that they hadn't minded the cursing, but also because when you're from the South and you have a chaotic family and sometimes you have characters do not-so-smart things in the books, you hope that your family isn't holding a grudge and secretly planning your demise or having a little white coat with the shiny back clasps specially made.

To Amanda Eschete, my daughter-in-law, and to Nicole, my youngest son's fiancée—it's a joy to have you both in my life. I couldn't have asked for better additions to our family. To new addition Angela Grace, who never ceases to make me smile, I can't wait 'til we can read books together. To my sons and in-laws (Patsy and Marion), thank you for everything. And to my mom and dad,

ACKNOWLEDGMENTS

Al and Jerry McGee, words here would completely fail. You have always been a shining example of tenacity and love and hope.

Finally, for my husband, Carl: You already know you are the world to me, and my best friend, and the one who makes me laugh the most. Thank you.

DOUBLE CROSSES.
SHOOT-OUTS.
HOSTAGES.

Just another day for Bobbie Faye...

Bobbie Faye's good-for-nothing brother has been kidnapped, and Bobbie's the only one who can get him back. Luckily, she knows how to handle guns, outwit angry mama bears, drive a speedboat, and get herself out of (and into) almost every kind of trouble. If only that pesky state police detective (who also happens to be a pissed-off ex-boyfriend) would stay out of her way . . .

"If you like Janet Evanovich, if you're looking for a lot of **unlikely action,** or if you're simply having a bad day, go out and find Bobbie Faye. She's an **outrageous hoot."**

—*The New Orleans Times-Picayune*

Available wherever books are sold